CURSE OF DRAGONS

SERA'S CURSE
BOOK TWO

CLARA HARTLEY

A SUPER BIG THANK YOU TO MY AWESOME BETA READERS, EDITORS, AND READERS WHO MADE THIS BOOK POSSIBLE.

CHAPTER ONE

WHEN FOUR PRINCES fought over who could please you more with their dragons, you knew you were the luckiest girl alive.

It was pleasant weather that day in Constanria. The skies were blue, with not a rain cloud in sight. Aereala had decided to bless us with her goodwill, and everything was supposed to be peaceful.

Supposed was the keyword here.

Finding peace amongst the four dragon men was close to impossible, not with their sibling rivalry and constant contests that got more ridiculous each time Kael suggested something.

"Let's see who can make Sera blush more, or laugh more, or *fart* more."

I couldn't remember how the last one came up, but that was *not* a good day for me.

Today, I'd decided to take the day off. The princes forced me to take one every month, because they said I needed to loosen up from work and spend time with them. I agreed with them. Work with the council never ended, and I always promised too much, letting responsibility after responsibility pile up. I was also trying to garner better impressions from others, so others stopped viewing me for my curse alone.

We stood over Gaean's pit, a mountain range next to Raynea, the capital of Constanria. Kael had chosen the location because he said he knew it well. Its jagged rocks and steep valleys did *not* look safe. The cliff we stood on had a sharp fall and ended with a smattering of spiked rocks. If I accidentally slipped and hit the unwelcoming bottom, I had no doubt I would die. *Great idea, Kael.* Perfect place to go flying on the backs of dragons.

There ought to be no chance at all for me to slip and fall to my doom, not with their scaly, slippery backs. Yep, no chance at all. I could trust them completely for my safety... except for that one time Kael slipped the wrong mushrooms into my soup to make me fart, or when Kael forced me to spar with a draeox to sharpen my skills with the blade. *Or* that other time when Kael suggested I put rocko candy into the fizzy drink and it exploded in my face, nearly blinding me. He was rolling on the floor for a good five minutes after that, grabbing his stomach and wiping tears from his eyes.

Note to self: avoid riding Kael's dragon if I want to survive.

I was still planning my next big comeback. Kael was going to get his just desserts from me, and I had to make sure it was especially sweet.

I looked at my four princes, who never failed to be gorgeous. Rylan, the crown prince, had the side of his hair in a braid as usual; Gaius, his twin, wore his constant grumpy frown that hid the fact that he had a soft side; Micah, their half-brother, beneath his red fringe, looked collected but encouraging; and Kael, the third oldest, was rubbing his hands together with a devious smirk inching up his lips.

And me? I probably had the words *I'm about to shit my pants* written on my face.

But I couldn't touch anyone else, since dragon-kind seemed to be allergic to my skin. It made them hurt. *A lot.* So I was stuck with the princes, whether I liked it or not.

But I *liked* it.

An eagle cawed in the distance, punctuating the ominous atmosphere of Gaean's pit. "Uh... guys... isn't there someplace safer to fly?"

"Nonsense," Kael said, pushing out his chest and waving away my comment. "This is the best place. It allows for sharp turns and large drops because of how narrow yet deep its valleys are. It's great for being adventurous and showing off our skills."

"How about *not* showing off your skills? Why not fly across a nice, serene landscape, where we can enjoy the view?"

"The view here isn't bad," Rylan said, completely missing my point. "Different... but not bad."

"Somewhere grassier? With soft, bouncy hills that won't completely skewer me should some accident happen?"

Micah reached out to hold my hand. My gloves lay on the ground next to us. I didn't see a need to have them on next to the princes, and a light tingle, the one I always got whenever I touched the princes, tickled my skin. Micah brought my hand to his lips to kiss it. I should have gotten used to their little grazes here and there after being with them for two months, but I hadn't, because a blush crept up my neck. "Don't worry, Sera-kit, I won't let any harm come to you." His eyelids were hooded, and his lips soft and inviting. Often when he looked at me like that, I was reminded that he wanted me. They all did. And yet they hadn't acted on that desire, which frustrated me to no end.

My heartbeat sped up. "It's not you I'm worried about." One day I'd get used to how blue his eyes were, but so far, that day hadn't come.

"Right," Gaius said, patting Micah on his shoulder. "So there's nothing to worry about."

No, wait. Yes there was. There was *everything* to worry about.

"Let's shift, then," Gaius continued. "And the one who Sera deems the winner will get to cuddle with her tonight."

"Just cuddling," Rylan added.

"Which is annoying," Kael said, almost with a groan.

Micah's expression didn't change.

I rested my hands on my hips. "I didn't agree to that. Although I wouldn't mind, but you guys have been so difficult about this sleeping thing for the last few... What are you doing with your pants—"

Gaius fumbled with the hem of his pants before stripping them off, leaving his glory-thing on display.

Out of reflex, my eyes darted away. But then curiosity returned... and why should I be the one to look away? They were *mine* now, weren't they? They said so. I should have every right to look and ogle, because we were a thing, and people in relationships got to see each other naked.

Thus, shamelessly, I looked.

They all had their pants off but were walking away, besides Kael, who stood winking at me. I didn't get to see their *ahems*—except for Kael's, which was no doubt impressive—but butts were a nice consolation prize, and theirs were firm and completely pinch-able.

I am not bothered by their nudity was what I tried to convince myself, but of course I was. Still, I stared onward as if it was my life's mission, because I might as well get used to it.

Rylan reached back and smacked Kael over on the head. Kael scowled, but turned around to follow the others.

With his back to me, Rylan said to them, loud enough so I could hear, "There won't be any way to talk to Sera once we shift, so let's be civil about it. She'll take turns riding us. Once you're done, come back here and set her down, and she'll get on the next in line."

"I'm first," Kael said, raising his hand.

"We're going by age. Oldest to youngest."

Amongst the brothers, Kael had the firmest butt.

Kael let his hand fall. "Hey, that means you're first."

"Exactly." I heard the smile in Rylan's tone.

Or maybe it was Micah with the firm butt. Or Gaius… or Rylan. Actually, all of them had firm butts, and this was impossible to decide. I had to give each of them a good grope later, just to test out the effectiveness of their firmness.

For scientific purposes, of course.

I was a scholar first, horny post-adolescent girl second.

"How about the other way around?" Micah asked. "Youngest to oldest?"

Rylan fastened his hands on his hips. "Because it makes more sense that way. I was born first into this world, so I get to go first in everything."

"Okay, now that is just horseshit—"

"I pick oldest!" I shouted. Only because that put Kael lower on the list.

Micah turned around to flash me a dejected expression.

My heart fluttered, and I regretted what I'd said. I quickly corrected my mistake by saying, "I rode on your dragon's back once already—better to let the others have a chance."

His expression lightened, and I felt relieved that my excuse appeased him. They squabbled for a bit more, until Rylan got too impatient and went ahead, shifting first. The others took that as a cue to summon their dragon forms too. I'd never seen the transition between human and dragon form before. Bones clicked and morphed into multiple times their size. I'd expected it to look grotesque, but much of the shifting was obscured by magic that shimmered with an iridescent bright yellow. Through the light I could see faint hints of human limbs growing into claws, and heard the cracking of their skeletons. The ground shook as they morphed, and I had to bend my knees and reach my arms out to balance myself. The glow continued to grow in size and brightness, until it hurt to stare at it directly and I had to glance away.

When the magic dissipated and I looked back, four dragons were in the princes' places. Two black ones and two white. Gaius's dragon was black like Rylan's, and was exceptionally large. He had the friendliest face, however, which was strange, because his human face wasn't friendly at all, although undoubtedly handsome. The dragon forms of the other brothers had ridges protruding from their faces in different patterns, which added to how menacing their dragons looked.

Their wings spanned buildings. Their forms were sinewy, every inch muscled yet graceful. Smoke rose from their nostrils. Rylan puffed out some fire, probably to show off. Kael stepped up and released a roar, which startled birds and made them flutter to the skies. I assumed that was him trying to impress me. But instead of impressing me, the force made me stumble backward. Luckily, I stood far enough from the edge of the cliff, or I would have plummeted to my doom.

Rylan was up first, so he stepped forward, his form rippling as he moved. He neared me. Up close, his eyes were a gorgeous, shocking yellow.

"You know," I said, "the four of you are scarier in dragon form, but also quieter. You guys losing the ability to talk makes life a lot more peaceful."

He snorted at my remark and shrugged. He swung his tail in front of him and allowed me to hop on. I hoisted myself over his frame and steadied myself on his back, gripping one of his protruding scales to use as a handle. His hide emanated heat, which was a comforting lukewarm temperature. It seeped through my pants—*yes*, pants, because robes were too impractical to go dragon-riding in—and sent a comforting sensation through my body. I leaned over and rested my torso over his frame, because it gave me better balance, and also because it felt nice.

Rylan growled, which I assumed was his way of asking if I was ready.

"Fly away, big guy," I said.

He lifted his wings from the ground and beat them against the cool winds of Gaean's pit. As he lifted, my heart dropped. My breathing quickened, and I couldn't decide if this sensation was exhilarating or terrifying. I'd been on Micah's back before, but that had been a while ago, and I had to adjust to the experience again.

Then I remembered I actually enjoyed riding on Micah's dragon, and that helped to calm me down. Still, Micah did take me to a much nicer place, with pretty vines, trees, and soft grass.

I tried to ignore how this landscape looked like a death trap.

Think pretty things. Que sera sera—as they like to say in ancient dragon tongue.

Rylan's back did feel safe enough, as long as he didn't do anything too abrup—

He dived toward the sharp rocks, dropping at least a castle's length. I lost my breath and a scream ripped from my throat. I liked it when Micah did the same maneuver, but this was way faster, and I believed Rylan had dived too close to the rocks on purpose, because I heard the crunch of them as they crashed into Rylan's feet. I pulled my face from his scales and opened one eye. *Still alive.*

But... I had to admit—that was pretty fun. "Not fun at all," I said to Rylan. I gave away my lie through a giggle.

And, because he and the boys were so gratingly adventurous, he took my laughter as permission to do whatever in Constanria he wanted.

In the next few minutes, we swept past all sorts of cliffs. Steep cliffs, rounded cliffs, cliffs with caves in them. I thought it was inadvisable to try and squeeze through all of them, but Rylan did anyway, nearly beheading me at one point. There wasn't much to see in Gaean's pit but rocks, and maybe some fanciful, colorful birds, but I had no time to take a closer look because Rylan went by so quickly that they blurred.

I was nauseated by the time we were done. We reached the plateau we'd started on, where three other dragons perched and lumbered, waiting for us. "I think... I think you could have slowed down," I said.

Rylan's wings glided against the air. When he halted, his feet made a loud *thud* and the ground shook. I slipped off his back. When my boots touched the ground, my legs wobbled beneath me. I rested on his frame for support. Pressing my hand to my forehead, I sighed. "Now that's done and over with." I was ready to go home.

But three other sets of dragon eyes fell on me. They shone with eagerness, and I knew they weren't going to let me go until I rode on their backs. The day was only beginning.

I shook my head. "Why does everything have to be a competition?"

Gaius lunged forward and pushed Rylan aside. He swayed his back side to side, and a low rumble vibrated from his throat to travel through my bones.

I palmed my face. This *had* to be a competition. There was always one when it came to these four.

———

"Micah wins," I said, pointing with my thumb.

Micah held me in his arms as we flew back to Raynea. A splendid rainbow arched through the blue sky, framing the wonderful, picturesque landscape of Constanria. Many of the leaves had begun browning—oranges and yellows replaced the greens, giving the setting warm autumn tones. It looked like a painter's dream.

Bright light shone through the clouds. It split into fanning rays that shimmered over the city. *This* was a view. Not like the terrible rocky edges of Gaean's pit. I would have preferred it if they showed me this view on their dragons' backs—slowly, and not with the up-and-down whirlwinds they put me through. Rylan, Gaius, and Kael seemed to think the faster they went and the more risks they took, the more impressed I'd be. Rylan's ride was choppy, but Gaius was almost twice as bad.

And Kael's?

It was surprising how I could still stand on two feet.

"I knew I should have went last," Kael muttered.

Weren't they complaining about who got to go first?

I sniffed. "That's not it. Micah's the only one who actually let me *enjoy* the ride, and I didn't feel like hurling after he finished."

"He didn't even look like he was trying," Gaius said.

"I think the rest of you tried too hard. It doesn't have to be a game."

Kael shrugged. "It's in my nature."

I shook my head but didn't retort. Arguing with Kael was

like arguing with a child—he always pulled arguments out of nowhere, and how ridiculous they sounded didn't bother him at all.

"Did anyone else feel what I did in our dragon forms?" Rylan asked. A deep frown creased his brow.

"Yeah," Gaius said.

"Feel what?" I asked.

"Like we needed to... needed to mate with you," Rylan explained.

My stomach tightened and my breathing quickened. I'd been trying to be more suggestive, but they never took the bait. "How so?" I asked. I thought the reason being suggestive never worked was because of how terrible I was at it. I knew how to charm my subordinates for political gains. But men? I didn't know the first thing about seducing men.

Rylan replied, "I can't spell it out. It was a strange feeling. Not overbearing, but my awakened dragon seemed to really like the thought of you being solely ours... That I should... *claim* you? Is that the word? These terms are coming out of nowhere, but they feel right."

"They're the words the dragons of the old used," Gaius said.

Rylan nodded. "I can't describe the feeling any other way."

"Could we be Sera's mates?" Micah asked.

Rylan narrowed his eyes. "How can she have four? Even if mates existed?"

"She's special," Kael said, smiling smugly to himself as he continued to glide through the air with his shimmering white wings. He seemed pleased with himself, as if his hypothesis explained everything away.

I sighed. "And none of the spell books have a hint about what's happening between us." I hadn't been too motivated to find clues. I was content with what we had, except for their apparent lack of interest in going any farther than kissing.

Something about our relationship had them worried.

"We're running tests to try and figure it out," Rylan said.

My mood soured. "Yeah..." I was going to have to participate in another one of those experiments once I got back. The thought of it made my skin crawl and my stomach sick. I had to go through with it. In exchange for peace with the princes, I'd promised King Gisiroth I'd partake in experiments, to figure out why my curse worked as it did, and why the princes could touch me while everybody else couldn't. "I'm tired today. Can we skip this week's meeting?"

"Father wouldn't be happy about it," Rylan said, looking somber. He gazed into the distance, then continued, "But we don't have to listen to everything he says. He'll be grumpy and give me another reprimand, but one day shouldn't make a difference. If you're tired, rest."

A scolding from Gisiroth didn't sound fun. "It's all right. I'm not that sick."

"Are you certain?" He turned to me. His cool, gentle gaze brushed my skin.

"I'll be all right. Once we reach home and I get a cup of water, I'll be fit and fine again."

"I'm serious—don't let what Father thinks get to you."

"I am certain! You're making a fuss."

Rylan frowned, but I knew I had convinced him, because he nodded and said, "All right. If you insist."

We'd reached Raynea in half an hour. It would have been much faster on a dragon's back, but I wanted no more of that, and the princes obliged. Micah's strong arms and their half-dragon forms made me feel safer than their slippery scales, especially after what I'd just gone through. We flew over the wonders of the palace, with its towering waterfalls and flowing rivers, and reached the outhouse where King Gisiroth assigned the experiments to be held.

The small, rickety building paled in comparison to the grandeur of the palace.

I hated this building. Gisiroth picked the outhouse that I had been banished to when I was separated from the princes. He wanted this to be a reminder of my not belonging here. He wanted me to know my place.

I didn't let it faze me. I knew where my place was. It was next to my princes. This weak attempt to convince me otherwise did nothing.

We opened the wooden door, and the princes slipped through it, into the dilapidated building. The interior had changed from the bedroom I used to live in. These days, it held only one chair, which stood alone in the center of the wooden floors.

Micah, Rylan, and Gaius entered first. I trailed after them, but Kael pulled me aside before my foot went through the door.

He rested his hands on my shoulders and leaned in so closely that I thought he might kiss me. He had a loose strand of hair dangling in front of his strong-jawed face, so I brushed it back and helped him tuck it behind his ear. As I did so, he grabbed my wrist and pressed it to his cheek. I licked my lower lip, and his eyes darted there.

I sucked in a deep breath. "What is it?"

"Do you hate me, Sera?"

"What?" My lips curved downward. "No, of course not. Why would I?"

"Because of all my mistakes. I was careless when trying to play, and I did stupid things that put you in danger. Sometimes I get too comfortable, because you fit in with us so well, like a missing piece of a puzzle we'd spent years searching for and now we've finally found. Sometimes I forget you're not entirely like us."

"Oh? If I'm not like you, then how am I like?"

"Fragile. In need of protection." He kissed my palm. The electricity between us sent a thrill through me. "You're human. More vulnerable. You're not like my brothers, who can take everything I throw at them. I shouldn't forget that."

I quivered at his touch, but his words struck the wrong chord. I didn't want to be seen like that by the princes. I wanted to be more than a burden they had to guard.

It was why I put myself through with these experiments, and was still working hard at the council. If I stopped looking like a damsel in distress to everyone, then the princes would gain favor with the court, and Vancel would stop using me as a weapon against them.

"I'm alive, aren't I?" I told him.

"You fell so sick."

Kael had worn guilt on his face for days after the mushroom incident. I kept telling him it was all in the name of fun—not *good* fun, however. It was fun of a more disastrous nature.

I peered into his blue eyes. "We still laugh over the incident sometimes. You were playing around."

"The others do," he said. "Not me."

"You're amazing, Kael," I said, reaching up so I could run my fingers through his silky white hair. He stood too tall, so when I tiptoed to kiss him, I couldn't reach. He figured out what I was doing, so he bent down and captured my mouth with his, feeding me his ocean-like taste. I reached my hands up and placed them on his hard stomach, tracing over where I thought the tattoos might be. A small sound escaped the back of his throat.

That was when Micah interrupted us. "We're right here, you know?"

Kael parted from me, brushing the tip of his nose across mine right before he stepped away. Micah's eyes flickered to dragon yellow for a second. He walked up toward us, grabbed my hand, and dragged me through the door to kiss me more fiercely and passionately than Kael had.

Micah was possessive. More so than the others. That was saying a lot, because as alpha hidraes, they all bore some level of possessiveness.

Every time Rylan, Gaius, or Kael kissed or touched me too long, Micah would step in to claim the same. He made me weak at the knees doing so, because I felt how much he truly wanted me. But sometimes how passionate he could be also scared me, because his behavior could be overwhelming.

His sweet scent never left him, and I let it surround and envelop me as I hummed into his lips. His hand slipped into the curve of my back and he pressed me deeper into his frame. My heart raced. I wrapped my hands around him.

"That's enough," Rylan said, dragging Micah away. A hint of sourness took his expression, and he dropped his gaze to my flushed face. My lips were likely swollen from how hard Micah had kissed me. My breathing was unsteady from the intensity of it. "The officials should be here soon. We shouldn't be in the throes of lust before they arrive. Micah, control your dragon."

Micah growled. His eyes had shifted into a full yellow. He moved away from me, his boots smacking on the wooden ground, and sat in the chair that was supposed to belong to the test subject. Propping his elbows on his knees, he bowed his head. "Why can't we have her?" A husky quality had taken over his voice.

"You know why," Rylan said.

"I don't care for propriety. The court cares little for me."

Rylan sighed. He folded his arms and leaned against one of the barren concrete walls. "You are part of the Everbornes, dear brother. And you will be judged like us."

"A lesser version of an Everborne."

I scooted over to Micah and bent down, tipping his chin so his blue eyes met mine. I forced a smile. "You are just as wonderful as your brothers. Never think for once that you are lesser. The councils are stupid and shallow and can kiss their own uptight asses, because I and your brothers will always be here for you."

His expression remained serious for a moment, and I wondered if my words had gotten through to him. When the sides of his lips curved up, that made my smile genuine.

"You're right." He cupped my face and brushed his lips over my temple, which made me quiver all over again.

I cleared my throat. Feeling curiosity rise, I turned to Rylan and asked, "But why?"

"Why what?" He raised an eyebrow.

I bit my inner cheek. "Why can't you have me? Is it because you don't want me?" I'd whined about it and acted out in frustration a couple times, but I'd never asked directly why, and they'd never bothered to explain.

Rylan's brows crept further up his forehead. "I thought you knew."

I shook my head.

"There is the matter of contraception."

"There were spells for them ages ago."

Gaius nodded. "Yes, but those belonged to the witches of the old, and the spell was lost in the first queen's ban."

Rylan continued, "Should a child be born without us having said the vows, the name of the Everbornes will be sullied, and Vancel will use that to spout more untruths and bring more harm. We can't do anything until you are wed to one of us."

"Wed?" My mouth gaped.

A force tugged at my shoulder, and I found myself pressed against Gaius's hard body. He took my chin between his fingers and searched my eyes. "Are you growing impatient, Sera-kit?"

Was it obvious that I was salivating? "Wait... then..." I looked at Kael. "Have you... have you fathered—"

Kael raised his hands. "We used acecia berries with the other women, but I don't think you want that experience."

I'd heard of it. The woman had to take it before intercourse, but it made her sick the next week. It worked by wounding the subject's womb, making her momentarily unable to bear children. After that, it took time for the womb to recover. The scholars still hadn't figured out how it might affect women's future ability to bear children. It was a common form of contraceptive because people didn't have many other options.

"No." I pursed my lips. "That doesn't sound pleasant."

Gaius smirked. "So, Sera, who would you prefer to wed?"

I couldn't look at him, or any of them, for that matter. How could I decide? They were all equal states of charming. I could feel Gaius's breath on my skin as he ran his lips over my neck—he used touch as a way to persuade me, and I had to admit, he was being incredibly persuasive.

"Can I have all of you?" I asked.

Rylan laughed, a low, mesmerizing sound. "That is not how our marriage system works. You can only have one partner."

Kael said, deepening his voice, "Then it is time for the final competition—"

"Sera," Rylan said, a hardness in his tone. "If you marry me, you will be crown princess. The future queen."

Numbness traveled through me, and my mind fuzzed into blankness. I'd wanted to climb up the ladder... at least I had before. Surely being queen would trump whatever position the council could give me, especially since I stood no chance at being the head of the council anymore. What would my parents think? Could I prove them wrong with this? But wasn't I supposed to get up through my own abilities?

Gaius continued to trail kisses up my neck and to my jaw. I wondered if he knew what his getting carried away was doing to my insides.

"I... I don't know," I said breathily. I gripped Gaius's forearms, which were thicker and more muscular than the others'. "I'll need to think about this."

I spotted Micah over Gaius's shoulder. A darkness took over his features. A growl ripped from him and he stood up.

"Micah?" I asked.

He stormed out the door. I pushed Gaius away. Had I hurt Micah's feelings somehow? I gave chase, wanting to circle my arms around him and ask what was wrong, but the officials stood in the doorway with the test subject. Micah shoved past them, and they blocked my way, not letting me run after him.

"Sera Cadriel," the official in front said. He was an armored male. Dark-skinned with a thick mouth. A subject from the Council of Fortitude. Tindyll, current head of the Council of Intelligence, stood next to him, wielding a clipboard for her notes.

"Apologies for being late." The male official bowed to the princes. "Your Highnesses."

Rylan gestured for them to enter, and so they did.

I looked at my latest victim, and my stomach dropped.

CHAPTER TWO

A BOY.

An innocent child, who looked no older than ten. He was fair-skinned, with doe-like eyes and round cheeks that emphasized how innocent he looked.

He was to be my next victim.

Previously, the officials had made me torture convicts. Men of the lowest of society. They had been gangly, burly, or simply downright hideous, and they bore the most terrible scowls, together with the meanest of dispositions. It was still difficult to use my powers on those convicts, but I used how horrible they were as a distraction—a way to justify whatever torture I had to inflict.

But this boy... with his head of brown hair, angelic face, and wide, curious eyes...

I couldn't hurt him.

He sat in front of me, on the wooden chair, the sole piece of furniture in the room. The chair seemed too large for his tiny, fragile frame.

"No," I said. "I can't do this. Bring me someone else."

"He is the next in line," Tindyll said. "This is something you must do." She glanced at my gloves warily. She had never shed her fear for me, not even after all these months. I took as many precautions as I could, and made sure no incidents like the ones with Mei reoccurred, but it was more difficult to cleanse a bad impression than make one.

"What is the point of all this?" I asked. "I touch them, they go through the pain. Sometimes their minds break, and I'm left with nothing but guilt, and we don't learn anything."

Tindyll snorted. "And I thought you were smart."

"I'm smart enough to recognize meaningless torture when I see it."

"It is not meaningless," Tindyll said. "We have catalogued every one of their reactions, and noted down the different traits of your victims. You have tested your powers on hidraes, drerkyn, draerins, and darmar alike, and we have come to a conclusion."

The boy looked at me with his round eyes. "Where's my mom?"

"What's your conclusion?" I asked Tindyll.

"Those with more dragon blood react more violently to your powers. There's excruciating pain for all of us, yes, but the breaking of minds comes quicker to stronger dragon-kind. Take that sole hidrae convict you touched, for example. His mind broke in a mere three seconds, while the darmar suffered your touch for a whole minute, and nothing happened."

I remembered that particular experiment with the darmar. I'd wanted to let go. Each time I did, they made me repeat the experiment, lengthening the amount of torture the darmar had to go through. So I latched on and begged time and time again for them to let me stop as the torture went on, but they kept asking me to hold on.

"But that doesn't explain the princes," I said, looking at Rylan, Gaius, and Kael. They stood in a corner, watching over me like guardians. I was grateful for their company. I knew Rylan still had lots of work to do, but he took the day off just to spend time with us.

"No, it doesn't," Tindyll said, sighing and adjusting her monocle. "That, unfortunately, is still a mystery we have yet to figure out. Perhaps they have blasphemed as much as you."

A low rumble vibrated from Rylan's chest. "I would watch your words, Elder Tindyll."

Tindyll clicked her tongue against her teeth. "A mere observation, Your Highness."

"It was not."

Tindyll swallowed. "Then I apologize if I sounded offensive."

"The boy?" I asked. "Why must it be him?"

Tindyll regarded the test subject, and a thin-lipped smile sliced across her face. "Dear, could you shift for us?"

The boy closed his eyes and furrowed his brow in concentration. Moments later, a single scale, green and small, appeared beneath his left eye. If not for me staring and actively looking for a difference, the detail would have flown right past me.

Tindyll gestured. "He's a darmar, but one so weak he is almost human. We wonder if he will experience pain from your curse. We also know of a little human girl from Aere

Grove, who apparently does not have the same curse you do. We will send for her next week, and you must test on her, too."

"Aere Grove? My town?"

"Yes, perhaps there is something special about that place... or vile. There must be a reason why dragons are losing their powers there. We have sent some soul magic wielders there to carry out some research, but so far their findings have been inconclusive. Back to the matter. Will you please just carry out the sole duty the king has requested of you?"

I had other purposes, although Tindyll liked to pretend they were as inconsequential as dust. For one, I still led the team in the council, and favor for me was returning. We'd done as much as we could to dispel the rumors Vancel had spread. We tried improving relations amongst other officials, and I worked harder to prove my worth. These days, it wasn't for me to climb the ladder, but to protect the princes. I wanted to be useful so I could stick by their side no matter what.

"The boy might not get hurt?" I asked.

"If our assumptions are correct," Tindyll replied, her features as cold and hard as her heart.

Fear rose in the boy's face. I flashed a reassuring smile, even though I wasn't reassured in the least bit myself. I slipped off my glove and rubbed my thumb across my fingers, which felt clammy because of how nervous this made me.

"This will only last a second," I said. "Open your palm."

The boy lifted his hand. It was shaking. I heaved a deep breath and reached my fingers out. I skimmed my touch over his finger. He winced, but didn't cry out in pain as all of the others did.

"Did that hurt?" I asked him, feeling my chest pound from the beating of my heart.

"I don't know."

"Oh, for Aereala's sakes," Tindyll said. "I have an appointment to rush to shortly. Grab his hand and be done with it."

Rylan gave me an encouraging nod, while Kael grinned, understanding the promise of this situation.

I steeled myself and took the boy's hand in mine. This time, a soft grunt escaped his lips, and his features contorted. Still, there was no screaming and wailing, and he merely looked like he'd eaten something bad. "Ow," he said, trying to tug his hand away.

I let him go, seeing no point in causing more agony, even though his pain paled in comparison to the other test subjects. Relief washed over me. At least I didn't have to break a little child's mind, and the damage I'd done, even though uncomfortable, was something I could live with. "You all right?" I asked the boy.

"You're mean," he replied, pouting. He rubbed his hand and scrunched up his nose. "I'm going to tell Mother."

"Go ahead."

"You mother will be paid handsomely for your sacrifice," the military official said, smiling at the boy. So far, I hadn't heard him speak much, despite the many times we'd met. I didn't realize he had a tender side. I had guessed that he was serving as a guard for Tindyll, and was here to protect her from the convicts who got sent to me. He was likely a formality instead of a necessity. Tindyll, as a powerful draerin, could manage herself just fine.

The boy slipped off the chair and strode to the military official. The official offered his hand, and the boy took it eagerly. "I want to go home."

The official led him away. "And you shall, soon. You were very brave."

"I want to go home too," I said to my princes. My inner thighs were beginning to ache from all the "fun" we'd had in Gaean's pit, and I wanted nothing more than to sleep the rest of the day away. I had a pile of work waiting for me tomorrow, but that could wait a little while longer.

"And you shall," Rylan said, parroting the official's words. He shot me a look that told me he thought I was brave, too.

I padded over to his side, and he embraced me with open arms. I found comfort in his warmth, and his presence let hope rise in me. It felt like these tests would be over soon, but what would the next ones be now that we'd figured out the correlation between dragon blood and my curse? Whatever they were, I could face them as long as I had the support of the princes.

Rylan tucked a strand of my blond hair behind my ear. "Now, let's go find that silly brother of mine, shall we?"

"Let's." I needed to talk to Micah about his outburst, whatever it was. Having four dragon princes sounded nice, but tiptoeing around their emotions could be difficult at times.

Tindyll, the boy, and the official left. We followed them out. Outside, Frederick, the greatest friend in all of

Constanria, stood next to the door, arms crossed and waiting for us.

His robes had been upgraded with more decorations and a shinier blue material. In the last few months, Frederick had managed to get a promotion. He now led two teams in agriculture, and was ranked higher than me. Ambition finally did catch up to Frederick, and he was beginning to accept that the way his family viewed him did matter to him.

At first, I'd felt jealous of Frederick, because I wanted to be the one with all the accolades, and believed my curse had torn my opportunities away. It didn't take long for me to realize that was petty, and that as a friend I should be happy for him, because that was what good friends did—they celebrated each other's achievements despite whatever competition stood between them. Frederick had showed me that.

His face was gloomy, and he shifted his feet about.

"What is it?" I asked.

He turned to face me, straightening the long sleeves of his robe. "The king has called for an audience with both councils. He sent out word that you, specifically, had to be there."

We strolled away from the outhouse with the princes behind me. The evening had passed and the moon had risen, glowing as a beautiful white orb in the sky.

"That doesn't sound promising," I said. "You could have sent a messenger to fetch us."

"I know. I just wanted to see you about it. It's got me worried." He rubbed the back of his neck. "I was beside myself trying to romaine calm. There are terrible rumors frying about."

Those silly puns. Months had passed, and he was still trying to use his vegetable puns. He'd begun recycling a lot of them. I believed they were now in Frederick's speech patterns and it was too difficult for him to unlearn the habit.

"What did Vancel do this time?" I said, sighing. Vancel's tricks were beginning to tire me.

"It wasn't him. At least, I don't think so. They said it has something to do with prophecy. And—"

"Prophecy?" From Princess Anatolia? She had the ability to see visions from the future. "What about it?"

"That's the thing. It's not out yet, but Gisiroth hates you—"

"Thanks."

"—so I'm assuming it's something bad."

"When is it ever good?" Everything was always a constant climb.

"You know," Frederick said, "you talked about ladders once, but sometimes I don't even think it's that. You're not climbing a ladder. You're stuck in some terrible ditch someone shoved you in, and you have to claw your way up with bloodied hands that are missing a few fingers."

"That's dark."

"But we're here to help," Kael said. "Just that we're trying to fly you out but we can't, even though you're strapped to us. Because you're too heavy."

"What is that even supposed to mean?"

"I don't know," Kael said, shrugging. "Frederick went all philosophical, so I tried to find an analogy myself."

"Wait." I pinched myself through my tunic. "Are you calling me fat?" I'd actually been trying to cut down on the sweets and eat more vegetables.

Gaius elbowed Kael's arm.

Kael raised his hands. "It was an analogy! I don't call women fat. Not unless I want a death sentence."

"You called Fat Marbora fat," Gaius said. "In fact, you gave her that nickname."

"But have you seen her?"

Frederick cleared his throat. "On to a less sensitive topic"—because Frederick himself could lose a few pounds —"there's also the news of the Jura region losing the entirety of their autumn harvest."

That stopped us in our tracks.

"What?" I said.

"Probably not the best day to take the day off," Frederick said. "Tindyll gave us the briefing right before work ended."

"But..." I looked at Frederick as if he had Constanria's biggest mystery plastered on his face. "That shouldn't be it. We solved the food crisis, which isn't supposed to be happening at this time of the year anyway. I thought the high summers were the problem."

"Apparently not. All the crops just died." Frederick snapped his fingers. "Poof. Gone. Dead and blackened to ash. Apparently for no reason at all."

"So, we're going to have to defend ourselves from Vancel again today," Rylan said.

We all looked to him.

"If you think he's not going to tie this in with Sera's curse, then you must have missed everything he's done so far. He'll say that we blasphemed by keeping her alive or something, and use this incident to sully the Everborne name." Rylan looked at me. "Maybe you shouldn't be there."

Gaius shook his head. "That'll make it worse. It'll tell people that Sera has something to hide. She should be facing the accusations head-on, because that's what an innocent would do."

"My innocence doesn't matter at this point," I said. My nails dug into my palm. "They don't see me. They'll just see my curse as something to blame again." I thought we were over this, that my new findings solved the problem and, with hard work, we could slowly rebuild our reputation. But things could never be that easy. Aereala simply liked throwing shit our way.

"I should have ice cream ready after this," Frederick said. "To cheer us up."

"Ice cream?" I said.

"Oh, you haven't heard of it?" he said. "New invention from soul magic. It's happiness in a bowl, pretty much, and it'll make you feel like all your problems can melt away in your mouth."

I tucked my tongue between my teeth. "I don't even know if we'll have time to eat ice cream after this."

"Oh, there's always time for ice cream."

CHAPTER THREE

WE COULD HAVE FLOWN to the throne room, but I didn't want to leave Frederick behind, so we walked the rest of the way, which took about thirty minutes.

I was in no hurry anyway, because what awaited me was nothing pleasant, and we needed time to think about what we had to face.

"So," Gaius said. "Do we have a plan?"

"At this point, all we can do is refute whatever Vancel is saying," I replied. "After this, we'll regroup and try and come up with something better to prove him wrong. I'm thinking we should do what he always does. Fight dirty. Dig up something in his background to use against him—the same thing he always does to us. But that's for after this meeting. Right now, we can't do much but take the hits while trying to lessen the blows."

"What if they're too heavy?" Frederick said. "What if you can't recover?"

"Oh, I will." I flexed my jaw. "Because that's what I do, right?"

"That's the spirit, bunny monkey."

"Bunny monkey?" I asked.

"I don't know. I'm playing around with nicknames."

I cracked my knuckles because that made me feel stronger—maybe because of how masculine the action seemed—and stepped through the entrance of the throne room. A wall of warmth hit me. The throne room was warmer than most of Raynea due to the sheer amount of people gathered.

Moonlight shone through the windows, lighting the majestic place. Hundreds of people sat in rows, in tall marble chairs, that faced a blue carpet that ran up to where King Gisiroth perched. His hawkish blue eyes fell on me the moment I stepped in, which sent a spiral of fear through my gut. I knew the princes would protect me from their father, but that man, with how sharp and overbearing he was, could make anybody cower with one look.

Queen Miriel and Princess Anatolia sat at his left, in two golden chairs that were grander than the officials'. On his right, four chairs, probably for the princes, were lined up next to each other. Micah was already in one of them.

"Once you marry me," Rylan said, "or any one of us, for that matter, you'll be up there, too."

"I don't know if I like the sound of that," I said. "What if I needed to make a really ugly sneeze? Everyone would be watching."

Rylan laughed. "It's impossible for you to look ugly."

"Even with my messy hair in the morning?"

"It's cute."

Other people were also strolling in as we did, but they didn't give me the wide berth they used to.

"I should head to agriculture," I said, "and you four should go to your fancy seats."

Gaius turned to me. "I thought you liked fancy?"

"Not when it's right next to Death."

Kael snorted. "My father isn't Death."

"He might as well be, with how gloomy he looks all the time."

A squire, female and with a rose-tinted face, stopped in front of us. She lowered her head, greeting the princes, then turned toward me. "His Majesty has asked me to escort you to your seat."

"I have one," I said, pointing.

"He's assigned a different seat for you."

She led me to one awfully close to the front, right next to Tindyll. Frederick parted from us to find his, and the princes left me to go to where they belonged. Tindyll flashed me a sour look, her face pulling down and making her graceful features uglier than they should be, and scooted her chair away from mine.

"I won't kill you," I said, not bothering to glance her way.

"You might, Sera," she replied. "Your ignorance might be the death of us all. Why must you be this stubborn? Isolate yourself for the sake of the country."

"Because my curse isn't the answer."

"Maybe today will prove otherwise."

"It's a scapegoat."

Vancel Gavril, cousin to the princes and also head of the

CURSE OF DRAGONS   33

Council of Fortitude, sat right across me. He had one leg crossed over the other. Like the princes, he didn't wear a shirt. It was to show that he was a hidrae. Today, his slacks were a simple black.

When everyone entered and settled, a loud bell rang through the throne room, signaling the start of the larger-than-life meeting. Gisiroth tucked his hands behind his back, as Rylan often did, and stood from his throne.

"I'm sure many of you have heard the news," Gisiroth said, projecting his voice through the audience. "All the crops in the Jura region have withered away. There is no way to revive them, not even through soul magic. There'll be a famine this winter." He sighed. "If we don't work this out, many will die."

His last three words knocked into me like a hammer on wood. *Many will die.* This wasn't petty politics, simply to save my or the princes' reputations. I kept thinking about how this might affect our positions, but it was bigger than that. It had real repercussions, with real lives at stake. Lives that Vancel would simply use to fight for the throne, instead of working together to save.

"Are there any details as to how it happened?" one elder from the Intelligence Council asked.

Gisiroth bore himself with gravity and melancholy. "Unfortunately, we don't know the cause. It's not likely the high summers. The crops in the Jura region all died at once, with no warning and without leaving behind any clues. In one moment, they all went gray, and citizens reported those crops tasting like ash in their mouths, inedible for the most part. I will need arrangements to start rations for that region.

Times like these are when the nation is put to the test, and we'll have to judge the compassion of our people. Send out a call for donations, see how much food we can salvage from the capital. If there isn't enough from the capital, send more requests to further regions. If that fails, we will have to put out a demand—"

Vancel stood, his chair screeching.

We all knew exactly what he was going to say, and I steeled myself for what was to come.

With one breath, he voiced what most were likely thinking: "Your Majesty, I am sorry to interrupt, but don't you think this might be related to the curse Sera bears?"

Gisiroth frowned. "It is rude to speak when your king does."

"I apologize, but the thought burned so passionately in me that it made it difficult to hold my tongue. I worry so much for our country that I couldn't help but raise my concerns—"

I stood. "This incident happened more than a hundred miles away from here. How you think me, or my curse, for that matter, might have caused it makes me question how your mind is so dull as to make such a leap in logic."

Vancel looked at me, raising a brow. A catlike, completely punchable smile split his cheeks. "The deaths of those crops are one supernatural phenomenon, and you another. Surely you can see the correlation."

"One fundamental rule of scholarship is that correlation doesn't equal causation. Can you not understand basic principles? Should you need lessons, I'll be happy to tutor you." My voice ticked up in volume as I went on.

The throne room burst into chatter. Hopefully, into conversations that supported me.

Vancel faced away from me, regarding the king. "The crown prince and his brothers have been spending too much time with Sera. We Constanrians have a belief. We think the state of the royal family affects the fate of the country. Perhaps Sera's interaction with the princes has caused this phenomenon."

It sounded completely illogical to me, but Vancel didn't have to be logical. He merely had to appeal to the emotions of the people.

Gisiroth nodded. "Yes. I understand your fears. And that is why they will not be spending any more time with Sera. Nobody will."

What? He couldn't stop the princes from being with me, could he? The king had tried earlier, right after that council vote. The princes outright defied him, and he couldn't do anything about it.

Rylan stood. "Father, I—"

"My daughter received a vision this morning. It's a succinct one, and I've deliberated long over how to deal with it." The king was looking over the whole court, commanding their attention with his presence. "Before you say anything else, listen to what my daughter has to say. Anatolia?" Gisiroth turned to gesture at his daughter.

Princess Anatolia had grown a few inches in the last few months, but she was still a child.

She strode up to the edge of the steps, heaved in a deep breath, and said loudly, "Sera must die." Her gaze shifted to the ceiling, then to her mother.

I jolted at the harshness of her words.

Most of Anatolia's prophecies came true, and she'd had another one regarding me and the princes a few months back. She had been the one to predict Vancel's winning of the head position in the Council of Fortitude.

"Explain, Anatolia," the king said, resting his hand on his daughter's shoulder.

All the princes were on their feet. Kael had his hands on his daggers, Rylan and Micah's on their swords, and Gaius's on his axe.

Vancel's expression had morphed into one of distaste— his grievances were not with me, but with the royal family. He wanted to use me to sully their name, but now that Gisiroth had so brutally cut me from the Everbornes, I was nothing but a useless pawn.

I liked that Vancel's plans had been foiled, but this alternative wasn't an improvement.

Anatolia continued, "I had a vision, of death and destruction, of the ashen crops described from Jura. But this time, it was not merely the crops in Jura that died, but everywhere." Her lower lip quivered. "Too... too many deaths, and dead bodies everywhere. And in there I saw Aereala."

Aereala? The goddess? Questions were murmured through the room.

Anatolia straightened herself. "And she said—I think she was talking to me in that vision—that Sera must die."

Quietness punctuated the atmosphere. I felt everyone's eyes on me. Their gazes were sharp and pierced through my skin.

Vancel sat down, even though I'd expected him to spout more lies. He must have thought there was little use for him to continue his slander, and so he kept his words to himself.

King Gisiroth broke the silence. "You've all heard my daughter. As ruler of Constanria, I must do my duty, and sentence Sera Cadriel to death."

———

Hearing that verdict made my mind go blank.

I woke up, hearing clashing and yelling all around. What had happened?. I was in Kael's arms, and he was carrying me. My cheek... it bled? *That's right*... Guards had swarmed from every corner after Gisiroth gave his sentence. Rylan had refuted his father's verdict, but the king stated that if his sons didn't adhere to it, their ties would be severed.

And Rylan... he'd actually given up his position. He told his father he didn't care, and his fist flew right across Gisiroth's face.

I wasn't sure why I went into shock. Maybe because the verdict sounded like a nail in the coffin. Or perhaps that pounding at the back of my neck had something to do with it too. Did one of the guards knock me over the head?

He might have. The side of my head hurt like hell.

I blinked harder. As my vision cleared, I recognized the pillars of the castle's corridors.

"Sera?" Kael said. He sounded anxious.

"I'm here." I gripped his arm. He lunged forward and made a maneuver that sent nausea through me, and drops of warm liquid landed on my face. I reached up, touched the liquid, and looked at my fingertips.

Blood.

Holy Aereala—I was a scholar, not a fighter, and no amount of Kael's training could make me one. Blood and I did *not* go well together. I looked at where Kael had aimed his dagger and regretted it at once. I didn't think holes were supposed to exist in dragon-kind bodies, especially not such garish ones.

"Couldn't you have, um, poked them a bit more gently?" I asked him.

"That's your kind of thing in bed, huh?"

"This is not appropriate."

"Do you know how hard it is to fight with you in my arms? It's ridiculously awkward."

"More reason to be gentle."

He laughed. "They're trying to kill us, kit. We're not getting out of here if we're 'gentle.'" I heard another squelching sound. Micah was in front of us, clearing a path. I buried my face into Kael's chest, where it was hard and warm and safe, distracting me from the terrible battle playing out around us.

"Scared?" Kael asked. "We'll keep you safe, Fragile-kit."

Fragile-kit was not a nickname I approved of. If acting scared made me deserve it, then I had to act differently. I pried myself away and stared ahead, watching men get knocked aside, wounded and screaming.

"They're your fellow soldiers," I said. "Why are you killing them?"

"They'll live," Kael said. "Dragon-kind heal quickly. It's not like we're smashing their heads in."

Micah turned around. "You don't have to watch if you don't have to."

"I have to." Something told me that life from now on would be filled with more of this, now that Gisiroth had made me an enemy of the state, and I had to harden myself to the violence. "Maybe you should let me down."

"No way in Gaean's balls will I do that," Kael said. "You'll get yourself killed, and that's not going to happen on my watch."

"Makes sense."

I tried to ignore the violence and scanned the perimeter for Gaius and Rylan. "Where are the other two?" The smell of iron filled the air.

"Gaius is up front, trying to give us clearer passage."

Just as Kael explained, I spotted Gaius. He looked even more menacing when serious in battle, wielding his battle-axe clunkily (because Gaius was Gaius), but also with a brutality that made the palace guards cower before him. Magic blasted out from the soul beads around his belt, curling into icicles that cut through his enemies.

"How about Rylan?" I asked.

Silence passed between us. Kael abruptly dipped, whirled, and kicked a guard who came out of nowhere. The guard flew across the corridor at an angle and hit the wall, cracking it.

Kael continued jogging forward, as if what he'd just done wasn't amazing, and replied, "Rylan might not be coming."

"What?"

"He stayed back to try and talk to Gisiroth. I don't know what's going to happen to him."

"Then we have to go back for him!"

"He'll be fine." But the tic in Kael's jaw sent doubt through me.

"Kael, please."

"There's an army of guards between us and him, and he stayed of his own volition. We won't make it. At least you won't, and I'm not going to lose you." His grip on me tightened. "I can't."

I fastened my hands over his arms. "We can't leave him behind. Not like that."

"He'll be fine," Kael repeated, this time with more conviction. "It's now or never. We have to get out."

A *thud* sounded beside us. A draerin, in full dragon form, landed on the roof right across from us. I thought Kael and his brothers might be able to take on one, but then more dragons appeared, one after another, both hidraes and draerins.

"That doesn't look good," I said.

Kael grunted. "The entire military's coming for us." He set me down, as if I were some piece of porcelain. I hated having to be treated this gently. I wanted to be able to blast these enemies away like the princes did. Then I realized I *could*—because my curse was actually a boon in moments like these. I shed my gloves and pocketed them.

It didn't seem like I needed to use my powers, because Kael turned around and zapped electricity at the platoon of guards rushing toward us. It took most of them out. He drew his other dagger and made quick work of those remaining. The dragons who landed on the roof closed in as he did.

Rubble fell behind us—were Gaius and Micah shifting?

When Kael finished clearing out the guards, he turned to me, smiling. "That should buy us a few seconds."

I reached behind him and grabbed the wrist of a guard he'd missed. A sword almost sliced Kael's skull in two. The guard wailed in agony. Kael spun around and thrust his dagger through the man's stomach.

"Sorry, Andre," Kael said. "But you're trying to hurt me."

"On orders," Andre said, wincing.

"Say hi to your wife for me. She makes the best stew."

"Will... do..."

Andre slumped onto the ground, falling unconscious.

"I have to stop wanting to squeal whenever you do that," I said.

"He'll wake up tomorrow morning, good as new." He took off his pants. "You ready?"

"Ready for what? To ride your dragon?"

"Control yourself, Sera Cadriel!"

"You know what I mean." I rolled my eyes.

He smirked. He looked so devilishly good when he did that. "We'll save the naughty things for next time." Striding away, he said, "Try not to get crushed." He gestured for me to step back, and so I did, quickening my footsteps into a sprint. Bright light reflected off the walls as I heard bones clicking and cracking.

A draerin leapt out in front of me, its teeth bared and face full of menace. I let out a battle cry—or at least what I hoped sounded like one, but if I was honest with myself, it probably sounded more like a girlish shriek—and lunged at the draerin's feet. We'd tested out my powers on dragon form before, and they worked just as well as on dragon-kind in human form. The creature roared its pain. I glued my hand to his scales for a few more seconds, making sure he wouldn't be able to move after that, before letting him crumple to the ground.

Another opponent charged at me. This time, a guard in human form.

I was *so* ready to embrace my violent side, when I realized he was covered in full metal plate. *Great*, now my powers were useless.

The walls around me shook. Kael in his white dragon form bit the guard with his enormous mouth. He flung the guard across the courtyard.

I rushed up to Kael and jumped onto his back, using his tail as a stepping stone. I didn't have time to fasten myself there when he took off, leaving behind the palace guards. I almost slipped and fell, but caught my balance before it was too late, and sank against Kael. Arrows flew toward us. Kael banked right, blocking the arrows with his hide, and the arrows dropped to the ground like dead flies.

Draerin and hidraes pursued us, but Micah and Gaius came to our rescue. They looked at Kael. They were growling, communicating to each other in dragon form— dragon vocal cords didn't have the same frequency as humans'. But they could still speak to each other in dragon form, even though my ears couldn't make out what they said.

Kael nodded, before making a wide turn and zipping into the clouds. The icy air prickled my skin, sending shivers through me. I leaned against Kael, and his warmth seeped into my body, mitigating the cold.

"Micah and Gaius," I said. "We can't leave them behind, too." They were obviously outnumbered.

Kael made a nonchalant grunt.

I tensed, clutching Kael more tightly. The princes would know what to do.

They'd be safe.

And this was going to be one hell of a ride.

CHAPTER FOUR

WHAT WAS I supposed to do now? The whole country was after my neck. I couldn't even go back to my parents in Jaerhel's Honor, and had to grasp at straws. My first plan was to ask the princes to drop me somewhere obscure. They could move on with their lives and I could try and live in hiding. But that sounded awfully lonely.

Was there any other way?

I needed to have a long talk with the princes over what just happened.

"Where is this?" I asked as Kael soared through the skies. Stars littered the sky in colorful shades, but beneath them, darkness greeted me.

Kael, of course, couldn't respond, so I let him carry me with his wings. I closed my eyes and relaxed against the comfort of his scales, trying to stop the whirring in my mind. The scent of dirt and leaves hit me—earthy, almost like how Gaius smelled. I heard the rustling of flora, and the faint whistle of the winds.

After I opened my eyes, I still had no clue where we were.

As Kael landed, his body shook, and the ground with it. I slipped off his back, and my boots crunched against a branch. Kael flew off, leaving me in the dimness of the night. Only the moon provided light. I could vaguely make out the edges of trees and bushes.

"We're at Greta's Pines," Kael said, walking back.

Most of the trees were tall and stretched to the sky. It was commonly known that the pines around here never died, and many were as old as the first king.

Kael had his pants on, and his daggers along with them.

"What?" he asked, catching the question in my expression. "You didn't think I'd leave them behind, did you? I threw my items in a sack us hidraes often carry around in dragon form before taking it with me. I can't lose these." I thought I might have seen him doing that. He patted the hilt of one of his daggers. "These are my babies."

"Are they?"

"You shouldn't have left your blade behind. I even named her for you. This is the second time you've lost one of my weapons."

"*Pointy* is not a name. It's a description."

"You're not saying it lovingly enough."

"I really have no idea how you're supposed to say that lovingly. Also, shouldn't names of weapons be commanding, or at least threatening? *Lefty* and *Righty* aren't exactly names I'd give daggers. Especially not ones as exquisite as yours."

He shrugged. "Makes it easy to remember which belongs where."

We'd had this conversation before, and frankly, I was too tired to joke about silly things. My mind reached back to what Anatolia said—*Sera must die.* Was that a lie weaved by the king to rebut Vancel's accusations? Or was it true? What if I wasn't wrongly accused, but the villain causing all of this?

I had to let my mind rest. This was a bigger problem for more troublesome days. Frankly, I just wanted to sleep. Everywhere ached.

Right now, we had plenty of other problems in front of us, and I had to worry about Rylan, Gaius, and Micah. "Why are we here? And when do you think the others will be here—"

Kael hugged me. His body heat surrounded mine, and only then did I notice how cold I was. Winter was only a couple of months away, and the clothes I wore now, despite working perfectly fine in Raynea, couldn't provide proper warmth around the outskirts.

"You're shivering," Kael said, his voice low. "Let's get you someplace warm."

"We were supposed to just have fun today," I said. "Not exactly what I had in mind."

He tipped my chin up and gave me a peck on the lips. "It's exciting to me."

"Will you go back?" I asked, searching his eyes and attempting to ignore the chattering of my teeth. I couldn't see his eyes clearly in the darkness of the forest, but after looking into them countless times, I knew they were beyond beautiful.

"To Raynea?"

"To your family."

"You are my family. Ours."

My breath stilled. I clutched Kael's arm, telling myself he was *real*, because right then, he felt too good to be true. Even my own mother never said I belonged with my family, and hearing the words from Kael's lips made me a little numb.

He rubbed his thumb on my arm, right below my elbow, making comforting circles. "Rylan sent us here. He has a hideout in the pines, one that we know of, so we'll head there to meet up. After that, we can think of a better course of action."

"But Raynea—"

"Is still governed by our father." He smiled. "We have hundreds of years left to live; there is plenty of time to figure this out." His last words weighed heavily between us—we still weren't sure what my life span would be, but chances were it was similar to any human. I'd be lucky to live to a hundred years... probably less, if what Anatolia said was true, and the princes would continue living years later, moving on without me.

"What about the famine?" I asked.

"What about it?"

"We can't just... just let it happen."

"It's not your job to solve it."

It felt like it was. After finding a solution last time, it felt like the responsibility to fix the problem lay on my shoulders, and now that my suggestions had backfired, I had to come up with a better idea.

I frowned. "I could be a farmer. It won't be that bad. It'll be back-breaking work, but at least it's not like going through the latrines."

"Look, Sera," Kael said, "Constanria has a whole council of scholars, many with more experience and expertise in these fields. This is their problem now. You? You simply have to focus on surviving, and we'll help you through it."

I sank into his hard body. The shivers had melted away under his touch, and I could almost sleep in his arms because of how dependable they were. *Wow.* I never thought I'd call Kael dependable, but that was what he was in this moment of need. "Hmmm... for an absent-minded prince, you're talking a strange amount of sense."

"I always talk sense. And that's why I named my swords what I did, because those names make sense."

"Sure," I replied. *And he's back.*

"Let's get to the hideout, shall we—"

Two dragon forms landed in the distance. If not for the *whooshing* of their wings, and the *thumping* of their feet, I wouldn't have noticed their presence in the darkness. It was so dark in these parts. The moonlight wasn't enough to illuminate the place.

Gaius and Micah shifted, and as they neared, their features vaguely came into view. I scanned their clothed forms and sighed relief when I determined they weren't injured.

Rylan wasn't with them.

"You're all right," I said, more for myself than for them. "Good. That's good." I hugged the both of them, one by one, letting the solidness of their frames remind me of their presence. Despite all the blood and violence we'd gone through, we were mostly unharmed.

"Sorry it took us so long," Gaius said. "They were hard to shake off."

"Are you still mad?" I asked Micah, remembering how he had stormed off earlier in the day.

He flashed me a warm smile, one that made my heart race, and replied, "I shouldn't have been in the first place. Right now, I'm just worried about what just happened."

"We'll come up with something together," I said. I thought about settling around the Mishram Plains. Maybe the princes could join me, and try and farm, too. How would that work? I couldn't imagine them in commoner garb. Even then, they might attract too much attention.

We strode through the trees of Greta's pines. I couldn't see clearly and might have tripped, so I held both Gaius's and Micah's hands. They would catch me should I fall.

Then Gaius fell. He tripped over a branch, so I caught him, but he was too heavy, and I was dragged along with him. Micah steadied the both of us, and luckily, I didn't get debris on my outfit.

Cicadas played a repetitive tune, chirping as we strode through the forest. Our feet rustled the leaves and scraped past the shrubs of the forest floor.

"Will I ever go back?" I asked them. I missed Frederick already. Did this mean I was never to see him again? The thought sent anxiety through me.

None of them answered. The question hung in the air,

shrouding us in the uncertainty of the future. With my princes leading me, we trekked through the forest.

We reached a cave. Its entrance was huge, its top thrice my height. It was covered with vines that draped over it.

We entered. The cave was far larger than I thought it would be, big enough to fit a dragon, some furniture, and even books lying about. In there, a campfire lined with stone, orange and flickering with a soft glow, waited for us. Next to it stood Rylan.

"You guys are slow," Rylan said, with a teasing smile that smoothed his edged features.

I let go of Micah and Gaius and ran to him, nearly tripping but catching myself. Rylan accepted my embrace.

"Good," I said, clutching Rylan's arms to support myself. "The four of you are alive."

"Happy to not be dead," Rylan replied.

———

"I can't eat it like that," I said to Gaius, who offered me a piece of raw meat. Kael had caught us a balebeast, a creature shaped like an ox, for dinner. Two large horns protruded from the creature's head. They were larger than my arm. The princes didn't set the head aside while they feasted. I tried not to look into the beast's haunting eyes. It seemed to be questioning why I was eating it. That made me lose my appetite.

The night was still young. Rylan sat in the corner of the cave, with a gravity I didn't like. Kael was juggling his daggers, as he often did, and Micah tended to the campfire.

"How else are you supposed to?" Gaius asked. He burned the meat with his fingertips. "Or do you prefer it like that?"

I pushed away the half-raw mess Gaius was offering. "I might get sick eating this."

"How?" Since I couldn't stomach it, Gaius began biting into it himself.

"Not all of us react well to raw food. Haven't you seen what the servants give me during our dinners?"

"It looks bland, with no depth in flavor. Sometimes I wonder how you put up with it."

I cocked a brow. "They give me the best food in all of Constanria. Sometimes I think you four live in a separate world, unlike the rest of us."

"A world you're a part of now," Gaius said, smiling.

Initially, I wouldn't have thought so, but Gaius had a sweet side. Half the time it rivaled Micah's, when he wasn't being a complete asshole the other half. He was brasher and more temperamental, but because he was so loyal, he treated whoever had his allegiance with the utmost care. Ever since he'd stopped trying to push me away or bite my head of, I'd grown to love him.

"So, how do you want this cooked?" he asked.

"I have no experience surviving in the wild. But preferably cooked thoroughly, with no raw meat, and no burned edges, either. Usually you have to do it slowly, and I don't think dragon fire from your fingertips is going to cut it." I searched around and found an elongated piece of rock. "We could use this as a plate over the flames, perhaps? Wash it first."

When I turned around, Gaius had crouched in front of the campfire. He stuck his whole hand above the flames, and was cooking the food along with it.

My eyes widened. "Gaius! You'll hurt yourself."

He looked at me, amusement lighting his eyes. "No I won't—flames can't hurt us. We're hidraes. Can't promise food like our chef does it, but you won't go hungry today, at least."

I was about to crouch next to Gaius when Rylan strolled up to me and grabbed me by my arm. "Sera, I'll need to talk to you for a moment," he said.

"I'm all ears," I said. "Now, about that farmer thing."

"Farmers?"

"Are there any less populated plains around?"

"We're not doing that. The whole country's going to be looking for you, and we need a better plan than that."

I nodded, feeling a little disappointed. The more I thought about it, the more interested I became in seeing the princes in country garb. "Right, so let's discuss it."

"I need to talk to you. In private, please."

I remembered the last time he'd been withdrawn like this. My stomach made little somersaults.

I sighed. "All right."

We left the cave, striding into the cold of the night. It was still dark, but Rylan held me tightly with his hand, and I felt safe next to him.

"How is Frederick?" I asked. "They didn't do anything to him, did they?"

"He's safe. Still in his council position and not implicated in what happened for the most part."

I nodded. "That's good. Didn't want anything to happen to him. Especially not because of his association with me." Everyone knew he was my greatest supporter. That might give him some problems.

"He'll have more trouble with Vancel, perhaps, now that you won't be around as a target anymore. But I'll make sure he's all right."

"But you're here with me now. How are you supposed to do that?"

Rylan walked onward. I sensed dread brimming in my heart, and I squeezed his hand more tightly. "You're not staying, are you?"

"I wish I could," Rylan said. "But I can't. I wanted you to myself, at least just for this moment."

"I know. The kingdom is important. Your family name is. You can't discard it all just for me, and that makes perfect sense." I still couldn't stop my heart from crumbling, however, because I hated having to lose him again.

"I care for Constanria, but that's not all there is to it," he said. He spun around and hugged me so tightly that my breath slammed out of my lungs. Before my face reached his shoulders, I saw anguish in his expression, and that sent the same emotion through me. "I want you to come home, to Constanria, and continue to build a life for yourself and with us. But that's not going to happen, not if no one's there to protect your name and try to redeem you in the eyes of the court."

"There's no redemption after what just happened," I said. "It won't come. Not after a death sentence from a vision."

"I'll find a way. Perhaps I can question Anatolia more. She wasn't exactly clear on why you must die. I'll overturn Father's decision, or convince my mother to appease him."

"Queen Miriel..."

"She likes you."

I'd been nagging at her sons to visit their mother more, and they had. I didn't think much of it, but it seemed to have won me favor. "She has little power over Gisiroth."

"He listens to her sometimes."

"Not in matters like this."

Rylan kissed me so hard and with so much fervor that I couldn't breathe. He was usually more reserved, and to feel so much emotion pour from him made my chest ache and my mind numb. I felt his muscles tightening around me.

He drew back and tucked my hair behind my ear. His touch grazed my cheek. "I hate the sound of Anatolia's visions. If they are true, then I'm terrified."

"They're not always accurate, are they?"

"They're not easy to decipher, but this one... it sounds so resolute. The resources are all in Raynea. I'll need to go back and look more into this. To figure out what's causing this famine and how it's related to you."

"I wish I could come with you."

"It won't be long." He smiled, but it didn't reach his eyes. "I'll get to the bottom of this, regardless of what it takes. I won't fail you. I hate to fail."

"You don't have to go back," I said. "It'll be all right. As long as all of you are with me." I'd miss the palace—I'd spent many years there, after all, but I could get used to new surroundings. But maybe to Rylan, it still mattered. He was crown prince, raised to be the kingdom's future ruler, and not even I could change the way his past shaped him into who he was today. Unlike his brothers, he couldn't discard all that he'd been trained to care for.

"One year," Rylan said. "Give me one year to fix things. Then I'll come find you. Regardless of where you are, even if you're stuck at the ends of the earth, or across the continent, in Gaia."

"I..." I wanted to say I could live with that, but a year felt like forever when parting with a loved one, so I said, "I'll miss you." I paused, searching his gaze, then continued, "What are we going to do while waiting? I still say we go to a field."

He shook his head. "My brothers and I have plans. You don't have to worry. We'll keep you safe." He sighed into my hand. "I'm going to miss being able to sleep at night," he said.

"I promise to haunt you in your dreams."

His laughter rang out. "I'm looking forward to that."

He brushed his hand over my face, so tenderly that I felt like a treasure to him. He captured my lips with his once again. His body forced mine back. I feared I might trip, but not for long, because he kept his grip steady against my back, until the bark of a tree pressed against me, the coarseness contrasting with the smooth edges of his face.

"I want you," Rylan said. Even in the darkness, I could see the yellow of his dragon eyes. My heart raced.

"Then take me," I said.

He traced my bottom lip with his thumb, and as he did, a low growl shook from his chest. "My brothers won't be happy. We promised to share your first."

He took my lips one more time—each time he did, it felt

like he kissed me harder than before. I wondered where this aggressive side of Rylan came from—perhaps it had always been in him, and now, because we had to part, he'd let it out.

"When I come back," he said, his voice breathy, "when all of this is over, and I know we can raise a child together with no worries, I will make you my queen, and I'll mate with you then." Increasingly, more of his dragon seeped into his words, layering bestial hunger into them.

I didn't want to wait a year. I wanted him now. But we couldn't betray the others, so I wrapped my arms around his neck and nodded. "Okay," I said.

We kissed for a good, long moment, until my lips went numb and I couldn't feel my legs anymore. Then, even though I hadn't had enough, Rylan lifted his lips from mine.

"Your face is flushed," he said. If the sun was out, perhaps I might have caught a twinkle in his eyes.

"Yours is, too." But I could hardly make out the color of his skin in this darkness.

"Liar," he said. He cupped my cheek. "Let's go back. The others are probably wondering if I've kidnapped you."

He walked me back, the same way he did when we'd left. I tried to take in as much as I could of this moment with him. I wanted to tell him to stay with me, but I knew I couldn't convince him, and perhaps it would be selfish for me to. Rylan belonged on the throne, or at least close to it, and I hated myself for making it difficult for him, for making him have to choose between two things he loved.

I hated this. I had the princes and wanted to protect them, but I felt like a nuisance instead of someone useful.

I squeezed Rylan's hand.

"What's wrong?" he asked.

"Trying to figure out how to make all of this right."

CHAPTER FIVE

Rylan hugged his brothers and said goodbye. I couldn't pry my eyes from him the entire time. What if I stormed through the doors of the palace and demanded that Anatolia explain?

I recalled all the guards chasing us. *Nope.* That wasn't going to work.

I wanted all four of us to stick together, but life just wouldn't have it that way. If Aereala stood in front of me now, I'd stick a middle finger in her face and ask her about the crazy visions.

"Hey," Kael said. "You better not worry yourself out when you're gone. Sera won't be happy if we find you looking like an old man, with graying hair and all that."

Rylan smirked and pointed to Kael's white head of hair. "She doesn't mind you."

Kael scowled and punched his brother on his shoulder.

Gaius was the most upset of them all. He and Rylan were twins, and perhaps the closest of the four. "Are you sure I shouldn't head back with you?"

I'd lose two of them, but seeing Gaius leave with Rylan would also give me a peace of mind. Rylan wouldn't have to be alone.

"Sera needs all three of you," Rylan said. "The entirety of Constanria wants her dead now. There are probably patrols looking for her. Remember our plan about Beyestirya. Protect her for me."

Beyestirya? Was I going to be a farmer there instead?

I needed to stop with that farmer thing.

Rylan patted Gaius's shoulder, then turned to his youngest brother. "And Micah? I love you, brother. I don't know what's gotten you so pissed and looking at me like that, but whatever it is, I'll still miss you."

Micah let some of that anger simmer away. He accepted Rylan's embrace, hugging him with as much love as a brother should, before they parted.

I studied Rylan as he talked to his brothers, trying to burn every last bit of his image into my mind—his beautiful, slender, but masculine features, the way his earring hung from his ear. The pattern of his tattoos, which hugged his muscled frame.

Then he turned to me. I gave him a final embrace, before he gave me one last, gentle kiss, and took off into the forest.

And he was gone.

Just like that.

He'll be back. It hurt, but there was no need to waste tears over this, because I was going to see him again soon.

I turned around, facing his brothers.

I saw utter chaos.

One mattress lay on the ground. The fires were dimming.

Next to the campfire were the remains of our dinner—bones and shredded pieces of meat, and even drops of blood, dirtying what I assumed was to be where we had to rest tonight.

I was *not* going to sleep next to the carcass of a balebeast. Disgusting.

"You men are strong, right?" I asked.

Kael grinned, and used my statement as an opportunity to show off. He rested two fists on his hips and flexed his pectorals, letting the muscles bulge. Impressive, but not really what I wanted from him right then.

I continued, "Then why is it so difficult to lift a few pieces of waste? Clean this up." I'd do it myself, but it looked too heavy, so I needed their help.

"Clean?" Gaius said, cocking his head.

"Have you never heard that word in your life?"

"It's the most mysterious word in the dictionary," Kael said.

Gaius nodded. "Isn't it something peasants do?"

Peasants like me. Gaius was never going to shed that haughtiness, was he? I sighed and began picking bones off the ground. "Come on, we don't have all night. I don't know about you, but I'm exhausted. The sooner we clear this, the sooner we can get some shut-eye."

Why were balebeast bones so heavy?

Gaius folded his arms. "I don't know. If we let it rot, the meat will fall off and the bones will be left behind. It'll look interesting. Fancy. I think Rylan might like this new piece of decoration."

I rolled my eyes. "That's your excuse? Are you going to help me or not?"

It was going to take forever if I did this myself.

They obliged, making quick work of the carcass. Gaius disappeared with most of it, and some of the blood got on his clothes, but he came back later without a stain. "There's a river nearby if you want to wash up tomorrow. Probably can't see it now, but this place is actually something to see in the daytime."

After we'd dealt with the carcass, we simply had to figure out where to sleep.

We only had one mattress.

Micah started, "I presume it goes to Sera—"

Kael flopped onto it.

Gaius proceeded to kick him off the mattress. "Ladies first."

"Hey! I have needs, too." Kael scowled, rubbing his neck, then looked at me. His expression softened, and a bit of guilt showed. "All right... Sera should sleep on it."

I shrugged. "One of you can have it. I can sleep on the ground."

Micah snorted. "It's cold. It's nearing winter. You'll be sick in the morning. Or if not, at least extremely uncomfortable. We're dragons, so sleeping on the ground should be second nature to us."

He had a point, and although I wanted to say no for formality's sake, it was a waste of time, so I took the mattress, while my princes slept next to me. Kael had been filled with life throughout the day, but as soon as his head hit the ground, he was knocked out. He snored. Somehow, even when snoring, he looked attractive. Micah and Gaius took their places next to me, and I used their warmth to try and calm myself after the events of the day.

The events raced through my mind regardless of how much I attempted to abate them. My body was tired but my mind refused to rest.

Micah's breath on my neck interrupted my thoughts. He circled me with his arms and dragged his body closer to mine. I hummed a soft sigh, unable to help myself. Often the princes avoided sharing my bed—perhaps it was too tempting. Plus, they were trying to hold themselves back. We should have had more moments like this, but they were rare, and when they did come, I delighted in them.

"Don't marry Rylan," Micah said, his voice raspy against my neck.

"What?"

"Don't. Just... You can't."

I turned so I faced him. I frowned. Micah sounded... defeated, and afraid. I cupped his face and shot him a questioning look. "Rylan's gone, Micah."

"Not for long. He'll return a year later, or when all this blows over , and you'll marry him because of all he has. He's always had everything, and with him, you'll be queen. With me—you'd never choose me, because I'm the bastard child of the king and I'll make you look bad."

"That's not what I see."

"But it's the truth."

"No." I shook my head. "Of course it's not. You're strong

despite what life has thrown at you, and you're the sweetest, and one of the cleverest, men I know. You make me feel special, Micah." Sometimes more so than his brothers, but I couldn't admit that—it'd start a fight should I be overheard.

He brought my hand to my lips and kissed the back of it. His lips were slightly chapped, and the coarseness sent tingles through me. "Promise me you won't marry him."

"Micah—"

"He has everything, Sera. And now he'll have you."

"I belong to all of you. Regardless of status." I brushed the back of his crimson hair and looked into his striking eyes. I had to make him see that I cared for all of them equally. Maybe I shouldn't marry Rylan. Maybe belonging to just one of them, despite it only being in name, would ruin everything. "We'll look at the circumstances."

Micah heaved a huge sigh. His breath sent heat through my fingertips. "All right. I'll have to convince you some other way, then."

My eyes widened. "Wh-what are you doing?"

My cheeks lit with fire, and so did the rest of my body. Micah rested his hand between my legs, and there, he began stroking. I couldn't keep the air in my lungs, and a huge, shocked breath rushed from them.

A smirk lit Micah's eyes, and with his inviting, chapped lips, he said, "What I've wanted to do for a long time. I'd always thought there was a code between us. We've been walking on a tightrope, wondering what to do with you. But now I'm thinking I should tell the code to fuck off."

I was turning into a puddle.

He reached to cup the back of my head, and pushed his lips to mine. There, he took control, guiding me through the kiss. My toes curled. A heady sensation took over, and for a second it felt like I was floating. When Micah dipped his fingers into my folds, I thought I might die.

Behind me, Gaius stirred. "What are the both of you doing—"

I muffled a moan and pressed my fist onto my lips. With my other hand, I gripped Micah's arm, the one that was pleasuring me.

Gaius started, "Micah, you cheeky—"

Micah merely winked at Gaius, and that made him look more irresistible. Aereala curse him for the brothers' ridiculously good looks.

Gaius turned me around, and as he did, Micah didn't let go. He caressed my center, working his way deeper and wider, spreading me apart, until I wasn't sure if I liked it or if it was too much for it to take.

"Look at me," Gaius said. Commanding much? But I liked how assertive it sounded. I opened my eyes, not having realized that I had shut them, and saw Gaius's yellow eyes, which had shifted from blue.

Gaius claimed my lips, while Micah wouldn't relent. Gaius's hand edged down the curve of my back, until it reached my ass, and he cupped it, pulling me closer to him, as if trying to snatch me away from Micah.

"You can't have her all to yourself," Gaius told Micah.

"Sometimes I want to," Micah said. They were both whispering, in tones so low and rough that they made me want to squeal, but that would completely kill the mood, so instead, I restricted myself to a soft mewl.

"Then you're going to have to fight me for her."

A low growl, followed by a chuckle, came from Micah.

In the background was Kael's light snoring—he was sleeping through this entire thing, and some part of me wanted him to wake up just to see how he'd react. He was the one constantly boasting about his sexual prowess.

"You're making this difficult for us," Gaius said to Micah. "We've been trying not to have her. And now I can smell how much she wants us."

"Oh well," Micah replied. "Tough luck."

"I think you guys should... should stop trying... to hold back," I said. Or, at least, I thought that was what I said. Most of my words were probably incoherent, because I couldn't manage much more than a gasp.

Micah's hardness pressed against me. *Oh gods.* He rocked his hips back and forth.

"I need you, Sera," he said into my neck. His breath was hot and tickled my skin.

Kael was completely oblivious to all this. Hearing his snoring somehow made this more exciting, because it felt like we were doing something wrong, even if it *felt so right*.

The tension in my center built. I hugged Gaius, moaned into his chest, and my body shook. I rode the waves of pleasure that pulsed through me. Micah quickened his fingers, making me buckle against his grip. I hissed out a curse, wondering why we'd waited so long if this was what I'd been missing out on.

The waves settled, leaving me thoroughly satisfied.

I thought it was over, but Micah bit my ear and whispered, "Again?"

"No... it's too much." Did my words come out? My mind was fogged and I didn't have a proper grip on reality.

"I'm not sure we should," Gaius said. "It's making it hard to hold back."

Micah continued to stroke my folds. "But she's enjoying it."

Gaius lightly tugged my hair back and nipped my neck. A low rumbling, animal-like, vibrated from his throat.

Micah wouldn't stop. I gave in and threw away my cares, letting myself sink into the pleasures Micah and Gaius gave me.

———

Micah must have been incredibly talented with his fingers, because it seemed like he'd sent me straight to heaven.

Heaven? Maybe it wasn't that exactly. Being in a dream made more sense.

What if I'd died in my sleep? If I had, well, that smelled like Gaean's balls, but at least I'd had a painless death, which was more than most people could ask for.

Heaven was gorgeous, but also kind of creepy. The sky here had a blanket of purplish clouds, and everything seemed ghostlier, with forms that wavered and misted as I walked past. Flora littered the ground. The tufts of grass here reached out in a mesmerizing bluish-green, with not a withered blade in sight, but as I stepped over them, they vanished into smoke before misting back in place once I passed.

I stood in a meadow. It was the strangest meadow I'd ever come across. I continued to walk aimlessly. Heaven should have more forms of entertainment. An eternity in this endless landscape, despite how pretty it was, seemed more like hell than heaven. Or perhaps I did deserve hell... maybe the gods had deemed my curse too terrible and wanted me in hell instead.

If that were the case, the gods must have been quite sadistic, because they'd given me my curse in the first place.

As I continued to walk, I spotted a giant tree looming in the distance. I had nowhere in particular to go, so I waded toward it, trying to get used to the ethereal nature of everything around here. The tree bore bluish-green leaves, same colour as the grass. It was gigantic, and the closer I went, the more its branches seemed to encompass the skies.

Faint, misty birds chirped in the tree. They twittered—then one of them dropped dead.

Yep, I was increasingly convinced that this was hell. Nobody said hell couldn't be pretty.

"Baa...llaaannnceee..."

The creepy voice startled me. I walked around the tree, and there, next to the trunk, was a woman perched on a pink rock.

She looked...

She looked like me.

And that made me ready to wake up from this dream.

She was creepy, making my hair stand on end. It felt like I was looking into a new and improved reflection of myself. Was this some kind of trick the gods were playing on me?

Her head lolled as she continued, "Neeeeddsss... Restoreeddd..."

"Hello?" I said. I waved my hand in front of the woman to try and get her attention. She continued to stare up ahead, her eyes glazing over, kind of like Kael when he magically emptied his mind. "Helllooo?"

As I inspected her, I was more convinced she was my twin sister... or something like that. Her features were mine—just infinitely more refined. A shapelier mouth, the same blond hair, although her hair was wavier, with a sheen that sparkled under this pink sun. Her eyes were slightly rounder, the green of them brighter than mine. She didn't seem much taller, but her figure and curves had such amazing proportions that she looked even more beautiful than Miriel.

Me. Just more perfect. No, beyond that—not just flawless, but a beauty who transcended words. However, I doubted she'd fare well in the dating scene. She was pretty, but she'd scare men away with the way she cryptically spoke drawled-out words in her eerie voice.

"Heeellooo?" I tried again, waving my hands in front of her like I was carrying out a strange dance.

"Baallaaannnceee," she said again. Her voice sounded like an echo, reverberating through the air.

I got frustrated and reached out to touch her. My plan was to shake her until she acknowledged my presence.

My hand misted through her.

Was there no way to get her attention? I frowned.

It took me a second to realize I'd been mistaken. I did get

her attention, because when I looked up, her green, crystalline eyes were on me, lit by a smile.

"Sera," she said. "Nice to meet you."

I opened my mouth to respond, but my consciousness tugged in another direction, and moments later, my eyes flung open.

I stared up at the walls of the cave. Micah and Gaius lay next to me, sprawled awkwardly on the mattress, which was too small for the three of us. Gaius had his hand over my face, which was too heavy and giving me a headache. I had to pry it away to save myself. My two princes slept, eyes closed and breathing softly.

I lifted my hand and rested the back of it on my forehead, trying not to elbow Micah in the face as I did. What had just happened left me utterly confused.

So that was a dream? Not heaven or hell? But it felt so *vivid*, and my dreams usually consisted of non-vivid, nonsensical things, like a cabbage chasing Frederick or Kael cheating on me with Tindyll. Kael received a scolding after I woke up from that one, and I'd left him flabbergasted. It was right before the time of the month that day, so my hormones were acting up, and waking up from that dream made me unreasonably mad.

"What?" he had said. "Me and *Tindyll*? What in Gaean's balls?"

I had answered him by throwing a pillow at his face.

I did apologize for my outburst, but his brothers wouldn't let him hear the end of it for an entire week, making jabs about when he was going to ask Tindyll out on a date. They'd exploded into laughter each time the council head strode by. It did little to improve her impression of us.

The memory made me smile.

I closed my eyes to force myself back to sleep, but moments later, an orange glow seeped into the cave. The sun had risen, which meant I had to get up.

Or not.

Five more minutes.

CHAPTER SIX

Would Kael miss Lefty if he found his dagger missing? Or maybe I was holding Righty instead. I couldn't tell them apart. They both had the same blades and hilts, with embellishments of dragons on the sides and a comfortable grip. I didn't know how *he* could tell them apart.

I breathed out a deep sigh, going through the motions Kael taught me before. Fire stance, with my elbow raised and pointed up, to water, which was more a fluid motion than a stance. It was imperative I could quickly switch to different styles, to make sure none of my moves were predictable.

I wondered if I looked like a fool, standing in the forest clearing, swinging my dagger in what I hoped were *not* aimless motions.

Gaius was right about the pines looking much better in the morning. The forest had morphed into an entirely different creature, and the place glowed with golden and red leaves. The constant humming of the cicadas had switched to the chirping of songbirds.

But in the beauty, I saw some burned leaves. Ashen—like how accounts from Jura region had described the plants. As I guided my dagger through the air, I thought about what that strange woman had said in my dream.

Balance? How did this world lack it? It was gorgeous, and Raynea, despite having grown into a flourishing city, embraced nature and embedded it into its landscape.

Maybe she'd knocked her head into something. It certainly seemed like it, by the way she couldn't form a coherent sentence.

A *whooshing* came from above me, and when I looked up, I saw a draerin flying past. My heart dropped, but the dragon left quickly, not spotting me. I wondered if it was one of the king's men—guards, on the search for my presence.

I tried to ignore it and return to training.

I dipped into stone stance, before rising in fire stance, but lost my balance and ended up landing in what I called my-butt-hurts stance. I sounded an *oomph,* then moaned a complaint about not being blessed with grace.

No matter—if I worked hard enough, I would earn that grace. And then I'd give Kael a run for his money with his sword-fighting skills.

I had to believe that, because starting with success in mind was the best way to find it. I envisioned Kael falling to my feet because my skills awed him so much, kissing them while begging me to teach me his ways.

I chuckled at that image.

I didn't see the need to train in battle before, but now, with a whole nation wanting my head on a pike? Fighting skills were probably more important than agricultural knowledge.

A yipping sounded next to me. I startled, whipping my head around to its source, and my heart almost froze.

Oh, this creature...

It was... was...

It was *so* cute!

An ingoria puppy stood behind me, with its tongue out and tail wagging. Ingorias were a subspecies of canine, related to ingors, but they were wilder and larger.

This ingoria, however, was small and a still a fuzzball. It had a babyish face and a tiny snout. *Adorable.* So adorable I almost wanted to strangle it—what was with cute things and their tendencies to make people aggressive?

"Hey, little guy," I said, the pitch of my voice rising a couple notches. I dropped my dagger and turned around, offering my hand for it to sniff.

It bit me.

The little devil.

I flinched, before realizing it wasn't attacking me, but play-fighting, and its nipping didn't hurt much. I laughed and scratched the back of its ear, musing at how soft its white fur was.

More yipping came from the bushes, and two more pups came out, looking for its sibling. I made a silent prayer to Aereala, thanking her for making my life a little fairer—yesterday was a shitty day, but today was getting off to a great start.

One of the pups circled me. I played with them, picking them up and pushing them on their backs to rub their bellies.

Their bright yellow eyes shone with eagerness. The smallest one ran ahead, suddenly deciding it'd had enough of roughhousing, and flopped onto its belly. It licked its tiny paw and yawned.

"Tired?" I asked.

Its ears perked up, but it didn't lift its head.

I chuckled and continued messing around with its siblings.

A growling, instead of more yipping, rumbled from the bushes. A huge figure swept the branches aside, and an enormous ingoria, almost twice the size of me, emerged from the branches.

It did *not* look happy.

Aereala bless me. If I ever saw her, I needed to give her a slap. Screw eternal damnation and whatnot if she'd decided to give it to me.

I leapt to my feet and grabbed Kael's dagger. My hands shook. I didn't want to use it, not against a mother with three little cubs.

The puppies continued to wag their tails and bounded toward their mother, seemingly without a care in the world.

Traitors, I thought.

The full-grown ingoria padded forward. Its eyes were sharp, menacing, unlike its puppies. It drew back the top of its lip, growling, showing off its canines, which were the size of my hand. The sinew of its muscles rippled as it stalked me. I felt increasingly smaller as it neared. I gripped the hilt of my blade tighter.

"I was just playing," I said. "I'm just going to go and head off now, if you don't mind." I took a step back and raised both hands in a surrender. I continued to walk backward, pivoting to the left to turn around.

It lunged.

I attempted to dodge, but a sharp pain sliced across my leg. My body landed at an awkward angle. An ache shot through my left side. I groaned and spun around to inspect my leg. I'd suffered a wound. Shallow—nothing too serious.

My heart pounded. My hands became so sweaty that it felt like I'd lose my hold on the dagger.

I jumped up to my feet. Did I really have to fight? I didn't want to kill this beautiful creature... or be killed by it.

"Let's... let's call a truce, shall we? You don't want to fight me," I said to the ingoria, mostly for my benefit. I was absolutely terrified.

The creature could smell fear. It seemed to grow more aggressive. I inched back again, and it pounced.

I cursed internally. The ingoria slammed me with its side and I flew across the clearing, hitting a tree. The back of my head knocked against the wood. I hissed.

"Come on, I promise to leave you and your cubs alone." My entire body ached and I wanted to return to my princes' arms. I looked around, hoping they'd appear—weren't princes supposed to rescue maidens during times like this?

Not a hint of them. Kael was probably still on his face, snoring.

I had to somehow face this terrible beast.

The ingoria pulled its lips up, snarling. It stalked toward me. My heartbeat quickened with each step it took. I held Kael's dagger with both hands and readied myself to counter an attack.

The ingoria snapped its jaws and pounced at me. I flinched, imagining the beast's teeth sinking into my flesh.

Nothing.

I pried my eyes open. Warm blood trickled down my hand, and a limp, furry body slumped from my dagger and onto the ground.

Crap. Through some miracle, I'd killed it. The creature had impaled itself on my Kael's dagger. Blood continued to leak from the ingoria, staining its white fur an ugly red. Its tongue lolled out of its mouth, falling to the ground. The ingoria's eyes were still open, staring at me, as if accusing me of its murder.

I was panting so hard that I heard myself breathing. I wiped my stained hands on my pants.

"Hey!" Kael's voice woke me from my shock. He had his wings out and was shouting to me from above. Micah and Gaius emerged from the canopy of the trees too, with their wings fanned out behind their backs.

Took them long enough to arrive.

They swooped down and landed in front of me.

"Sera!" Gaius called. Anger laced his voice.

Well, I should have been the one angry, because the princes didn't save the damsel.

"She found us breakfast," Kael said. He rolled the ingoria to its back with his foot and plucked his dagger from the beast. "I'd been searching everywhere for Lefty. Aereala's teats. Sera's got you all bloodied up, didn't she? Poor Lefty."

I frowned. "Isn't that what daggers are supposed to do? Poke things and get bloody?"

"Take care of the things you borrow!" He looked at his

dagger and tried flicking blood off it. "I'll need to wash this in the river."

"Oh geez, thanks for your concern."

"You're fine."

"She's hurt," Micah said, inspecting my leg. He turned around, waving Gaius to come closer.

"Oh," Kael said, turning to me and seemingly forgetting about Lefty.

Gaius, wearing the same serious expression as Micah, knelt next to me. "We don't have an unlimited supply of magic, not like in Constanria."

"It's for Sera."

Gaius nodded. He murmured a spell that was so soft I couldn't hear it. A cooling sensation tingled over my wound. It closed up, stitching back together, and the scratch disappeared.

I blinked.

"And that was at least three oxen worth," Gaius said, sighing. "Why are healing spells so expensive?"

"You could have let it heal naturally," I said.

"But you might have been scarred."

Kael shrieked—or did that count as a shriek? It was a weird, muffled sound. "There's a scratch on Lefty."

Micah smacked him over the head. "Priorities, brother."

Kael sniffed, running a finger across his nose. "I'm glad you're healed, Sera." He walked over to one of the cubs. I felt a pang of guilt—I'd killed their mother. I had to, or I probably wouldn't be standing here right now, but knowing that didn't stop me from feeling like an asshole.

Kael picked one of the cubs up by its nape. "And she got us dessert, too."

I balked. "You are not going to eat that poor thing!"

He chuckled. "I'm kidding. Their mother is plenty."

Not because they were innocent and cute?

"You are incorrigible."

"It's the food chain. But yeah, they're kinda cute." Kael scratched the pup's chin, but the pup didn't react. It was grieving over the loss of its mother.

"You're not eating their mother."

"What?"

I folded my arms and walked from the tree. My legs didn't hurt anymore because of Gaius's magic, but I needed to wash the blood from my hands. "None of you are. Have some respect. We're burying her." It was my half-assed attempt at making it up to the pups. Was this weird? It felt kinda weird. I'd just killed their mother, but hey, the creature was about to eat my head.

"But that is just a waste of—"

"I want a proper burial. The ingoria was a majestic beast. That's the least it deserves."

Micah shrugged. "I'm with Kael. You don't see us performing funeral rites at dinner every day."

"It's different when you played a part in slaying the beast." I'd seen it as a living, breathing creature. Not to mention its children now stood in front of me. Eating a mother in front of her offspring was nothing but cruel. "We're burying it."

Gaius sighed through his nose and scratched his temple. "But I'm hungry—"

"No buts." I lifted a finger in warning. "Find another breakfast."

"All right, all right."

We found a nice site, next to a lake. Micah shifted into a dragon and dug a hole for us. The pups were scared out of their wits. They hated me—for five minutes—before warming up to me again. I guessed children, regardless of species, had no real concept of death.

We buried their mother, and I said a poem commonly recited by priests. Micah swept his claw over the dirt, covering the ingoria.

"It's a whole lot of trouble for meat," Kael muttered as he patted the dirt down. I found a shiny rock and placed it over the grave, marking it.

Micah flew away and returned moments later, clothed.

"Why is my dragon always acting up every time I shift?" Micah said. "It's so adamant that Sera's our mate. And I keep telling it that mates don't exist."

The big, beautiful lake next to us shimmered under the morning sun.

"Same here," Kael agreed.

Gaius pressed his lips together. "She can't have four mates."

"She's one of a kind," Micah said. He kissed my cheek and hooked his arms around me. "Maybe she really belongs to all of us."

Four. I sighed. Without Rylan around, it always felt like something was missing.

The three ingoria pups splashed around in the waters. I was beginning to be able to tell them apart. There were two males and one female. Strangely, the female pup was the biggest, but also the prettiest, with a snout that curved out gently.

"We can't stay in the wilderness forever," Gaius said. "Not after what just happened. Sera needs to be someplace safe." He looked at the ground, in deep thought.

"I took care of myself, didn't I?" Perhaps I was learning to be dexterous, just like Kael—or maybe I'd been lucky. The second option seemed more likely.

"Barely. The ingoria might have torn you apart."

I gestured to myself. "Still alive."

"And you might continue stealing my weapons," Kael said.

"I'll take Gaius's axe next time, or Micah's sword."

Both their faces scrunched up with distaste.

"They're just things," I said.

Kael narrowed his eyes. "You shouldn't speak such blasphemous words."

I cocked a brow.

"We've had these weapons since we were teenagers. And we've been taking care of them since—"

"On to the matter at hand," Micah said. "Rylan had suggested we go to Beyestirya before he left. To Kaldaross."

"To Kaldaross?" I asked. It was the capital of Beyestirya. "What's there?"

"We have a cousin."

Kael groaned and buried his face in his hands. "Not her."

"Vanjar," Gaius said. "She grew up with us, and won't turn us away. She's also in a powerful position there, so she'll have the resources to take care of you. We won't be plagued by patrols there, because if Gisiroth keeps sending them over, it'll strain the relationship between both countries."

"Not Vanjar," Kael said.

"Why not?" I asked.

He knocked his head onto his fist. "She's mean, vindictive. She will eat our hearts out—"

"She's really nice," Micah said. "Don't let what Kael's saying get to you."

"Okay..." I didn't know whom to trust.

"Do you need to pick up anything from Rylan's hideout?" Gaius asked.

"I didn't bring anything along," I replied. "Not that I had a chance to. Since we were running away from guards." I wished I had. I desperately needed a change of clothes.

"All right," Gaius said. A smile inched up the side of his lip. His blue eyes had never been so gentle. Was he still worried about what happened to me yesterday?

I was more worried for him. Did the princes often spend this much time out the palace?

"We're really going to Beyestirya?" Kael whined. His face had turned into a field of morbid bleakness.

"Yes," Micah said. He stripped off his pants.

My brows reached to the top of my forehead. "I need to get used to that."

"What?" Micah asked, not caring that he stood stark naked.

I twirled my index finger in a circular motion, gesturing to his oh-so-exquisite frame. "Can you tell that I'm salivating?"

He smirked. "Yes."

I ran my tongue over my bottom of my lip, and Micah tracked that movement with his eyes.

Kael and Gaius took off their weapons and pants, too, acting like me ogling solely Micah peeved them. I'd gone past trying to be proper. I fully embraced my pervy side, and took in what I could.

They shoved their items into their sacks and swung them over their shoulders.

"We're shifting to dragons," Gaius said. Gratingly so, or maybe deliciously so, he managed to look amazing while talking bare-bottomed. "It takes too long to get to Beyestirya otherwise."

"You're staring too hard," Kael said, his eyes twinkling. He turned around, his ass fully on display. I wasn't sure if he was tightening the muscles on his butt on purpose.

"And you're ha—" I bit my tongue, deciding I didn't want to go there.

They proceeded to shift, summoning bright yellow light from their frames. There were some trees in their way, and they had no choice but to knock them down as they grew in size.

The three pups whimpered and ran to me. They pawed at my legs. I scooped them up into my arms, feeling my fingers sink into their soft fur.

CHAPTER SEVEN

I PRESUMED I'd have gotten used to heights and flying by now, but apparently, riding for a few minutes was entirely different from riding a couple hours on dragon-back. I was feeling giddy from being in the lighter atmosphere for too long, and I wanted to rest on solid ground to calm my nausea.

I sat on Gaius's back, and we flew across a plethora of beautiful landscapes. The princes had to take a huge detour to avoid Raynea, where lots of the search patrols were. I caught sight of some dragon silhouettes in the distance, and Gaius sped up when he saw them, avoiding them. Luckily, they didn't give us any trouble. Perhaps they thought we were another patrol.

I spotted the peaks of Gaean's pits in the distance, and rows of green fields and fruit. There were trees and some dirt roads beneath us, and they were bright with yellows and oranges.

I thought everything was scenic, until my eyes caught the blackness of fields of dying crops. We must have passed the

Jura region as we went, and only then did I truly manage to visualize the horrors of what the farmers there had spoken of. Never had I seen something so ghastly—had we wronged the gods?

"It's terrible," I said to Gaius.

Smoke billowed from his nostrils. Was that him agreeing?

I clutched the ingoria cubs closer to my chest.

They'd stopped freaking out and had calmed down. It was a huge conundrum trying to balance them on Gaius's back. I didn't want to commit to pets, but if I'd left these pups behind, they would no doubt perish in the harshness of the wild.

Oh, and did I mention they were cute?

Gaius continued to glide through the winds, his wings flapping through the air. Eventually we left the morbid fields and soared over a large expanse of snow. The snow stretched on for miles, a blanket of white over the vastness of the Drae Lands. I managed to see a huge group of mammotharians trekking, their feet forming a huge trench in the snow.

Despite the fun sights, I was not in good shape.

It was *cold*. Even the heat from Gaius's dragon form couldn't stave off the coldness, although I thought it was the only reason why I wasn't dead of hypothermia yet. I should have searched for thicker clothing before agreeing to come here.

The Beyestiryan mountains stood colder, sharper, and icier than any other mountains I'd seen—even more so than the ones in Gaean's pits. We passed by stretches of mountain ranges, so endless that I began to question when I'd see the end of them.

The winds here blew relentlessly against us, and one gust was so strong that the cubs and I almost slipped off Gaius's back. I held to them for dear life. We needed a better way to transport these cubs, because me holding them like this was *not* reliable. I was surprised they'd even made it this far.

The ride neared an end when I spotted a wintry palace sprouting between a valley of mountains. Relief spread through me.

Painters never missed the iconic palace when painting Kaldaross. Beside the breathtaking icy structure was a mass of buildings that sprawled and fanned out from the palace, which looked like the epicenter of the view. Gaius and his brothers dipped their wings, and we began our descent.

The palace grew larger as we neared.

Gaius reached the ground, landing in front of the massive structure. The force of his landing shook through me. The pups yipped again, as if announcing our arrival.

The palace was so huge that I couldn't even see the top of it when I arched my neck to peer up. My inner thighs ached from sitting on a dragon's back for too long. My muscles there had not yet been trained. When I lifted my left foot to swing it toward my right, I winced from the ache.

The ingoria pups slid off before I did. They walked around with tentative steps and sniffed the ground, recovering from their fear in a blink of an eye. Their fur protected them from the cold, and they weren't as bothered as I was.

A group of guards strode down the entrance's steps. "Who's there?" They were dressed in thick armor, and had their faces covered with scarves—clothes that looked comfortable and warm. Clothes I needed.

Kael and Micah began shifting back into human form.

A guard picked up the female pup. During my long ride, I'd decided to name her Aura, because she deserved a pretty name like that. I named one male Mayhem, because he seemed like the most playful of the bunch, and the other male Grunt, because he wouldn't stop making strange noises.

"D-d-d-don't hurt it-t-t!" I shouted, teeth chattering. "W-w-we c-come in peace."

"We're looking for Vanjar," Micah said in human form. My eyes widened at how he stood completely naked in the cold. He didn't shiver or bat an eyelid. My initial reaction was to worry he might freeze his (firm and pinchable) ass off, but then I remembered hidraes like him could control their body temperature. Micah slipped into his pants and fastened his weapons to his leather strap, as did Kael.

I pushed myself off Gaius but hugged closely to his body as I slid from his frame. I wouldn't last long if I didn't have his warmth. The cold of the ground seeped through my boots, chilling the soles of my feet.

"What do you want with our queen?" a guard asked, voice guttural. He had his pike pointed at us.

Queen?

"First," Kael said, "clothes for our human here. She's not taking well to your cool weather."

Cool? This wasn't cool weather. Cool weather involved prancing about, perfectly content with how nice and gentle the winds were. This was one step away from standing in a straight-out blizzard. It was a freeze-your-eyeballs-out level of cold. I rubbed my arms. At least the city was a tad warmer than when up in the air. The lower altitude and being surrounded by more dragon-kind likely made a difference to the temperature.

I *needed* to get some clothes on myself. I was close to ripping those comfortable woolen clothes off the soldier myself.

The soldier set Aura down, much to my relief.

"Who are you?" another soldier said. He seemed to be one of the chubbier ones, though I couldn't tell very well from their wooly garments. Maybe it was his triple chin that made me think that.

"Your worst nightmare," Kael said, lowering his voice. I withstood an eye roll, and Micah elbowed him. He laughed, despite the guards tensing up and edging their spears closer toward us. "I'm kidding, kidding. We're the princes from Constanria."

"Princes—"

"That's enough, men, lower your spears," a woman said, bursting out the front gate. She was the most beautiful woman I'd seen, with long chestnut locks. She had smooth and tan skin. Her eyes were gray like smoke. Each of her movements exuded allure, and I wasn't sure if she was consciously being this sensual, or if she simply was this way. "Cousins," she said, a wide grin splitting her face.

As I continued to stare, I realized her complexion and features reminded me of Vancel.

"Wait... if you guys are cousins..." I said to Gaius, despite knowing he wouldn't be able to respond. "From which side of the family?"

Gaius flared his nostrils. Vanjar... Vancel. Were they siblings?

Why in the world would the princes trust Vancel's sister?

She looked to be just as foxy as he was. Perhaps even more so. As she tipped her chin up, she nudged her breasts. Her soldiers immediately dipped their gazes to her chest.

My brow creased. Was she doing that on purpose?

"Somebody hurry up and get this girl a cloak!" Vanjar said, raising a hand.

The soldiers scampered away like ants.

She walked down the steps, each of her movements graceful, fluid, almost entrancing.

And because I was a woman, and because women often got jealous, I hated her.

She was too *perfect*.

Except for that strange boob-touching habit she had.

But that wasn't enough to make me like her. Her beauty didn't rival that ethereal woman I'd seen in my dream, but maybe they were just peaches and apples.

Vanjar strode up to Kael and Micah. Micah gave her a hug, and I wanted nothing more than to pry her grimy hands off my prince. Kael looked mortified when Vanjar approached him and offered an embrace.

"Still hate me?" Vanjar said, lowering her arms.

He growled.

Her laughter was like a songbird's. "We were children, Kael."

"Doesn't mean I have to like you."

"Pity."

"I'd beat you at the sword now," Kael replied.

"No doubt you will. I'm out of practice."

Kael harrumphed.

"I still remember those times you cried and called out for Mommy."

Kael stuck out his tongue.

A servant girl came up to me, holding a thick cloak made out of fur. I sighed in relief and hastily took the garment from her, wasting no time in slipping it over my shoulders. I'd been out into the cold too long, and needed a warm fireplace and a bowl of hot soup to stop the chattering of my teeth. Still, the cloak brought some reprieve.

Only when I clothed myself in the garment did Gaius dare shift back into his human form.

Moments later, I stood next to his nude body.

"Gaius!" Vanjar called out.

"Sh-sh-she's Vancel's sister, r-r-ight?" I asked.

Gaius nodded. "Yep."

"Wh-wh-why?"

"Why what?"

Before I could explain, Vanjar threw herself around Gaius, not seeming to mind his nudity, so I wanted to wring her neck.

Vanjar peeled back. "I've missed all of you. It's been so long since I've visited Constanria, and with Bael newly ascending the throne, there's less time than ever for visits. Where's Rylan?"

She needed to get her sticky paws off *my* men. Her perfect, *perfect* skin looked completely slappable.

"It's a long story," Gaius said, putting on his clothes.

"You can explain as we walk. And who might you be?"

Vanjar turned to me. Strangely, because she asked, I liked her a little more. I knew how small I looked next to the princes. Not like her—she was as tall as they were. And it wasn't difficult to overlook me when I stood next to them.

But having reason to like her fueled my jealousy. How could she be this beautiful *and* nice?

"S-s-era Cadriel," I answered. "I w-was a s-ch-sch-olar—"

Damn me and my chattering teeth.

"Sera! I've heard all about you."

"Y-y-you have?" I tucked my lips between my teeth, hoping that would stop them from knocking against each other.

"Come; there is much to discuss." She gestured at the palace, inviting us in.

She walked us up the steps and in through the front gate. It was *so warm* in comparison to outside. I huffed into my hands, thanking Aereala for the respite. The interior had cool silvers and blues. Chandeliers hung from the ceilings. They were box-shaped, with glass panes tinted with blue to add to the color scheme.

We walked across the patterned, tiled ground. My boots clicked against the pavement, but the princes didn't bring their shoes along and were barefoot. The pups followed us, sniffing around with their inquisitive noses.

"We're... somewhat fugitives," Gaius explained. "At least Sera is."

"Why is that?" Vanjar asked.

Gaius proceeded to give her the entire story of what had happened, and why Rylan stayed behind. He left out the part about Anatolia condemning me to death.

She flashed me a wide-eyed look. "Gisiroth and the Constanrian courts are quite dull, aren't they?"

"What do you mean?" I asked.

"They don't see a gift despite it hitting them in the face. We Beyestiryans think differently."

"You're Constanrian, too," Kael muttered. We all heard him.

"I've switched allegiances, dear cousin," she said. "It's been a hundred years since I've married off, and my heart is now irrevocably Baekeil's."

How did she move with such grace? It made me want to shake her until she imparted her knowledge of moving so seductively to me.

Even my new pups loved her. They wound around Vanjar's feet as we moved onward.

"Now," she said, "my husband has a say over everything here in Beyestirya, and I must ask him for permission if you lot are to stay. He will likely say yes. This is just for formality's sake."

We strode up a stairwell. The pups followed us. We stopped in front a door fit for a king. I guessed that it was the king's study.

Vanjar rapped on the door. Did she realize she shimmied her hips when she did that?

"Come in!" came a gruff voice.

She pried the doors open.

The Beyestiryan king was not a neat man. His documents were strewn about the place, and he seemed to have a thing for pelts. His hunting trophies decorated the walls, their mouths gaping open on their severed heads. I recognized most of the animals—a balebeast, a drearbear, and even an ingoria.

The pups pranced in as if they owned the place. Mayhem sniffed around and lifted his leg. I panicked and scooped him off the ground before he peed on the king's carpet.

"Don't you dare," I said to Mayhem.

His tongue lolled out, making him look like he was grinning.

The king had a gigantic spear, with its tip in a strange arched shape, lying on top of his documents. He paid no mind to his logistical duties, and was instead sharpening and cleaning his weapon.

"Deary," Vanjar said, in a tone I didn't think anyone would dare use on this man.

The king rose from his seat, setting his weapon aside gently, but knocking some sheets of paper to the ground. He strode toward us and smiled. "Love! You have visitors."

He had long hair, which he wore in a braid on the right side of his face. He fastened the braid with one gold clip. He wore no shirt, like the Everborne males, but had no tattoos. Around his waist hung a thick pelt, which probably served as fashion instead of function. Hidraes didn't need to keep warm.

"Can they stay?" Vanjar asked. "They're my cousins."

King Baekeil's grin widened. He regarded us four before nodding. "They can."

Vanjar smiled at us.

Baekeil rested his fists on his hips. "If they can best me in a duel."

My jaw slackened.

"Send out your best warrior, fellow dragons, and if you can defeat me in battle, I shall allow you shelter."

Vanjar groaned. She brought her palm to her face and shook her head.

———

King Baekeil was crazy.

A *sane* king would have listed the political implications and question our motives instead of outright asking for a duel.

It was Kael's kind of crazy.

Without hesitation, Kael stepped up to the challenge, pleasing Baekeil with his eagerness. The king ushered us downstairs, into a wide, blue, and snowy courtyard that was sparsely decorated with furniture. I didn't want to step outside so soon because of the cold. Micah, the intuitive one, hugged his arm around me, pressing me closer to keep me warm.

Vanjar, Gaius, Micah, and I stood aside the royal courtyard.

"What's happening?" I asked. My mind reeled from the absurdity of this.

Vanjar shot me a sorry look. "My husband likes to challenge people to duels. He thinks how one swings a blade tells a lot about character, though I constantly remind him that there are more civil ways. He's a Beyestiryan through and through. They tend to think with their impulses instead of their minds. I'm sorry about this."

"What happens if Kael loses?" I asked.

"He'll kick you out of the palace."

I looked at her incredulously.

She smoothed a hand over her hair. "It'll be hard to convince him otherwise."

"Is the king any good?" I asked.

"The best in Beyestirya. Or so I'd like to think."

I turned to Gaius. "Kael can beat him, right?"

"I've never seen the king fight before. I asked Kael to not make him lose too badly," Gaius said. "But maybe he does have to give it his all."

Kael had Lefty and Righty drawn, both ready to slice. He twirled both daggers so quickly my eyes couldn't follow, threw one, and caught it in his hand, all without batting an eyelid. *Show-off.* Baekeil wasn't fazed. He smirked and made a spinning motion with his spear, taunting Kael.

It seemed like this encounter might be fun, but I wasn't looking forward to it. I didn't want Kael to get hurt, and there was also that problem about getting kicked out if he lost.

Baekeil attacked first. He leapt at Kael, not giving the courtesy of announcing the start of the fight.

"Beyestiryans are brash like that," Vanjar explained.

Kael spun, dodging Baekeil's attack, but when he stopped, I saw blood dripping from his cheek. I tensed, and my first instinct was to rush up to him to wipe the blood away. He did that himself. The wound healed as soon as he got it. He dashed toward Baekeil, going faster than I'd ever seen him, and skidded when he reached Baekeil. The king summoned his wings—they were red—before Kael could trip him up, and he sought to the skies.

"I hope he doesn't get hurt," Vanjar said.

"I hope Kael doesn't," I replied.

"One of them has to."

It was then I realized Vanjar wasn't on our side. She was so friendly that I thought she might have been. But her loyalty belonged to her husband. Of course she'd root for him to win.

Baekeil tossed a sharp object at Kael. It sliced through the air with a metallic sound. Kael yelled in pain as it pierced his skin. My heart dropped. Blood dripped from Kael's wrist, and he dropped one of his daggers on the ground. I bit the inside of my cheek.

Maybe Kael had finally found his match.

Kael shrugged. He plucked the knife from his wrist and placed his injured hand behind his back. "I can do this with one hand."

The king laughed. "Don't be foolish and admit defeat before it's too late."

Kael made a taunting motion with his uninjured hand, which was still holding Righty.

"I asked him not to show off," Micah muttered.

"He's not doing a good job of showing off," I said.

"He hasn't even gotten started."

"Uh. Isn't he the one bleeding?"

Kael and the king resumed with another series of maneuvers. Both of them smiled feverishly as they clashed, their wings fanned out behind them. White and red. It took me a moment, but it shocked me to realize I recognized many of their movements. Fire, stone, water. Those were the stances Kael had taught me, but they'd altered them slightly for air combat. How quickly they moved made it hard to follow, but having prior knowledge about the stances made it possible, at least.

The king elbowed Kael's chest, knocking him aside. He used Kael's distraction to fasten his hand on Kael's neck. Baekeil pushed him down to the snowy ground. Kael landed on his back, the king pinning him down with his boot and pointing his weapon at Kael's throat. Fighting with one hand had proved too difficult after all.

"I guess we're sleeping outside," Gaius said, sighing.

"You underestimate our brother," Micah replied.

The king tipped his chin. "Say you lose and admit defeat, Constanrian."

"Have I?" Kael said. With a move so quick it might as well have been sorcery, he shoved the king's spear away. In less than a second, it was Kael who had King Baekeil beneath him, daggers in a crisscross around the king's throat. "Or did I just want to save you from looking bad in front of your wife?"

Gaius groaned. "He's making the king look worse by toying with him. What if he decides to toss us out anyway?"

"He's improved," Vanjar said. Her gaze was fixed on the fight.

The king didn't seem to mind Kael's toying. He let out a loud guffaw. Hearty, but also strange. King Baekeil had the ugliest guffaw I'd ever heard. It was completely unfit for a king. It alternated between a high-pitched shriek and a snort.

"You put up with that?" Gaius asked Vanjar.

She smiled. "I love every aspect of him."

Baekeil patted Kael on the shoulder. "Help me up, comrade. You are a good fighter. I will accept you into my abode."

Vanjar added, "Even if I did find his laugh strange at first."

Kael grabbed Baekeil's arm and pulled him to his feet. "You're not bad yourself." They both retracted their wings.

Baekeil wrapped his pelt, which had fallen off during the fight, around his waist. I rushed up to Kael to look at his hand. The wound there had healed shut, but splotches of blood marred where it'd been.

"You don't have to worry," Kael said. He tipped up my chin to kiss me on the lips. "I'm not so fragile."

"I don't like seeing you get hurt, even though you deserve it half the time."

"Aw, it's cute when you're worried." Grunt barked and wagged his tail. Mayhem was behind his brother, trying to bite off Grunt's tail, while Aura just sat next to them, licking her paw, as if frolicking with the likes of them was beneath her.

"This is good!" Baekeil said, wrapping an arm around his queen. "I like this new company. Let us show you to your quarters, then we shall wine and dine and feast tonight!"

"Has anybody mentioned Baekeil's strange way of speaking?" I asked Vanjar, whispering as softly as I could so his dragon ears wouldn't be able to pick my words up. "It's kind of archaic."

"He likes historical novels," Vanjar explained.

I nodded, accepting her explanation.

CHAPTER EIGHT

I woke up in my new, huge bed, still feeling full from the feast last night. I'd expected to meet the strange, ethereal woman in my dreams, but she didn't come. Instead, I dreamed of a food fight, but instead of food being tossed around by the princes, it was the food tossing the princes around. Maybe it was because the meal last night hadn't been satisfactory. It felt... lacking, in many ways. The Constanrian cooks had been spoiling me.

Usually, my dreams never made sense. Some poets and scribes had fantastic dreams they could weave stories about. Stories made from my dreams belonged in the bin.

I craned my neck, peering up at the ceiling. Everything in Beyestirya was bigger—the ceilings were higher, the rooms larger... but the serving proportions were, strangely, much smaller. I wasn't sure what Baekeil meant by "feast," because what we'd had was hardly one.

But the beds were larger. This bed could have fit all five of us. And there still would have been extra space. Too bad

Rylan wasn't here. And we still hadn't explained to Vanjar about how we all were a thing, so the princes got their separate rooms.

I wondered how she would take that revelation.

My initial reaction to her was hate. She was too perfect to not dislike. Then she warmed me up with her friendliness. I gave her bonus points about sharing with me stories of the princes' childhood. When he was still a child, Rylan had held the wrong woman's hand in court, and he burst out in tears because he was embarrassed.

I couldn't imagine calm and collected Rylan doing that, but the story made me smile. I imagined child Rylan being utterly serious. The moment he came out of his mother's womb, he ordered the servants to have him cleaned and bathed.

I laughed at the thought and stretched, and a yawn took control of my body.

The Beyestiryans had a thing about icy color schemes. This room was white, like snow, and the sheets of my bed were a cool blue. The duvet was exceptionally soft and comfortable. I reveled in the sensation of my head resting in the fluffy pillow and softly hummed. I missed the four portraits up in my bedroom in Constanria—they were my favorite pieces of decoration—but this bed was *divine*.

I heard my door creaking open.

I hoped it wasn't Vanjar, because I hadn't combed my hair.

Kael stood in the doorway, wearing his cocky smirk. Of course, it was Kael. It was always him whenever somebody didn't knock on the door. He sauntered in, shutting the door behind him. He wore his daggers at his sides—he didn't leave them behind often, because the princes had been trained in their warrior tradition to always be ready for combat. "Morning, messy head," he said, unstrapping his daggers from his waist and putting them at my bedside.

I combed my hand through my hair. Tangles caught between my fingers. I winced and gave up. "I'm not in the mood to get up yet." I lay back down and wiggled myself in my bed. Kael slipped under my sheets and hugged his arm around me. He tugged me closer to his body, until mine was pressed against his.

It wasn't a bad thing to wake up to.

I ran my hand down his chest, across his stomach. "What's up with you?"

"Missed you," he said. His voice sounded raspier and lower than usual.

"You're normally not this sweet."

"It's been a rough week."

"You said it was fun. Beyestirya seems like just the place for you."

He brushed his lips over my forehead and lifted the hem of my nightgown. He rested his hand on my stomach. "Nothing's like home. I'm so used to our palace."

"And its tiny corridors?"

He grinned. "They're *my* corridors."

"Your father's."

"The same thing."

I breathed in Kael's warmth. "I miss Rylan."

"I do too," he said. "But his absence also means there's more of you for me."

Sometimes the screws in Kael's head seemed to tighten. He wasn't always acting crazy, and moments like these did come. They were just few and far between. I dug my face deeper into his neck. When he wasn't picking a fight or teasing me, he could be pretty nice.

"I couldn't sleep last night," Kael said.

"New bed?"

He chuckled. "No."

"Didn't like the food?"

"I was thinking about Anatolia's vision. I think I know why we were crying in her first one. Damn, Sera, I'm scared. The others are, too. Anatolia's visions do come true. They're hard to decipher, but they're accurate for the most part."

"Might be some convoluted message."

"I can only think of one thing that'll make me want to cry."

"Losing Lefty and Righty."

He scowled. "That sounds terrible. That'll make me pissed, but no." He grabbed my hand and blew a sigh into it. As he did, his eyes caught mine, seeing through me. "It's losing you, Sera."

He said it with so much conviction that it was almost weird, because Kael never committed to anything. He was a touch-and-go kind of person. But he hadn't dumped me when he got bored, not like Gisiroth said he would. It had been months and he was still here.

"Everybody wants to know the future," he said. "But when we actually figure it out, it's better not knowing."

"Nobody's taking me away, Kael." I kissed the side of his

neck. "Even if Aereala herself came for me, I'd knock her teeth right out and tell her I'm sticking with my boys."

He smiled. "Sounds like something you'd do." He smoothed his fingers over strands of my hair.

"It's so weird to hear you speaking philosophically," I said. "What happened to the real Kael? Did you eat him?"

"I want to eat you."

"What?"

His hand, which had been calmly resting on my belly, trailed to the side of my waist. He gripped my waist and pressed me so tightly against him that I couldn't breathe.

"Kael?"

He took my lips with his, feeding me his taste. Giddiness took over me. His hand on my waist traveled to my back, and there, it sank to my ass. He cupped it and drew my hips against his.

I wanted to ask questions, but why fight what he was giving to me? I let him kiss me as hard as he wanted to, let him assault me with his tongue.

Looking at me with hooded eyes, he said, "I did say I enjoy the more bodily form of pleasure, didn't I?"

"Yeah, but so far you haven't been making good on your promise."

"About time. Micah and Gaius taunted me with what they did last night. They said you liked it, but they never went into any detail."

"Did they?"

"Tell me, Sera-kit." His voice dropped so low that when he used my nickname, my stomach turned. "What did they do to you?"

I bit my lower lip as Kael's fingers brushed the insides of my thighs. "You shouldn't have slept through it."

"How did they touch you?" he asked, brushing his fingers across my center. "Like this?"

I sank my fingers into his white, silky hair.

A devilish smirk lit his face. "Or were they more adventurous? Did they go deeper, like that?"

A curse word was at the tip of my tongue. I traced my lips across the edges of his hard jaw. "Micah was better," I lied.

His blue eyes flashed to yellow. He licked his top row of teeth, and his canines seemed to have grown pointier. "Is that a challenge?"

"Maybe," I said.

He took his fingers from my center. I almost hissed out his name and wanted to force his hand back there. Aereala bless me—what else was better to wake up to in the morning?

Kael disappeared under the blanket. I felt his hair brushing my stomach, which he had exposed by lifting my nightgown. Then his hair tickled my inner thighs.

My stomach coiled with anticipation.

Oh my gods. He knew how to work a tongue.

I lifted the blanket to look under. Kael peered up at me, grinning, mischief twinkling in his eyes. "Was Micah still better?"

"Yeah." I bit my lower lip.

"We'll see."

I pressed my fist onto my lips and threw my head back. I began rocking my hips back and forth, and Kael used that as encouragement. He hooked his hands around my thighs and sank his tongue deeper.

My eyes caught the gleam of the chandelier hanging above me as Kael made me want to melt.

The knot in my stomach tightened, coiling around itself, until it became too much to take.

That was when someone else knocked on the door.

No. Not yet.

The knocking grew louder. Kael lifted his head, leaving me wet and more desperate than I cared to admit. So desperate that I contemplated getting violent, but that wasn't too sexy... not unless that was what Kael preferred.

What *did* he prefer?

"Come in," Kael said, emerging from the blanket. He turned to me and said more softly, "Maybe if you said I'd won earlier, I wouldn't have stopped."

I wanted to slap him.

Or shove his lips back down to my center. Both options sounded pleasurable.

Micah and Gaius opened the door. I pulled my nightgown down, though that did little to hide what had just happened. They probably could tell from their heightened sense of smell.

Gaius leaned on the doorframe. "Oh? What did we miss?"

Kael brushed his hand through his hair. It fell back neatly into place. I wished my hair did that. "Trying to convince Sera of something important. I think I did well."

"Something important, huh?" Micah folded his arms. He knew exactly what Kael was talking about, judging from the flashing of his blue eyes. "Did he do well, Sera?"

I kicked Kael's butt, but I couldn't make him budge, since

all four princes were as sturdy as mountains. "No, no he did not."

"She's just being stubborn," Kael said.

Micah lifted his chin. "Or maybe you're not that good."

"Oh, I am."

"Anyway," I said, sitting up. I brushed my hand through my hair like Kael had, hoping it would neaten in a similar fashion. Nope. The tangles wouldn't relent. "Why are all of you barging into my room in the wee hours of the morning?"

"Wee hours?" Gaius said. "It's almost noon."

"What?" I slipped off the bed. My lazy bones seemed to be rebelling against all my late nights today.

"We were debating whether you died in your sleep or something," Micah added.

"We don't have anything planned, do we?" I said. "Actually, is there a way to talk to Rylan now that we're here? They should have piegfowls in Beyestirya, right?" Piegfowls were birds with blue plumage. They were trained to always return to specific locations, and were used to send messages. They used to have sparrow-vellum back in day, before the first king, but those were thousands of years gone. Sparrow-vellum were spelled sheets that could transmit letters over long distances.

"About that," Gaius said. "That's why we're here. Vanjar suggested she give us a tour of the compound. There are many here looking forward to meeting you, but I can't for the life of me figure out why."

"Me?" I squinted. "Are you sure you guys aren't talking about yourselves?" Because everybody—girls, especially— wanted to meet the princes.

Gaius shook his head. "She specifically mentioned your popularity here. I have no clue. Beyestiryans are strange."

Curiosity piqued in me. "I'm up for that."

"Hair," Micah said, gesturing to my bed head.

"Right," I replied, and turned toward the bathroom.

I entered it, but not before turning to Kael one last time, who dragged a tongue over his lips.

I tried to ignore how attractive that looked, but failed miserably. The ache between my thighs returned.

I willed myself not to blush—to little success—and zipped away.

———

Could anybody else see the blush on my face? Because I could feel it. It was red hot and prickling my cheeks, and I couldn't stop looking at Kael and the others because holy Aereala. The thought of him being between my legs never simmered down. In fact, it grew as time went by. Kael turned to me and winked as we strode onward. The asshole knew exactly what emotions he'd left lingering in me.

I needed a change of undergarments, and I was beginning to regret that I'd let him stop.

Why didn't I just worship his mouth, erect a shrine for it or something? I didn't have to stupidly compare it to Micah's. If I did that for Kael, then he'd never stop, because the best way to get Kael to do something was to stroke his ego.

Vanjar, completely oblivious to whatever had just happened, led us down the corridors. We'd left the ingoria puppies behind to settle in and be cared for by the servants here. I hoped they didn't give the servants too hard a time.

I hadn't gotten used to how tall the ceilings were around here. She pushed up her boobs—I was unconvinced that she wasn't doing that on purpose—and said, "I've heard that you were a prominent scholar in Constanria. I thought I might show you the Assembly of Scholars first. Perhaps it might intrigue you."

"Those days might be behind me," I said, feeling an unexpected pang of longing.

Vanjar waved her slender fingers dismissively. "Nonsense. Once a scholar, always one. One doesn't simply shed a pursuance of scholarship."

"Are you one?" Because she sounded like one.

"I have queenly duties, but I do dabble in it as a hobby."

We stopped in front a bronze door that had a strange shape. There weren't any door handles.

Vanjar hit a button, and the strange-looking doors opened. I gaped. How were they moving on their own? Magic? I glanced around, surveying the princes' reactions, and they were just as intrigued as I was. Vanjar smiled to herself, pleased.

In front of me was a boxlike room, not larger than a few dozen square feet. A dim light lit it. We stepped into the room, and the doors groaned, shutting. The metal shook. I gripped Gaius's hand. This place didn't look safe. All I wanted was to send a message to Rylan.

"It's not magic, if that's what you're thinking," Vanjar said.

"Not... magic?" I asked.

"A new contraption, invented by one of our scholars."

The room began to rumble. It emanated a squeaky noise before descending.

Vanjar continued, "He calls it an *atira*. Named it after his daughter. The darmar are grateful for his invention. They used to have to take endless flights of steps, while higher dragons could use their wings."

"How does it work?" I asked.

"It's quite fascinating, really. He used dragon fire as a way to generate energy, to power this strange contraption. And it controls a system of cables and pulleys fastened to this box, to lift it up and down. He thinks this energy can be used for many other uses, too."

"He thought of all of this himself?" It sounded incredibly impressive.

"He found some ancient records from a few thousand years back. Did you know there were many wars after the first king? Dragon-kind are prone to conflict. All these wars moved civilization back each time they happened."

"Interesting," I said. I knew about the wars, but this mechanism was something to investigate.

I still didn't feel safe in the box. What if the cables snapped, and the box plummeted all the way down? It sounded like a painful death.

The *atira* croaked to a stop. The doors opened, making the same creaky noise they did when they closed.

Beyestirya's Assembly of Scholars was... dim. Sun didn't shine through it, not like the Council of Intelligence. But it was also *big*. It was lit by dull yellow lanterns. Compared to the brightness of the council back home, I wondered how anybody got anything read around here.

We stepped out into the large hall, with staircases that spiraled up to countless floors of books, scrolls, and reports.

"The letters we'll send to the piegfowls are written on the third floor," Vanjar said.

"It's so much larger than the Council of Intelligence," Micah said, eyes lighting up. He looked ready to gobble up every piece of information they had here. He could memorize a page with one look because he was a savant, but with this much to go through, it'd still take him years to learn it all.

"Baekeil's father was a stickler for records and history," Vanjar explained. "A thousand years of nitpicky scribing leads to this."

"Sorry about the loss," Kael said, as if just remembering something. "We received the news of his passing last week."

Vanjar waved her hands. "We lost him years ago. His mind left him before his body did. The succession, however, that's something I'm sorry for. It was a mess."

"Wait," I said. "So you're a new queen?" I hadn't heard much news from Beyestirya. I'd been too concerned about the happenings in Constanria.

"Freshly crowned last week, along with my dear king." She smiled.

Groups of scholars had stopped their activities and were looking at me. Their gazes made me uneasy. Was it because of the curse?

"Why are they staring?" I asked as we walked onward.

Vanjar rested her hand on my shoulder. "They're eager to meet you."

A brown-skinned scholar, dressed in a peach robe, walked up to us. The robes here were different to Constanria's. They were thicker, woolier, with fur at their hems, and instead of drooping to the ground, they ended mid-thigh. The scholars here wore pants under their robes. Most of them wore boots, although I spotted one person wearing sandals. Why would someone wear sandals in a place this snowy? Then again, lots of dragon-kind didn't have to care about their feet getting cold. The princes still had their torsos bare, much to the pleasure of all these women staring over here.

I clutched Gaius's arm and pulled him in. *Mine.*

The men, however, shrank back whenever the princes stepped too closely. They had the right idea.

"Your Majesty," the scholar said. "The lead would like to speak to you."

"I'm attending to guests." Vanjar gestured to us.

"It'll only be for a minute." The scholar dipped her head.

Vanjar regarded us with a sheepish grin. "You can send your messages there." She pointed to a table with stacks of paper on them. It was a couple floors above us. "You can ask around if you get lost."

"We might," I said. "This place is a maze."

"I'll be right back."

She strode off, following the scholar.

We walked up three flight of stairs, like Vanjar had asked us to. I spotted more *atira* at the edges of the hall, which the scholars probably used to get to the higher levels, because this place, although built underground, was taller than any other building I'd seen.

"I hate this place," Gaius said, wearing his signature scowl. A few more people shied away after looking at him. The princes, Gaius especially, had this imposing air about them.

Most people didn't know their true natures. Not like yours truly. The thought made a smile curve my lips, springing haughtiness through me.

"Same here," Micah replied.

"It's nice," I said. "Looks cozy." And filled with texts—my kind of thing.

Gaius scowled. "Dragons aren't meant to hide underground."

"You like caves." They often brought me to caverns and caves if they had free time.

"There are ways to fly out in caves," Micah said. "Over here? It's just a little *atira*. What if it breaks down? Leaves us trapped."

I pointed as we climbed up to where the letters were written. "Looks like there's more than one *atira*."

"The both of you are just scaredy-cats," Kael said, stretching. He moved his neck in a circle. "I am perfectly comfortable."

Micah rolled his eyes and elbowed his brother. He then said to me, "He won't admit it because he likes to act brave and manly."

"Nonsense," Kael said. "I'm just not one to fear."

"See?"

I shook my head. "Let's hurry up and send Rylan that letter." *And then maybe we can investigate the famine.* I was seeing dead crops lying on tables around here. The scholars here were studying that. Maybe I could get a lead, which could redeem me in the eyes of the Constanrian court.

We reached the table Vanjar had pointed to, but the two women manning it looked busy. One was crying, while the other comforted her.

"I'm just... just... I don't know what to do," the woman crying said. "They should have sent more word. I could have tried to get them more food."

"It's all right," the other replied. "You'll be all right."

Kael, the insensitive ass-hat, cleared his throat. I elbowed him, but he'd already interrupted them and gotten their attention.

The crying woman looked up meekly, and when her eyes met the princes', she looked livid. Her gaze dropped to mine. There, it softened into one of... I couldn't understand why she was looking at me so strangely. Fear, hate—confusion, even. I could understand those.

This look was foreign to me. Awe, perhaps?

"I... I need to go," the crying woman said. "I'll see you around, Rena."

Rena gave her a hug. "I'll be right here."

The woman nodded and scampered away, avoiding the princes.

"What can I help you with?" Rena said to us. She was fair-skinned, like most of the Beyestiryans, with ginger hair like Frederick and a sprinkling of freckles over her cheeks and nose.

Gaius cocked his head. "What did we do?"

"You're the Constanrian princes, aren't you?"

Most people were afraid of the Constanrian princes. But Rena had balls—figuratively speaking, of course.

Gaius tipped a brow up. "Yes, *and*?"

"Then you bloody well know, don't you? It's because of you that Sascha's brother is ill. He doesn't have enough to eat. *Families* are dying because there's not enough food, and here you are"—Rena gestured to us rudely—"acting all innocent with a 'what did we do?' attitude." She blew out an exasperated breath. "Your kind tick me off."

"Careful," Micah warned her.

Rena stuck out her tongue.

"We sent relief," I said. I recalled Frederick talking about it in the Council of Intelligence, but I had been busy with the new crop I'd invented a few months back, so I wasn't sure about the specifics. "We're experiencing the same problems too. And if I'm not wrong, we have helped as much as we could."

"Oh, and you're the beacon of light everyone's counting on for no apparent reason." Rena rolled her eyes. "I seriously don't see why. You're wrong. Wrong in every way."

Beacon of light?

"All those stupid names they're calling you," she muttered, then continued more loudly, "Anyway, what do you want?"

Kael folded his arms. "I don't like you."

"Yeah, well, I don't like you either, ugly."

"Ugly?" Kael unfolded his arms and straightened. He swept his hair back, and I wasn't sure if that was him trying to prove a point.

"We want to send a letter," I said. "To Constanria. Their crown prince."

"We've stopped sending letters to Constanria," Rena said.

"Wait. What? Why?" I asked. "We were supposed to have treaty."

"I don't know. Orders from the higher-ups. Ask the queen. You guys were being chummy with her, though I guess she's your kind, too."

"The piegfowls," Micah said. "You guys should still have them, right? Where are they kept?"

"In the stables, above the training grounds. Can you leave me alone now? Looking at Sascha and then looking at you makes me sick."

I frowned, wondering why the queen had sent us here in the first place if she knew we were only to be turned away.

I eyed the letters on the table, almost annoyed that they existed, while I was denied sending a message to Rylan.

Vanjar took her time in getting back to us. We ended up wandering around, exploring whatever they let us put our hands on. Beyestirya's spoken language was similar to ours, although they had strange accents, but their written texts were completely unreadable to me. Micah and the princes had spent time learning Beyestiriayan in their childhoods, so they had no problem finding reading material.

Kael wanted to get their texts on battle tactics, but of course they wouldn't let the prince of a foreign nation read their most important ones. Micah was content to memorize some of their histories, while Gaius got his hands on their less important information on soul magic.

We lounged at an empty table, waiting. I found a book of

interest myself—one of visions. It was written in the Constanrian language, so I could read it. Apparently, Anatolia hadn't been the first to experience visions of the future.

Kael swung his dagger and pointed it at Gaius. "As if you don't know everything written in there."

"You shouldn't do that in a place this crowded," I said.

He dismissed my comment with a wave.

Gaius ran his fingers over the book. "Their spells... They're more sophisticated, actually."

"How so?" I asked.

He took out one of his soul beads. "*Glacialia pravata.*" A whisper of smoke weaved out of his bead. It formed the shape of a snowflake above the table, before chilling the spot where it hovered above. Did this count as property damage?

Gaius narrowed his eyes. "Looks like they'd altered many of the original spells while we simply took them as is. Hey, where are you—"

I stood up and strode to a table I'd been eying for the past minute. Someone—the scholars here seemed to work individually instead of teams—had left a dead, ashen leaf untended. I hadn't had the chance to inspect a dead crop.

I picked it up with my gloved hand. It just looked like a leaf, but a weird color.

I ran my fingers over its texture. It had lost the waxy feeling of most leaves. "Still looks edible," I said. I sniffed it. It didn't have a rotten smell.

"It tastes terrible," a scholar said as he walked up to me. "Like paper. Just worse."

"Really? Is it safe to eat?"

"We've tried putting people on diets of these crops. It was a stretch, but we're desperate enough. They lost too much weight and it didn't keep them full, but other than that, no signs of poison."

Out of curiosity, I put it on my tongue. *Ugh.* It did taste like ash.

But when I looked at it again, the ash had fallen away, and green returned to the leaf.

Holy Aereala!

I shared a wide-eyed look with the scholar next to me.

"Guys?" I said, turning around.

The nearby scholars reacted even more quickly than the princes did. They rushed up to me and pried the leaf from my hands. They passed it around. Some took out magnifying glasses and monocles to take a closer look, as if the green itself wasn't apparent.

Gaius swung his arm around my shoulder. "Guess my sister's premonition was wrong."

I stood in place, slightly awe-struck. "This... this is strange."

CHAPTER NINE

"This is wonderful!" Vanjar said, clapping her hands together. The *atira* creaked and rumbled as it ascended. I still didn't feel safe in this thing.

"I don't know," I said. "My powers don't stretch far enough to solve the famine." I'd touched a few more plants after our revelation, but so far, only the small leaves reacted. Some branches did regain color, but only tiny parts of them. Nothing of significance.

Vanjar continued smiling to herself. "It is promising, dear sister."

I'm upgraded to sister now?

"You are *hope*. Our people have been devastated ever since crops started dying off. At first it was the high summers. As you know, Beyestirya is a country filled with ice, and we rely on our outer provinces for food and agriculture, but so many of our fields died out in the high summers. And now, with crops dying en masse around those regions, we're losing all hope. Even the fish. There are less of them in the big lakes."

"I've changed the color of a few leaves."

"Which is the only positive thing that has happened since. You are *hope*. A good sign."

Wow. *A good sign*. Those words stunned me even more than seeing that leaf change. It shocked me more than anything I'd ever heard, because nobody ever said I was *a good sign*.

"Constanria has been trying to help by sending relief," Gaius said.

Vanjar shook her head. "It wasn't enough. We're grateful, cousin, but truly, a disaster of this nature can't be solved by donations from Constanria." She clapped her hands together one more time. "I have to be honest. I suggested this tour more for my benefit than yours. I wanted to show you around, to bolster the confidence of our troops and scholars."

The *atira* opened again, and we stepped out, into the corridor.

"Troops?" I asked. "Is there a war?"

"Oh no, not at all," Vanjar said. "We have to deal with barbarians south sometimes, but they don't attack anymore. There is nothing for them to steal. Half of them are probably dead now. It's just so terrible." She sighed. "I just don't want my people to die. We're next."

Kael's skin was tickling mine because of how closely he stood. He placed his hand on the small of my back. I wasn't sure if he did it consciously, but it felt nice. Much better than the bleakness that Beyestirya had to face.

Vanjar continued, "Beyestirya is a country with a strong

warrior tradition. And my husband, he's always believed in always being prepared."

"So, we're going to the training grounds?" Kael asked. His eyes lit up.

Gaius smacked his shoulder. "Not for you to beat up Beyestirya's soldiers. Pick on someone your own size."

"I'll be teaching them to learn through failure," Kael said.

We left the back gates and strode outside. Luckily, I'd brought thick clothing today. The weather, despite clear skies, was just as cold as the day before. Without my cloak, I'd have frozen my knickers off.

The moment I stepped out, my feet sank straight into the snow, which reached up to my knees.

"It'll be easier if we fly," Vanjar said. She summoned her wings, which were a light pink. They fanned out to her sides. The princes did the same. Every time they summoned wings, I liked to imagine that I could do the same, too. My wings would be red and fiery and awesome.

Alas, I had none, so I rode in Gaius's arms.

"You know," he said to me, as we soared through the skies, "my dragon has been more protective of you since we left."

"When we left Constanria?" I asked.

He nodded. His breath tickled my skin. "When those guards were chasing you, I think it clicked in me that one wrong move, and I could have lost you forever. I will do everything in my power to make sure you don't get hurt. I swear on it."

"Even if it meant having to fight a piece of inca meat?" I blurted, my mind traveling back to my dream. Because that piece of inca meat was *relentless*. It kept throwing Kael after

Kael at me, and all the Kaels were cackling maniacally, which was something he would totally do if he were a piece of food in a food fight.

Gaius frowned. "What?"

"Nothing," I said. I hugged his shoulders and kissed his jaw, which was growing a bit of stubble. "I know you'll protect me, Gaius."

"I mean," Gaius said, "it depends. Was that inca meat seasoned by Julius?" Julius was the head chef that Gaius had made friends with.

"Yes?"

"Then I'll gladly eat it for you. Only because it's to save your life." He nuzzled my neck, and I made a humming sound.

We reached a huge platform of rocky ice. The Beyestiryans had set up rows of tents on it, and next to them, sections of troops trained. Dragons, hidraes, and draerins flew above the platform, their tails curling behind their wings. A stretch of pine trees lined the horizon. The massive encampment stretched toward it.

"This isn't just a training ground," I said, eyes widening. "It's an army."

Vanjar flew closer to us. "Too many people came from the outer regions after the famine. After the fields died, they had nothing to do. We had to find a way to put them to work so they wouldn't be wandering aimlessly." Vanjar chuckled, but it sounded strained. "Baekeil's trying to treat this as a hobby."

"This is a hobby?" I said. I wasn't sure if I should have

been more scared or amused by Baekeil's strange way of thinking.

"Are you implying something about Baekeil?" Vanjar raised an eyebrow.

I tried not to give away how this sight disturbed me. I shrugged. "He's a weird fellow."

"I like your honesty." She gestured to the troops. "It is what he wants to see Beyestirya become. A strong nation. Strength through troubled times. It's what's keeping us alive."

As Vanjar flew ahead, leaving us behind, Gaius turned to me. His eyes darkened. "I don't trust this."

"No," Kael said. "We shouldn't. This number of troops... It makes Constanria's pale. I thought we had the strongest army in all of the Drae Lands. How did Baekeil amass this many soldiers? Beyestirya is supposed to be less populated."

The answer became apparent as we neared and walked through an encampment. The soldiers weren't made up of just men.

Children and women trained alongside the men.

I felt my mouth go dry at the implication. "But... but this is... You can't be thinking to make children into soldiers?"

"Baekeil really might be nuts," Micah said.

Vanjar glanced over her shoulder. "No, of course not. We're planning for the future. Years later, when our soldiers grow old, others have to replace them. Plus, like I said, it gives them something to do." She cupped her hands over her lips. "Akirya, Sanjar! Come greet your momma."

Two children, a boy and a girl, dropped their spears. They ran up to Vanjar, their cheeks flushed red from the cold. They looked no older than ten, and the way they smiled, so filled with wonder and innocence, made me want to smile, too. Vanjar opened her arms, inviting the children into her embrace. She picked up the little girl and rested her other hand on the boy's blond head. The girl resembled Vanjar more, with brown skin and full lips, while the boy resembled Baekeil. He was pale, and had the same deep amber of his father's eyes.

"My children," Vanjar said. "I wouldn't send them to war. They're here to learn, as many others are."

Kael grinned. "You didn't tell us you had children!"

"It's been many years," Vanjar said. "And my emissaries don't send word of *everything*."

Gaius wore the same smile Kael did. "You should have told us. I can't imagine *you* of all people being a mother."

"Oi," Vanjar said. "Not in front of them. And when are you having children, hm?" Her eyes fixed on me.

My heart skittered. "What?"

"The four of you have a strange thing going on. Don't think I haven't noticed. How will you know which one is the father?"

"We haven't... haven't done anything." After all, despite my amazing experiences with Micah and Kael, I'd never bedded anyone. I was unused to this kind of talk, and felt like a sore thumb whenever someone spoke of it. I looked at the boy—Akirya, I presumed—and he waved at me. He walked toward me, flashing a toothy grin, and grabbed my hand.

"Akirya," Vanjar said. "Don't go randomly touching our guests."

"Is she magic like they say, Mom?"

"Yes, yes she is."

"What have your people been saying about me?" I asked Vanjar.

Vanjar pressed her lips together. "They think you have won Aereala's favor."

"Yes, with a curse," I said. Sounded silly to me.

"No, Sera. A boon. You have the strength to win any battle against those with dragon blood. That is essentially everyone in this world. It's great power. Us Beyestiryans recognize strength. You have this. What else can it be, other than a boon?"

"I can't touch those I love."

"You can with my cousins. Perhaps that was the goddess giving you another favor. You're the answer to all this."

"Can I touch her bare hand, Momma?" Akirya asked.

I tugged my hand away. The boy frowned and peered up at me with a dejected expression.

"I don't want to hurt him," I said.

Vanjar patted Akirya on the head again. "Perhaps another time, Akirya, when you're older. You're too young for this."

"I can take it," the boy said. "I can take him." He pointed at Gaius.

Gaius reeled back. "Huh?"

"He's the biggest one of the Constanrians. Small, still." Akirya scrunched his nose up. "But he can still be a worthy opponent. Let us duel."

"Little brat," Gaius said.

"Are you scared?"

Vanjar grinned. "Come now, cousin, you're not afraid of a little boy, are you?"

"Kids." Gaius grunted. He shot a look of challenge at Akirya and cracked his knuckles. "They don't know their place. All right, then, fetch your spear. I'll show you who's boss." Wasn't he just talking to Kael about picking on someone his own size?

I looked at him and said softly, "You're not really going to show him, are you?" Akirya had run back to where he'd left his spear—the little spitfire. Vanjar's daughter hadn't said a word during this whole exchange. She was the quiet type, still shy and not yet grown into her confidence. It was only a matter of time. She had Vanjar as a role model, after all, and her mother was not the least bit shy.

Shy women didn't grope their own breasts like that.

As Gaius walked to position himself, he tripped and fell flat on his face, crashing into the snow. I tried not to laugh, as some others did, but I couldn't control myself.

Akirya cackled. "And you think to face me!"

"Watch your mouth, brat," Gaius said, wiping the snow off his clothes.

Gaius and Akirya stood face to face in a clearing of flattened snow. Gaius twirled his large axe. That sparked excitement in Akirya's eyes, and the boy hopped from foot to foot, as if unable to contain the energy bubbling inside him.

"Gaius wouldn't hurt your boy," I told Vanjar.

Gaius dropped his axe on the ground. "I don't even need this against you."

"But he can't help but show off," I added.

"He might be surprised," Vanjar said. "My boy has a lot of potential."

"You'll regret that!" Akirya shouted. He sank into fire

stance with his spear. That probably was him trying to be menacing, but I wanted nothing more than to pinch his cheeks.

The fight started, and Gaius was *not* surprised by Akirya's abilities, not like Vanjar suggested. I actually expected something because of how confident Akirya was. Then again, all children were like that. They were huge egos caught in bodies too small for them.

Gaius pretended to let the boy win at first. He even acted like he'd tripped, falling onto his back, and Akirya lunged at him with the pointy end of his spear. Gaius evaded it expertly, but he feigned a moan right after.

"No, no, mercy!" Gaius cried.

"My cousin is a good sport," Vanjar said. "Sorry about this. Akirya likes to look down on others sometimes, judging people by their skin and class."

"That makes two of them," I muttered.

"Kid deserves to have his ass kicked," Kael said, scrunching his nose. "This just gives him a false sense of victory."

"So, if you were in Gaius's place, you'd knock Akirya off his feet?" I asked.

Kael nodded. "Undoubtedly."

"Pointless," Micah said. "You should explain to him his place, not shove it in his face."

If I shared a child with these princes, he or she was going to have the strangest parenting.

Gaius gave a bad show of trying to pretend. He wasn't fooling anybody, not even Akirya. "Ow, ow, it hurts!" But the spear was lodged in the hard snow. "Mercy, please!"

Akirya scowled. He let go of the spear and ran back to Vanjar. "Momma, he's toying with me! I hate him."

Gaius sat up. "Oh, thank you for your mercy, great battle lord!" He made a bowing motion with both of his hands raised.

Akirya spun around and stuck his tongue out. "Next time, take it seriously. Then I will, too."

I helped Gaius up, although he didn't need my help. I brushed some snow off the top off his arms. There was still a lot on his head, but I couldn't reach high enough.

"Little brat," Gaius said. "That'll show him to know his place."

"You'll make a good father," I said. That was all I'd kept thinking while watching their exchange.

Gaius's eyes twinkled. "Then we should hurry up and make me one."

"I... I didn't mean..." It'd been *months* since we'd started being this close. Why did I keep blushing when around the princes?

Gaius chuckled and kissed my temple. He parted from me and picked up his axe, fastening it to the strap of leather around his torso.

Vanjar walked up to me. "Would you care to give the men here a demonstration, Sera?"

I cocked my head. "A demonstration of what?"

"Of your powers."

My eyes flicked across the encampment. Many of the soldiers had stopped their activities, and now looked at me with expectation on their faces.

"Vanjar," I said, "whoever I touch suffers *immeasurable*

pain."

"We know."

"And you want to demonstrate anyway?"

"We're eager to see." Vanjar turned to the crowd and raised her voice. "Aren't you eager, men? Don't you want to see what the Beacon can do?"

Beacon? Was that my new nickname?

Cheers echoed through the encampment. The troops clapped and whistled their excitement.

My stomach turned.

I swallowed a nervous gulp. "How do you want me to do this?"

And who's going to be the unlucky fella?

―――――

The unlucky fella was apparently *me.*

"What do you mean I have to fight him?" I said, pointing to the brutish guy standing across us. He was *huge.* Not larger than Baekeil, because nobody was bigger than Baekeil, but his massive arms and sword looked like they could cleave me into two in a single swing.

Vanjar continued to wear that silly grin of hers, as if there was nothing wrong in the world, and like she wasn't asking me to sentence myself to death. "Don't worry; Keistus is a friendly giant."

He did look friendly, with his thick red beard, wrinkly eyes, and the way he made his unassuming finger wave at us.

"That doesn't stop him from being a giant!" I said, turning back around. "I thought you were going to just make me touch someone. That's how the power usually works."

"Look," Vanjar said, "that'll be too easy a win. The Beyestiryans won't like that. They'll want to see you fight for your right to be called our Beacon."

"I don't need to be called that."

"I want you to."

"And?"

"If you don't agree to this, I'll have to make you leave the castle." Vanjar's eyes narrowed.

Micah frowned. "Why are you so insistent on this?"

"I won't let Sera go through this," Gaius said.

Kael nodded. "Agreed. I'm not letting Sera fight that monster there. Over my dead body."

Vanjar's features softened. "Please. Resolve amongst our people is weakening. I need something to strengthen it, and Sera's just the thing. I'm sorry to threaten you. I'm doing my duty as queen."

"To have your guests killed?" I said.

"I've asked Keistus to make sure you're okay. And if it goes too far, I'll stop it. We have healing potions for you, too. It's a show for the people. A ruse. Almost like entertainment, but a meaningful kind, to bolster their hearts." She twisted her fingers together. "We *need* this."

The princes looked skeptical. I was, too.

Vanjar shook her head. I could sense the sincerity from her. The desperation. "It will be so much help to me. To my country." She sighed. "And I'm serious about withdrawing my welcome. In exchange for your protection, it's only right that you give something to us Beyestiryans, too."

She had a point, but I wasn't inclined to agree with it.

I looked back at Keistus. He spread his lips to flash me what I assumed was a grin. His teeth were stained with yellow. There were black patches that looked like bits of food. Or perhaps that was decay that never left his teeth.

"You promise he won't hurt me?" I asked Vanjar.

"I... I can't promise that entirely, but you'll have your head intact at the end of it."

"I don't like this," Micah said.

Right... that wasn't much of a promise. My head could be intact, but if my legs were broken, that didn't sound good either.

"Fine," I said.

Kael growled. "What?"

"No," Gaius said. "Absolutely not."

Kael stepped forward. "I'll fight Keistus for Sera."

Vanjar pursed her lips. "That will do nothing. You can't win her battles for her. We all know that you're good with your daggers, Kael. They need to see a display of Sera's strength."

"I *am* what makes her strong. My support strengthens her."

I smacked his shoulder. "No you're not."

He shot me wide-eyed hurt.

"I'm not a kid for you to baby, Kael," I said. His stepping in gave me more motivation to fight Keistus. Vanjar was right. I had to win my own battles. Maybe it was me wanting to prove that I was something other than an outcast. I wanted to be worthy, and for the first time in a long while, I could be accepted by the people.

Keistus had both his forearms exposed anyway. "I don't have to wear my gloves?" I asked. "And Keistus is dragon-kind?"

"The whole point is for you not to wear your gloves," Vanjar said. "Embrace your powers."

It was still difficult to get used to the notion of embracing my curse, but this new way of how others viewed me was undeniably refreshing.

Vanjar continued, "You shouldn't have to keep hiding yourself."

I slipped my gloves off and passed them to Micah. "Then let's do this."

The three princes narrowed their eyes at my statement, but they didn't stop me. As I prepared, putting on the armor they provided, and picking a sword that reminded me of Pointy, the princes constantly gave me reasons why I shouldn't go through with this. But I trusted Vanjar enough—Keistus would leave me alive.

And I never was one to turn down an opportunity to prove myself.

When I stood in front of the sparring area, with the princes behind me, I was horrified to see my advantage promptly taken away. Keistus had put on more armor, leaving little of his skin exposed. Of course he'd put on more armor—I had, hadn't I?

I looked at my thin, although versatile, sword. That would do little against the giant man. I tossed it aside. "Kael! Pass me one of your daggers." I'd had experience with them, too, since I'd trained with him a lot. I hoped he was a good teacher and most of the skills stuck.

"Which one?" Kael said loudly. "Lefty or Righty?"

"Any one. I can't tell the difference."

"Righty's usually more reliable," he said.

"Are you sure it's not because you're right-handed?"

"He has more luck."

He threw me the dagger. If it were Rylan, Micah, or Gaius, they would have caught it by the hilt and looked cool. I was not about to try that and slice my palm. The dagger skidded to my feet. I picked it up, weighed it in my hands, and settled into neutral stance.

"Hey, meathead!" Kael shouted. "If you hurt her, I'll make your life a living hell!"

I could hear the princes bickering behind me.

"She shouldn't be doing this," Micah said.

"We can't stop her if she wants to," Gaius replied.

"Oh, and if she wants to hang herself, we should let her? This is exactly it."

Kael added, "She's just trying to have fun, isn't she?"

"Dying?" Micah said. "If that's your definition of fun then you need to get your vocabula—"

"She's not going to die," Gaius said. "Vanjar promised."

"That man is twice the size of her. Or are you blind?"

"I've beat beasts twice the size of me," Kael said.

"But you're not Sera."

What was that supposed to mean?

I tuned out the princes, finding it touching they squabbled over my safety. I was coming out of this fine, however. I wondered where all my confidence came from— maybe it was because of the way the people here looked at me. It made it easier to trust myself.

A horn bellowed from my left, signaling the beginning of the fight.

Keistus and I circled each other. He wore a dirt-filled grin, which was disconcerting. I summoned courage from my pool of confidence and made the first move. I shifted my sprint into a skid, swiping Righty across his ankles, where the fabric looked thin.

Keistus jumped away before my dagger touched him. He slammed his sword down. Out of pure instinct, I rolled aside, and the sword grazed my hair.

I pushed myself to my feet. The transition went less smooth than I wanted it to, since I still hadn't trained enough to be nimble yet.

Keistus swung his sword at me. I sank into stone stance and parried his sword with my dagger.

Wrong move.

His strength surpassed mine by far. Using his sword, he pushed the dagger to my torso. I gritted my teeth—I couldn't slide my dagger away, or his sword would slice right past it and hit my face.

Keistus punched my side. I let out a cry of pain but kept my dagger in place.

I thought he was supposed to take it easy? Was this the Beyestiryan style of taking it easy? Because I thought it was pretty tough.

With one big push, he tossed me off my feet. I landed on the ground, my bones cracking beneath my own weight. I bit back a cry and sucked in a breath through my teeth.

"Stop, stop it!" I heard Micah shouting from behind.

I tried to get up, but Keistus lunged at me. He sat on my

waist, pinning me beneath his weight. Panic flared in my vision. "Now would be a good time to start taking it easy," I told him.

He gave me a crooked smile. I smiled back at him, hoping his reaction meant he was done being mean.

He answered with a punch to my face.

My ears rang. I must have lost some teeth with that one. My vision blurred and unbearable pounding flooded my temples.

He punched me again.

And again.

Crracckk.

Fear gripped me. I couldn't breathe, and I wasn't sure if it was because my nose had caved in, or because I was so scared I'd forgotten how to.

I'm not going to make it through this.

Why had I gotten overconfident?

Why had I trusted Vanjar? She was Vancel's sister. Of course I shouldn't have trusted her. I'd let reassuring smiles fool me. I'd been played.

Craackk.

Was that the sound of my skull breaking? I could taste my own blood. It was metallic and bitter and I hated it. Kael, Gaius, and Micah... they were shouting in the background. I heard the clashing of metal, mixing with their yelling.

"Stop this!" I couldn't tell which prince said it.

"I will," Vanjar said. "Just a little longer. Sera needs to prove herself."

The sound of Keistus's fist hitting my face soon drowned out the other noises.

Why weren't the princes stopping Keistus?

Death by punches. There were better ways to go.

My vision cleared for a second. I saw Keistus's feverish expression. His fist was raised to the side of his face, ready to give me another punch. Keistus, in his fit of bloodlust, had left his neck open. His bare skin was exposed.

Yes... I still have my curse...

My gift.

I reached up as quickly as I could.

My cries blended in with his. His deafening scream broke through the ringing in my head. I kept my hand there, unrelenting and unwilling to let go. Memories from my childhood came to me. The boy I drove mad. The incident that made my entire town shun me. And I tried to ignore them, to get over the guilt, because this was a fight and I had to be tough to survive. He continued to scream, to beg. He looked like a drerkyn to me. That meant the pain would be far worse compared to a damar.

"P-pl-please," he muttered.

Or at least I thought he'd said that, because my vision was too foggy for me to concentrate.

He slumped to my side, his body brushing across the hard snow, and that was when I let go. His breathing was labored next to me, echoing mine.

I turned my head, facing my princes, seeing a mass of knocked-out soldiers around them. More soldiers had their spears pointed at their necks.

Vanjar clapped. Her hands moved but I couldn't hear her very well. She tugged my elbow and helped me to my feet. My head felt too heavy to lift up.

"Sera Cadriel, everyone! A Beacon fit for her title." She pulled her own sleeve over her hand, took my wrist and forced my hand up. With her other arm, she passed me a mug, filled with suspicious brown liquid. "I'm sorry about putting you through this," she said, her voice still muffled. "I will try and make it up to you. It was a test, and you passed. Medicine, for your wounds, imbued with soul magic and saved for the direst injuries, and only for important soldiers. It'll patch you right back up."

I eyed the liquid. It split into two images, dancing and wavering in front of me. I wondered if I'd be able to bring it to my lips without me spilling any. I really didn't want to trust Vanjar anymore, but I figured she couldn't do much more harm to me. I was already on the verge of death. I downed the liquid. Just the act of swallowing sent fire through my throat. I winced from the pain.

My vision started to clear. The spectators were cheering, chanting my name. Their voices grew louder as my hearing improved through the help of the medicine.

"Sera! Sera! Sera!"

I blinked hard. Hearing my name said with such reverence and excitement left me dumbfounded. Physically, I felt so small in this crowd, but mentally? This experience was larger than life. More people continued to join in the chant, and soon it felt like the entire army was shouting my name.

It was no longer the whispers behind my back. I recalled how my mother's loving smile morphed into a scowl of disappointment. I wondered how my family was doing back in Aere Grove. Hopefully the famine didn't affect them.

Vanjar clasped my shoulder. "You are our hope."

The princes pushed past the soldiers. Now that the fight was over, the soldiers dropped their spears, letting them past.

Micah was the first to hug me. His body crashed against mine, and he pulled me into a long, hard kiss. He gripped my shoulders and bent down so we were eye level. "Don't you ever do that ever again, you silly thing. I was so worried."

He wrapped his arms around me and pressed me tightly against his body. A sharp pain spiked through my chest—my ribcage might have broken. He caught my reaction and loosened his grip. His breathing was strained. "You almost killed me, Sera. Don't you ever do something so foolish again."

"I won, didn't I?"

Gaius pulled Micah away from me and caught me in his embrace. "We were about to shift into dragons. Destroy the encampment. I'm going to rip Vanjar's head off."

The chanting hadn't ceased. *"Sera, Sera, Sera!"*

"But I won."

Kael joined our embrace. "I can't believe she won."

"Yep," I replied, beaming.

I could get used to my name being called like that.

CHAPTER TEN

THIS NEW GLORY was getting to my head, and I wasn't certain if I wanted to stop it from doing so. I was important, to not just the princes, but an entire nation. The people here would kiss my feet if I asked them to. So many of them had rushed up simply to shake my (gloved, of course) hand. Some mothers had asked me to bless their children. I didn't know how to, so I mumbled some silly words that sounded awesome and pretended I did. After that, they regarded me as if I were Aereala herself. Some people would get embarrassed from all this attention. Me, however? I soaked it all in like the spongiest sponge in all of the Drae Lands.

Vanjar explained to me that the fight would have never gone too far, although I thought it had already. She wanted to see how far my abilities would take me before making Keistus back off, and that if the fight was real for the most part, the people would be more likely to believe. It sounded like horseshit, judging by the way things played out.

Or maybe she had a point.

These people wouldn't be looking at me the way they did now if things didn't go as she planned. And her healing potion really did work. Besides the ache on my shoulder, I felt nothing.

Aereala bless me, I loved having positive attention for once.

We sat in a red tent, reserved for the generals, and were having lunch around a table. Vanjar and the princes dined with me and the generals. The tent was lit by lamps that glowed with prolonged *lucio* spells. It was interesting to see how openly the Beyestiryans used soul magic. Even though King Gisiroth allowed it in Constanria, most still used it secretively because of the controversial nature of it.

Lunch here looked far less appetizing than what Constanria offered. Even the generals in Beyestirya mostly ate gruel, thin and watery. They said they were lucky enough to get dried meat and eggs. A far cry from the ingor meat the princes usually devoured.

The dried meat was rubbery. My jaw hurt from trying to chew it.

Kael scooped up some of the gruel from his bowl. He let it dribble down his spoon. He eyed the thin strand of liquid as if he'd never seen anything more intriguing.

I forced a spoonful into my lips. It had turned cold. *Yuck.* Instead of showing disgust, I forced a thin-lipped smile.

"Ooh, you really were something," Sylus, the general of this company of troops, said.

"Which part of the fight did you enjoy?" I asked, then continued wryly, "The part where he smashed the left side of my face in, or that other part where he punched my right side and nearly took my hearing?"

Sylus threw his head back and let out a guffaw, acting like I'd made the funniest joke. He drew a hand through his icky beard. "That part where you *won*."

"That's my favorite part, too."

Micah sat across Vanjar. He wouldn't stop giving her daggered stares. Sometimes I caught his eyes flicking to yellow, and I wondered what exactly his dragon was telling him to do.

Gaius kept staring at me and, when we were walking here, every rock in front of me. His extra caution served him well, because he hadn't slipped once since the fight, which for him was a miracle. Unconsciously, he sucked in a spoon of gruel, and made a disgusted face right after.

And Kael? Kael was still playing detective with his food. I did catch a few glances in my direction, but he liked to emphasize how his life's mission was to not care and have fun, even though his feelings for me were making him go against that. So, he pretended all was good and well.

My mind reached back to Rylan. How would he react? He probably would have stepped in before the whole fight and set out the terms, so such a disaster wouldn't have happened in the first place.

Gods, I missed him so much. I needed to get that letter out quickly.

Sylus, from the sounds of it, needed more training, but not in battle. He had no etiquette whatsoever. Dribbles of gruel had caught in his thick blond beard, which seemed to cover too much of his thin, but tall, frame. He fought with a piece of jerky and said as he chewed, "Constanria must be filled with fools to shun Sera like that. They don't know a gem when they see it."

His comrades—a smattering of generals around the table —murmured agreement.

"Have you heard about the news of her powers?" Vanjar asked, eating with a pinky up.

Sylus looked up. "What? Her power to strike fear in her enemies' hearts?"

I laughed sheepishly. "I wouldn't go that far—"

"Her ability to bring the plants back to life," Vanjar said.

Sylus's mouth gaped open. He'd apparently forgotten he had been chewing. He lifted his half-eaten piece of jerky. It jiggled in his hands. "That's interesting. You're going to solve the famine, young lass." He gestured to his bowl of gruel. "I won't have to keep eating this piss. You'd be perfect if you were a true Beyestiryan. Not like one of those Constanrians."

"What's wrong with Constanrians?" Gaius said.

"Now, now." Vanjar shook a finger, ignoring Gaius. "Her powers don't extend so far. She can bring small portions of the ashen plants back to life, but she's not able to bring entire fields of crop back. Not just yet."

"It's a good start," Sylus said, and went back to chewing with his mouth closed, much to my relief. "But maybe we're overthinking this."

I peered down at my gruel and stirred it, delaying my eating it. How could they finish this? It tasted worse than anything I'd ever had, and that was saying a lot, because Mother and Father could never afford anything. Many soldiers out there had thinning frames. They weren't naturally this thin—the famine had extended farther than I'd imagined.

Even the generals were lankier than they should be, and it explained the small-portioned "feast" we'd had last night.

If the higher-ups had to starve, then what of the people?

A servant slipped into the tent, carrying a medium-sized, roasted beast. A wyngoat. It could only be found in the wild.

"Just for you," Vanjar said, eyes crinkling. "We were saving this for a special occasion, and I believe this is it."

The generals broke out in cheers. They looked at me gratefully, as if I had bestowed upon them their prize, while all I'd done was taken a beating before coming here.

I shook my head. "I'm... I shouldn't—"

Kael reached for the wyngoat. "That's the way it—"

Sylus snarled, reached forward, and slapped Kael's hand away. "Beyestiryans first. You Constanrians have had enough."

What in Aereala's name? That was brash.

I looked at the generals and frowned.

Gaius's eyes lit with fire. He unfolded his arms and straightened, his eyes locking on Sylus. "Repeat that."

Sylus growled. He tugged his upper lip up in a sneer and continued, "Do I need to elaborate? Constanrians are selfish and barbaric. Even their princes do not know etiquette, and the entire nation is filled with scum who have not a clue what empathy means."

I thought he was being unfair to judge our entire country simply through Kael's reaching for the wyngoat first. I knew someone trying to pick a fight when I saw it, and wanted this whole thing to smooth over.

Kael shrugged. Micah sat there with his unreadable expression.

But Gaius wouldn't take this lying down. He was always the most devoted.

And the most temperamental.

He stood, knocking his chair over to its side, and reached for his axe, which had been propped at the side of the tent.

I started, "Gaius, don't—"

"Okay, tree-face," he said to Sylus. "Do you want to take this outside?"

Tree-face? Now that Gaius mentioned it, Sylus's face did look a little like the bark of a tree. But that wasn't what was important.

"This one's a bully." Sylus turned to his generals, shaking that piece of jerky he was taking too long to eat. "And because he's not content to gloat at our suffering from his own country, he's here to rub it in our faces. Constanrians... unable to appreciate—"

A metallic sound pierced the air.

A carving knife stuck out from Sylus's chair, next to his tree-like face. Its blade caught some of the sunlight seeping from the tent, and a yellow spark glinted from it.

I knocked my head back and stifled a groan. This was supposed to be a good moment. *My* moment. Why couldn't the princes just dine in peace? And why did Sylus have to let his mouth go off like that?

But the princes were troublemakers, through and through. I loved them for that. A lot of the time, however, that caused a lot of inconvenience. Especially now, since we were in a foreign land, where not everybody seemed to like us—

well, *them.* They worshiped me. *Praise Aereala.* I liked this change in circumstances, although it would have been better if everybody got along.

Sylus plucked the knife from his chair and stood up. He tossed the knife at the table, and it lodged into the wyngoat, its hilt pointing up at a forty-five-degree angle. A collective gasp chorused around us. The generals eyed the wyngoat as if it was the king's babe about to get thrown down a pit. A shifty-looking general leaned forward and carved a sizeable piece for himself, eying Sylus like he was a storm about to blow.

"All right, pretty boy," Sylus said, rubbing his hands together. "You and me. I'll show you what real Beyestiryan fighting is, and you can cry after we're done." He dragged his palm down his beard, which only smeared the gruel more. *Note to self:* to look intimidating, it was also important to be able to eat neatly, because all I could think was that Sylus reminded me of a tree stump that a child had just vomited over. Not exactly the most fearsome image.

Gaius tightened his grip on his axe. "You better be ready for—"

I placed my hand over his. "Gaius, stop this."

"What?"

"We don't have to make this worse. We can talk it out."

Vanjar shot me a grateful look.

Gaius frowned. "Why are you stopping me?"

I rubbed my forehead. "Come on."

He ignored me and looked back at Sylus. "You better be ready for—"

"For enjoying a nice meal, Sylus," I said, turning around

to face the general and straining a grin. "Come with me, Gaius."

Gaius reeled back, stunned. I patted his chin, reminding him to shut his gaping mouth, and led him outside, where we could talk without others hearing.

I grabbed my cloak and slipped it over my shoulders.

The cool wind of Beyestirya hit me once I walked out, and although my first inclination was to lean closer to Gaius to steal some of his warmth, I doubted he was in the mood for getting cozy.

His signature frown had deepened. "Sylus was being a rude—"

"You didn't have to escalate it. I mean, why couldn't we have a nice meal? We're their guests, and yeah, Sylus was kind of mean, but if you'd ignored what he said—"

"What is wrong with you?"

"With me?"

"Why are you defending them instead of us?"

"They were nice enough to offer us food they weren't used to having. To us. Strangers."

"You're not a stranger to them now," Gaius said, narrowing his eyes. "You're their god, and you're letting this get to your head."

Was I their god? Was I letting it get to my head? And was it wrong to relish in some glory after being shunned my entire life? "That's not the point..."

"He insulted Constanria. He insulted us. You wanted me to take that lying down?"

"You didn't have to get violent."

"Whose side are you on, Sera?"

"What?"

Gaius's face darkened. "Whose side? Constanria or Beyestirya? I don't trust these people. And if it came down to it, where do your loyalties stand?"

My mouth dried up. What did I owe Constanria? All its people had judged me, hung me up as a target, and never given me a chance. And here... I'd barely been in Beyestirya and they'd given me a status I'd never imagined I could have.

Where *did* my loyalties lie?

The answer was obvious. "With you, silly." I stood with the princes. I'd follow them to the ends of the Drae Lands, and I hoped they'd do the same for me.

But if they wanted to beat up our starving hosts, even if they had rude words, I should stop them, right? What if what they wanted to do was wrong?

Gaius's features softened, but he put on his mask of anger so quickly that I would have missed it if I hadn't been looking closely at his expression. "Well, it doesn't seem like it."

"Gaius? Gaius, don't walk away." I didn't like leaving fights unfinished.

He turned around and trod away. I quickened my footsteps, trying to keep up with him, but I couldn't. He summoned his wings, black against the snowy mountaintops that surrounded the training grounds, and lifted off the ground.

"Gaius!"

I was left standing like a fool in the middle of the encampment. I shifted my jaw and turned to look at the faces who were gawking my way.

Smile and wave.

I was becoming an important figure, after all. Important in a good way. Not some kind of scapegoat for blame, but a *Beacon*.

A little boy standing next to a woman waved back.

I stomped over the icy ground and made my way back into the generals' tent.

Most of the wyngoat had been eaten. Its carved carcass stood out from the center of the table, cleaned and picked to the bone.

"Saved some for you," Vanjar said. She wore the afterglow of having had a nice meal.

I glanced down. The portion on my plate amounted to a spoonful. "Thanks," I said wryly.

Kael picked his teeth with a tiny bone. When he saw me, he wriggled the bone at me.

I gave him a flat look. "I appreciate it."

CHAPTER ELEVEN

"VANJAR TOLD me I can send out messages to Constanria from here," I said to the stable boy.

The boy looked around fifteen, with the lightest complexion I'd ever seen. His fairness was marred by dirt from tending the stables, which speckled his face. He wore a thick cloak that gave away that he had to either be a drerkyn or darmar, since hidraes and draerins could generate their own heat and didn't need thick clothes.

"Sorry, ma'am," the boy replied, shaking his head. "Orders from the king. No more messages are to be sent to Constanria, not unless given royal approval."

A horse whinnied next to us. The stables were built with wood and had many cubicles that housed different animals.

"And why is that?"

He shrugged and scratched the back of his ear. "Not a clue. I'm just listening to the higher-ups. Don't look at me like that."

"One message will suffice. I just want to ask of my family's well-being." *Family.* Because that was what the princes had become to me, more so than my real one, who probably were still getting fat in Jaerhel's Honor.

"None allowed, ma'am. I'm sorry. You'll need to get royal permission to—"

"But I do have it."

"A seal, or written word, would be required."

"Don't you know who I am?"

The boy cocked his head. "Someone important, I presume? Even then, you're not a royal."

Seemed like my status of being the Beacon could only go so far. Apparently, not everyone was in on it.

"So I'll have to drag Vanjar here?" She was busy drinking with her generals. Food was scarce, but alcohol, apparently, was in reasonable supply, at least for those of higher status.

"Yes, ma'am." The stable boy turned around and fed a horse a piece of hay. Even the horses here looked underfed. One of them had its ribcage sticking out, and I'd never thought horses could have sallow cheeks before.

Gaius came up behind me. "Let her send that letter."

I spun my head around. Wasn't he off to sulk and brood?

The boy shook his head. "Sir, I'm sorry, but only royals."

"I am a royal."

The boy rose a brow.

"Not of this country."

"Then you have no command over me."

"Do you want to test that?" Gaius cracked his knuckles.

I placed a hand on him and wanted to ask him to stand

down, but Gaius wouldn't hurt a boy, and the last time I'd tried to stop him from doing something was moments ago, freshly burning in my mind. It hadn't gone well between us.

The boy tightened his jaw. "The king—"

"Is my cousin-in-law. I'll have a word about it with him and you won't be held accountable."

"You certain?"

"Yes. Now stop wasting our time."

The boy crinkled his brow. When Gaius stepped forward, the boy shrank back a bit, before finally obliging. He led us around the corner, where the piegfowls were kept. The birds flittered about in their stacked, boxlike cages. Some chirped, others simply perched there. I saw a few dead ones that had dropped from their roosts.

The boy tapped the edge of a box. "These are the ones trained for Raynea. You'll need to have your letters ready. Once you're done, just slot your letter, which can't be too big, of course, to those little tubes attached the feet of one of these piegfowls." He peered at the sky. "Then send them flying."

"Why are there so few birds for Raynea?" Gaius asked, frowning.

The boy shrugged. "I don't have the answers, so stop asking me like I do. I'm just here to do what I'm told and make sure the geckari and horses don't die." He strode away, leaving me alone with Gaius.

The winds around us had calmed, and the air didn't whistle as it blew. The horses from the stable nickered, and some geckari made a guttural, ghastly sound. They punctuated the silence between Gaius and I.

I had a sheet of paper which I'd folded and torn at its creases so it would be small enough to strap to the piegfowl. On it was a message I'd written to Rylan in the Assembly of Scholars.

"What did you write to Rylan?" Gaius said. He stood close to me. I could feel his heat emanating from him.

I wasn't mad at him, but the tension and awkwardness between us was hard to ignore.

"Took me a while to figure it out," I said. "I've been wanting to speak to him so badly that I kept thinking about this letter yesterday. But really, it's just the simple things. Has he been eating well? Sleeping well, because he has insomnia? Have the politics there been giving him too many headaches?"

Gaius smoothed his hand down my arm. I felt it through the thick fabric of my clothes. "You wrote that?"

"I didn't think I had enough space for rambling. Not on this tiny piece of paper. It's simple."

I'd written down two short sentences:

I love and miss you. Take care.

Perhaps too simple, but I hoped they put across what I felt for Rylan well enough.

"Good," Gaius said, lifting his own piece of paper up to show me. "We don't want to waste too many pigeons, and I have more important things to say."

I scowled at him. "You're a prick."

"You love me."

"Yeah, but that doesn't stop you from being an asshole ninety percent of the time. What's so important?"

He peered around. "This army, for one. No king gathers

an army, summons both women and children, simply as *a hobby*. Beyestirya *says* it has good relations with Constanria, but you've seen their generals—they're desperate and they're beginning to hate our people. Kael and Micah agree with my sentiments."

"You think they're going to attack Constanria."

"The more I stay here, the more I think it's a possibility. I knew they've experienced famines, because of the letters they sent us, but I didn't think it'd be this bad. Most of these soldiers look half of what they should weigh."

I frowned. "So, what are you going to do? Why are you here if you're so convinced they're the enemy? And why would they bring the princes here to gawk at their strength if they're going to attack? Wouldn't it make more sense to take you guys as hostage as soon as they can?"

Gaius shook his head and took my letter from me. He rolled both of our letters into little tubes. "I don't know what they're playing at... What Vanjar's playing at. But she *is* Vancel's sister."

"You guys said you trusted her." That was why I went with trusting her so easily, because I had faith in the princes' judgment.

"To an extent. We used to get along and she would have our backs, even though Vancel liked to stay out of our games as children. But she said so herself: she's Beyestiryan now. And her country's at its wit's end with the famine."

I wanted to doubt Gaius, but too much of what he said made sense. Countries—no, *people*—would do whatever to survive. A thousand-year peace treaty meant nothing if they weren't going to live another year. But didn't it make more sense to work together? That was why the treaty existed, right? The effects of the die-out were beginning to affect us, too, and them attacking us would waste more resources rather than help the matter. In the long run, even if they won, all of us would perish if the crops continued dying. Could Baekeil be this short-sighted?

I recalled his challenge when we first got here.

Yes—yes, he could be.

I watched as Gaius pried open a cage and caught a piegfowl. The piegfowl's eyes looked wide and terrified as Gaius held it by its neck. He slid our rolled-up messages into the small container attached to its leg. Then again, piegfowls always looked the same, regardless of what they felt. This piegfowl could have been turned on by Gaius's warm touch and I wouldn't have known.

Speaking of Gaius's touch...

I needed to stop thinking stupid thoughts.

He let go, and the piegfowl took to the skies. "Let's hope this one gets to Rylan."

"What did you say to him?" I asked.

"To be wary of Beyestirya. And I gave an estimate of their troops. Plus, I reminded him not to go overboard with Father and get himself punished or killed by the courts. I'd hate to go back and see his head on a pike. I'd slap him for it."

"I don't need that mental image." Gaius meant it as a joke, but that went too far for me. A pang of fear spiked up my chest at the thought. Could Rylan actually get himself killed? He couldn't, right? He was their crown prince. But what if Vancel decided to spring a coup or something? I wouldn't put it past him. If that happened, then Rylan's head would be one of the first to go.

I wanted to receive his reply soon. Just to know he was safe.

Bah. It had only been couple days since we got chased out of the palace. Was my cycle coming up? Because I always overthought things then, and when it came by, the princes always tiptoed around me like I was some kind of fire spell waiting to happen.

Gaius shrugged. He shut the vacated cage and spun toward me. "That thing I said earlier. About your allegiance?" The bright, wintry light reflected off the snow, shining into Gaius's blue eyes, making them shimmer. "Sorry." He slipped the tip of his thumb across his perfect nose.

"You had every right to be angry. I could have dealt with it better. Shouldn't have undermined you in front of the others."

"I could have held my temper."

"And solved the famine at the same time." I snorted. "You're not the kind to hold your temper, Gaius—tempers hold you."

"Wouldn't hurt to try. I blame my dragon. It always wants to burn things down."

"How does it work, exactly? Is it like a voice that's talking to you in your head? Another personality?"

"It's more like... like an instinct, which sometimes project itself as words."

"So, you hear nothing now, and it flares only during certain moments?"

"Oh, I hear something."

I raised a brow. "What's it saying?"

"It's giving me an urge." He smirked.

"Your dragon wants to go pee?"

His smirk fell. "You had to go and make it unsexy, didn't you?"

"Are urges supposed to be sexy?"

"The right ones are." He dipped his eyes to my lips. "The ones my dragon has when it looks at you. *Wants* you."

He hooked an arm around my waist, and even though it was cold outside and there was so much fabric between us, I could feel his hard body against mine. "It's when I get really mad at you, and my anger dissipates. After that, all that energy goes to craving you, and thinking about ways to have you."

I held his gaze, which had deepened into a darker, entrancing shade. "Are you asking for me to piss you off more?" Why was I saying so many silly things? Maybe it was my brain flubbing about when he looked at me this way. My inner self was jumping and squealing and slapping herself because Gaius, when in heat and giving that *smoldering* stare, was too attractive for words and made me want to explode.

"There are better ways to arouse me than make me mad, Sera."

Arouse? Did he say arouse?

Maybe he meant *a brow*, or *eyebrows*, because I could eyebrow him really hard right now. They could reach to the top of my forehead, or perhaps a frown was more appropriate.

Stop thinking—or saying—stupid things! Of course, he

meant what he said. Who *eyebrows* anybody? What did that even mean?

Gaius's fingers lingered over my lips. "Kael had tasted you, Micah touched you, and now I want a part of you to myself. And I'm thinking about where first." He traced the edges of my lower lip with his thumb. "Your mouth…"

His touch wandered. I couldn't feel all of it, not with the thick clothing, but that didn't matter. It was the way he looked at me—how a man wanted a woman, or a beast wanted prey. "Your breasts…" He slipped his hand through my cloak and rested it around the curve of my waist. There, it traveled lower. "Or your—"

A *thump* plucked me straight out of the moment. Gaius stumbled backward and fell on his butt, sliding snow out of his way as he did. He pressed his palm against his head, sat up, and let out a groan. A cinder block lay next to Gaius on the frozen ground. "Ow! What in Aereala!" He snarled.

Kael sauntered up to us, with Micah lingering behind.

"What was that for?" Gaius said. He rested his head between his knees and groaned.

"Kael's had a bit much to drink," Micah replied.

"Beyestiryan ale tastes like something!" Kael bellowed. "Almost like piss, actually. But that's better than the water Constanrian liquor tastes like. I think." His cheeks were flushed. "And I'm not drunk. I just like throwing things. At Gaius in particular." He beamed at me.

Gaius shook his head and pushed himself to his feet. "You could have misjudged and hit Sera instead."

"No, no I couldn't have, because I'm a better aim than

that, and I would never in any circumstances hit Sera." Kael blew me a kiss.

I blew one right back. "Where's Vanjar?" My body was lighting up, but I tried not to show it.

"Playing with her children," Micah said. "She said we could spend as much of the day we wanted around here, since there's lots to explore. But tomorrow she's going to have to show you around the courts and introduce you to more of their political officials, because of your potential to be of use to them."

Of use, huh.

"And Gaius thinks she sees us as enemies," I said, pointing to him with my thumb.

Kael hugged Gaius and nuzzled into his neck. "You're so punchable, brother." Gaius was trying to get Kael out of his face by pushing at it.

Micah pressed his lips together. "What if she does?"

I folded my arms. "She wouldn't let her enemies venture around her army unchecked."

"Maybe that's the point. She wants us to let our guard down by lowering hers."

"It's a bit of a stretch."

Kael made another kissing motion at me, before flipping off a random soldier who walked by.

"How much did he have to drink?" I asked.

Micah looked at Kael, then back to me. "A few barrels. He was challenging Sylus over who was the fastest drinker. They went as far as Vanjar would let them, before she decided their supplies couldn't take any more of their fooling around."

I pursed my lips. "Best drinker. Not the best title to vie for."

"Kael vies for everything, as long as it's a game."

I nodded, agreeing to every word of that statement. "So, what now?"

Gaius slipped a dagger out of Kael's sheath and tossed it across the ground, and Kael went to fetch it. "We take this chance to figure out as much as we can of their army," Gaius said, "and maybe, if we have some extra time, you can play around with our dragons again."

"Your big dragons, or your baby dragons?" I asked.

Gaius rolled his eyes. "We seriously need to work on your sexy talk. Don't call it a baby dragon." He strode up to the cages and plucked another piegfowl out of its box.

"I've heard worse. Some scholars back home used to call it a baby arm." I attempted my sexiest voice, which wasn't very good. "*Oh*, darling, let me pleasure you by running my fingers over your baby— What are you doing?" Gaius shoved the piegfowl into my satchel and tied it closed. He went for another one. It was somewhat disconcerting to be carrying a struggling creature. I felt it knock against my thigh.

Kael strode back with a pissed-off look on his face.

Another cinder block was flung Gaius's way, but Gaius shifted his head, dodging it. The block bounced off the stable. "I'm keeping them in case we need to send any more findings to Rylan. I don't want to keep coming here to use their piegfowls. We're less likely to alert the Beyestiryans this way."

"So I have to go around the rest of today with this?" I

asked, pointing to my satchel, which looked like it wanted to fight me.

Gaius grinned. "You'll manage."

"Hey," the stable boy said, peeking out from the corner. "Are the both of you done?"

That was when Kael drop-kicked Gaius, and more of their roughhousing ensued.

CHAPTER TWELVE

In my second day in Beyestirya, I found out the princes enjoyed spending time with the military. I didn't. I hated the cold, and most of the encampment was out in the open.

But Vanjar thought I should spend more time there, too. Something about bolstering their confidence. I didn't see how it made sense. But I was inclined to follow her wishes. She said it'd make the people here like me, and I realized I wanted that.

I loved being accepted for once, and she said my presence alone made a difference. That was something to be pleased about.

I just needed to find a balance between Beyestirya and the princes, and then all would be well. Because when push came to shove, I had to stand with the princes no matter what.

We sat under a tarp canopy, watching the soldiers spar. Women fighting children. It looked so odd.

Kael balanced two daggers in his hands, one belonging to the Beyestiryans; the other was Righty.

"Mine's better," Kael said.

Gaius sniffed and hit his hand against the table. "Of course it is. How is that even a surprise?"

"No, but their dagger is *almost* as good. Definitely not refined craftsmanship, but still quite amazing for something meant for a common soldier. It looks like their blacksmiths here are more advanced, too."

"Give me that," Gaius said, snatching the dagger from Kael. "Hm. You're right. Beyestiryans. Why are they developing all these war-related things? I don't trust them." He placed the dagger down.

Kael took the dagger back and placed it in his mouth.

"What are you doing?" I asked.

He unsheathed Lefty and got up before adopting stone stance. Taking the Beyestiryan dagger out of his lips, he said, "Trying to invent a new style."

"And that is?"

"Kael style?"

"Huh?"

"If dual wielding is more effective, surely triple wielding would be better, no?"

Gaius set his mug of ale down. "Fool." I preferred to call their ale Beyestiryan piss. Not that I'd had a taste of it. But I did get a whiff, and it smelled *pungent*.

Micah joined us, sliding a chair beside me and sitting down.

"What did you get?" Gaius asked.

Some snow was melting on Micah's head. I helped him

brush it off. Micah replied, "Their army is twenty thousand strong, and I've got a map drawn out of most of the place."

"Twenty thousand?" Gaius echoed.

"It's more than ours," Kael added. "Twice as much."

I leaned forward, resting on the table. "You can't be counting the children."

"There's a reason why they're there," Micah said.

I nodded. "Vanjar did say they needed to put people to work."

But what if Beyestirya truly wanted to attack Constanria?

"Better safe than sorry," Kael said. "I've made some sketches of the geckari experiments they've been working on, and I have the numbers of their cavalry. Their weapons... They're hard to get to, so I couldn't make a proper count. But I've also drawn a map of their training grounds in case we need it."

Micah placed a large scroll on the table. He looked around, to make sure we didn't have anyone else's attention, before unrolling the large sheet. An intricate, beautiful map was splayed across the table.

Sometimes, I forgot about Micah's abilities. That he was a savant. He was usually so quiet about it.

I frowned. "Snooping around? It doesn't feel right..." These people treated me nicely. Should I be betraying them?

But I was Constanrian.

Damn this all.

"We're being careful," Gaius said. "Might as well use the opportunity, since we have it."

"In the event of war"—I squinted—"will they even let us

have the chance to use these? We'll be locked up before we know it."

"That's why I'm going to try and send these to Rylan with the piegfowls."

"You'll have to be good with summarizing."

Said piegfowls were now in cages, hiding in my room. I hoped the pups didn't get to them. I'd covered the piegfowls with fabric and told the maids they were a rare species of bird, never to be touched.

We spotted Vanjar waving to us from a distance. She wore an alluring, hundred-watt smile and had just finished talking to her children. Micah quickly swept the map up and clasped it against his leather belt.

She strode up to us. The bluish snow made her tan skin seem to glow even more. "I hope you lot have been making yourselves comfortable."

"Too comfortable, perhaps," I murmured.

"Your hospitality is unparalleled," Kael said, using all his charm. "And it would be even more so if you let us see those strange geckari your men have hidden."

Vanjar laughed. "Don't want to be *too* hospitable. It'll inflate your expectations, then it'll be harder to please you next time." Sidestepping Kael's question, she turned to me. "Sera, I have made arrangements for you."

All their eyes fell on me. I licked my lips. "Arrangements?"

She waved for me to follow her.

Moments later, I found myself face to face with a jolly-looking fellow. He had to be a draerin, if not a hidrae, because he kept his muscled arms out. He was clean-shaven, with a thick jaw and nice head of blond hair. He was as tall as Gaius, and when we closed in on him, I felt Gaius tightening his grip around my hand and saw him standing straighter.

"Hoistus is going to be your new trainer," Vanjar said.

"Trainer?" I asked, sizing up the man. I recalled the incident with Keistus. I had no desire for a repeat of that.

Vanjar nodded. "In sword fighting, and the martial arts. I thought it might be good for the people here to see you in battle, and it'd be to your benefit to sharpen your skills."

Kael stepped forward. "She has me."

"Your time can be put to better use, cousin," Vanjar said.

"Kael never puts his time to good use," Micah replied, which made Kael hit the butt of his sword on Micah's forehead. "But it's true that this is unnecessary. If you want Sera to be trained, she has the three of us."

"Perhaps she could benefit from different learning experiences. Hoistus here is trained with Beyestiryan martial arts. It varies from Constanria's."

Kael sniffed. "It's worse."

"I'm not letting Sera into a fight with another Beyestiryan," Gaius said.

"I promise she won't be hurt," Vanjar said. "This isn't like last time."

Maybe she was counting on me to say yes, like I did with Keistus, but I recalled the way he hit my face and how much it hurt.

I also recalled the cheers after that.

"I shouldn't turn down an opportunity to learn," I said.

The princes looked at me, mouths gaping open and each with the same level of befuddlement.

"Oh no," Gaius said. "We've done this before, and it did *not* go well. I'm not letting you go through that again."

I pursed my lips, uncertain about my decisions. But I recalled the cheers those people gave me, and wanted to prove myself again. "It'll be all right."

"Why does this sound so familiar?" Micah said.

"I want none of your soldiers around us," I told Vanjar. "So the princes can step in should they feel like they need to."

"I promise," Vanjar said, pressing her boobs together, as if it were some kind of secret handshake.

Gaius snarled at her. She gave him a poised, practiced smile.

Hoistus and I exchanged greetings. He wasted no time before beginning his teachings. When he wrapped an arm around my waist to guide me, I heard growling from behind.

Kael said, "This is completely unnecessary." I found the princes' reactions to this worth the extra trouble. They were cute when jealous.

Kael strode up to Hoistus, interrupting the training session. "You and me." He gestured with two fingers. "We have a go at it. If you, by some miracle, win, then I'll allow you to train Sera. If not, kiss my ass."

Hoistus gave him a respectful bow of his head. "I'm sorry, Your Highness. I was under Vanjar's and the Beacon's instruction to start this session. You'll have to take it up with them." His eyes twinkled as he regarded me.

I made a shooing motion. "You heard him."

Kael grunted out his frustrations. He gripped his dagger until the whites of his knuckles showed.

I wondered if I'd gone too far. Kael stalked to where

Micah and Gaius waited and folded his arms. He glared at Hoistus as if he were a demon, and looked ready to pounce should Hoistus do anything remotely out of line.

I spun around and gave him a little finger wave, absorbing the feeling of being special and wanted.

"Right," Hoistus began. "So the Constanrians call this the stone stance. Us Beyestiryans are usually larger and taller, so we've altered it a bit. We lower our center of gravity by doing this. It won't be as useful for you, but it's good to note if you face one of us. It'll allow you to think more quickly."

Hoistus demonstrated, and I tried to follow. My two left feet got in the way, but he was more patient than Kael, and I eventually managed to catch up.

We finished our session in about thirty minutes. I felt winded, reminding me I needed to work out more.

"Thank you," I said to Hoistus, shaking his hand. My face was still intact.

"No." He shook his head and pressed his hand to his heart. "The honor is mine."

"Training me is no honor."

"Of course it is. You're the Beacon. Our symbol of hope."

"Why? Because I can hurt people?"

"Because you have great power."

I was at least two heads shorter than Hoistus. That didn't feel too empowering.

"I don't see what's the fuss," I said. "I haven't done much for your people."

"Oh, but you have."

"It's been two days."

"My men have been smiling more. Talking more. I can

see fire in their eyes again. We thought we had no more hope, that Aereala and Gaean had forsaken us. But here you are, a symbol of their favor. Maybe through you they can save us. Talk to us."

I frowned. "Uh huh." The Beyestiryans had the strangest way of thinking. I'd beaten up their comrade. Aereala wasn't exactly known for her warring tendencies. She was the goddess of pasture, creation. Gentle and kind.

"I'll see you around, Hoistus," I said, waving goodbye.

"Wait," he said. "Before every one of my pupils end a session, I spar with them, to make sure they've understood the principles I've drilled into their heads."

"Sparring?" Like with Keistus? I shifted my gaze to the princes. They visibly tensed. "Can we do this next time?"

"You might be the Beacon, but I don't make exceptions for anyone."

I sighed, caving in. We were fighting with wooden swords, so I supposed no one was going around piercing anybody. Still, Hoistus was twice my size, and he could probably crush my skull with his hands if he wanted to.

But there weren't any soldiers around, so the princes could jump in should it go awry.

I slipped into a neutral stance. My heart raced. My body stiffened with the promise of the fight.

"It'll be quick and simple," Hoistus said, grinning unassumingly.

Keistus had done the same.

Hoistus's smile did little to ease my worries. Maybe this was a bad idea.

Without warning, Hoistus lunged at me. Three quick

strides, and he closed in. My training kicked into motion, almost out of instinct. I slid into water stance and dodged Hoistus's blow. It was nearly too easy.

I knocked his ankles twice with my training sword. He let out a groan that sounded faked and pretended to stumble.

What was going on?

He attacked again, raising his sword above his head. Before it landed, I shifted my weight to my left and sidestepped it. I kicked his back and forced him forward. He flew into the snow.

My kick didn't have that much force.

The lunge-and-dodge scenario repeated a few times, each time leaving me more confused than the last. Hoistus had lost all the grace he'd demonstrated during our lesson. Each time he fell to the ground, it wasn't because of my doing, but his own. It felt like he was throwing himself onto it.

Eventually, he raised an arm, admitting defeat.

"What was that?" I offered Hoistus a hand and pulled him into a seating position.

"*Sera, Sera, Sera!*"

The same cheers I'd heard during my fight with Keistus echoed. But these felt much emptier.

"I'm sorry, Beacon," Hoistus said. "The queen wanted me to make a showing. She said it'd be good for morale."

"Your people have a strange way of being encouraged."

Hoistus chuckled. He stood up and brushed the snow from his trousers. "We like fights."

More soldiers closed in around us. They brimmed with joy. I wanted to tell them it was all a lie and that they shouldn't be rejoicing, but they were starving, and had little to look forward to.

I didn't feel good about it, but why take their celebration from them?

I forced a smile through my cheeks and waved.

———

I liked to think of my visit to Beyestirya as a forced vacation. I'd been chased out of my country and sent to somewhere exotic to relax.

Not that I wanted to relax while everyone else was starving to death.

The Beyestiryans, however, didn't seem keen to let me do anything.

"Your baths will be prepared to whatever temperature you prefer," Vanjar said. She stood with me in the *atira*, which shook as it descended. "You'll have your pick of dresses, and if you want more food, we'll try and manage it. Don't strain yourself too much. You seem like the type. I see the fire in you. We don't want anything to happen to our Beacon."

"Is all this necessary?" I pinched my dress, which Vanjar had asked me to change into after my fight with Hoistus. It was *huge,* but wooly and kept me warm. It reminded me of the dresses Mei used to wear to the council, just three layers thicker.

"Absolutely." Vanjar nodded. "Image is very important for Aereala's chosen. And we want to make sure you're happy here." The princes had gone off to do some hunting, because they complained the food here was absolutely atrocious.

"Aereala's chosen?" I asked.

"What the people have been calling you, other than the Beacon. It is good that you have your three ingorias with you. The people here adore ingorias. They're beastly creatures of the wild. Gaean's favorite animals, or so lore says."

I glanced down at Grunt, who was sniffing around. He had adorable, round eyes. Not the least bit terrifying or beastly. I had the three of them in collars and leashes. "I still don't understand why they're so into this." The whole of Constanria were insistent that I had to die, and this country, even though I was a stranger to it, was giving me everything.

"Get used to this. It's a lot of responsibility."

But very little work.

Was it strange that I missed the familiarity of it? Most other people preferred to escape it, but I'd found comfort in it through the years.

The *atira* creaked open and we stepped out. Vanjar shoved a scroll in my hand.

"What's this?" I asked.

"Your schedule."

"Schedule?"

"I want you to be seen around the castle, and perhaps we'll let you tour the city, too. Everyone here is feeling better. It'll be good if others work more vigorously. But most importantly, you bolster their morale, give them reason to think the future isn't bleak." She looked at the ground and smiled. "I'm just so happy that things aren't as gloomy for once. Thank you so much, Sera, for being here with us. My people... I haven't seen so much light in their eyes for a long time."

"You're welcome?" I decided to go along with it, even if I didn't understand. I trailed after Vanjar into the Assembly of Scholars. I looked at the scroll. It didn't have much for me to do, just places for me to visit, listing when and where.

"Make sure you don't miss those times," Vanjar said.

"Uh, why?"

"It'll... unnerve me a little."

She was a little uptight, wasn't she? It made sense now that she was dressed so primly.

She left me alone to talk with her scholars. I had to wander around the assembly with little to do, stuck in the dimness of its yellow lights.

I picked a cozy spot and took out my book on visions and seers—that was what they used to call people like Anatolia, because she hadn't been the first. Lots of these accounts were nonsensical. Many hadn't come true. There had to be fakes amongst all those who claimed they could see the future.

I went through two to three books over the course of a few hours—I could read quickly.

One particular paragraph struck me as something to use:

There are many hypotheses for where spells come from. The gods seem to have gifted users, just as they have gifted seers. Artemes Remus once suggested that spells might be a way to channel spiritual energy (what he believes is the supernatural force surrounding our globe). This supernatural force is then what we call "souls," the energy that we use in magic. Some channels are more effective than others, and perhaps seers are a different kind of conduit.

"Beacon?"

I looked up, tearing myself from the hypotheses of Artemes Remus. I didn't agree with all his points. He seemed to mix too much religion in his findings, but he also had intriguing ideas.

A dark-haired woman strode up to me. The ingorias sniffed her ankles, making her uneasy. I shooed them away so they wouldn't scare her.

"How may I help you?" I asked her.

In her wrinkled hand was a leaf, gray, like many here in the assembly. "I was wondering if you could bless me and my sons." I focused on the leaf in her hand.

These gray leaves... they did look like herbs that were missing their bright souls. Souls harvested could be split into two parts—dull and bright. Dull ones existed the same way in every living creature, while bright souls gave the being its special properties. I didn't often do the harvesting of magic, but I'd seen some workers do it before.

"Bless you?" I asked the scholar.

"They say you have the power to fix all this."

"Um..." I shifted my gaze to the side, before looking at her again. "I don't know if I can promise as much."

"Have more confidence." She smiled. "You do. The goddess has yet to truly shine through you, but it's only a matter of time. Please, will you bless us?"

"And how do I do that?"

"A token from you would be nice. I was hoping you could bring this leaf back to life, then I will keep it with me for as long as I can, as a reminder that this isn't the end."

"Okay," I said, still uncertain. Maybe what I'd done

before had been a sham, and the leaf wasn't going to respond. I obliged and took off my glove. I blew out a sigh of relief when the leaf turned from gray to green.

Could I restore the bright souls in beings somehow?

I dropped it into the old lady's palm. "Here."

"Thank you." She kissed it. "Thank you so much."

"It's nothing. Really."

A bald scholar came after her.

"You want one, too?" I asked him.

He nodded. "I would be most grateful."

After him, more people came, and a long line formed behind them. I must have gone through at least a hundred leaves in an hour, and for some reason, it was taking a physical toll on me. I felt my shoulders slump, and my energy drain. A channel... Maybe I was one.

And then the power stopped working. The very last leaf I touched didn't change color. I looked up sheepishly at the next in line, seeing the freckled-faced girl I'd met two days ago.

If I remembered correctly, her name was Rena.

"Guess I'm out of luck," she said, shrugging. She turned away. "Your power isn't infinite after all. Some leaves here and there, who would that feed? One person for a day?"

"Hey," I called to her. "Is your friend okay?"

"Sascha?" Rena asked, spinning around to face me. "Brother's still ill from not having enough food. If that's what you're asking. Parlor tricks aren't going to feed him." She placed her hands on her hips and looked at me.

I didn't like how judging her gaze felt. "Why are you here, then? If you don't care for these tricks."

"Sascha's been talking about you nonstop, saying how you're going to save her little brother. Thought a leaf might cheer her up." She threw her ashen leaf to the table beside me. "Oh well. I just hope she's not too disappointed when she finds out you're not going to be much help."

The crowd dispersed after I announced my powers had stopped working. Many said they'd come back tomorrow, hoping I'd be able to do it again. I picked up the leaf that Rena left behind and shook it with my bare hand.

Nope.

It continued to stare back at me with its gray color, telling me how useless I truly was.

These people were counting on me. I shouldn't be walking around lying.

An idea sparked in my mind. I went around, looking for soul beads, and a few helpful scholars were eager to give me what I asked for. If I was a channel, and the spells another one, would combining both be effective? Maybe I could take more energy from the "spiritual realm," as Artemes put it, and restore the bright souls of these plants.

The scholars passed the soul beads to me and trailed behind me after I thanked them and strode away. They didn't make it obvious they were following, and kept a distance, but I noticed their eyes flicking in my direction every so often.

I picked up a branch that was lying around.

"*Arcio involus,*" I said, summoning my magic. It was the growth spell Gaius had used a few months back, when we were trying to solve the high-summer problem.

The soul beads reacted, glowing and spilling out power.

The spell worked.

I felt exhausted after that, but the branch reacted to my touch and spell—it changed color, just like the leaves, and even grew a little.

"Holy Aereala," I said. "It works!" I stood up and showed it to the scholars around me. They beamed, just like I did. "We can solve this."

I let them lead me to the granary, where they kept most of the food. Lots of scholars followed, eager to see what I was going to do next. They gave me a whole bag of soul beads. Our route to the granary caused a huge commotion, and more followed as we went.

My footsteps were quick and had a spring to them, but my legs couldn't seem to travel fast enough.

In the crowd, I spotted Rena. She was still looking at me all judging, but I was going to show her that I could make a difference. I didn't need their worship if it was just empty. That fight with Hoistus still bothered me, and I wanted to change that.

The granary was a structure made of stone, dug into the ground. Snow covered the rocky cavity. Stairs led to little doors around it. Of course there were a ton of stairs. Beyestiryans loved their leveled structures. In a corner was an *atira*, too small for the group of people who had gathered behind me.

"They tried harvesting some plants that died out, to see if they could make any use of it," Rena told me.

"Where do they keep them?"

"You're lucky they haven't cleared it yet. They were going to next week. Come with me."

I trailed after her, trying to keep up with her quick

footsteps. She was the first down the stairs, and me next. The group made way for the both of us. We reached an outcrop with a blue wooden door on it. The granary was *deep*, and the floors slippery. I hoped not to slip and fall. A drerkyn opened the door next to us and flew out, carrying a sack of food with him.

"In here." Rena pointed to the inside. "These ashen plants start rotting after a while. We tested it in warmer areas. But here in Beyestirya, the cold keeps them from rotting." She dragged a sack of food toward me.

I was still grasping the branch in my hand. In my other was the pouch of soul beads the Beyestiryans had gifted me. I turned around and looked at the crowd. There were so many people, all expecting and hoping for something to happen.

I sucked in a deep breath. *"Arcio involuntis."* The magic dragged from the beads in the pouch.

My belly started to hurt and an ache traveled through my arms. I pushed harder. This *had* to work. I *needed* to solve this famine.

The power surged through me. The whole sack of grains glowed, pulsed, came to life.

And then dimmed.

Rena pulled open the sack. She reached into it and pulled out a handful of corn. It spilled from her hands, yellow, like liquid gold.

The crowd behind me erupted into cheers.

"Could you do another one?" Rena asked. "We could use this to feed the neediest first."

Sascha's brother. I was going to save lives with this.

I smiled but shook my head. My energy had completely dissipated. "I think I need to sleep. You can try."

"I'm not sure," Rena said, frowning. She took the soul beads from me anyway and chanted the same spell I had over another sack of food.

Nothing happened. More people stepped forward and tried, all without result.

Rena looked at me. "I think it's only something you can do."

I glanced down the food standing before me. "That's all right."

Because this was progress.

This was good.

CHAPTER THIRTEEN

Two months had passed since the incident at the granary. I tried going back to restore more grains, so others could be fed, but the spells seemed to take a toll on my body and required too much soul magic. I thought the princes could pull it off, because they were just as adept with the art as I was.

They couldn't.

Each day at the granary made me more exhausted than the last. Eventually, I simply couldn't keep up. This method of trying to feed the people simply wasn't feasible.

It did, however, spark even more stories, and the tales of me grew to new heights. I felt like I was constantly being watched, albeit for better reasons than in Constanria. I needed some time alone, without people judging me, expecting something out of me. I'd turned so many leaves from gray to green that my power ran out, and one time, I had to wait three days before it came back.

"Hey," Rena said to me one day at the assembly. She was reading and walking at the same time. "You're looking down."

I often saw her around, and she had warmed up to me. She got books for me whenever I requested them. "I've been trying different spells, but they're not working. I feel stuck, you know?"

She patted my back. "You've done enough good."

"Didn't fix it."

"One step at a time." She scribbled something on her paper and looked up at me. "We're not expecting you to solve the whole famine. But you helped. *A lot.* Sascha's brother is now better. And so are many others. You've managed to feed families."

"I did?" I lifted my brows. "I salvaged so little food every time."

"It added up. You salvaged a thousand sacks of grain, Sera. *A thousand.*"

"That many?" My pulse quickened with excitement.

She nodded and smiled.

I'd converted Rena to my side. That made me feel a little good about myself.

But then I went to the medical bay, and I saw people there still dying from hunger. No matter how much time I bought these people—people who seemed to count on me so much—it wasn't enough. I needed something else. Simple spells weren't going cut it.

I wasn't thinking big enough.

I needed something to work.

Something *grand.*

I needed a walk outside.

"Vanjar said I shouldn't go out alone," I told Micah. "That it'll be terrible should anything happen to their symbol, and that I should stay where she can find me."

Micah hovered his fingers around me as he muttered an illusion spell. We were standing in my room, with the three puppies (they were much larger now) sleeping, and the birds on top of my cupboards, draped in fabric.

Micah cocked his brow at me.

"And," I continued, "Vanjar is incredibly uptight, isn't she? Thanks for doing this."

The castle in Kaldaross didn't have much to explore compared to Raynea's palace, and it was easy to start feeling claustrophobic in it. Most things were built bigger around here, but the castle itself didn't have as many buildings, because it was only home to the royal family and its servants.

Its corridors had begun closing in around me, and the Assembly of Scholars, despite being so tall, was too dark.

It didn't help that Vanjar had given me such a strict schedule—from mornings to afternoon, I was to be at the assembly. I'd then have meetings with people after lunch, before moving to the training grounds in the evening to "show off" my warrior side. The training bouts were usually staged, to give the Beyestiryans the false impression that I knew my way with the sword. The princes absolutely hated Hoistus's guts.

But maybe I *was* getting better. Training every day did have that effect. Still, it was a lie I was living.

Micah shrugged a vest over his torso, before whispering a spell over himself. His crimson hair turned into a deep brown, but his striking blue eyes stayed there.

"It's fun to see how the people here treat you," Micah said. "They're finally recognizing how amazing you are."

I patted his cheek. "It's all lies."

"There's a lot of truth in it."

"I need to do *more*. To make sure there is truth. But we're back to trying out different spells that don't work. It feels like what we did in Raynea all over again."

"You'll come up with something," he said.

"Now you're starting to sound like them."

He hugged me by my waist. "Well, even if you don't, that's all right."

"Why?"

"You wear this pout that makes me want to kiss you." He rubbed his thumb across my lower lip.

"Since when was anger a sexy expression?"

Micah chuckled. "Every expression you make is sexy."

"Could have fooled me." I shrugged. "Considering how you guys aren't acting on it." Of course, we couldn't do anything yet because Rylan wasn't around. They had a promise to share my first time together, and they were still worried about that whole pregnancy problem.

I really wanted Micah and Kael to work their fingers more, however. I didn't dare ask. I was too inexperienced in these matters to muster up the courage.

Micah smirked. His gaze dropped to my lips, then to my boobs. My upper portion of my chest was exposed because of the design of this top, but after I walked out, I had to don a cloak to cover my skin. He spun around. "Let's go." He made a circling motion with his finger. "You wanted to explore the city, didn't you?"

I dragged my cloak around my shoulders. Because of the illusion spell, no one would see me as Sera for a while. I didn't realize how freeing it could be to wear a different skin. "Vanjar will freak out if she comes to my room and sees it empty."

"My cousin always liked having things in order," Micah said as he led me down the corridor. "She's a bit of a control freak, if you ask me. She used to decline lessons because her tutors didn't wear what she wanted, and her dolls... they were arranged in such a tidy fashion that it was almost creepy."

Now that Micah mentioned it, Vanjar's hair was incredibly neat, despite how wavy it was. It was like she had planned where each curl should fall.

"I didn't assume she'd be the type," I said. "Not with how silly she acts sometimes."

"She wants things to be perfect. It stresses her out often, but she's good at hiding it." He grabbed my hand and squeezed. "Hopefully, you won't have to put up with it much longer. I don't know what Rylan has planned, but once he tells us he's won your position back, we'll go home."

I nodded. "Yeah." Still no word from Rylan. It had been two months. I was tempted to send one of the princes back there myself, to make sure he was okay. But what if I was sending them to danger, too?

"Shouldn't we invite Kael and Gaius to come with?" I said to Micah.

"Can I be selfish for once?"

I squeezed his hand back. "Okay. It'll be nice to just spend time with you."

We walked outside, where the skies were open, cloudless,

and blue. Micah summoned his white wings, which blended with the snow. With his smooth complexion, he looked like an angel in this backdrop.

He scooped me into his arms and took to the skies. It got increasingly colder the higher he soared, but we needed to blend with the clouds to sneak past the guards.

I hugged his body, which he brought to a higher temperature for me. My cheeks warmed with his touch, and I blew out a sigh, which misted in the cool air surrounding us.

"The Beyestiryan cities are much humbler than Raynea, aren't they?" I said as my boots hit the cobblestone pavement. The buildings didn't tower over us like in Raynea. They were usually one story high, two at most, and were made of gray-bluish wood. Most of their sloped roofs were covered with snow. Someone had probably cleared the streets of snow earlier, for most of it had been shoveled to the side.

"Any idea where to go?" I asked Micah.

"You're the one who wanted to explore. This is my first time here. So, feel free." He gestured at the street.

We strode, hand in hand, across the buildings. The stores looked dreary, many derelict. I wondered whether we'd stopped by the wrong district.

There were plenty of beggars lining the streets. "This isn't as fun as I thought," I said.

Micah peered at me. It took me a while to adjust to his disguise. "They are going through a famine. From what I've heard, it's gone on for a year."

"Constanria has been prospering. Why didn't we help more?"

"I didn't think it was this bad. From the emissaries and

letters, it simply felt like Beyestirya was being greedy. We used to always supply them food, and famines aren't uncommon around here. We thought they'd work through it, like they always do. We couldn't snatch too many resources from our own people."

A little girl, who looked too frail to even walk, sat in front of a store, tending to some wooden dolls. They were no bigger than my thumb. She picked up a doll and reached out to me. "Would you like one, ma'am?" Her cheeks were a fiery red, but her lips had turned blue.

"How much is it?" I asked.

"This one's a good-luck charm for couples. Ten ruby gems."

I raised my eyebrows. Ten ruby gems was the equivalent of five silvers.

"It costs two rubies for a decent meal these days," the girl said.

Micah fished the money out from the pocket in his vest and passed it to the girl. I thought I saw extra in his palm.

The girl gave him the doll. "May your marriage prosper."

"Marriage, huh?" Micah said, smiling. He hooked his fingers in mine. "So, have you decided to marry me yet, Sera? Maybe this is a sign." He shook the wooden figurine between his fingertips. It was a young woman carved into a round shape, with two red cheeks.

I turned back to glance at the little girl. She looked so frail and weak. Like she wasn't going to make it.

"Marriage?" I said. Oftentimes when the brothers fought over me, it made me laugh and gave me a funny feeling inside. This, however, was something heavier. I couldn't give a thoughtless reply. "No."

His grip tightened.

"I can't... marry any of you. At least not just one. It doesn't feel right. Especially if you're going to fight over it. Not unless I have to."

"And Rylan?"

"I'll say no."

"But you'll be seen as a spinster as the years go by. You won't get the perks of marrying a prince. Or king."

"Does that matter? You guys will be with me, right?"

He smiled, but it didn't reach his eyes. "We will. I was hoping you'd belong just to me, however."

I couldn't think about this clearly, not with seeing the girl like that. I turned to her. "When was the last time you ate?"

"This morning," the girl said.

"Was it enough?" I asked.

She shook her head.

I took a scroll from my satchel and bent down to write on her table. She stared at me with wide-eyed curiosity. I passed my letter to her. It had my signature on it, so the guards would listen to its instructions.

"Go to the castle and show them this. They'll give you what they can."

"What's this?"

"Show this to your mother. She'll know what to do."

She nodded before lifting herself to her feet and striding off. Her footsteps lacked the bounce that many children's had, and each frail step she took broke my heart.

"You can't save all of them, you know," Micah said.

"It's better than nothing."

We continued on in silence. More stores showed up, manned by people who looked famished. There weren't many stores for food. I saw some women standing outside, with half their tops off, trying to sell their bodies for a meal despite the cold.

"This is depressing," I told Micah. "Let's go back."

I was beginning to hate Constanria for neglecting these people, even though I had no reason to. I was as blinded by my ignorance as the other Constanrians until I came here.

"Maybe that's why these people need you more than ever," Micah said. "Signs of hope don't come by easily."

"I'm doing nothing. And what then, when Rylan calls for me back?"

Would Vanjar let me go? Would these people, after I'd promised so much?

"Important figures are usually valued more by how they're seen instead of what they actually do. And it's up to you decide. I'll stay wherever you go."

"I don't know how you stand it." Micah had been scrutinized since he was a child. My powers, at least, only manifested when I was nine, and I'd managed to hide them for a long time.

We walked out of the street, past the gloom and misery. Micah spread his wings from his back, took me in his arms, and brought me to the skies. "It's almost refreshing how no one thinks anything of me here. To be a nobody. I'm a Constanrian prince, yes, but they see me more as a visitor who will be gone soon, not as a bastard member of the royal family."

"It's strange," I said. "All my life I've been trying to be someone to be looked up to."

Micah kissed my temple. "It's not that amazing."

"I don't know." I laughed. I loved being in his arms. I tried to put those images of the starving Beyestiryans behind me, to just relish this moment with Micah. "Being able to ask for anything and whatever I want isn't that bad."

"Don't get too lazy. It's the fight in you I enjoy seeing."

"I'll fight you with other things."

"Oh?"

"Hoistus said I'm learning fast with the sword. One day I'll best you."

He snorted and rolled his eyes, but chuckled. "Let me know when the day comes. I'll even submit to one of Kael's silly ruses if it does."

"You didn't keep your promise on the phallic hat."

"Then I will. Once you beat me in sword fighting."

"You're asking for it. I'll hold you to that. And if you dare back out on it like you did with Kael, I'll give you a hard time."

"*When* you can best me at sword fighting. I'm not sure if you can do that. Not even if you had a thousand years to train."

"It's motivation." My cheeks hurt from grinning. We traveled through the cold Beyestiryan air. It was one of the warmer days, with the sun shining brightly above us.

We released our illusions and swooped down into the entrance of the castle.

There, King Baekeil stood in front of a huge beast, one I hadn't seen before, with two long necks, heads, and two slobbering mouths laced with sharp teeth. Its tail swung out behind it, with thorny scales and a mace-like tip. It towered over the king's human form.

Baekeil, despite the beast's size, showed no signs of being intimidated. He leapt over it, bearing his spear, and nicked the creature's side.

"A draekari," Micah said. "I've never seen one before."

"I've seen sketches of it," I said.

"Cousins of the geckari. Was this creature what the scholars had been trying to create with their experiments?"

"Bah!" the king screamed, spinning on his heels. He wrestled with the creature. "You! Come here and help me."

Micah pointed to himself. "Your Majesty?"

"This wretched beast!" Baekeil dodged a blow from the draekari. "I've been trying to tame it for years. But it's as stubborn as Vanjar is."

Just then, Vanjar strode out of the castle gates. Her jaw hung open. She raised a questioning brow and crossed her arms. "What did you say, dear?"

"That you're as beautiful as this beast is!" He let out a round of laughter, ugly as it was, which didn't seem to help his case.

"I don't think that's what you think it means, dear," Vanjar said, pulling her upper lip up. Her gaze dropped to me, which made my stomach churn even though I didn't feel like I'd done anything wrong.

Micah walked up to the beast, coolly, as if it were a puppy instead of a creature that could rip his head off with one bite. He reached a hand out, almost in supplication, and summoned fire in his hands. "It's afraid."

"Afraid!" Baekeil hopped off the creature, no longer swinging from its back, and sauntered toward Micah. "Such a creature cannot possibly afraid. The draekari is feared by many, a creature with prowess unparalleled by—" Baekeil frowned. "Wait a second, how did you manage to get it to..."

The beast lowered both its heads, bowing before Micah. The serene look on Micah's face was almost breathtaking, enrapturing me with how he commanded the attention of the draekari. Micah lowered his hand and extinguished his flame. "I read it in a book once. I wanted to test the theories out. The common habitat of these beasts is volcanoes, and when they do not sense the flames nearby, they get antsy."

"So you calmed it with flames? Animals are often startled by them."

"Not draekari. They need them to feel safe."

A wide grin broke out across the king's face. His teeth were so bright that they reflected the sun. "I've been trying to tame these beasts for the longest time! You have saved me so much trouble, dear comrade."

He clasped Micah's hand and gave him a brotherly hug, accompanied by a rough smack on the back. "Now for the real test." Baekeil leapt onto the draekeri's back and mounted it as if it were a horse. "It is not resisting me."

Micah frowned. "I'd be careful. They are more aggressive than geckari, and are wild creatures at heart."

"I'll need to strap on a saddle and rein," Baekeil said. "I do not fear how wild it can be. It's not a challenge for a dragon."

Micah added, "You will need to expose it to fire more, or it'll go back to being skittish."

"That's no problem. I'll let the beast sleep next to it, bathe it in fire should it be necessary. You've made this a very good day for me, Michael. I can call you brother now, and we shall feast on my latest catch tonight."

"It's Micah."

"A brother, regardless of name."

The king slid off his new pet and strode away with Micah. He spouted accounts of his new projects, and seemed eager to learn of Micah's opinions.

I was left standing in the snow, facing Vanjar.

"I wanted some time for myself, all right?" I said, walking up the steps. "I'm sorry for not sticking to the schedule."

"You're not a prisoner here," she said. "You're free to do as you please."

"You're not mad?"

She twirled one of her perfect curls around a finger. "I need to get over my controlling tendencies. I'm just happy you're putting up with me."

"What's Baekeil going to do to Micah?" I asked.

The palace doors shut behind us.

She laughed. "Rant a lot about how he beat his brother in the succession, maybe. If we're lucky, Micah won't be bored to death."

CHAPTER FOURTEEN

"Come on now," I said, laughing on my bed. I sat on it cross-legged. "Sometimes I wonder how you guys have all this energy."

Gaius lay by my side, watching the ingorias with me. "They're taking too much after Kael."

Mayhem ran around, chasing Grunt's tail. Aura was stalking them from the left. Mayhem and Grunt were completely oblivious to Aura's shenanigans.

The three of them had grown to twice their size over the last two months. It surprised me to see how quickly they grew, even though I knew ingors and ingorias like them had large growth spurts. They were no longer the tiny fluff balls they had been when I met them, and were now the size of large dogs.

"Feed them," Gaius said, looking at the satchel in my hand.

Heat prickled between us. I knew he wanted me. I

wanted him. How we'd managed to last this long was a miracle.

He had a hand cupped over my exposed thigh. Was he aware of it?

"Don't you want to eat?" I asked my pets, trying to distract myself from Gaius. I fished a morsel from one of the satchels of food the maids had given me. They could only afford me dried, over-kept meat, completely unsuited and unpalatable for most dragon-kind, but the ingorias didn't seem to mind.

I tossed the scrap on the ground. Mayhem was the first to react, because he was such a glutton. He lunged for the food, but Aura pounced on him, knocking it aside. Grunt got to the scrap of meat first.

"There's enough for all of you," I said, throwing more food on the ground. Ingorias were messy eaters.

"They're as hungry as I am for you," Gaius mumbled.

I whipped my head to him. "Are you doing this on purpose?"

"Doing what?" He squeezed my thigh and shot me a smirk. The spark he sent there traveled straight up.

"Never mind." I sighed. Why did I put up with all this? Maybe I should simply rip my clothes off to see how the princes would react.

It would be really awkward if they just left me standing there to pick up the broken pieces of my broken heart.

The ingorias were slobbering all over the ground. When they finished, Grunt came up to me, tongue and tail wagging. He pushed Gaius aside. Gaius snarled at him, but Grunt continued swishing his tail in Gaius's face, causing the prince to look increasingly more peeved.

"I don't have any more," I told Grunt. He licked my hand, then my face, his ribbed tongue making my hair stand on end. I couldn't help but giggle and scratched the back of his ear. "Stop it, Grunt." But I continued laughing.

Gaius was staring at the ingoria with an expression I found hard to decipher.

"I like being licked," I said.

Gaius flicked his gaze to my face and raised a brow. "So is that how we're doing this?"

"I have absolutely no idea what you're talking about."

He pushed Grunt away and inched closer to me. "We're just making this harder for the both of us."

His hand was inching up my thigh.

"It's just you that's getting hard," I said.

He narrowed his eyes.

I stifled a laugh.

I *really* needed to work on my sexy talk and stop ruining moments with how silly I sounded.

A banging sound interrupted us.

The ingorias were making a ruckus. One of them had bumped into my shelves, and the birdcages on top of it shifted, almost toppling.

"Hey!" I said, tearing away from Gaius and getting to my feet. Grunt hopped off the bed. I walked to the shelves and dragged a stool over. I didn't have to climb it. Gaius reached up to the cage and grabbed for me.

"They're just piegfowls," Gaius said, passing the cage to me.

"Still have to make sure they're well."

When I pulled the fabric from it, my heart sank.

The piegfowl was dead.

It lay on its back, eyes clouded over with a layer of white, its beak open and gaping. It was happy and flapping just yesterday.

I frowned.

I got worried about the two piegfowl I had remaining. Gaius had sent out another one to Rylan.

"Let me check the other two," I said.

Gaius passed them to me.

When I peeled the fabric off to inspect them, one was preening while the other had its eyes closed, sleeping.

Good. They were fine. The one that had perished must have fallen sick or something.

Someone rapped on my door. Mayhem and Aura stopped messing around and raised their ears to attention. Gaius helped me place the cage back and covered it with fabric.

"Come in!" I shouted.

Vanjar entered my room. She wore a pretty, flowing gown, and had her hair pinned back in a delicate hairstyle today. "Am I interrupting something?" She carried a tray of tea in her hands. Her eyes darted to Gaius.

I forced a grin. "Oh, no, just playing with the pups before I head to bed."

Micah popped his head in. "Gaius."

"What?" Gaius asked.

"Hi?" I said. This was my room. "Why'd you think you'd find Gaius here?"

"I asked the maids," Micah said. "Anyway, Gaius, you have to come."

Gaius frowned. "What is it?"

"Kael's got into a fight with Hoistus."

"Hoistus?"

"I think he's going to kill him."

"Now I have to see."

"Excuse me?" Vanjar said.

"Don't worry," Micah said. "We'll leave part of him alive."

"Boys, if you end up hurting him, I'm going to have to withdraw my invitation—"

The door slammed behind us.

Vanjar looked at me, flabbergasted.

"What?" I said. "Don't look at me. I'm not responsible for what they do."

She placed the tray down on a small table. "Your ingorias can hardly be called puppies anymore. Soon enough you won't have space in here to fit them, and they'll have to stay in the stables."

I sat next to her and crossed my legs. Grunt ambled over to us—he was the sweetest of the three—and slumped down, resting his hand on his paws. His soft white fur brushed the side of my leg. "Maybe we'll all squeeze in this room," I said. "The rooms in Beyestirya are plenty big."

"It probably won't be enough to fit *one* ingoria. They are wild creatures."

"Like your husband's draekari?"

"I've been trying to talk him out of that for the last year.

He's insistent that a hidrae like him deserves a strong beast as a pet. Sometimes he thinks with his ego instead of his brain."

I poured myself a cup of tea and took a sip.

"You've lost weight since coming here," Vanjar told me.

I shrugged. "Everyone here has."

"We have plenty of food for you."

"Doesn't seem right to be stuffing my face when everyone else is trying to get something to eat."

We sat in silence for the next minute. I sipped tea, scratching Grunt's ear every so often. Why was Vanjar here?

"I'm sorry for putting you through everything," Vanjar said, breaking the silence. She poured herself another cup of tea. "For placing all this responsibility on your shoulders."

"All I've been doing is trying to make my presence known. You aren't exactly giving me work."

"It's not the work."

I knew what she meant. It was the expectation that I was to make things work.

I set down my cup and looked at her. "Do you believe in all this?"

"In?"

"That I'm supposed to be your 'savior' or whatever."

Vanjar pursed her lips and furrowed her brow. "I think I do."

"I'm a girl from a small town."

"Gifted with an extraordinary power. We've been looking for the answers all over. This famine... it's plagued us for a year. I didn't think much of it at first. I thought it would come and go. Then, a few months back, the plants started dying en masse. The livestock began dying out because we had nothing to feed them with. Then the people began to go, too."

She shook her head. "I'm worried, Sera. Worried for my children. My life... had always felt perfect. I could get along with everything and everyone, and at a young age I found the love of my life and thought I'd live hundreds more years with him. And now everything I love is being threatened by something I can't explain."

"I'm trying to find something. What if I can't?"

"You don't have to. We're waiting for another sign."

"From me?" I tilted my head.

"From Aereala."

"What do I have to do with Aereala?"

She paused and rested the rim of her teacup on her lip, as if considering whether she should tell me what I wanted to know. "We... we had a man, who told us he had a vision of Aereala years ago."

When she didn't elaborate, I said, "And?"

"You're the splitting image of her. He said so. He was amongst the scholars, and he told me on the first day. The rumor has spread. The scholars are convinced that Aereala will talk through you soon, to tell them what to do. We're all waiting."

"What?" It sounded like utter nonsense to me. But then I recalled the woman from that strange dream I had weeks ago... Was she...

No, that's ridiculous.

"You think too little of yourself," Vanjar said.

"What if Aereala never comes? That's likely to be the

case. Then what? What your people are doing... that's not a plan."

"We're grasping at straws at this point." She sighed and fished out something from the pocket in her long sleeve. A scroll. She unrolled it.

"Uh..." I squinted. "What is that?"

"Something dear Akirya drew for his father. He wanted me to show it to him."

"Is that... a king standing on a pile of meat?"

"My children are hungry," Vanjar said. "They miss the luxuries they used to be able to afford. This is his silly way of expressing that. It's cute, but as a mother, it breaks my heart. I wish I could have provided them a better world." Vanjar leaned back into the chair and rubbed her temple. I wondered if this was how the queen usually was, late at night with no subjects to look at her. Was she usually this battered? Because outside, she dressed herself in a bright smile and a carefree attitude.

"If it comes down to it," I said, "will you war with Constanria?" I resisted placing my hand over my mouth. Maybe I shouldn't have blurted that out. Maybe I was giving Gaius's plans away.

Vanjar looked at the ground. "We won't win. You Constanrians are better fed, stronger in numbers in terms of healthy men. We don't want war, but we are prepared for it. And should we need to, we will strike first."

"Why would you need to prepare?"

She released a tired breath. "I don't know either. That brother of mine..."

But she didn't finish her thought.

"All this talk about me being the Beacon. What if I want to leave? If I don't want to stay here?" What if, despite how badly Constanria treated me, home was home, and I wanted to return to Rylan's arms, and find Frederick, and go back to the life I'd wanted to grow out of, but finally realized I liked?

And my parents and sister... they were still in that country, and despite how badly they could treat me sometimes, I could feel some part of Mother still loved me.

It was a huge step to take, to commit to Beyestirya. It was as foreign to me as I was to it.

"I won't stop you," Vanjar said, her gray eyes deepening a shade. "But I'll appreciate it if you stay. What you've done here... It gave my people life. A reason to fight again. It gives them reason to hold on longer."

I tried not to let those words get to me, but my chest tightened nevertheless.

Vanjar stood, taking the tray with her. "I'll need to see my husband. I just wanted to thank you and say sorry for what I'm putting you through. You've been a dear all this while."

"I should be thanking *you*," I replied.

She gave me one more smile before turning around and walking out of the room.

I let my body sink into the chair.

What did I want?

Life used to be so simple before all these problems started showing up, but now I had too many choices, and the decisions were too hard to make.

———

When Vanjar left my room, she'd forgotten to take her silly drawing with her. I strode through the castle's corridors. I lifted the drawing out of my satchel and took another look at it—children could be so creative. Akirya didn't just draw meat. He drew different kinds, all cooked in interesting ways.

Why did the Beyestiryans have such a taste for *tall* things? Baekeil's study was on the seventh floor, and I had to climb up winding stairs to get to it. The flames on the wall flickered as I moved up, and my thighs protested against my weight by getting sore.

His door was wide open when I arrived.

"Hello?" I called, knocking against his door.

I entered the mess of his room, scroll in my hands. I wanted to leave his son's drawing on his table and be on my way.

Right before I pried my eyes from his desk, I saw Constanria's seal on one of the letters on the table.

Rylan?

If letters were coming from Constanria, why hadn't Rylan sent any to us?

I searched around, because guilt rose in my chest and it made me not want to pry. But my curiosity was stronger. I picked the letter up from the desk. I had to squint to read it properly. The room was lit by nothing but moonlight streaming in the windows, which wasn't much.

To His Royal Majesty,
Baekeil,

Your demands have stirred our Constanrian courts, and we are unhappy with the way you have treated us over the months. You have been unable to meet our gentle requests, despite how lenient we have been in regard to our territory disputes. Your people are claiming more of our lands, encroaching into our territories despite our many warnings. Let this be our last one before action is due.

Yours sincerely,
   Head of the Council of Fortitude
   Vancel Gavril

I placed the letter down, letting it sink in. *Take action.* What was that supposed to mean?

The knocking of footsteps sounded from outside. My heartbeat quickened, and I made for the door, but the torches cast sharp shadows on the walls, and I realized it was too late. I ducked into a corner, hiding behind a shelf.

Vanjar's voice echoed through the room. "There has to be another way."

Baekeil's voice followed. "The Constanrians are going to attack, love. We can't sit back and let them destroy whatever little we have."

"And my cousins?"

"Keep them away for now. Perhaps it's better to keep them warm and well fed. We don't need trouble here, not while there might be war at our borders."

"They only intend to send us a warning. What if they

decide not to come? Maybe my brother will finally listen to my pleas."

"They will come." Baekeil's voice was muffled. Their breathing grew heavier, and the sounds of wet kisses reached my ears. My stomach dropped at the realization that I was intruding on something too intimate for my ears. A blush crept up my cheeks. "I love you, Vanjar, and I know you love your country, but this is the only way. When they grow desperate, just like we do, they will demand more. They will take more. We have to end this."

"But my brother—"

"Is the one sending us these threats. He doesn't care for you. Your family is here, in Beyestirya. With me. You promised to be by my side no matter what."

"I don't want war, Baekeil."

"Please, listen. We have to ready our troops."

"Not like this."

"Constanrian forces are gathering around the mountains, love. They're planning to attack. We have to do so before they do. I'll ready the troops, and we leave in a week."

"Be safe."

"I love you."

I stilled my breathing as I heard Vanjar agreeing with a moan. I pressed my hand against my mouth, not daring to make a move. I wanted to drown out the sounds.

I shouldn't be here.

Vanjar's moans grew louder and higher-pitched. I didn't want to imagine what they were doing, but the sounds sent vivid images through my mind. I wanted to leave, but couldn't. If they spotted me, I was afraid of what they'd do to me.

Moments went by at an agonizing pace. I heard the door shutting from the front of the room, and ceased to hear their lovemaking, panting, moaning, or the knocking of their bodies against Baekeil's desk. I pulled my hand from my mouth and sucked in a sharp breath. I was giddy because of how I didn't let myself breathe. I waited for a few more minutes, staring at the brick wall in front of me, still not feeling safe enough to move.

Only when I was certain the coast was clear did I get on my feet.

The implications of what they'd said and what Vancel had written in the letter trickled through me.

Take action.

Beyestirya was being threatened by Constanria, and for that, a war was going to start.

Gaius had been right.

But in this scenario, it felt like Constanria was the country who was triggering war with its threats.

My mind whirled as I picked up the warning letter and shoved it into my satchel. My hands were shaking as I pried the door open.

I darted out to the corridor and down the steps as quickly as I could, my feet unable to keep up with the racing in my chest.

CHAPTER FIFTEEN

I sat on my bed, with a heavy heart and three pairs of curious blue eyes on me. The three ingorias were sleeping. Aura was the only one on my lap. I used Aura's fur to try and calm myself, but the whirring in my mind raged on like a tempest.

War.

And we weren't the good guys.

"It's late, Sera," Kael said, stretching. His muscles pulled his tattoos with them. He yawned. "Why have you called us all here? I was having a nice dream."

I passed them Vancel's letter.

"He replied?" Gaius asked, snatching it from me.

"Look again," I said.

They passed the letter around, each bearing serious expressions as they read it.

"So Constanria might attack Beyestirya," Micah said, summarizing what they all thought.

I massaged my temples with my index finger and thumb.

"Or the other way around. Beyestirya will order the first move next week." I did *not* want to go into the details of how exactly I'd found this out. "They're attacking Constanria with their full force soon."

"Then we must stop them," Gaius said, straightening. "We'll have to fly back to Rylan, tell him of Beyestirya's plans, crush their forces before they ambush us."

"No," I said.

"No?"

"We... we can't. Hundreds... thousands. They'll die if we do this."

"And if we don't, they'll gain the advantage."

I thought of those beggars I'd seen in the streets when I walked with Micah. Images of the Beyestiryans I'd spent time with, gotten close with, flashed in my mind.

They didn't ask for this. That little girl who'd sold me the doll... it was still on my bedside, supposedly a blessing for my marriage.

I shook my head. "No, we can't. Too many innocents would be caught in the battle if we did this."

Gaius kissed my lips and dug his hands in my hair, until his earthy scent encircled me and soothed me. I was stunned when he pulled back, and his eyes dug into mine, burning with questions. "I ask you again, Sera, where do your loyalties lie?"

I bit my tongue, not knowing how to answer. "I... With you..." That was what I'd said before. I cupped his face, where light stubble had grown, and pulled my thumb across his warm skin.

"Then we're going back to Constanria, aren't we?" Gaius asked his brothers.

Their expressions, even Kael's, were grim. They both gave him solemn nods.

But I wasn't so sure about my earlier response. I wanted to be with them, more than anything else in the world.

But could they stick by me?

"We can make this better," I said. "Let's stay. Try and fix this before they call for war."

Gaius frowned.

"We're here now, in a position where we can do something. Think about it. It's strategic. We're on the inside, capable of doing things other Constanrians are unable to." My gaze dipped to the ground. "And... I don't know, Gaius... I just don't want it to come to this. Constanria sounds like it's the one pushing Beyestirya into a corner." It wasn't black and white.

"I'll follow what Father and Rylan decide," Gaius said. But the other two brothers didn't look as convinced.

"Even if they're wrong?"

"They're family. You are." He sat by me. "Tell me you're with us, Sera."

"I am. That's why I say we try to work things out here. Where Rylan can't."

"Sabotage?" Kael said, crossing his arms.

It sounded worse when he put it like that. "Yeah," I replied.

Gaius grabbed my hand. His touch was warm, but not as comforting as I'd hoped it might be. My insides were going cold as I thought about Vanjar and her children.

These people merely wanted to survive. I'd talked to them, laughed with them, heard their concerns. They saw *hope* in me. Unlike the country I was born in, the country I should want to protect instead.

Micah could see the turmoil in my heart. He was the most perceptive. The bed sank under his weight as he sat. He grabbed my hand and placed it to his lips. "It's okay to feel the way you feel, Sera."

I shot him a grateful look.

Kael slackened the tension on his shoulders and sat on the edge of the bed too. "So, we'll try and avoid war, then. What do you say we do?"

"We'll need to give them reason to avoid it," I said. "Remove what they require for war. We can't kill their people, of course, since that's a last-resort thing." I thought back to Hoistus and his joyous laughter (he'd mostly suffered broken pride from his fight with Kael); my maids; Rena, who had warmed to me; and Sascha, whose brother had received the grains I'd brought back. "But we can get rid of their supplies—"

"Their food," Kael said. "Every army needs to be fed. Without that, they'll need to find more, and that's what they're going to spend all their energy on."

I smacked his shoulder. "They're already starving. If we get rid of their food, we might as well kill them."

"And Constanria won't be attacked," Gaius muttered.

"You really want to kill all these nice people who have been so accommodating?" I asked, giving the princes a flat look.

"I have no problem with offing Hoistus," Kael said. "I'll cut his head off myself."

I cocked a brow. "Vanjar's children?"

"Not the children, though. I like Akirya. Little brat's got a punch."

"Good, then we agree on something else." I clapped my hands together. "How about their weapons? Disarm them."

Micah leaned on my bed and stretched his arms. He didn't care that he still had shoes on and dragged his legs onto my sheets. "You might want to rethink that."

We all looked at him. "We're throwing out ideas here, but why?" I asked.

"Their armory is one of their most guarded places. It's going to be trouble trying to get in."

"Even for us?" Kael asked.

Micah smirked. "You really want to go there with our dragon forms? You'll end up surrounded with spears pointed at your throat and chained up in dragon stone in minutes."

"What's so hard about getting in there?" I asked.

"It's guarded on all sides by drerkyn and draerin," Micah said. "Plus, the structure that holds the armory has roofing made of dragon stone, so even if we wanted to go there as dragons and blow it up, it'll repel our fire."

"So, what now?" I said. I closed my eyes, wondering what else we could do. Get rid of their soul magic? Would they use much of it in the first place? How about assassinating Baekeil? Would that be too terrible? I'd much rather avoid that if I could. The man only wanted to protect his people.

But he did intend to use child soldiers, didn't he? I thought it showed just how desperate he was.

Gaius began, "We fly back to Ry—"

I slapped my hand over his mouth. "We scout the armory tomorrow, see if there's any way to get in other than force, and once we do, have some spells ready. We'll blow the place up."

"I'm telling you," Micah said, "it's not that easy."

"Since when is anything?"

———

The armory was as guarded as Micah had said. It was a structure that looked almost like Dragon Keep—a residence the first dragon king had called home. The Beyestiryans might have built this keep based on it, for it looked similar to how Dragon Keep used to be depicted, with the same towers, gates, and walls.

Dragon Keep, however, was said to house thousands. This was a smaller version of it.

"Twenty men at the top," Kael said. "Ten around the bottom. And draerin scouts all above. You weren't kidding."

"We could take them," Gaius said. "Think it might alert the rest of the army, though."

"You're always rushing into things," Micah said.

"Oh, like you rushed into pleasuring Sera?"

I set my mug of water down. "I appreciated that."

We sat a field's length away from the structure, sipping on Beyestiryan piss (more accurately, the boys sipped on ale while I stuck to water) and trying to blend in with the background. It was quite impossible to blend, though. The princes stood out too much. They were too gorgeous, too princely. And everyone around here knew who I was and loved to gawk.

The moon shone bright and white in the sky. It was a half-moon tonight. The wind was colder at night. The cold had seeped through my boots, and I had to bite the insides of my mouth to stop my teeth from chattering.

"We're not getting in there without a ruckus," Micah said. "I told you that already."

"You have your spells ready?" I asked.

Micah licked the foam off his upper lip. "Yeah, right here." He pulled them from his pocket and passed them to me. "Bombs. They'll go off once you utter the spell, and then it's fireworks."

"What's the spell?"

The little black pellets felt smooth and glassy. They had a decent amount of weight to them, too, reminding me of a handful of silver coins.

"I can't say or they'd go off," Micah said. "And since I invoked it, it has to come from my lips."

"Fair enough," I replied, placing them in my satchel. "So I just have to get these inside?"

"Good luck trying to get in," Kael said. "Give me two hours. Maybe I can take them all out. Quietly. If they sound the alarm, then that's too bad." He chugged his drink and set his jug on the shaky wooden table.

"I'm not risking sounding the alarm." I lifted myself to my feet and strode to the armory.

"Hey!" Gaius said, his eyes burning. He grabbed my wrist. "Where are you going?"

"Getting the job done."

"You're just going to waltz in there?"

"I'm going to try to. Being their symbol of hope has to come with some perks, right?"

"You can't do that," Micah said, shaking his head.

"And why not?" I asked.

"They can't be that dumb."

"No harm trying. The worst that could happen is them thinking I'm crazy and turning me away." *And Vanjar screaming in my face*—but I could take that.

Gaius and Micah shared uneasy glances. Then, sighing, Gaius let me go. "We have your back should anything happen."

"Yep," Kael said, his lips popping at the P sound.

I nodded, gritted my teeth, and strode up to the guards blocking the entrance. They grew taller as I neared—bulkier, too, and larger. Their pointy spears looked, well, *pointier*, as well.

I missed Pointy. She and I were forming a team.

They thought I was on their side, so they weren't going to attack.

"Oi!" one of them shouted. "You there! Halt." He had one hand raised as he strode toward me. I forgot about the chattering of my teeth. They knocked against each other, making me look even more suspicious.

"Beacon?" the guard said as he neared. "What are you doing here?"

"I'm... I need to take a look at your armory. I've got a thing about swords and shields and stuffs like that. You know. The stabby things. Thought I could familiarize myself. Uh. Hoistus's instructions?" I stopped myself from slapping my hand over my face. My explanation sounded dumber once it left my lips. "It's important I go in."

"I... I don't understand," the guard said.

His companion strolled up to us. This one wore a thick blond beard and had a shrinking belly. They both towered over me. I had to crane my neck up just to look at their chins. "What's going on here? Oh—Beacon!"

"Vanjar sent—" I held my tongue before finishing my sentence, because I realized I had something better as an excuse. The bombs were heavy in my satchel. I tried to ignore them as I continued, "Vanjar sent me here, because she said it was the right thing to do." I felt grimy because of how easily the lies came out. "I had a talk with Aereala. She wanted me to look at the Beyestiryan weapons. I told the queen, and she gave me permission."

The brows of the first guard crawled up his forehead. "Aereala talked to you?"

"She came to me in a vision," I said, wondering if it truly was a lie.

Blondie gaped at me. "So you are our savior!"

It was tough to ignore the irony of his statement.

Kael strolled up to me. He waved at the guards. I shot him a what-are-you-doing-here look, but he simply returned my expression with a sparkling grin.

Thinking quickly, I added, "Oh, and he's with me."

"The prince?" the first guard said.

"Hey, uh," the Blondie said, nudging his friend with his elbow. "I'm not sure if he should be allowed in."

"You don't have to worry about me," Kael said. "I'm only here for Sera. To make sure she doesn't get herself in any trouble. She has this thing about being clumsy sometimes. And that"—he pointed—"is an armory, after all. What if she trips and gets her silly little self skewered on a sword or something? Wouldn't want that to happen to your precious Beacon, don't we?"

I narrowed my eyes at Kael. It sounded like he believed what he was saying. I wondered if he had confused me with Gaius. Gaius was the one who always got himself almost accidentally skewered. I'd actually saved him a couple times by telling him to watch his step.

Kael patted Blondie's beard, before leaning back and scrunching up his face. He sniffed his hand. "How often do you wash that thing?"

"The cold winds keeps it clean, sir," Blondie replied.

"*Ookay* then," Kael said, grinning. "Good for you." He carried himself with so much confidence that the guards couldn't help but trust him. Hell, I trusted him, even though I knew we were here planning *sabotage*. Kael strode straight past the guards, and I followed him.

"Vanjar needs to give a decree asking her men to bathe more," Kael murmured. Blondie apparently heard that, because when I turned around to check, he was looking straight at Kael. I quickly spun my head back before our eyes locked in an awkward gaze.

"You didn't need to come here," I said. "They were more likely to let me through if it were me alone."

He turned to me, a glint in his eye. "My brothers sent me. We were squabbling over what to do, 'cause we were worried. And then I decided we couldn't take it anymore, and someone had to go along. So here I am."

"What if the guards got suspicious? Then the whole thing might blow up."

"That's what we're here for, isn't it?"

The guards hollered, and one of their companions pulled the gates open for us. It groaned under its own weight, and lifted off the ground, exposing the insides of the armory. Torches, flickering on the walls, lit its interior, but it was still so dark that I had to squint to make the objects in the fort clearer. I strode in, Kael behind me. I had to admit, having him around did make it safer.

Many weapons had been piled on top of each other in crates. Those must have been the less valuable ones. They should be keeping the more valuable ones in a safer location.

Other guards patrolled the interior, some wielding spears, others swords. Many of them leaned against the walls, or sat in corners, obviously bored from standing around doing nothing particularly important all day.

Gaean's balls. I didn't want them to be caught in the explosion. I knocked on a crate, attracting their attention. "All of you!"

So much for sneaking in.

My skin tingled with anticipation as their gazes locked on me.

"Beacon?" a guard asked.

I pointed to the entrance with my thumb. "Your superior's asking for you outside."

"For what?" another asked.

I searched my mind for an answer, but only silly ones came up, so I gave them one. "Food? I think he might have gotten some extra for you guys, but I might have misheard."

They all bristled at the promise of food.

One soldier, who looked like he was in his teens, stood up from his corner. "Which superior?"

Bah—why were they asking so many questions? "I didn't catch his name. The one with the scruffy beard?" Lots of the men had scruffy beards, so how far off could I be?

"She must be talking about Commander Yulerick," one said. "Let's go. A man never turns down free food." He was the first to walk out of the armory.

Kael looked at me. "Good thinking. Now we don't have to worry about getting caught when putting the bombs down." He backed me toward a crate. His hard body pressed against mine, and my breath hitched in my throat. At first I thought he might kiss me, but he reached across my waist and took one of Micah's spelled metals out of my satchel. "Let's get to work."

"Work?" I said. "Strange choice of word for you."

He shrugged. "I can compromise."

"Another strange choice of word."

He shot me a toothy grin. "Cheeky."

We made haste around the armory, placing the metal balls next to crates. I could sense the cool sensation the magic gave off as I placed them down. Hopefully, they'd do the trick. When I climbed to the second story, more guards stood around, albeit fewer than downstairs. I gave them the same story I told the others, and they quickly scampered off in the rush for food. The more valuable weapons were kept upstairs, hung neatly on the walls. Exquisite bows and arrows, swords that had been shined and polished. Some of the equipment looked downright disturbing—catapults and their heavy projectiles; large crossbows and bolts that looked specifically designed to crush a dragon's skull. Even some torture devices were kept here.

When Kael and I finished, we rushed out of the armory. My heart was pounding, the excitement of it all making me dizzy.

Kael wiped his hands together. "I deserve a huge reward for all that work."

"And what did you have in mind?"

He bent down, pointing at his cheek. I smiled at him, before tiptoeing to plant my lips there. But he abruptly turned his head. My mouth fell on his. I heard him sucking in a deep breath, as if he was relishing my scent.

His eyes twinkled as he drew his head back. "Now we just have to get Micah to finish his spell."

I blinked. Recovering from the kiss, I said, "Who's the cheeky one now?"

"It's always been me. I gave you a compliment, but don't let it get to your head."

Playfully, I shoved him, and he gave me a *thwack* on my ass.

That actually hurt. I rubbed my bottom and shot Kael a peeved look, and that only made him laugh.

We strode out of the armory, right out the gate, which was three times my height.

In the distance, I saw that a ruckus had started. The guards were crowded around who I assumed to be Commander Yulerick. They were talking with raised voices, wondering where their food was. Yulerick looked at me, scowling, and I shrugged, playing innocent.

We rushed back to Micah and Gaius, who were still sitting on the table. My gaze kept flitting back to Yulerick as I walked away. Their squabbling seemed to be getting violent.

Better a fight than lives lost.

Micah looked at me, his gaze flicking to Kael's hand on my shoulder. "They're placed?"

Kael gave him a thumbs-up. "Yep. All that's left is the remainder of the spell."

Micah took out his soul beads, which glowed, and said, "*Juraca borivilia.*" A sizeable amount of magic, probably all the princes had gathered, flowed out of the beads and toward the nearby fort.

I was feeling quite pleased with myself when I turned around. That emotion slipped away right after, and my bones grew cold. The men were walking back into the fort. The whole place was about to light up like fireworks and they were going to get caught in the explosion.

"Wait we have to stop them!" I shouted, starting to run.

But Kael fastened his grip around my waist. I could hear my own breathing as my vision blurred with panic.

Kael held me to his body. "It's too late."

"They'll die!"

"That's war."

"This isn't supposed to be war. We're supposed to prevent it." My heart slammed against my ribcage, its beating pounding in my ears.

Some of the men were laughing and roughhousing with each other, completely unsuspecting of what was about to hit them. Kael didn't let me act on my instincts, which was to sprint there and drag them away. I shouldn't care—usually I didn't. But these people *trusted* me. Betrayal, my own, tasted bitter on my tongue.

"This is war, Sera," Kael said again. "For the good of the many."

I watched as the glowing magic danced through the winds, winding its way to the fort. Such destruction in beauty.

The magic zipped into the fort, disappearing through its walls.

We looked onward with bated breath.

I counted the seconds in my head.

"Nothing's happening," Gaius said, breaking the silence.

Kael released me, and I stepped into the cold, losing the sensation of his warm, hard body on mine. He furrowed his brow. "That's strange. Does the spell usually take this long?"

Micah shook his head. "It should have gone off by now."

Part of me was relieved that the men were safe, but I knew this had put us many steps back. I ought to feel frustrated, but the relief overwhelmed that. I blew out a sigh. The cold made it fog in front of my eyes.

"They must have safeguards against spells, then," Gaius said, sitting back down. He rested his hand on his chin and closed his eyes. "This is annoying. Gaean's teats, why can't anything ever be easy? We'll have to think up something else. I still say we go back to Rylan."

"Give me more time to think," I said. "There has to be a way around this."

The men went back to their posts, unaware of what might have happened.

The exception was Yulerick, who looked at me with menace.

I put a smile on my face and waved at him, hoping to seem above suspicion.

I doubted he bought it.

CHAPTER SIXTEEN

Yulerick scooped up some of his slobbery meat stew. It slopped off his spoon and into his bowl. He did it again. And again. It made it colder, and everyone knew stew tasted better piping hot.

But he didn't care. He was mad at me, staring at me from across the table of generals. Sylus was there. Vanjar and the princes, too. It felt like a meeting called to interrogate me, even though Vanjar had said that it was to smooth over our differences.

Yulerick's gaze was glued to me, not relenting, and it made my stomach turn. I couldn't enjoy lunch—not that it was much to enjoy—with him giving me that angry glare.

I stifled a sigh. Why did Vanjar have to arrange this meeting with the generals? I wanted to dismiss yesterday as a failed operation and put it behind us.

The next time Yulerick let the stew dribble down, some of it missed the bowl and spilled onto the table. "Why am I here?" he said to Vanjar, who sat at the tip of the table. She wore a tight-lipped smile, which was her way of pretending that everything between us was peachy.

She'd just given me a long scolding before dragging me here. I thought she might have blown her pretty top off.

"Sera wanted to apologize about yesterday," Vanjar said. "Didn't you, Sera?" She turned to me, glaring with two beady eyes.

My pride told me to be more difficult, and I wanted to say something snappy, but that would only bring unnecessary drama. Plus, Yulerick had right to his anger. So I swallowed my pride and plastered a grin to my face. "It was unthoughtful of me."

"Do you know what she did?" He slammed his spoon on the table, causing the rest of the tableware to clink, and pulled his face into a scowl. He shook a finger at me. "This *Beacon*. I don't know why ever the fuck she's called that, because we should be naming her the *Bitch*. She got my men all riled up yesterday. They wanted a party and I came up empty-handed. They got pissed! Some abandoned their shift and I had to waste my breath screaming at their sorry asses to come back and do their job." He leaned forward and pulled up his sleeved arm.

"What's that?" I asked.

"Where they bruised me."

"I don't see anything."

"I'm a draerin, so it healed already. But I can tell you, it was bloody and it was bad."

"Okay?"

Vanjar nodded. "I understand, Yule—"

"Fuck you do! You invited her here, convinced us she's

some symbol of hope while she's just some symbol of trouble, and now my men feel betrayed! I had to beat those pussies back into shape, but they'd lost their fire, all because of her stupid prank."

My stew tasted bitter.

"Yulerick," I said, sucking in a deep breath and pulling the table straight. I stared into his fiery eyes. "Whatever I did, it wasn't for some silly prank."

Gaius reached under the table and squeezed my thigh. I didn't think he'd meant to do anything sexual, and had only wanted to warn me of the trouble I might cause, but his action startled me and made my heart race regardless.

"It's part of a plan," I continued.

Vanjar searched my gaze. "What plan?" she asked.

"Aereala's."

The people in the tent stilled, and the clatter of utensils stopped. All of their eyes fell on me, burning with questions. Even the princes stared at me with curious gazes.

"She talked to you?" Vanjar said.

"Yes," I lied. Using Aereala's name was starting to become too easy. *Aereala's chosen.* I abused the goddess's name, but it just made things go more smoothly. Once I mentioned her, everyone's doubt melted away, and they listened to whatever I said.

They were looking for an answer—a divine answer—to solve their troubles. And even as I lied through my teeth, they swallowed my words like they were sweet nectar.

I cleared my throat. "Sometimes she comes to me... in visions, and my dreams."

"Does she?" Vanjar said.

"The first one was in the forest when we first left Constanria," I said, mixing some truths with my lie. "And you're right. She does look just like me."

"What did she say?" Yulerick asked. He leaned back and tipped his chin up, stroking his beard.

My mind whirled. "She's... vague about things. She mentioned looking for something in the armory, and she promised food. I thought I'd let your men know, but I think I misinterpreted her words, which caused the commotion yesterday."

Sylus, who had been silently eating his stew in the corner, let out a huge half snort, half grunt. "She's playing you, Yulerick."

"I am not," I said, lacing my voice with false conviction.

"She's playing all of us. Look at her: she's a nineteen-year-old who's more inexperienced in everything compared to the rest of us. What good has come since she arrived? *Nothing* but her parading around, shouting to everybody about how perfect and strong she is. Maybe the only thing she's good for is to spread her legs and give us men a good romp. She's *Constanrian*. The enemy—"

"What's this about being the enemy?" Gaius said, folding his arms. His upper lip curled in a snarl, making his expression positively dragon-like.

Sylus shut his mouth. He regarded Gaius, then said, "I've been thinking of you guys as the enemy ever since your father decided to hog all the food for himself. It's just personal."

He'd just called me a whore, hadn't he?

"I don't know," Yulerick said. "What she did at the granary was something."

"Oh, so now you're on her side?" Sylus said.

"Don't want to make the goddess mad."

"Look at you." Sylus folded his arms, eying Yulerick. "She's got you wrapped around her pretty, deceitful finger."

I gave myself a mental slap, needing to wake up from the stupor I was stuck in. No need to let the old general spit venom all over my name. "I'm not playing you, Sylus. Was I the one who called myself the Beacon? It was some silly name you lot came up with on your own. I didn't 'play' myself into this title whatsoever. If you think I'm fooling anybody—I'm not. If what I say isn't the truth, let me remind you that these are *your* beliefs."

"Look at her," Sylus said. "Beating about the bush. Just stand up and tell us you're lying, you stupid whore. No need to act all prim and proper about it." He made a rude gesture at me.

The hard knock of a dagger sticking into wood resounded through the tent, slicing through the wintry blowing of the wind. It was Micah's dagger, and it'd shaved off part of Sylus's beard.

"Now," Sylus said, licking his top row of teeth. "You've threatened me enough, boy."

Vanjar squinted. "Sylus, stand down."

"You're letting them walk over you." Bits of food escaped his mouth as he spat out his words. His beard was still stained with remnants of his lunch. "If you're not going to stand for Beyestirya—"

"Stand down! It's an order from your queen!"

But Vanjar's command bounced off Sylus. He'd flung

himself across the table, toward Micah, his eyes yellow and flaring with dragon rage.

The generals rose to their feet, drawing their weapons.

"Guys," I said to the princes, "we don't have to do this."

Kael grinned. "About time something happened."

"No!"

He threw a bowl of stew in Yulerick's face. The entire tent erupted into a fight—Kael had mistaken it for a food fight, and it was amusing to watch him counter the generals with utensils and stew while they swung at him with sharpened blades.

He left a line of them covered with food, their noses steaming and flaring with anger. None of their blows hit him as he whirled around them, playing with them as if they were nothing more than toddlers.

Vanjar was screaming orders in a corner. A stray fork went flying toward her, almost splitting her forehead, but she caught it with a quickness I hadn't expected and flung it aside. "Baekeil will hear of this!"

I was both panicking and furious at the same time. "Guys! We don't have to do this!" We were supposed to be forging peace, not waging war on enemy territory.

I screamed at them to stop, but as I did, the tarp of the tent lifted over my head, letting the sun pour in. The ropes and stakes holding it down unfastened, snapped, and flew into the air. The wind hit my face, and so did some stew.

"Oops," Kael said.

"What are you doing?" I asked him, wiping it off my cheek. Luckily, it had already cooled down, and only gave me discomfort instead of a burn.

"Thought I'd mess around while my two brothers go crazy."

His two brothers had apparently shifted into dragons, along with the rest of the generals, and were causing a huge scene in the middle of the training grounds.

The soldiers stopped whatever they were doing, many dropping their weapons to the ground. They craned their heads up to look at the clash of dragons above them.

I smacked my forehead. "Holy Aereala. What are they doing?"

"I think they're pissed," Kael said.

"Why aren't you with them?"

He shrugged.

"They weren't supposed to lose their cool like that. This lunch was meant to re-forge the ties between the generals and us."

Kael rested his hands on his hips. "That went south, didn't it?" He bent his back, as if stretching—as if this wasn't an utter disaster.

Gaius, in his black dragon form, bit a piece off a smaller dragon. I winced. That looked painful. And my heart skipped a beat at the violence of it all.

Vanjar shook her head. "This is wrong. All wrong. You have to stop them," she said to me.

I cocked a brow. "There's ten dragons fighting in the skies." The booming of their brawling shook through me. "How am I supposed to stop them? Transform into the great, mighty dragon and summon Aereala's strength? Oh, that'll be easy. Just give me a second." I placed two fingers on my forehead and pretended to call upon it. "Nope, not coming." I gave Vanjar a thin-lipped expression.

"Aren't you going to help them?" I asked Kael, hearing my tone rise a few notches. "They're outnumbered."

"You're not supposed to make more join the fight," Vanjar said.

"It's too far gone." What mattered now was making sure my princes were safe.

Kael waved his hand across his face. "They'll be fine."

One dragon—thankfully not Micah or Gaius—lost half its wing and plummeted to the ground. It landed in some ashen trees and sent a shock wave. People began dispersing to find somewhere safer. Nobody—*praise Aereala*—got crushed.

Darmar soldiers huddled together, next to large structures, hiding from being crushed. Some drerkyn flew away. Many watched with wide-eyed, curious expressions.

The smaller draerin generals fell, one by one, crashing and spraying snow everywhere. From what I saw, Gaius and Micah left them with superficial injuries, but knocked them out nevertheless. The black and white dragon duo were a threatening pair as they commanded the skies.

And then it was just one blue dragon left, facing the two of them.

"That's Sylus," Vanjar told me. "The old fart has a lot of grit, doesn't he? I thought he'd be one of the first to fall." She seemed to be enjoying the spectacle as much as the rest, and had given up on shouting her head off. If I had popcorn, I'd give some to her, but we were undergoing a famine.

Sylus fell to the ground, his wing ripped, like many of his

fellow generals. We thought it'd end at that. Micah seemed to think so too. His white dragon strode away.

But Gaius had other plans.

His dragon lumbered toward the fallen Sylus. Large and domineering, eyes filled with rage and menace.

He's going to kill him.

"He has to be stopped," Vanjar said. "This will be worse for the war. It'll rile the generals. There'll be more bloodshed, too early, between us." She was muttering to herself. Gray wings fanned out behind her. She rushed toward the two dragons, but she wasn't going to make it on time.

"Gaius!" I shouted, my sentiments echoing hers. I sprinted toward the two dragons, although my dress was terribly difficult to move in. My call had alerted Gaius, and he turned his head. His yellow eyes fell on me. My heart stilled.

He spread his wings out—large and enough to span a few small buildings—and glided toward me. He knocked a few watchtowers as he did, but didn't seem to mind. Then he swooped down, lowering toward me.

I backed away. What else was I to do when a dragon came for me? But before terror could properly kick in, Gaius bit my clothes and lifted me onto his back. An uncomfortable sensation shot through my spine because of how roughly he treated me. I positioned myself behind his scales and gripped them, my fingers shivering, not from the cold, but from fear.

He lifted into the air as his growling shook through my body. The force of him dug into my chest, and I pressed my weight on his scales, steadying myself.

It didn't take long for the fear to dissipate—that was instinct, but I knew Gaius wouldn't hurt me.

The dragon lifted off the ground, causing huge gusts of winds with the flap of his wings. He flew off, taking me with him.

CHAPTER SEVENTEEN

The ride didn't last long.

As soon as Gaius found a rocky outcrop to stop at, he descended, landing on his four talons. I was panting, and my knuckles had gone white from how tightly I held on. He hadn't been gentle with the ride, and I'd almost fallen off a couple times.

"Gaius?" I asked. "What's wrong?"

He stepped away from me. His dragon form almost slipped off the cliff, dislodging rocks that fell down the steep drop. He regained his balance and shifted back. A few moments and some yellow glows later, his naked form stood before me.

My first instinct was to look away, but I decided I shouldn't be abashed about his nudity—he wasn't—and turned my head back around. Before my gaze fell on him, I felt lips crashing against mine, overwhelming and hungry.

His heat surrounded me, and I returned his hunger, fisting my fingers in his hair. His lips were locked on so tight that I had to breathe through my nose. When he realized I was struggling to breathe, he pulled back, giving me take a moment to catch my breath.

"Gaius?" I sounded like a parrot, constantly repeating his name, but he wasn't responding to any of my pleas.

"Let me kiss you," Gaius said. "Helps to calm the mind." His voice was layered with bestial undertones.

His lips claimed mine. His solid body pressed tightly to me, and I felt his member, hard and wanting, digging into my thigh. Heat traveled to my cheeks and inner thighs.

He pushed me to the ground. The snow softened my fall. Some of it slipped into my dress and tickled my back. Gaius spread my thighs apart. He rested his weight between my legs.

"I'm just..." he said, breathing just as hard as I was. "I can't control my emotions right now. It's a blur." I caught his eyes, and they still hadn't changed from their bright yellow. Right now, Gaius was all dragon.

"Okay." I circled my arms around his neck and dug my hands into his short, dark hair. His stubble grazed my jaw as he ravaged my lips, prickling against the skin of my chin.

His hips rocked back and forth, stirring desire and uncertainty through me. He grabbed my cloak, and for a second I thought he might tear it off, and take me on this mountaintop, but the sensation of his hand simply lingered there, next to my waist. It made me feel like I was going to die of a heart attack. Questions burned through my mind. They made me wonder how far he would go with this.

How far I would let him go with this.

"They're not here," I said, as he finally pulled his lips

away again to let me breathe. "Your brothers... We shouldn't..." I tried to focus on his face: handsome, rugged, and now filled with need.

"I know." He cupped the curve of my ass and pulled me closer toward him. I couldn't distract myself from the sensation of his length, which I felt as clear as day.

The rock and snow of the mountains were cool against my back, but inside, I was a furnace.

I knew we should have stopped, but Gaius was impossible to resist, and I was liquid in his hands. He could do whatever to me and I'd let him; even in this cold, these winds, his heat pulsed off him, closed around my body and made my veins throb with a desire I couldn't control.

"Gaius," I repeated, this time not as a question but a plea. He continued to consume me, and I hoped my touch consumed him as much as his affected me.

Doubt flickered for a second. What if I couldn't please him? I'd never lain with a man before. What if, despite all our good times, after we were naked and bare, he realized he didn't like what he felt, that I was just like the women he'd slept with—or worse than them, even. What if, after he saw my naked form, he thought my waist was too wide, or my thighs not smooth enough? Ridges had appeared on my thighs after I reached puberty, and they made me self-conscious.

I shoved those thoughts away. I could learn to get better at it, couldn't I? And what we had here wasn't so superficial. He wouldn't leave me simply because my thighs jiggled too much, or because my butt wasn't round enough.

We loved each other.

With that realization, I kissed him harder than I ever had before. A growl ripped from his throat, and his yellow eyes flashed brighter. I skimmed my hand across his body, letting it slip down his neck, across the ridges of his abs, and down toward his length. His yellow eyes watched me as I did, and that growl never left his throat. It continued to rumble across the thin layer of air between us, sending vibrations across my skin.

The sky was clear today, the sun shining almost too brightly amongst the blues. A mountain sparrow danced through the air, the sporadic way it flew mimicking the beating in my chest.

I felt his length—warm, pulsing, needy. My breath hitched in my throat. I'd never touched a man like this before. When I saw him react, letting out a soft sigh, my confidence stirred, and I drew my hand over his length.

He sucked in a sharp breath. "Sera. Oh, gods."

Everything stilled around me, and it felt like it was just me, Gaius, and the whistle of the wind.

"Serraa," he called. He cupped my face with his hand.

It sounded like I was doing something right, but I had no idea. My hand was moving awkwardly. Shaking, because of how nervous I was.

Gaius kissed me again, invading me with his earthiness. With my free hand, I clutched his back to pull him in, needing more of him.

We were alone.

Except for Kael.

Who tore Gaius off me.

I sat upright, dizziness swirling through my body, still

caught in the moment and wondering why it had ended so abruptly. Wintry winds replaced Gaius's warmth, and a lightness I wanted filled with Gaius's body drifted across my skin. My lips ached, mourning his loss. I wanted to tug him back down to me again.

Another growl ripped through Gaius. Talons lengthened from his fingertips. His fist flew at Kael, but Kael dodged, shoving him aside. Kael's eyes weren't blue either, and when he spoke, his voice dropped, echoing his dragon.

"I brought you pants." Kael threw them at Gaius.

"I want her," Gaius growled. His eyes raked over me, and despite my thick clothes, it felt like I wasn't wearing anything.

"We all do."

"We're in Beyestirya now. Who cares what the people in Constanria think!" Gaius looked just about ready to lunge at Kael. "She can have our child and we'll all be better for it."

"A child?" I said, chest thumping. Did I have it in me to be a mother?

"That wasn't what you were saying about the war. And we can't. Not without Rylan. It wouldn't be right." The winds blew Kael's white hair across his face.

Micah flew toward us in human form, his pearlescent wings fanned out behind his back. He stepped over the soft snow. It was deeper here, and his feet sank into it, until it reached his ankles. "We've gotten most of their generals injured, but they were knocked out because of—" His eyes dipped to me, then to Gaius. "What happened?"

"What do you think?" Gaius said, dragging a hand over his hair. He walked over and picked the pants from the ground. He was oddly comfortable with his nudity and wasn't in a hurry to put them back on. Instead, he slumped to the floor and plonked his butt into the snow. The color of his eyes slowly changed from yellow to blue, but his expression still burned with primal hunger—*intense*. "I still want her. I've wanted her since I first laid my eyes on her and knew we all feel the same. I hate how we've had to hold back, and I'm sick of it."

I pursed my lips. "It's cold," I said, despite the heat between my thighs. It wasn't going away anytime soon. I considered echoing Gaius's words, because I *wanted them*, but that would simply stir more need between us, and we had to keep level heads now. If Rylan came back after a year and found out we'd gone on without him? Well, that would just make him mad.

Kael picked me up in his arms and nuzzled my neck. His eyes were still yellow. I was surprised by how well he controlled his dragon side. "Let's get you someplace warm, then."

"I got mad that Sylus insulted you. Threatened you," Gaius said, clenching his jaw. "My dragon woke, asked me to protect my mate, so I acted on it... and after that, it was hard to calm it down." He paused. "It's not normal. This mate thing."

I looked at my bare hand. One of my gloves had slipped off during our make-out session. "Did it have something to do with my curse? Is it a bond of some sort?" I picked my glove up from the ground.

Kael, in an uncharacteristically gentlemanly way, took my hand in his and kissed the back of it. "Why do you need an explanation for everything?"

"It's how I'm trained to think," I told him.

"Maybe it's just that. You're our mate. All four of ours, and there's no need for an explanation. The old dragons didn't need logic behind why they needed to find their other halves, and maybe we're not a pair but a quintet. First of its kind." He smirked. "It's a little bit romantic in a crooked way, isn't it?"

"When were you the sweet one?" I asked Kael. I looked at Micah, who often said things like this to me in private. I flashed him a smile, which he returned.

Micah sniffed. "It's the first time Kael's talking sense because he's talking about something that doesn't make sense. But yeah. Not everything in life needs an explanation. You belong to us and vice versa. That's all that matters, right?"

"Okay," Kael said. "This is getting a bit too corny for me. Let's go back so we can resume hitting things?"

Micah rolled his eyes. "The only ones going to get hit are us. By a bombardment of questions because of the ruckus we caused."

Kael stepped off the edge of the cliff. His wings were spread out and they caught the winds. He flew while carrying me. "I'm not the one who started it this time. Surprisingly enough." The fabric of my blue, fluffy dress flopped in the air. Why did it have to be so *huge*?

I looked over Kael's shoulder to Gaius, who had slipped on the pants Kael had given him. They were fuzzy, tinted pink, and had garish trimmings on the back, which reminded me of a stubby tail. Kael couldn't just pick a normal pair of pants. He had to go for the silliest one in the batch.

Gaius narrowed his eyes at Kael. "I hate you."

"You're welcome," Kael said, spinning around and snickering to himself. "At least I brought you pants. Then you don't have to go flying around with your appendage swinging at everything." He spun back around to face the other direction.

Over Kael's shoulder, I flashed a reassuring look at Gaius. After seeing that disgruntled scowl on his face, matched with those fuzzy pink pants, I had to turn around and snicker too. I clasped a hand over my mouth, hoping he wouldn't hear me.

"She's laughing at me, isn't she?" Gaius said, projecting his voice across the distance.

"Yep!" Kael replied, joining my laughter.

Micah chuckled, and we flew back, feeling lighthearted. This wasn't going to last long, not with things brewing as they were, but moments like these were what made life seem not too bad.

CHAPTER EIGHTEEN

I WAS HEADING out of an *atira*, wanting to stroll where Vanjar often situated me, when she halted me. She tucked a strand of her dark hair behind her ear as she gave me a thin-lipped look.

Her gown was fancier than most of her others today, with extra frills around her breasts, and she wore more gems around her wrists than she usually did. But there was something different—her curls weren't as neatly placed, and the frills around her chest didn't look like they'd been ironed properly.

"I have to talk to you," Vanjar said. The yellow lights of the assembly lit the harsh lines on her face.

I frowned. I hadn't seen her since what happened yesterday with the generals. After Kael flew me back, we'd headed straight to our rooms, and nobody stopped us, although some soldiers gave us wary glances as they strode past. We expected more reprimanding, and even considered leaving, because after something so violent, it wouldn't be too far-fetched to think they'd throw us in the dungeons. We decided to go back to Kaldaross, however, for the chance to prevent a war.

Vanjar held my hand and pulled me aside. She folded her arms and leaned against the wall, before cocking a brow at me.

"Well," Vanjar said. "What do you have to say?"

"What do you mean?" I asked.

"About yesterday."

I pushed my lower lip forward and shrugged. "The princes got carried away. Dragon men are often like that."

"It looked terrible." Vanjar sighed. "The generals recovered quickly, and most healed within an hour, so they don't think the princes truly wanted to harm them. But still, two Constanrian princes shoving them around made them seriously unhappy. They want to have them punished."

"And are they?"

"Are they what?"

"Being punished."

"I spoke up for them," Vanjar said, kneading the bridge of her nose. "They're missing food for the next three days, I suppose, and Baekeil seems to have a good impression of Micah, so he helped me speak for them, which worked in their favor. They're my cousins, so I'll make sure they're safe, but if they step out of line, just one more time..."

"The three of them don't even eat the food here," I said. "They go out hunting their own."

"I know. Baekeil does the same thing. He tries to find game. Whatever animals are left around here, anyway. Animals around here are dying out too."

"They haven't been complaining about the food—"

"That's not what's important, Sera," Vanjar said. She blew out a breath and continued, "I'm just saying that the people here have goodwill for you, but that doesn't extend to the princes. You have to talk to them and ask them to tone it down a bit, so no more trouble happens."

"Sylus sounded like he hated me."

"He doesn't speak for all of us. The man hates all Constanrians. He's eight hundred years old and something happened with his brother. He's never told us the full story."

"Sylus is that old?" My eyes widened. Gaius and Micah had beaten up an old man. They should be mighty proud of themselves.

"Which explains why he's so grumpy all the time. Don't mind him. Even Yulerick's forgiven you. But remember, this leniency doesn't extend to the princes."

I dipped my gaze to the ground, wondering why they gave me so much goodwill when I didn't deserve it. I was fully intent on betraying their trust. The night at the armory still bothered me.

Vanjar placed both her hands on my shoulders. "Sera, there might be a time when you have to decide between helping us, and the princes."

"The princes and I..."

"Are in love. It's three of you and one girl, which took me some time to get my head around, but my cousins were always strange. It didn't take long for me to get over my surprise."

"I'll pick them," I said. "I always will. Regardless of the circumstances."

"Even if they were in the wrong?"

"I'd try and convince them otherwise, but we're not supposed to go against each other. We're a team." I considered lying to Vanjar, so she'd think I was on her side. But I realized that in this, I couldn't force myself to. "What about you and Baekeil? Would you side with him if you were in my position?"

She nodded. A crease formed in her brow. "All right. I guess you're right."

She led me back to my desk, and it was business as usual after that. The assembly was just as suffocating as it usually was, and I went through more texts on visions, hoping I found some related to mine.

So far, nothing good.

With Rena, I had dug out more books by Artemes Remus, but his writing had regressed as he got older. He began talking more about how the gods had forsaken them for a chosen few, and how everyone else was to die, but he didn't have anything to back up his statements.

"I need to find another book," I told the guard who Vanjar had assigned to me. She didn't want me to cause any more trouble.

"Of course, Beacon," the guard said. "You're free to do whatever you want."

I nodded and gave him a curt reply.

I slid from my chair and walked to the *atira*, before heading down the mechanical box.

Everyone was still bustling about, looking at those ashen plants that never seemed to change. I saw Rena and Sascha laughing together. Rena turned to me and waved, and I waved back.

I went around and picked up some leaves, trying to ignore how the people went quiet and stared as I strode past them.

The dead leaves were all over the place, as usual, left around from their failed experiments. Always one leaf changing to green, but nothing more.

"Um, Beacon," a wide-eyed scholar said meekly. "I-I'm sorry to bother you, but..."

I turned to her. "I'm happy to listen." She was taller than me by at least a head, but seemed so small from the way she talked.

"I was wondering... is there news of the goddess? I overheard some of the soldiers talking about it. They said you received some word from her... and they were convinced that this was all going to end soon. Please, I have a father who I don't want to... don't want to..."

"Uh..." More lies danced in my mind. It was starting to feel like they piled upon each other. Cover-up after cover-up, and deeper into betrayal I went. I hoped she didn't notice me scraping my palm with my thumb. How I felt like I was turning green from nausea because I was beginning to feel sick of myself. I squeezed the leaf in my hand tightly. "Aereala came to me in a dream, and she was not clear, but she spoke something of balance. That it's coming back soon."

Her lips parted in a grin. "That's good news."

"Yeah." I did have to lie back in Constanria, but that felt like it was necessary for political reasons. To protect myself.

It didn't hurt those I told them to. This just made my chest tighten. "I... I have to go."

"I'm sure you're very busy."

"Sure."

I turned, ready to skitter away.

There was one more spell Micah and Gaius had helped me come up with. I tried a new one every day. Some worked slightly better than others, but most failed and we still hadn't gotten anywhere.

But there was no harm trying. I picked up another branch, wanting to use the new spell for the day. Often, whenever I used my abilities, it felt like a surge of power simmering through my veins.

This time was different. The power seemed to be rushing *at* me instead of *through* me.

Dizziness hit me.

I wheezed.

It came in a sudden rush, taking me by surprise, and I worried that someone had poisoned me like Queen Miriel had before. But this dizziness was a different kind—it didn't hurt, but instead made me lightheaded. It felt like my body floated, the air around me rising.

"Beacon?" the scholar said. "The Beacon, she's—"

I tumbled forward, trying to get hold of myself. My legs felt the same airy sensation. I gripped a table, pressing the leaf against it and into my palm.

I was slipping.

It was difficult to hold on.

"She..." The scholar's expression filled with shock. "She's glowing! Wh-why?"

Glowing? I looked down at my hands. The leaf gave me a stinging, burning sensation, and I pulled away. My fingers were emitting a pink glow, ethereal, sparkling, but subtle in the yellow lights of the assembly.

I felt my eyes rolling into the back of my head.

And I passed out.

———

I blinked my eyes open and met heaven again. Or was it hell? I still hadn't found out what exactly this place was.

It was so much brighter and livelier compared to the dim yellows of the Assembly. I breathed in the scented atmosphere of this place.

It was sweet.

I was back. Back to its purplish clouds and ghostly forms, and the grass that misted into nothing and re-formed as my feet slid over it. The giant tree that I'd seen the woman sitting under before loomed in the distance, as imposing as it had been.

I walked there, my legs feeling lighter than usual, and brushed my hair to one side. A bird flew overhead. I watched it as it went, before poof, it became nothing.

I tried to convince myself that it wasn't creepy at all, but no matter what I said in my head, this place put me at unease.

The ethereal woman from before was sitting under the same tree, on a large blue boulder. How similar she looked to me still weirded me out.

I waved my hand over her face. She still couldn't see me. I made a silly face at her, then a rude gesture just for kicks, but she continued staring blankly ahead, not saying those weird things she had before. I remembered that only when I tried to touch her before did she look at me, so I placed my hand on her shoulder.

It didn't go through her, not like the first time I was here.

Her head whipped to me. She smiled, and her eyes looked brighter—more lucid. "Welcome," she said. She grabbed the hand I had placed on her shoulder. Her touch was so smooth, so tender, that it made my skin crawl.

It also felt like when the princes touched me. Like when two powers merged and caused a humming sensation.

I couldn't stop staring at her face. Her lashes were so long, her lips so plump. If I had her beauty, then maybe others wouldn't hate me as much. But why did she look so much like me?

"You're... you're Aereala, right?" I asked, blurting out the question which had burned in my mind.

"Look at you." She laughed, and it was like a song. Too melodic to be real, drifting and dancing through the air, far too surreal for mere mortals like me to grasp. "You look so puzzled... so confused. This is not the Sera who I saw grow up."

"You've been watching me?"

"Of course," she said. "I created you." Her green eyes sparkled like emeralds. When she smiled, her face didn't crinkle. Not a wrinkle marred her perfection. "Like I did all humans."

"Dragon-kind?"

"No. They are Gaean's children." She shook her head and sighed. Her breath fogged in front of her, glowing with a

pinkish color. Her eyes darkened when she mentioned Gaean's name.

It was awkward leaving my hand on her shoulder, so I tried to remove it, but she clamped her fingers over my wrist and took my fingers in hers, not letting go of me. She continued clasping my hand, letting her touch linger over mine. "Don't let go. That's the only way to keep the connection going. My power wanes as we talk, and even like this I'm not sure how long I can keep this up. Trying to connect the physical and the spiritual realm through sheer force takes too much energy."

"Why are you doing this?"

"There are important things to tell you."

"Okay, since we're on that topic... Why are the crops dying out? What do Anatolia's premonitions mean? What is this place—"

"Slow down. One thing at a time." She pursed her lips. Only then did I realize she was pale. Almost too pale. Her complexion was unblemished, but its color had faded into a gray that reminded me of those dead leaves. "I am balance, Sera. At least, one part needed to create it. Gaean and I exist in the spiritual realm, and together, we wanted more, for our powers are that of creation, and we had an urge to use them. I created the humans, the flora, and tried to maintain peace and stability. Gaean improved what we made, forced them to grow, gave them chaos. He is the master of beasts. He is always more imaginative than I am, and he made those creatures. There are so many kinds. I can't even keep track of them all.

"But Gaean is growing too powerful. I love him, but he can be too volatile sometimes. You see, he wasn't happy with just riling up the humans. He wanted a greater being,

something more bestial, more unpredictable, chaotic, of his own. I told him not to. I said that those beings, now called dragons, were too unlike his other beasts. They held too much power, and too many of them would destroy the balance in this world. He tried anyway, and because I loved him, I didn't stop what he was so passionate about. It didn't work, and by then he had invested too much to give up. So he gave up some of himself to ruin the balance, creating black magic and dragon-kind. He used the Dragon Mother as the seed for his idea, and it's uncontrollable. There are too many of them now."

I squinted, trying to follow. "This is..."

"A lot to take in. I know. Dragons and humans are both born from gods, but two different ones."

"So what does this have to do with it all? The famine. How did this cause the famine? And what of my curse? Why do I have this?" I looked at my hands.

"I have dominion over the flora. And balance is gone because there are too many dragons and too few humans. Gaean's presence in the physical realm is greater than mine. It's difficult to exert my power over the physical realm because the lack of balance is blocking me. The dragons are weakening, because Gaean is too, but even then, they multiply. And because my dominion over the flora is disappearing, crops die. Their bright souls are gone. That's the part that's me."

"What? So are we supposed to just kill all dragon-kind?"

She chuckled. "That is too crude a solution for me."

"And what of my curse?" I asked again, needing to know. Aereala sat before me as a vault of answers. This place felt too real, too vivid to be a dream. I felt like it was wasteful for me to be sitting here without pen and paper, for the right thing to do

would be scribble down everything she said and immortalize her words in a tome.

"Your curse is the solution."

"What?"

"The reason why you can't touch dragon-kind, Sera, is because I created you, in this world of dragons, putting much of my power into you so you will be prepared for what's to come. Your power is almost like poison to Gaean's corrupted presence. The presence that fills the veins of dragon-kind. You are the antithesis to them. That's why you can't bind with them without causing pain."

I didn't think I'd ever find the reason for my being this way. I never imagined how I might feel knowing the truth. Anger, however, was not one of the reactions I would have assumed. "You did this?" My pulse quickened, thrumming in my ears. "Why?"

"It was unfair on you, I know. But I need you, your curse, to buy them more time. These dragon-kind, they're not evil. I hated them, because I lost part of my Gaean to them, but I've seen them grow over thousands of years... learning, living, thriving. They are more chaotic than my humans, but I can love them the same. I don't want them to go. Not like the... Not like they did."

"Who?"

She opened her lips to answer, but closed them before she did. Thinking about it seemed to pain her too much. "My power is fading, so I can't reach past the spirit world. Not without a conduit. Thus, I created one. I sent a mass of my energy to the physical world. To your mother."

I spotted more dead birds around her, and I wondered if

the spirit world, too, was losing balance. "Me? I'm the conduit?"

"My vessel."

My breath stilled. I had been the outcast most of my childhood. The degenerate that nobody wanted to touch. And I was to save them all? With this curse they hated me for?

Aereala continued, "With you, I can enter the physical realm, if only momentarily. But with that, I can renew the energy in the world, and perhaps restore balance for the time being. It's a good plan. One I can repeat, should my power not continue to fade. And Gaean won't have to hate me so much for trying to stop him all the time. It's hard. At first I supported him, because I loved him and wanted to be by his side regardless of what he did. But he was wrong. So very misguided. I should have stood for what was right instead." She sighed and stared morosely at the ground.

I bit the inside of my cheek. "So... what happens after you reach the physical realm through me?"

"The famine will end, of course."

"No, not that." I should have been happy about the famine ending, but the implications of it all weighed heavily in my chest, and I was too selfish to celebrate for others when it felt like I had to give up so much. "What happens to me?"

She looked up at me, her lips turned down. "Your mind won't be able to take what I give you. It will be replaced by mine."

I stopped breathing entirely. "I... I'm okay with that," I said, more for my benefit than hers. I wasn't convincing anybody. Terror hummed through me. Not enough to make me *want to scream and tear my hair out, but enough to feel a coldness in my gut.*

A sacrifice.

My life hadn't been long. It could be likened to a worm compared to how old some dragon-kind were. But thought I'd fought hard during these short years, and it felt like it was finally going somewhere.

I hadn't worked this hard to be a sacrifice.

It wasn't like me to die for a cause. I wanted to stand for one.

"There has to be some other way," I said. "Not this."

She shook her head. "I'm sorry."

"Sorry doesn't cut it!" *The weight of the world felt like it'd landed on my shoulders. How could it be that it was my duty to die?* "There... there has to be another way."

"I just thought it'd be fair to give you some warning," Aereala said. "But perhaps ignorance might have been better."

"No, no it wouldn't have." *At least I knew the truth of what was happening now. Knowledge meant I could do something about it, right?*

"When my power is ready, I will come."

"No."

"I have to."

"Then what of the princes? Why can they touch me? That means that there are exceptions to the rules, right?"

Her expression twisted. "They... they are a conundrum."

"Please." *I would not cry—couldn't—because of how numb this made me.* "There has to be an alternative."

Spells.

They could be channels too.

"Wait. I have an idea—"

"I'm sorry, Sera," she said. She looked sorry, but sorry wasn't enough. I wanted her to do something about it. To save me. But of course, she'd pick the rest of dragon-kind. I had to as well. It wasn't really a choice when I had to decide between my own life and the end of the world.

"Just be prepared."

"What if spells could also help with—"

She let go of my hand. The grass disappeared beneath me, and I fell. I reached for Aereala, wanting to grab her. I needed to shake more answers out of her. But I couldn't reach the goddess, and the world faded away.

CHAPTER NINETEEN

MY HEAD HURT when I woke up. I let out a groan and pressed my hand on my forehead. The sun glared in my eyes too brightly.

What in Aereala—

The dream came back to me, sharp as a knife, vivid in detail. I couldn't forget the goddess. Nobody could, not with how ethereal and resplendent she was. Looking at her was like looking at the sun itself. It was too much for an ordinary person to bear.

I squinted against the sunlight, but I didn't have to, because a shadowed form blocked it right after.

I heard Gaius shout, "Guys!"

I released another moan and pinched the bridge of my nose. My headache was fading but not quickly enough. It pounded and ached and throbbed at the back of my head, along with the new revelations. My neck strained against the ache, and tingling had begun on the tips of my fingers and toes. "Where... am I?"

"Your room," Kael said, joining Gaius to stand next to me.

I blinked back the blurriness in my vision and saw their handsome forms more clearly. Kael had pinched some of his hair back behind in a messy ponytail, while Gaius looked more worried than angry.

I sat up, my skin sliding past the silk of the bed. It tickled with a soft coolness. Aereala's words were heavy in my chest. I now knew all the answers, but what was I to do with them? Could my idea with magic and spells really solve it? The gods played a part in this, and they created soul magic itself. Surely they'd use it if they could, since they were *gods*.

Maybe my imagination had indeed gotten out of hand, and my dreams were more vivid than I ever gave them credit for.

I wanted to believe that. With all my heart, I did, but what Aereala said had been too real.

Micah stepped into view. "You're squinting. Too bright?" He strode to the window, his shoes clicking against the marble floor, and drew the curtains hastily. "I told the maids to not keep them open. You need proper rest. Are you feeling all right? Thirsty?"

The new dim interior of the room was a reprieve.

I reached to my throat. "Water would be nice."

Micah rushed toward the jug as if his life depended on it.

Gaius sat on the edge of the bed. "Can you please stop passing out on us? This is the second time it's happened, and we were worried sick." He felt my forehead then slid his hand down to cup my cheek. "How are you feeling?"

"I've been better," I said.

"You've looked better," Kael said. He caught his tongue,

then continued, "Not that you don't look great all the time. You're the prettiest peach for miles on end, but right now you're just a little bruised on the side. But that doesn't mean that the rest of you is ugly. It looks delicious." He looked at me and smirked. "I'm not explaining this well, am I?"

"How did you manage to seduce those women?" Probably because he was so sexy. Kael could be saying the most ridiculous things in the world, and still all women of the Drae Lands would fall for him.

He shrugged, then flexed his arm. Winking, he said, "With these."

Playfully, I punched his arm, but ended up wincing because I might have broken my wrist.

"Careful," Kael said, taking my hand in his and massaging its sides. "Don't hurt yourself because I'm such a magnificent specimen of a man."

"Asshole," I muttered, smiling, before accepting water from Micah and taking a sip.

"What happened?" Micah asked, searching my face from under his red fringe of hair.

I didn't want to tell them the truth. It would break them. "I had a dizzy spell."

"Horseshit," Gaius said. "You were *glowing*. Everyone's been saying that Aereala summoned you or something, because you've been glowing since. Until now. The glowing stopped when you woke up. It was beautiful and terrifying at the same time. We didn't know what happened to you, and you wouldn't respond, no matter how hard we tried to wake you."

"How long was I out for?"

"Just a few hours."

Kael brushed his hand through his hair. It fell back to the sides of his face in perfect tousles. "The Beyestiryans continue to speak about what Aereala has done to you. They're incessant with their theories. Many are expecting a miracle to happen soon."

"Did you really meet up with her?" Gaius asked.

His piercing eyes looked like they were seeing through to my soul. "Yes," I said.

They collectively held their breaths.

"She said the only way to fix this famine is if I die."

Gaius's eyes were the first to flash. His grip around my bedside table grew too tight, and the wood crunched. "What?"

Kael started laughing. "She's teasing you, stupid." His eyes shifted to yellow. "Right?"

"Right," I said. I took another sip of water.

Gaius let go of the table. "Don't joke about things like that."

I forced a smile. "To answer your question—no, I didn't meet up with Aereala. I was knocked straight out. Nothing but darkness."

"Probably another side effect of your curse, then," Gaius said. "Why does this keep happening to you?"

"What does?" I asked.

"Shitty situations."

"At least it's not actual shit being thrown at my face." I'd experienced that before—well, splashes of shit I'd accidentally got on myself while cleaning the latrines. I still couldn't decide if I'd prefer that or sacrificing myself to a god to save the whole of dragon-kind.

They were different kinds of terrible.

Equally as bad? Maybe.

Gaius leaned closer. "They'll trust anything you say now, Sera. After that display? They're certain you're the messenger of the goddess herself."

"And...?"

"So you can end this all."

Micah thwacked Gaius over the head. "She just woke up. She doesn't need to hear this heavy nonsense."

Gaius ignored Micah. "It's important. And I want her to hear this before Vanjar comes in and takes her from us. That annoying cousin. She's been hospitable, but she's been hogging Sera."

"She needs me," I said. They all did. Constanrians and Beyestiryans alike. My chest tingled.

Gaius pressed his lips on the back of my hand. Sincerity poured from his blue eyes. Warmth spread from his lips to my skin, sending that familiar tingle that I often felt between us. "We all do. Aereala bless us, Sera, we've been so worried."

The irony of his words tasted bitter on my tongue.

As if on cue, Vanjar burst in. The door swung wide open, hitting the wall. She strutted in with her svelte form, head held high but hair disheveled—disheveled by her standards, at least, which was dragon lengths better than what my hair was probably doing now. She lifted her skirt up and strode toward me in a clunky manner I'd never expect out of her. "They told me you're awake."

I gestured down the length of my body. "I guess I am."

"What did Aereala tell you?"

"What makes you so certain it was the goddess?"

"We sensed magic all around you. Powerful magic that repelled ours. Power that could have only come from the goddess herself."

"Give her a break," Micah said, scowling. "She just woke up."

"She looks fine to me," Vanjar said. Her tense features softened. "I'm sorry. I hope I'm not stressing you out. It's just that we've been looking for so long..."

I nodded. "I understand." I ran my eyes over the princes. Kael had a teasing smirk on his lips, Micah seemed worried about my condition, and Gaius looked pissed, as always.

I sucked in a deep breath then said, "You shouldn't start a war with Constanria."

Vanjar stilled.

A heavy silence hung in the air, cloaking the room and thickening its atmosphere.

Vanjar shut her gaping lips. "When did you find out?"

"Not long ago. I overheard you and Baekeil talking." I didn't go into the details of under what circumstances.

Her gray eyes deepened a shade. She darted her gaze across the princes before returning it to me. "You're with them. You told me you were, whatever the circumstance. Do you know what your king has done? He has ordered raids on our outer territories, burning down villages as a warning. He's killed innocent Beyestiryans on a whim."

I stiffened at her words and noticed the same reaction with the princes.

Gaius's expression burned with more intensity. "If Father

did that, then he must have had a reason. He's not one to kill meaninglessly."

Vanjar rested her hands on her hips. "You might put your father on a pedestal, but don't be blinded by that. These are the facts."

I sighed. "The war. Don't start it. I'm only using what Aereala told me to advise you." I kept my eyes locked on Vanjar. "Believe what you will. But war is meaningless now."

"How can I trust you?"

"You wanted Aereala to talk through me, didn't you? This is it."

Vanjar's full lips thinned as she studied me. She took a step back and folded her arms. "Do not make me regret trying to make peace." Vanjar frowned. "Baekeil won't be so quick to accept this. But I'll request a visit with the Constanrian rulers. They'll come to my castle, under my rules, and should they be amenable, then perhaps my husband will order a truce."

"That sounds like a good step forward."

"For you, perhaps. I've yet to consider how this might benefit me."

"Maybe the goddess believes that war, when two countries should be working together to solve a famine, isn't the answer."

Vanjar looked away. "She could fix all this and not be pushing us into a corner in the first place. Isn't she supposed to be our god?" Loosening the tension in her posture, she continued, "But maybe this is her plan."

"She will," I said. "She'll fix this all. And she does have a plan."

"What else did she tell you? What is she thinking?"

"Nothing else," I lied, looking at the princes. "But when I met her, she seemed like she did. She won't let you all die. She loves dragon-kind." At least one part of that was true.

Vanjar cocked a brow, but I didn't elaborate.

Micah wrapped an arm around my shoulder. "Sera needs to rest."

"I'll send an emissary to Constanria," Vanjar said. "*If* the king isn't as difficult as he usually is, then it won't be long before they arrive."

Gaius stood. "We could go—"

"No." Vanjar fixed him with a sharp gaze. "Now that you're aware of the situation between our two countries, it's a wonder why I'm even letting you stand here. Don't test Baekeil's patience. He might order you locked up, and I won't be able to do much about it. I can't let you go back. Not now, while you know all our secrets."

"*You* can't let us go?" Gaius asked. "So what are we now? Prisoners, or guests?"

I'd been wondering about that. The line between the two had always seemed to blur.

"Guests," Vanjar said. "But on thin ice. I hope my goodwill can encourage your cooperation."

"And if we decide to leave?" Gaius asked.

"Then I'm afraid my hospitality might have to end. And Baekeil might step in." I saw the guards at the doorway. At least ten of them, waiting on Vanjar's orders.

Gaius snorted. "Like you can keep us here," he muttered.

Kael pushed himself from the wall, and Micah's grip on my shoulder tightened.

"Guys," I said, shooting them a warning look. "Calm down. It'll be fine."

Kael cocked his head. "That's the first time you've asked us to calm down. It's usually the other way around."

They stood down upon my request, but I could feel the tension prickling through the room, zapping around like electricity. Whatever Vanjar and the princes' childhood relationship had been, it didn't seem enough to keep war at bay.

I added, "Gisiroth and Rylan will be here soon if all goes well. And you can vouch for Beyestirya's goodwill. It'll all be fine."

"I'll be watching my back before I sleep tonight," Gaius said.

Vanjar clasped her hands together. "You have my word, cousin. Nothing will be done. Not unless war is officially declared."

She strode out, clothing sashaying with her hips as she walked, and shut the door behind her.

"You really think she's not going to do anything?" Micah asked.

"Not to Sera," Gaius said. "They revere her too much. But with us? Now that the truth's out?"

Kael stretched and yawned. "I'm sleeping out in the mountains tonight. And we should keep our guards up until Rylan comes."

"Vanjar mentioned she wouldn't let you leave," I said.

Kael laughed, stretching his arms over his head. "They won't even notice us gone. Not until it's too late."

"You guys are just going to leave me here?" How much

more time would I have before Aereala came?

Micah squeezed my hand. "We'll check up on you often. I just don't think we should stay here so much, since Vanjar has a reason to hang us now. Our cousin cares for us, but her country more."

"Speaking of which," Gaius said, lifting the fabric from one of the cages. "We should send a word of caution to Rylan. Since Sera's so adamant about it, maybe we should seek peace, but we should warn them of the meeting—"

The piegfowl in the cage was dead.

Gaius moved from cage to cage, tearing the sheets off to look inside.

I'd made sure the piegfowls had enough water and food. And when I was alone in the room, I uncovered them so they didn't find themselves too stuffy and warm under those fabrics. They had been fine yesterday when I checked.

"So much about sending word to Rylan," Kael said.

"All of them are dead," Gaius said.

I frowned. "I made sure to take care of them."

Micah walked up to Gaius and opened a cage. He inspected the underbelly of a piegfowl, and shifted its head left to right, looking at its eyes.

Micah clicked his tongue against his teeth. "Poisoned. It's surprising these piegfowls lasted until now. It's not your fault, Sera."

"So none of those letters ever got to Rylan?"

Micah shook his head. "Those piegfowls never would have made it."

Gaius growled. "Guests my ass. She won't even let me talk to my own brother."

CHAPTER TWENTY

I FLIPPED the leaf back and forth as the pups lay by my side.

It was green, as leaves often became when I touched them. Because of Aereala's power. If Aereala could channel herself through me, it definitely meant that I had a strong affinity to soul magic, right?

What was soul magic, anyway?

How did the words for spells come about?

I glanced down at the pups.

They seemed to have grown even more, now definitely bigger than most larger breeds of dogs. They made me seem larger than life when they walked beside me, even though it wasn't me who looked regal but the ingorias.

They'd bonded with me. Watching them sit by my side, licking their paws and making cute whimpering sounds, I couldn't see them as anything other than my babies.

Staring at the leaf, I called to Aereala. "Can you hear me?" I muttered. "Or do you just come and go as you please?

Maybe you're too busy doing god things. What do gods do in their free time? Could you just hear me out?"

No response.

Of course there wasn't any. What did I expect? I was talking to myself like a fool.

Didn't hurt to try.

The princes were away in dragon form, probably looming over some mountains somewhere. I hadn't seen them for two days, and they said they'd visit. What happened to checking on me?

Or maybe they had, but if so, they were being awfully sneaky about it.

Luckily, I had the pups to keep me company.

Someone rapped on my door.

"Come in," I said.

Vanjar entered.

I hadn't seen her so dressed down before, still in her nightgownt and not wearing her elaborate boots, but slippers that looked fluffy and comfortable. Her hair was tidy, as she normally had it. The ingorias liked her. Mayhem slipped off the bed and stuck his tongue out, inviting Vanjar in. She strode in and bent down, patting the ingoria's head.

"It's late," I said, shifting so I faced her.

She carried a stack of letters in her hands, all rolled up and neatly tied. "They're arriving tomorrow."

"They agreed?"

"The Council of Fortitude threatened to skin my emissary alive, but he made it back in one piece."

I blew out a sigh. "That's good to hear."

"So, Sera, come clean with me."

I tilted my head and stopped myself from licking my lips nervously. "I have."

"Have you truly? Is this what Aereala wants or what you want? I'm already at my wit's end. Mothers come to me begging for food with their dying children, and fathers are willing to sell themselves into slavery to keep their family alive. But we don't have enough supplies to feed everyone and we have to turn them away, as much as it breaks my heart."

"I don't see how war is the answer to this all."

"You don't know what the Constanrians did, or what they're demanding, do you?"

I tensed. "No."

"They want the remainder of our arable lands, and they've stopped all aid to our country."

"Gisiroth isn't the kind to do this."

"More children are dying every day because of their demands. They've burned many of our remaining fields, and our soldiers have been trying to hold them back. This final assault is to stop them from continually bullying us."

"Gisiroth is a good king. He's stern and deals a harsh hand, but he's always tried to be fair." I never liked the man, but that didn't mean I couldn't judge him properly.

"I love my cousins, but Constanria has been difficult for Beyestirya. Times are hard. Knowing all this, do you still want to barter for peace? Their demands might get worse, and more might die. Is this truly what the goddess demanded?"

"The goddess didn't demand anything," I confessed.

Vanjar narrowed her eyes at me.

"It's what I assumed was best from what she told me."

"You shouldn't be making decisions for her."

I breathed in, then let out everything Aereala told me, about the world losing balance, and about me being the vessel. "Aereala will be here soon. The famine will be resolved and there won't be any reason for us to fight anymore. We simply have to hold the peace for a while longer."

She looked at me for a long, silent moment, and I could almost see her trying to work over my words in her mind. Slackening her shoulders, she said, "I'm sorry, Sera."

"Sorry for what?" I said, letting out false laughter and trying to ignore the truth before me.

"Do the princes know?"

"I'm still trying to decide how to tell them."

"You should soon. It'll be painful to hear, but they shouldn't be left in the dark."

"Yeah..."

Vanjar strode toward me with the letters and dropped them to my bed. There were five of them.

"What's that?" I asked.

"They belong to you. I'm sorry I've been keeping them away. I couldn't risk it, not with what's been happening between countries. If Rylan spoke to his brothers, the princes would have given us a hard time."

I unrolled the first letter. It was brown and a little torn at the sides. I recognized Rylan's handwriting. Before reading it, I reached for the next and unrolled it too. These all were from him.

"I'm sorry for keeping them from you," Vanjar said. "And

the piegfowls, too." She looked to where the cages had been. Since there weren't any birds to perch in them, I'd ordered them to be cleaned away. A half-smile brushed her lips. "I want to be the first to make peace."

Should I thank her? But these letters belonged to me in the first place. "Revealing that you've been hiding things is a strange way to make peace."

Laughter rang from her, deep for a woman but melodious and sensual nevertheless. "That's one way to look at it. Good night, Sera. You must be excited to see Rylan tomorrow. Or are you just with the other three?"

"We... The four of us—"

"My cousins truly are strange. Dragon men aren't supposed to like sharing." She crinkled her brow, but the smile was still on her lips.

"We're happy with it."

"Most Constanrian women must think you're the luckiest lady alive."

"They're wondering why I'm alive in the first place," I muttered.

Vanjar's frown deepened, but she didn't press further. She waved me goodbye and slipped out of my room. I blew out relief. Vanjar had taken that well, which was more than I could have hoped. At least she was being understanding about it, and it seemed the truth had swayed her my way.

I redirected my attention back to the letters. The first was dated two months ago.

Dear Sera,

How are you holding up? I hope you're in Beyestirya. I suggested to my brothers to go there to keep you safe, but they do get sidetracked.

It's hard to sleep without you, and I'm sad to say I can't find a proper replacement. Kael made me a doll that resembled you a few weeks back as justification for why I don't need to go looking for you at night. It's disconcerting to look at the blasphemous object, and I'd prefer to avoid it.

Beyestirya has a food shortage, but I hope the castle isn't as affected and you all are eating well. Father has decided to cut the free flow of food and is starting to give out rations. The famine is hitting us harder than expected, and the courts are getting riled up over it.

I miss you. It hasn't been long, but I think of you more than I believe is healthy. I imagine you warming my bed, amongst other things that are inappropriate for this letter. But I've considered waiting before our consummation and realize I don't want to anymore.

My brothers have been accommodating to what I've been saying, but if you do bear our child, would that be too bad? To hell with the courts and my father. Perhaps a child might be a cause to celebrate.

It will completely ruin the Everborne name. Maybe this is me still being mad at Father for enacting that sentence.

I'm rambling now. If the Beyestiryan officials see this letter, that would be embarrassing now, wouldn't it?

With all my heart,
   Rylan

A blush warmed my cheeks as I read the letter. I pried open the next one and read it, letting each word soak into me as I did:

Dear Sera,

I worry for the state of Constanria now. It would be easier if you four were with me, but alas, this might be a burden I must bear alone. I received Gaius's piegfowl, and your message that came along with it. I love and miss you too.

The Beyestiryan numbers concern me, however.

Things are difficult in Constanria. The Everbornes are not safe in this current predicament, but I won't worry you with the details.

If Constanria is like this, then I'm afraid of what is happening in Beyestirya. Perhaps I shouldn't have sent you there in the first place.

Love,
   Rylan

I went through the other two. They were written under

increasing states of duress, but Rylan never went into much detail. He kept asking why I hadn't responded and questioned me about the brothers. He mentioned he might stop sending letters, because he worried they might not have reached me in the first place.

Then, in the last one, he wrote:

Dear Sera,

Home is safe enough for you to return to now, but I worry you are the one who is not safe. My spies in Beyestirya tell me of your being there. You seem well, but I'm afraid they've made an unknowing hostage out of you. If you are sending letters, no more are coming through.

I will have you back.

And Baekeil, if you are reading this and withholding this from Sera, note that this makes me more inclined to send my armies against you.

Sincerely,
   Rylan
   His Royal Majesty
   King of Constanria

My eyes ran past the last three lines. Over and over again. But they wouldn't sink into my mind.

Rylan... was now *king*?

My mouth went dry. Sensing my unease, Mayhem perked his ears up. I held the letter out in front of me and flopped on my bed. I kept tracing the letters with my fingers as if that would make them seem more real.

I stayed up all night staring at the ceiling, unable to comprehend what I'd just read.

What had happened while we were gone?

CHAPTER TWENTY-ONE

ONLY TWO MONTHS had gone by since Rylan had parted from us, months short of his promised year, but it felt like a lifetime had passed. I'd experienced a new world in Beyestirya. One that made me less sure of things.

When Rylan strode out of the ashen forest his dragon landed in, he didn't look how I remembered him. Those couple of months had aged him, shedding the tinge of boyish charm he used to wear. He no longer stood in the shadow of his father.

He was now a king.

I stood on the steps, next to Vanjar and Baekeil. Vanjar leaned closer to me. She whispered in my ear, "He mentioned wanting to see you first."

Rylan trod through the snow, the soles of his boots making imprints in the ground. Behind him, Kael, Gaius, Micah, and a few soldiers, wearing the blue of the royal family, followed. Rylan had his hair tied up, together with his braid. Rylan's elegant, slender features had a harder edge to them, and his eyes seemed darker, more piercing as he searched through the landscape. He was in a dark blue pair of pants, tucked into boots. His torso was bare, as it usually was, with its intricate tattoos carved over his frame. Like always, he had a sword on his hip, just like his brothers who wielded leather-strapped weapons against their frames.

When Rylan's eyes fell on me, they softened, and a smile spread across his face.

He strode straight past Baekeil, ignoring the king's outstretched hand, and tugged me into an embrace. His smoky scent surrounded me again, and his body pressed against mine, lighting fire in my veins.

I wrapped my arms around him and inhaled his intoxicating scent. "Rylan..."

"The others told me you passed out a couple days back," he said, his voice smooth and velvety. He drew back and cupped my face in his hands. The humming between us, when the princes and I touched, vibrated through me. He sucked in a deep breath, the sound causing the thumping in my chest to quicken. "Are you better?"

"Much." I grabbed his hand with mine, pressing it harder to my skin, needing more of his warmth on me. "But what happened, Rylan? Where is Gisiroth?"

His features hardened, and with a weighty sigh, he said, "King Gisiroth is dead."

My mind went numb. "Your father..." I looked over Rylan's shoulder to the other princes. They weren't showing the joy of seeing their brother, but the sadness of losing their father. Their shoulders seemed heavier, their steps dragging more than they usually did.

"Are your mother and sister okay?"

"They're fine."

"What happened?"

"It was Vancel," Rylan said. I flicked my gaze to Vanjar, who didn't react to Rylan's words.

Baekeil cleared his throat, the noise rough and grinding. It caused Rylan to flash annoyance before pulling away. He never fully parted from me, and his hand slipped to mine, hooking our fingers together.

"I was only just alerted to the news," Baekeil said. "Congratulations on your ascension to the throne."

Baekeil was inches taller than Rylan, but their presences paralleled each other. Baekeil glanced at his outstretched hand, which Rylan accepted grudgingly. It was the first time I'd thought a handshake could be aggressive.

"Welcome to Beyestirya," Baekeil said. "The officials are ready to gather at a moment's notice. They're eager to meet—"

"I'd like a word with Sera first." Rylan tugged me closer with his arm around my waist. "In private."

Baekeil nodded. "She has a room over here. I can lead you to it."

"Not here. Not around Beyestirya and with your people surrounding us."

Vanjar started, "We can't allow her with—"

"She is to be my future queen," Rylan said, his voice not rising in volume but booming all the same. "Starting negotiations with holding my queen captive isn't a good way to begin, is it?" I knew Rylan had a calm rigidness to him, but I'd never seen him this authoritative. So reassured.

Vanjar's expression tightened. "Sera, is this true?"

I remembered my promise to Micah, and despite all the lies I'd been spouting, this was something I couldn't do. Not if it'd hurt his feelings. Micah tensed as I replied. "It is... a possibility." Albeit a faint one.

Rylan wasn't perturbed by my hesitance.

Baekeil narrowed his eyes. "She shouldn't leave this place. If the people see her go, they'll lose something special to them."

"What is she to you?" Rylan said, seeming taller than he had only a moment ago. "I love her. I want to share my future with her. My country's future."

"She's our Bea—"

"Your pawn. You've been parading her around, using her to control the minds of your people, regardless of how this might affect her or how she feels."

I gripped Rylan's hand tighter. "Rylan, it's not like that."

He shot a glance at me, which was sharper than I expected, and I shrank back, doubting if I should have questioned him in front of his enemies.

If Kael, Micah, and Gaius were surprised by the change in their brother, they hadn't showed it. But there was none of their usual playfulness, and I found myself missing that.

"You've kept her prisoner," Rylan said. "Even as I asked for her to return home."

How he twisted my experience made me uneasy. "Rylan, let's go."

"Do come back for refreshments," Vanjar said wryly.

"Lest we call for war," Baekeil added.

We had to come back. Mayhem, Grunt, and Aura were still in my room, so we had to go fetch them.

He squeezed my hand and pulled me away. We walked down the steps, and as our feet touched the snow again, his black, leathery wings, filled with more splendor than before, folded from his back. I clutched his arm, reveling in the strength of his body, and he took to the air.

The *whoosh* of his wings beating against the cold reached my ears. Closing my eyes, I sank into his warmth and breathed in a deep sigh.

Rylan was back, and he was different, but he was mine again.

———

"Why are you king?" I asked, as soon as he was gliding through the skies. The familiar feel of his arms tightened around me, but as much as I wanted to muse at how good it felt, the need to know what had happened was stronger.

He smirked. "Does that bother you?"

"How it came to be does. Why is Gisiroth dead?"

His smile fell. "A coup."

"By Vancel? If that's the case, why are you king?"

His three brothers trailed behind us. They must have met before coming to the castle. Rylan must have told them the whole story before they met me, so they'd probably heard all the juicy details.

This wasn't how I'd expected our reunion to be. I imagined smiles and bickering, but the cloud of mourning hung in the air.

Gisiroth was more king than father, but their father nevertheless.

The trees beneath me were completely ashen. Gray. Soulless. They hadn't been like this when I got here. They were barren from the cold, but merely hibernating. These branches, however... they showed no life. The physical realm was disintegrating quicker than I'd expected it to, and I was afraid that Aereala didn't have much time left to gather her power.

Rylan looked ahead. "It was a rough two months. I spent the first week or two trying to convince Father to let you come back, and I was trying to get more information from Anatolia, but she simply said that the goddess wanted you dead, refusing to give me any more explanation. The famine got worse after that. It expanded from Jura to the Emilia region, and soon people got worried about what to eat. At the same time, Beyestirya was demanding more aid, and they threatened to start war should we not give it to them—"

"They did?"

"I suppose they wouldn't have told you."

Rylan had aged in the time we were gone. Perhaps it was the kind of growing up a man could only get from losing his father. He continued, "Vancel saw this as a good opportunity to undermine my father's power. He called for Gisiroth's indictment, saying my father was too weak to be king during a difficult time such as this. That Gisiroth could only rule during peacetime. Vancel appealed to the war-hungry of those in the military, and it stirred much trouble in the court, partly because they no longer had you to blame, and because everyone was worried about whether they'd have enough to eat. He went ahead and carried out orders without my father's approval. It became apparent Gisiroth was losing control. Beyestirya received mixed messages. They weren't sure whether we would attack or not."

The wintry trees beneath me stretched on for miles, and the cold was starting to bother me, despite the heat of Rylan's body. I hoped we reached our destination soon. A fog hovered over the landscape today. It had snowed last night, and the barren branches bore stretches of white snow, contrasting with their ashen color.

Rylan dipped his blue eyes to me, and I reached up to cup his cheek. He'd grown some stubble in my time away, and it added a certain ruggedness to his slender features. "Father was killed in his sleep, or at least that's what I prefer to think." He paused, letting a dead silence hang between us briefly. "He survived the rebellion, fought through it. But perhaps he did grow weak and complacent during peacetime. His guards weren't enough to hold back the planned assault, and he wasn't the agile man he used to be during the rebellion.

"The night Father died, some shuffling woke me up. When I opened by eyes, I found six men in front of my bed. They were hidrae. They thought they could assassinate me, but I managed to escape and alert the guards. Father didn't make it. The next day, they found him on the ground, unarmed but his talons lengthened. His throat had been slit open. His guards were all dead, too. Some with arrows shot through the head, others... It's too gruesome to describe. Servants got caught in the fray. It had been an elaborate plan that must have taken months.

"Vancel made for the throne as soon as the news broke. He made it quite obvious it was him who planned the attack. He wouldn't have been so daring if he didn't have the support. He started a scuffle with Beyestirya, sending troops in Gisiroth's name, to make a point. He tried to stage a coup with his generals. He hadn't expected me to survive. If I hadn't made it through, he would have easily won the coup. He didn't know that Gaius and I had been anticipating this for years. That so many of those letters I'd sent at night had also been to garner favors. Kael helped, as much as he won't admit it. He often went to the Council of Fortitude to train their men. Bond with them. Gain their trust. And so I subdued Vancel and here I am."

"Where is he now?" I asked. Rylan had had to go through so much. Alone. And I'd taken his brothers from him.

"Sadly, not on a pike." His jaw tensed. "He fled. We haven't been able to track him down, not even with soul magic. He took Mei with him and he disappeared."

Gisiroth... I still couldn't imagine him dead. And found next to his bedside, too. He had been such an imposing figure, the pillar that the country leaned on. Gone. His seven-hundred-year reign over in a blink.

Beneath us, an encampment sprouted amongst the empty spaces from the trees. It wasn't large—I counted three medium-sized tents. A campfire sat in the middle, smoke and ash rising from it. Rylan slowed the flap of his wings, descending to the camp. His boots sank into the snow that had piled up here, reaching halfway up his calves. The soldiers sitting around the fireplace stood to his attention, saluting. "Your Majesty," they chorused.

Rylan regarded them with a nod. "Leave us until it is night. Don't come close to our tent."

They saluted again and continued to stand at attention until Rylan carried me into the largest tent. As soon as the flap of the tent fell, the warmth of the inside encompassed me. A thick mattress lay on the ground, covered with multiple blankets and so many pillows that I was comfortable just looking at it.

"Until night?" I asked. "Why that long?"

"I wanted to give us enough time." He smirked. His brothers entered after he did, and Micah's eyes flashed to yellow. Kael's dark expression lit into a grin, and he licked his lower lip in a manner that was far too sensual.

Nervousness stirred in my belly, and I hugged Rylan tighter. Voice lowered and raspier than I expected, I asked, "Enough time for what?"

"You've wanted it, haven't you?" he said, setting me down onto the sheets. He peeled my cloak off and tossed it aside. The blanket was silky and cool against my touch, but Rylan's body was on fire, and I ran my hand down his hard stomach. My throat dried. It was like all the wetness from my mouth had disappeared to between my thighs. Could he hear how my heart raced for him? For *them*?

"But the courts..." I said.

"I'm king now. Vancel is gone. There's no one to oppose me. I can do what I want."

"The thing about the child..."

"Would that be bad?"

My breath hitched in my throat. Would it be okay to bear a child with the princes? How would they know which one was the father? Did they care? "It's all right," I finally answered, after staring into Rylan's intense eyes.

He grabbed my wrist, pulled off my glove, and kissed my palm, before he trailed his kisses down my arm. Each kiss he placed caused the tingling warmth to reverberate through me. Usually, his kisses felt comfortable, but this time, it made my insides twist. Looking at me, he said, "Did you change your mind? Do you want to go back to the castle?"

"No," I replied, wondering if I'd replied too quickly.

Micah came beside me. "You promised, Rylan." *Promised?* What was promised? Micah gripped my waist. A growl rumbled from his throat as he nipped my ear. He was looking at Rylan, a challenge in his eyes.

"Do you want to back out, Sera-kit?" Kael asked me, brushing his hair from his face.

I shook my head, clutching at Rylan, who continued to kiss me. "No."

"No?" Rylan said. "No what?" His eyes, too, flickered to yellow.

He wants me to beg. He was teasing me, like he had all this time. I swallowed a nervous gulp. "No... I want... I want all of you."

"To?" Rylan said.

My cheeks were probably completely red now. "To—"

"Stop teasing her, Rylan," Kael said. "That's my job."

Rylan chuckled. "You're not doing it properly."

"It's her first time," Micah said. "Let's make it easy for her." Gently, he pushed me to face him and guided my lips to his. His tongue slipped into me, pressing against mine and demanding my attention. I tried to tug my arm away from

Rylan, to place it at Micah's side to steady myself, but Rylan had a firm grip on my wrist. He tugged on it, pulling himself closer, and his mouth met my neck.

Kael dipped between my legs, lifting my dress. I recalled what he'd done before with that magnificent tongue of his. It caused anticipation to rise in my chest.

"You guys are going to break her," Gaius said.

I pried myself away from Micah to look at Gaius. He was standing across us, arms folded, just watching. It felt like his gaze was picking apart my every movement, which made more tension coil between my legs.

"Let's take this off, shall we?" Kael asked, lifting his head. His lips were glistening. He caught a mass of fabric from my dress and tugged at it.

They'd never seen me nude before. No one had. Fingers shaking, I reached for the knot behind me and tried to loosen it. My clumsy fingers couldn't seem to find it.

"I'll do it," Micah said, brushing my hair out of the way. He pried the knot open, and my dress loosened from my bodice. Kael tugged the dress from my frame. I expected him to struggle with it because of how big the dress was, but he tore it off expertly.

My heart raced. It was suddenly much colder in the tent, which made my body quiver. But the coldness was quickly replaced by the heat of the princes as they closed in on me.

"Don't be scared," Rylan said, running his lips down my neck and to my chest. "You're beautiful." His words tickled my skin as his breath brushed past me. Gaius joined in, and he ran his hands, coarser than the others, around my naked body. I arched my back, baring myself to them. Most girls worried about their first time with one partner, but I had four dragon princes to please, and that sent me into a panic. I steadied my breathing.

I want this. The princes did, too and we were meant to be.

"Don't be scared," Rylan said again, and I anchored myself to his calming voice, letting its strength course through me.

This was all too much to take. We were a tangle of limbs and moans and grunts, and my mind was growing weak from what they were doing to me. I was vulnerable to their whims. They could toy with me like putty. My stomach dipped again and I let them take the reins.

It was Micah who tugged off his pants first. He positioned himself in front, parting my thighs and resting his weight between. His cock was hard and pressing against my slick center.

He was large—too much for me to handle. I'd tried slipping two fingers in before, and that hurt. Micah looked like he might tear me apart.

Growls sounded from the princes. Their dragons had taken over, and their eyes were all a deep, gem-like yellow. Gaius had his lips locked around my nipple, and his fingers sought the nub of my center.

The tension built in my core, rising, tightening. Before, I had tried to imagine how I'd be in bed when mating with someone else. I'd liked to think I'd know how to pleasure a man in every way. That I could take charge and know exactly how to move, where to touch.

But, of course, I was still a virgin, and I was fumbling

about like a fool, muttering the princes' names and getting confused by all the sensations.

"I don't like it that you're first," Rylan said to Micah. "But I'll allow it."

A rumble sounded from Micah's throat. "You don't have to allow me anything. This is what you promised. What we agreed on."

"Be gentle with her," Kael said, releasing my mouth. Their scents mixed together, swirling in my head.

"It's difficult," Micah said. "I've been wanting to tear her apart since I laid eyes on her." I could feel his need throbbing against me, which only made me more impatient but nervous at the same time.

"We know," Rylan said. "Be gentle anyway."

Micah leaned into me, his hips digging into mine. The tip of his cock entered me, and it was already too large for me to take. My toes curled as I fastened my hands around Rylan's and Gaius's arms, trying to bear the pain.

A grunt ripped from his throat as Micah's entire length spread me apart. A moan slipped from my lips as tears prickled my eyes.

It *hurt*.

I'd overheard other girls talk about this, how the first time was the worst, but silly, naive me thought my first with the princes would be different. More perfect. We loved each other this much, after all.

Micah stilled in me. Over the hard breathing of the princes, I heard the blowing of the wintry winds from outside.

"D-don't move," I said, wrapping my legs around him, trying to still him.

"That's a tall order, Sera-kit," he said. His yellow eyes lit up, and he smiled at me. Despite being laced with need and hunger, that smile was almost sweet.

Gaius pulled his lips from my breasts. He stroked my cheek, and I tried to focus on the tingling sensation he gave me from that strange power we shared between us. "Can you take him, Sera? It's all right. We know it's your first."

I bit my lower lip, trying to ignore the sharpness between my thighs. Hesitantly, I nodded. Micah began to move his hips back and forth. Slowly, almost imperceptibly.

As he did, I felt three other pairs of eyes watching, gauging my reaction.

I tried to deal with it. I didn't want to disappoint them, but I must have gripped Rylan and Gaius's forearms too hard, because they could tell I was hurting too much.

"Micah," Kael said, "you should stop."

"You want to fucking try?" Micah said, frustration in his voice. "She feels so good."

Kael snapped, "I would've, but we decided to give it to you."

"I can take it," I said, panicking. "The pain is going away. Maybe it'll start to feel better." I was lying. The pain continued to throb. It ached, slicing each time Micah thrust into me. I just didn't want to disappoint them.

Rylan brushed his lips across my cheek. His hand was resting on my stomach. Or maybe that was Gaius's hand. It was difficult for me to tell at this point.

Micah groaned. A hiss escaped his lips as he pulled out. Cold air replaced his heat. He brushed his crimson hair away from his eyes and threw himself backward. "You guys owe me," he said.

"We owe you?" Gaius said. "You got to be Sera's first."

Micah ran his hand across his jaw. "This is torture. I didn't want to stop."

"We can try again," I said.

"The first time is always the worst, Sera," Rylan said, hugging me closer. "Don't worry about it. It'll be better. Give yourself some time to heal."

"You... you aren't mad?"

He laughed. "Why would we be?" The sound brought relief to me.

"Because I can't pleasure you. Any of you." I wanted to tough it out, but my body was too weak for this. I wasn't the amazing sex goddess I'd pictured myself to be.

Rylan snorted. "Oh, you can." He tucked my hair behind my ear, and only then did I realize how much I'd missed him doing that. "Just give it time. Then you won't be able to have enough of us, or us of you."

He laid me down on his mattress. I sank into the soft sheets. I wanted their hard bodies on mine.

But I didn't want to give them nothing. I wanted to help them find release. I reached down where Kael and Rylan's members were waiting as bulges in their pants. Tentatively, through the fabric, I rubbed my palms across them.

Kael moaned. A smile split his face. He caught my wrist, but didn't drag it from his member. "You're driving me crazy, Sera." I used that encouragement to be more adventurous,

CURSE OF DRAGONS 285

and I slipped my hands into their pants, against their bare skin.

I didn't manage to help them find release, but their enjoyment was evident on their faces. When my hands grew tired and my eyelids heavy, they let me rest. My center continued to throb with soreness. Micah had been too large for me. And I worried that when I returned to the castle, I wouldn't be able to walk properly.

We lay together on the mattress, which was still not big enough for all five of us. We were a tangle of limbs and hair and warmth, and I was perfectly comfortable in it. With Rylan back, the five of us were now whole again.

I fell asleep shortly after, probably with a smile on my face. There were terrible things to come—negotiations with Kaldaross awaited, and there was still that problem about the famine—but this moment was more than I could ever ask for.

CHAPTER TWENTY-TWO

I T WAS the first time I'd encountered a blizzard since I came here. Micah held me tightly as Rylan led the way. The blizzard covered their half-shifted forms, but their wings were strong enough to beat through the relentless winds. There seemed to be an endless amount of snow—oceans of white that incessantly poured down upon us.

My eyes caught the silhouette of the castle in the distance.

When we arrived, I wasn't sure how the guards managed, but they saw us, too. They opened the gates for us, and all five of us slipped in.

My teeth chattered as we entered. I held on to Micah, borrowing his heat, trying to still the shivering of my hands. It wouldn't cease. He took one hand and blew at it, and only then was it warm enough to calm the chattering of my teeth.

Vanjar greeted us as the door. "Took you long enough."

Rylan strode toward her, shrugging snow off his bare

torso. "I didn't expect the blizzard. We didn't want to travel in the night while the snowstorm raged."

We ended up spending the night together, all the way till this morning. The storm hadn't let up despite our waiting.

Vanjar led us down the corridor and toward the throne room. "I'll notify my husband and the rest of the officials. You were inconsiderate. Now many of them are disinclined to agree to a treaty."

"I hope the blizzard is a good excuse," Rylan said. "I wanted to spend more time with Sera, and was not expecting it to come so quickly."

"It's not a good excuse," Vanjar said. She took us to the throne room.

"You're colder than I remember," Rylan said to Vanjar.

"Must be weather."

It was the weather, all right—the phenomenon of crops dying left and right. When I first arrived, Vanjar was not nearly this stern. I wondered if she was being this way because she viewed Rylan as an enemy, or if the harshness of what had been going on had finally hardened her.

We strode to the seats she'd pointed out to us. She sent a servant to fetch Baekeil and situated herself in front of the throne room, at her seat.

Kael wiped his hands together. "Now that Rylan's king, we can call for more national holidays." It felt like he was trying to hide his sadness over Gisiroth's death. The smile on Kael's lips didn't feel the same as usual. But he couldn't help but joke around. That was him.

"My kingship is not for more of your antics," Rylan said.

"Of course it is. Everyone loves a ruler who knows how to

poke fun. What about inca dog day? It's an important food item, but nobody seems to respect it enough."

"What's next?" Gaius asked, staring at the ground. "A day to honor vegetable puns?"

"Frederick would love that," I said.

"Exactly what I was thinking of."

"I think a day to honor me would be best," Kael said, pointing to himself.

"And what exactly about you is worth honoring?" Micah asked. "Terrorizing the hearts of too many ladies?"

"You could learn a thing or two from me."

"I have Sera."

"I don't need you to terrorize my heart," I said. "I have enough to worry about." Turning to Rylan, I asked, "How is Frederick? Did the coup affect him?"

Rylan smiled. "He's better than ever. You don't have to worry about him. In fact, upon return, seeing him again might surprise you."

"How?"

"It wouldn't be a surprise if I told you, would it?"

As we talked, more officials entered. They watched us with wary glances, though sometimes, when their eyes met mine, hope shone from them, and they gained a little more confidence.

Confidence they shouldn't be having when looking at me. I promised myself that I'd side with the princes no matter what. I simply had to hope they'd choose the right thing, and nudge them in the right direction the best I could.

Speaking of which...

"Rylan?" I said. "You'll try and strike peace with Beyestirya, won't you?"

"If that's what's best for Constanria, then yes," he said.

Gaius folded his arms and leaned back in his chair. "I'd still be wary, brother. Don't trust everything these people say. I've never seen a military force this large—although many of them might be weak from lack of food and some are too young, their numbers will still prove a challenge. They've been rearing beasts of combat as well. Those will tear some of our men apart."

"Will our forces hold up?" Rylan said.

"They should," Kael replied. "If they haven't gone lax."

"Twenty-six thousand, five hundred, and sixty-two soldiers," Micah said. "At least, that's how many I've counted over the past couple of months. I can give you more exact numbers should you need."

Rylan nodded. "I'd like it written down and sent to me once we head home. Accounts of their armaments, too, and how they're structuring their units."

"Wait," I said. "Why are you all talking as if you're already planning war? This is supposed to be a peace negotiation."

"It is," Rylan said. "But we have to be prepared."

"We should be preparing for how to collaborate with Beyestirya, not how to decimate their forces."

"You were stuck in the Council of Intelligence," Kael said. "Not that of Fortitude. You wouldn't understand—"

"I wouldn't understand?" I assumed I'd been in a good position to, since I'd seen both sides of both countries. Kael's words sent rage through me. "I expected more out of the four of you."

"You're cute when you're angry," Kael said, patting my head. "But you can leave the governing to the big boys."

"Governing is *hard work*. Something you've been allergic to for the last couple centuries." I pinched Kael's ear, and to my surprise, he reacted with a groan and by scrunching his nose. "Ow, don't do that."

So I actually did have a way to hurt the princes. Not that I'd wanted to find one. "I thought you'd said you respected me?"

"I do," Kael said. "But not in matters of war."

"That's what we have to prevent!" I wanted to strangle Kael, but I sank into my seat instead. I looked to Rylan. "Promise me you'll do whatever to keep the peace."

"If it benefits Constanria, yes," Rylan said.

"It will. Aereala—" I held my tongue. I couldn't let them know—not during such a dire moment.

No one caught my slip-up, because Baekeil entered soon after, garnering the attention of the entire hall.

Baekeil had his wings outspread when he entered the throne room. He came in through a separate entrance, wielding his pike. He landed next to Vanjar and folded his wings back into his skin. Most of the officials had arrived, so he commenced the discussion.

He knocked the bottom of his pike on the ground three times, which sounded loudly and stilled the place into silence. He didn't waste time getting to the specifics. "Let us welcome King Rylan Everborne, who has come all this way from Constanria. He's willing to negotiate a peace treaty.

We're in troubled times with difficult decisions to make. I hope we come to the right one today."

Rylan cleared his throat. He stood, and although the size of the throne room dwarfed his human form, his presence loomed over the compound. Everyone's attention was drawn to him.

Had Rylan commanded this much presence before? Or had he gained this from his time alone in Constanria? He looked like a different man as he spoke. "King Baekeil. I'm surprised our discussion is on such... open grounds."

"What do you mean?" Baekeil replied.

"Often, in Constanria, discussions of this nature are kept behind closed doors."

"Are the Constanrian royals that ashamed and filled with cowardice? So much that they must hide behind secrecy as they talk over matters of the state? Us Beyestiryans have enough decency to let the people hear what concerns them."

"Are you implying Constanrians have no decency, then?" Rylan asked, tipping his chin up. "This isn't a good implication to make when starting a peace negotiation, is it?"

Nope, not a good start at all, I thought.

Baekeil knocked the base of his pike on the ground again. "Are you here for peace, king of Constanria? Or are you here to goad?"

"I'm here to see how we may mutually benefit each other."

"Before we start, explain the raids and the loss of innocent lives amongst our borders."

"They were a warning, although ones I had no part in."

"Villages, which were already starving... decimated."

"Those were ordered by Vancel, your wife's brother. It was his attempt to make a bid for the throne, to appeal to the violent tendencies of his generals."

"Then you have no control over your own court."

"Vancel was under the last king. I can assure you there will be no such atrocities under my rule."

Baekeil shook his head. "You do not answer any of our pleas. That is an atrocity in itself."

"If I do, my people would starve. I can't forsake my own for yours. I protect my own kind."

"Your granaries must be full from a healthy harvest. Your crops lasted through the season, while ours shriveled and turned ashen before we could pick them. Surely, you can spare—"

"I had to debate risking civil war. The wealthier are protective of their harvests. To tear it from them is to spark seeds of rebellion. And the harvest in our granaries... it's only sufficient to tide us through this winter. If we share it, many of my people might not make it. Or are you too foolish a king to understand this?"

"You don't want to risk civil war, and so you risk a blown-out war with another country."

"This is why I'm here, aren't I? To try and prevent something of that nature."

Then why was each one of Rylan's words laced with so much venom and threat?

Baekeil frowned, obviously unconvinced. "And what do you offer?"

"Not to send our troops against yours, for one," Rylan said, narrowing his eyes.

Baekeil snorted a laugh, while Vanjar placed a hand in her husband's. Baekeil said, "This is hardly a negotiation. You're just here to boast of your country's well-being, even if you won't admit it."

Rylan raised a hand. "You didn't let me finish. I've talked with my scholars. They are willing to help and are offering assistance. Surely if two countries are working on one problem, it will be easier to solve?"

Baekeil harrumphed. "Constanria trails behind us when it comes to soul magic—"

"And I have asked them to tally our rations against what we need. There might be a little food we can spare, even if it's not much."

"Not much?"

"Perhaps ten dragon shipments' worth."

Baekeil pressed his lips together. "That still can feed many. It won't solve the problem, but it can help us save some lives. More will make it through the winter, at least."

"What of Sera?" Vanjar said. My eyes darted to her.

Rylan's shoulders tensed. "What of her?"

"Will you take her back?"

"I did say we're to be wed."

"The people of your country detest her, want her dead. We here need her. She is the key to Aereala."

"I will not allow her here to be gawked at and used as a means for you to spread propaganda."

"She is a symbol here," Vanjar said. "If she returns, her potential will be wasted."

The time with my princes felt borrowed.

I wanted to spend it with them.

But I also caught Rena and Sascha in the crowd. They were looking at me hopefully, as if begging me to stay with their eyes.

Vanjar opened her mouth, wanting to add something, but Rylan halted her by saying, "This isn't open for discussion. Sera is coming home with me, regardless of what your plans for her are. I won't leave her here for the picking."

Vanjar tugged Baekeil's hand, trying to get him to retort. Baekeil sighed. "It seems like you might not be interested in peace after all."

"The terms are clear," Rylan said. "That is what I offer. But you have yet to offer my country anything."

"We have a large army," Baekeil said. "It is good enough we don't send it to your doorstep."

I wanted to slap both kings. One did not bargain for peace by threatening war.

A growl rumbled from Gaius. I turned to him and saw he had his lips up in a sneer. I reached over to squeeze his hand.

"That isn't much to offer," Rylan said.

"We don't have much food to give," Baekeil replied.

"Fabric, weapons? You did say your army is large. And my brother told me of your new experiments. Surely you could spare some creatures?"

Vanjar shot a look of betrayal at the other three princes.

"We could spare some," Baekeil said.

"Good." Rylan clapped his hands together. "Then we have come to a truce."

Baekeil didn't look happy with the outcome, but he knocked his pike to the ground and nodded anyway. He faced the rest of his council. "If any of you have opinions to voice, do so now."

Mutters broke out through the throne room as the officials discussed their opinions.

"What of the Beacon?" was the first one voiced aloud. "Will Aereala no longer see us in favor if she leaves?"

"She comes with me regardless," Rylan said without hesitation.

Another official added, "Can we come to an understanding, then? Perhaps send her here every few months? It would be unfair if communication to the goddess is only allowed for Constanria."

"It is not open to discussion!" Rylan's voice boomed over the court. Hushed silence befell everyone. I'd never seen Rylan let loose an outburst before, and it made me stiffen in my seat. He turned to Baekeil. "If that is all, we shall leave."

Baekeil straightened. "My officials have yet to—"

"I wished to only talk to you, not your officials. The fact that you've put me here as a spectacle, and that I have condoned it, is grating in itself. We have come to an agreement. I don't need to hear your complaints."

Baekeil flexed his jaw, but didn't say anything.

Rylan took my hand in his. The rest of the princes stood with him, and together with Rylan's soldiers, we strode out of the throne room.

Vanjar left her seat and ran up to me. I slowed my footsteps, and the princes did too when they noticed. Vanjar reached for my hand. "Sera, please."

Rylan pried Vanjar's hand away from me. "She's coming

home. You lot have kept her here long enough. Home is now safe for her to return to."

"I don't want to see my people lose that light in their eyes," Vanjar said. "The people look up to her. Please, Sera. Don't abandon us."

I shook my head. "They look up to my curse. Not me. If I stay here, the remainder of my life will only be viewed for my curse."

"So you're picking them?" Vanjar asked. "You can do so much more here."

"I'll always pick them," I said, turning away from Vanjar. But a niggling doubt began to start in my chest.

———

Vanjar watched me from a balcony as the princes and I strode out of the castle. My three ingoria pups trailed behind me as we did. Although they were huge now, they hadn't lost the playful liveliness of children.

"They don't like me," Rylan said, scowling at Aura. At first they growled at him, but after he growled back, they tolerated him, giving him a wide berth.

"Maybe you're becoming too serious," I said. "They abhor anything that isn't play."

"They must love Kael, then."

"Oh, they do."

Three large metal cages, with hooks attached to them, stood in front of us. Treats lay in waiting for them. I couldn't carry the ingorias, not like I did last time. They were too large. So we had to transport them through cages, which were to be hooked onto a soldier in dragon form.

"I hope they fall for it," I said.

They did. As soon as they saw the snacks, they bounded toward the cages and threw themselves inside. Rylan's men shut the cages and locked them up. The treats distracted the ingorias.

Grunt was the first to turn around. He shot me a dejected look. "Sorry, love," I said. "We'll get you out as soon as we get home. It won't be so cold anymore." The soft whimper I heard sent a *thwang* through my chest.

I turned around, seeing all four brothers gathered and bickering amongst themselves. They hadn't argued this much since Rylan left, and now that their oldest brother was back, things had returned to normal. It seemed like a team of three didn't leave enough people for them to shoot jabs at.

"I don't understand why you're the one insisting on letting Sera ride you," Gaius said to Micah. "We let you have her, didn't we?"

Micah folded his arms. "And that's why."

"I don't get it," Kael said, pressing a thumb to his lip.

"It was torture. So this is a way to soothe the ache."

Gaius looked at Rylan. "I think he wants me to knock his teeth out." The pain of Gisiroth's death had lessened, although it peeked out every so often. Gaius seemed much happier now that his twin had returned.

Kael brushed his hair back. "Sera rode Gaius from Constanria to Beyestirya. Rylan carried her back to the castle—"

Rylan rolled his eyes. "That's not even remotely the same."

"—Micah is a prick who isn't grateful for what he had. So that leaves me." Kael stood straighter and placed his hands on his daggers. Things were shitty all around, but when all five of us were together, at least we could lock ourselves in our own little bubble of fun. They annoyed me in a good way. I loved them for it.

"Guys," I said, "I thought we were over this? I haven't heard you squabble about this for months."

"Oh, we have," Gaius said. "We just do it prior, so we don't waste time. Sometimes we draw lots."

"Then draw lots now."

"No paper," Kael said, raising his hands.

"Really? That's why? This is getting old."

"I guess we'll have to leave it to Sera to decide," Micah said. He gave me a look that screamed "pick me," and I was about to, because of how intimidating it was, but then the rest of the brothers gave me the same look. They towered over me with their muscled forms, making me feel smaller.

Kael leaned closer and whispered into my ear, "If you decide to ride with me, when we reach home, I'll show you pleasures you never dared dreamed of."

I blushed then placed my hand on Kael, and because I had a shameless side to me, I blurted, "I'll pick Kael."

Three other pairs of blue eyes narrowed at me.

"We heard that," Gaius said, scowling.

"Did you?" I felt my cheeks warm even more.

Micah shot me a judgmental look. "We all did." He sniffed, then strode away.

"Hey," I said, raising both hands. "he offered me something I couldn't refuse."

Rylan was looking at me incredulously.

I just shrugged.

Kael hooked his arm around me and pulled me in. "I've yet to figure out where you like to be touched."

"And you're going to give me unimaginable pleasures, how? You don't seem to have the knowledge required." The blizzard had settled into a trickle of snow, leaving a fog over the landscape.

Still, Kael's eyes glimmered through it. "Finding out is the pleasurable part." He licked his lower lip, which made my insides crawl with tension. Mimicking his actions, I licked my lip, and his gaze dipped there, hungry yet playful.

I was burning up when he stripped to shift into a dragon. Their bodies, all of them, were all chiseled, and it sent a thrill through me knowing I had touched them just yesterday. Yellow glows erupted from all over, fighting through the fog. I had to look away so the light wasn't so blinding.

Kael's white dragon form towered in front of me as the glowing dissipated.

A rumbling, which was probably a dragon's laughter, shook from his chest as I climbed on.

Gaius, who hadn't shifted yet, continued to look peeved. I blew him a kiss, which made his expression soften.

"Kael won't be able to please you like I can," he said to me, loudly.

We weren't supposed to discuss such matters in public! I avoided the judgmental glances of Rylan's men, and the Beyestiryan soldiers on standby, as they turned to me.

Kael swung his tail toward his brother. Gaius leapt over it, dodging Kael's attack. He flipped Kael off and strode away to shift into his dragon too.

As Kael lifted into the air, I turned back to look at the castle.

Vanjar was still standing at the edge of the balcony. She had rested her forearms on the railings. I couldn't make out her expression at this distance, but just looking at her silhouette made me uncomfortable. Beneath her, at the castle's entrance, was a swath of Beyestiryans, sending me away. Some women were crying.

Crying? Why should they cry over me?

I bit my inner cheek and turned back around.

I was doing the right thing.

What else was I to do? Leave Rylan and the others? Even though we'd just reunited?

I haven't seen so much light in their eyes.

Vanjar's words echoed through my head, but I pushed them aside.

I clutched Kael more tightly, telling myself I couldn't be afraid, and that I shouldn't doubt my decisions.

We soared through the skies, and the atmosphere grew warmer as we went. Soon, I had to take off my cloak because being in it was sweltering. My ingoria pups whimpered in their cages. Riding with the dragons made them swing back and forth. I was going to have to give them plenty of treats later.

The epidemic had spread farther than I'd expected. Stretches of forest laid to waste, grayed out, as if their souls had been sucked from it. It got better as we neared Constanria, but even then, much of it looked like death itself.

The grand structures of Raynea poked out from the clouds.

Home.

It had only been two months, but that was enough to suck the life out of it. The streets lay empty, littered with trash and no longer filled with the lively activities that used to dance through it.

"What happened here?" I muttered.

Kael's dragon moved its neck side to side, surveying the difference just as I was.

Gaius and Micah swooped in next to Kael, and the three of them shared worried looks. I pressed my weight against Kael and peeked over his neck to get a better view.

I'd hoped that coming home would be the end of it all, but it seemed like just the beginning of our troubles.

CHAPTER TWENTY-THREE

"I NEED TO TALK TO RYLAN," I said to my bodyguard. One of the *ten* bodyguards I had next to me. He had brown hair and looked like an old drerkyn. His name was Ayren, and he was the captain of his team.

I thought I'd go back to my life in the Council of Intelligence and try and help with the famine there, but it'd only been two hours since I got back and things were looking strange.

Or, at least, *pretend to* help with the famine. I knew fixing the famine required more than cheap tricks like heat-resistant plants or fast-growing crops. Hell, I doubted the Dragon Mother herself could have fixed it. This was the stuff of realms, gods, and goddesses.

I needed a talk with Aereala. Sit her down, have a heart-to-heart, get all the details, and then maybe we could think this through together.

What has gotten into me?

I wanted to bargain with the goddess herself? Then

again, I couldn't give up and die without trying to find some other way.

Me and my far-too-many guards stood in the hallway. It was awfully hard trying to get around with these clunky figures blocking my view.

"We're leading you to him, Your Highnesss. But we think he might be busy talking to his brothers." Stupid Rylan, summoning his brothers and leading them away, and not inviting me into the conversation.

Oh, and that title—*Your Highness*—all the servants had been calling me that ever since I got back. Apparently, rumors had been going around that I was going to be the next queen, even though I'd said nothing to Rylan about his proposal. They'd probably started those rumors before I'd even landed in Constanria.

I was going to keep my word to Micah. I couldn't marry his brother, not if it meant ruining the dynamic between all five of us.

"I can't see a thing," I said. "You guys are just this wall of metal." It didn't help that I was *at least* a head shorter than all of them.

"You don't have to worry about looking around, Your Highness," a guard with an oafish voice said. Virgyl, was it? Or was it Vergen? I wasn't sure. There were too many of them. "We'll do that for you."

"Um, thanks but no thanks?"

"His Majesty asked us to protect you from all sides," Ayren said, "and at whatever the cost. Your head is wanted by many around here."

I'd forgotten how *friendly* Constanrians could be. I'd gotten too used to how nicely the Beyestiryans treated me.

"Fine," I said, sighing. "Lead the way."

I'd almost tripped on the stairs while walking up, because I was so distracted by this strange experience. Before my face hit the ground, Ayren caught me, made a huge fuss, and made me promise not to trip ever again. I rolled my eyes and pretended to swear to it, as if his demand had been reasonable, and continued on my way.

We reached Rylan's new study—now the king's study. Ayren spoke to the guard outside the room. He was a short fellow, about my height, with his hair in a bun. Ayren requested Rylan's audience.

"He said no, Your Highness," Rylan's guard said, shutting the fancy door behind him.

"No?" I said.

"He said he'll come find you later."

"Well, tell him to let me in now or he *won't* be finding me later."

The guard looked a bit perplexed, but he returned inside.

When he walked back out, he looked more worried than he had the first time. "He... he asked you to wait."

"*Tell him*"—I raised a pointed finger—"that if he doesn't let me in, I'm going to let everyone know what exactly he's afraid of."

Cockroaches.

Kael still used them to prank Rylan before we left for Beyestirya. Wouldn't be nice if the cat was out of the bag.

The guard's eyebrows crawled up his temple. "And what is the king afraid of?"

I waved his question aside. "It's a secret. But I'll let everyone know what about it if he continues to hide from me!"

"I'm not hiding!" Rylan's voice echoed from the room. "Let her in!"

The guard manning the door regarded me with a glint in his eye as he pulled the door open, letting me through. I walked across the carpeted ground.

As I entered the room, I raised a hand at Ayren. "Stay outside." I put pressure on my forehead. "I've had enough of the clinkity-clunking of your metal suits."

They looked at each other but did as I ordered.

As I turned back around, I started, "Rylan, those bodyguards have got to go. They're making me claustrophobic. There has to be a better way to—" I frowned. "What are you guys doing?"

Rylan sighed and sank back into his chair, which was lined with fur. "We hoped to keep it from you till the last minute. But you can be so stubborn sometimes." He rested his arm on the table. His brothers were next to him. Kael was standing, and Gaius and Micah both sat next to the table.

A table with a map on top of it.

Wooden pieces, almost like those from a board game, had been placed on top of the map.

"You're planning war," I said. I strode toward them. "But... but you promised Vanjar a truce. Before we left, you told her you'd start sending her emissaries—"

Guilt plagued Rylan's expression. He fiddled with a wooden doll, the shape of a dragon.

Micah answered, "We're worried about their numbers. Now is the best time for attacking—"

"Attacking isn't going to do anything!" I paced around in frustration. Why couldn't they see that fighting wasn't the answer? "You have to talk to them, try and save as many people as you can, at least until this famine is over."

"This famine isn't going to end, Sera."

"It will."

"How can you be so sure?"

"Because..." I shifted my gaze to the ground. "I have a feeling for these things." Maybe I should tell them. Would that make them more violent?

Gaius shook his head. "We don't run countries based on feelings, Sera. We look at the facts. And right now, we know that our granaries are light and theirs are empty. They might not attack today, tomorrow. The treaty has bought us time. But they're desperate. Desperate enough to want to send their children to war for more food. They will attack."

"Vanjar said that they were there only to learn."

"And you believe her?"

"Even if she were lying, must we do this?" What was happening felt so *wrong*. I wanted the princes to do right, but I supposed that was too much to ask.

"We have our own people to feed," Rylan said. "Our own to protect. It's the hard decision, but sometimes that's what rulers must make. I'm sorry you can't stomach this, Sera."

The four of them shot me sorry looks, and it was then I realized they saw me as weak.

Weak?

Because this was going too far and I finally had to say something about it?

Rylan went back to the matter at hand, treating me as if I weren't standing there, furious and mouth gaping. "Kael," Rylan said, "I might need you to take up arms."

"No problem," Kael said, as if this were a game.

"Not like that. I want you to command troops."

Kael made a disgusted face. "So, I'll have to lead armies and the like? Deal with orders?"

"You're the one going to be giving them."

"Orders, nevertheless. Me and rules don't go well together. How am I supposed to do this?"

"It is well within your abilities." Rylan looked down at the map. "Where do you think is best to strike first?"

Kael sighed. He searched the map, then stuck his finger on it, pointing. "The south border, here, at the Aes Mountain Range. They won't be able to see us coming because of the fog that builds up there, and the high topography. And I read that's where they liked to keep many of their livestock. It'd tighten their supplies, give them less to work with early on—"

"You're getting rid of their food?" I said. "That'll hurt them."

"That's kind of the point," Gaius replied.

I couldn't stand for this anymore. "Please. Please just reconsider."

"We know you have good intentions," Rylan said. "But this isn't something I can do just to placate you. I have a country to protect."

"And I'm saying this isn't the way."

Rylan scooped up another wooden piece and placed it on

the map. He was arranging them according to Kael's suggestions.

The princes didn't respect my decisions in governing and war enough. I hoped they would. I thought loving each other meant we'd be able to listen better.

I wanted to hit something. Hard.

I needed to scream out my frustrations and maybe slap the life out of a cute stuffed toy.

Instead, I settled for leaving. Anger boiled inside me right then, and I had to give myself some time to cool down. Maybe then, when I talked to the princes, I'd be able to reason it out better, rather than vent like a child.

When I left, I was met with the wall of guards again. I threw my hands up and groaned. "Back off," I said to Ayren.

"Your Highness," he replied, "we were told to keep close."

"Not that close. Please step away before you end up on the ground..." Those Beyestiryan fighting lessons wouldn't go to waste. I raised my gloved hand. "Or start shrieking in pain."

Despite how fearless they'd seemed at first, the guards apparently hadn't forgotten about my curse. Swallowing nervously, Ayren stepped back, leaving me a comfortable distance. The rest did the same.

I brushed my hair out my face and walked forward. They no longer crowded around me so closely, although they still flanked me on all sides. At least I could breathe now, and look at the color of the ceiling.

I needed a nice, long nap.

———

After my very eventful but also troubling conversation with the princes, I walked back to my room. Still my old room. Rylan hadn't shifted out of the princes' quarters despite being king. He'd kept most of my things in place, much to my delight.

The guards led me back there. I had to climb the many flights of stairs up to my chambers, suddenly wishing Constanria had the *atiras* found in Beyestirya.

When I arrived, a shuffling, knocking sound startled us. It came from my door.

"Your Highness," Ayren said. He drew his sword from its scabbard. "You might want to stay back."

"How did it even get in there?" I said. "I saw guards right outside."

"We're not sure, but you better keep away to be safe." He wore a grave expression. We gestured at me and his companions to back away, and so we did. Heaving a deep breath, he strode forward and kicked my door down.

"Help!" A male's voice sounded from my room. It was high-pitched, almost like shrieking. "Heeelp, please! Oh, Aereala bless me. I'll be a good boy! I'll stop leaving the seat up after I'm done!"

"Frederick?" I said, cocking a brow. He was being "attacked" by the ingorias, who were slobbering all over him with their kisses. They'd knocked him over and he was wriggling on the ground.

"Sera! Oh gods! Get these things off me. I think they're preparing me for the main course. I don't taste good! My diet is terrible and you'll only get a tummy ache, you beastly animals! Mercy!"

I whistled, calling to my pups, and they backed off Frederick to come greet me.

Frederick was still swatting the air, eyes closed, absolutely terrified.

But Frederick didn't look like Frederick at all. It seemed like a stranger had stolen his voice.

"You can stop wetting your pants now," I said.

"I did?" He blinked his eyes open and sat up, glancing down at his crotch. "No, I didn't." His blue robes had been torn and scratched by the ingorias.

"Figure of speech."

He eyed the ingorias like they were the Dragon Mother herself. "Those things shouldn't be here." Scowling, he reached up and wiped some of the slobber off his face.

"It's good to see you too." I offered a hand and helped him to his feet. I would've given him a hug, but my ingorias had truly done a number on him.

He squinted and scrunched his nose. "I was so excited when the other scholars started talking about your return. I came here as soon as I heard. The guards let me in, and once I opened the door, *those things* attacked me. I nearly died of a heart attack, but that wasn't the worst of it. They knocked me off my feet and wouldn't stop trying to season me."

"I think they like you." I scratched the back of Aura's ear. The pup wagged its tail as it looked at Frederick.

"Like me? They wouldn't have tried to eat my face if they did. I think you shouldn't be so close to them. Stay away before they attack you too."

"They're my pets."

"Your pets! Ingorias?"

"Never mind that." I gestured at him. "What happened to you?"

"To me?" His eyes widened, and he reached for his cheek. "Did they get me? Oh, tell me there isn't a scratch."

"Not that. I'm talking about, uh... you! In general. What happened to..." I gestured in circles. "Half of you. It's gone." If not for his voice, I wouldn't have recognized him.

"Oh," he said, wearing a pleased smile. He flipped his hair. "You mean *that*. Like it?"

"You lost weight. Is what I'm trying to say. I thought you mentioned you'd rather die knowing you had your favorite meal that day than die looking good but hungry."

"That was until the healer told me I'd shorten my life span if I kept my old habits up. I wasn't going to make it past sixty, even with my darmar blood. To be honest, both options you mentioned don't sound good to me. I'd prefer not dying at all."

"How did you do it?" I was pretty impressed. That was a *lot* of weight he had managed to shed in a relatively short time.

"Self-inflicted harm, is all I can say. You look thinner yourself."

I rested my hands on my hips. "No. Really. How?" He didn't have a chiseled body—not like the princes—but he'd lost most of the blubber he used to carry around. I almost didn't recognize him when I first saw him. But that shrieking couldn't have belonged to anyone but Frederick. "Was it the famine?" Was it so bad that it affected the nobles this quickly?

"I ate my vegetables," Frederick said.

"You always do."

"And exercised."

"Exercised?" Who was this person standing in front of me?

Frederick got on the ground and actually started doing push-ups. I gaped at him like he was the answer to the famine. "These are actually easy for me now," Frederick said.

"Are you sure? Because I think you're doing them wrong." His elbows wobbled, and other soldiers I saw bent their arms much more.

"They're easy, okay?" He stood up, already breaking a sweat and catching his breath.

"Okay," I said, still not convinced.

It was good to see Frederick again. With all that was happening, he was someone I could count on to always talk to me and not give me too much trouble.

Oh, don't get me wrong. I loved the princes, but they had trouble written all over them.

"Come on, it's been two months," I said. "Let's go for a stroll, and we can leave my little puppies behind—"

"Little puppies? I'm corn-fused."

"—and you can tell me all that's been happening here in Constanria."

It took some time for Frederick to get used to the armed men, so that made two of us. The architecture of the palace hadn't changed much, but the atmosphere around it definitely felt different. The palace had always intertwined the natural features, borrowing life from them.

But nature in the Drae Lands was withering away, and the beauty of the palace had suffered for it.

We stopped in a courtyard the princes and I had often enjoyed visiting. It used to have beautiful flowers all around, and when I left, the leaves had only just begun to change into gorgeous oranges and reds.

Many of the branches were empty. Not all of the flora was dead, but it seemed like this place was experiencing the beginning of a disease. A fireoak tree that used to bear a vibrant red bark now lay in the center of this courtyard, gray and gone. It was the most prominent dead thing here.

I peeled off my glove and placed my hand on it. Some of its reddish beauty fought to come back, reaching for Aereala's power, but it wasn't enough, and the red melted back to gray.

"How did you do that?" Frederick asked.

"It's a long story." I wondered how Frederick would take my death. Or if the princes could handle it.

Probably not.

A large part of me still believed that death wasn't the only option. I just needed that talk with the goddess. Maybe I'd be able to figure out a way. There was always one.

This was me falling into a spiral of careless optimism. Aereala was ageless. If there were a way, surely she would have figured one out by now. But I wanted to keep hoping.

I was supposed to be the Beacon, right? Hope was kind of my thing.

"You lead two teams in agriculture, don't you?" I asked Frederick.

"Things haven't changed that much. Save for the scenery. I think the palace is going through a teenage phase, acting all mopey and the like."

"How are the food stores?"

"We're using magic to preserve them. They should be able to last the city two winters. Food prices are going up everywhere, which is terrible, but it's helping with my diet. I'm not so sure how the outer regions might fare."

"Then we don't have that much to spare. The extra food will be used for rations, yes?"

"Most likely."

"So we can't bribe Beyestirya to keep their army at bay."

"Keep at bay? What do you mean? Are they going to attack?"

"The princes seem to think so. They want to make the first strike so Constanria has an advantage."

Frederick frowned. "War? But we can't afford war now. It'll drain our supplies."

"No country can. But everyone's too hungry—literally—to see that. They're thinking with their stomachs, not their heads." I tucked a strand of hair behind my ear and sat down on a marble stool. I stretched my feet out, staring at them as if they had all the answers written on them.

The answers weren't on my feet—*duh*.

I knew what it was. It was so obvious.

But also, so painful.

"Hey, Frederick," I said, "have you ever felt like you were being torn apart?"

"Yeah, when you touched me that one time. Hurt like

Aereala's teats, Sera." He scratched his ginger hair and cringed as he recalled the experience.

Wouldn't Aereala teats feel good? "Right. Sorry about that. But I don't mean physically—"

"That time when I took a really huge shit count?"

"Ew? No." I was trying to be serious here. Why did he have to mention that?

"It was tearing me apart, all right. I thought it might never come—"

"You don't have to elaborate."

He stared at me with a frown for a long, awkward moment, before adding, "I think it might have been the vegetables. Eating too much caused my bowels to—"

"I don't need to hear about your bowels. I'm not talking about that, okay?"

"Okay... then what are you talking about?"

"Being torn between two choices." I dragged my hand down my face. I wasn't sure how to continue this conversation, not with what Frederick had just gone on about.

But Frederick pressed on. "What are they?"

I blew out a sigh, then began explaining everything that had happened in Beyestirya to Frederick.

"So," I continued, "I thought about it, and I know I can't do much here. I want to support the princes, but I can't. I promised to stick by their side no matter what, but what they're doing isn't right. And I can fix it."

"But you'll have to leave," Frederick said, finishing my thought for me.

"The people in Beyestirya will listen to me. They see me

as Aereala's messenger, and I might be able to have a say in what they do with the military. Nobody will hear me in Constanria. They'd rather have me die. Also, if I'm there, physically, the princes might hold off their attack. I can act as a mediator if I join Beyestirya. A voice between both countries. I have the support of the princes, and the support of the Beyestiryan people. I'll have more political power this way, and I'll be able to make a difference."

The other option was having Aereala fix everything, but she was too unreliable. Once she came down, problem solved, but she didn't work with the timeline of mortals. The war might be over before she decided to do anything.

Frederick sat next to me on another stool and stretched. "The answer's pretty clear to me."

"And?"

"You need to stick up for what you think is right. That's the you the princes fell in love with in the first place. If you're not true to yourself, how can you expect others to be?"

"When you're not talking about silly things like vegetables and poop, you can sound kind of wise sometimes."

"It was really big, though."

I held up a hand. "That's enough." I needed to go back to moping, because this was the kind of situation people ought to mope about. Leaning forward, I rested my elbow on my thighs and pressed my lips together.

"You look kind of like that statue in the council," Frederick said. "The Brooder."

That made me smile. "You're awfully hard to mope around, you know that?"

He tapped his chest twice and spread his arms out.

"That's what friends are for." Dropping his grin, he said, "So what are you going to do?"

"I don't know yet. It's a tough choice."

"If you go, I'll miss you again. But I'll also like the fact that you'll be preventing enemies from storming our palace, so I'm just as torn as you are."

"Sure." I snorted.

"Do what you have to do—" He yelped and leapt to his feet. "Eep! I'm late. Oh, Aereala, he's going to kill me."

"Who is?"

"Torley."

"Who?"

"My date."

My jaw dropped. "You have a date?"

"I mean, we're not anything yet, but I'm hoping it's going to turn out well. He asked me out last week, and I think I nearly died, and I really don't want to mess this up." He checked his watch again. "So I have to go."

"Good luck," I said.

"Think I need it." Frederick fastened his satchel to his body and sprinted—Frederick sprinting was a strange phenomenon to me—off. He almost slammed into one of the guards, but managed to stop himself by a hair, and he disappeared through the corridors unscathed.

I was left alone in our empty courtyard, underneath the fireoak tree.

Time to assume the position of the Brooder, I guess. With Frederick gone, I could mope properly.

CHAPTER TWENTY-FOUR

*D*EAR *V*ANJAR,

I have reconsidered my decision to leave. I hope it's not too late to return. Circumstances have led to disagreements between the princes and I, and although it took too long for me to come to my decision, I've realized I can do more good returning to Beyestirya.

Sincerely,

Sera

I read through the letter once more before I rolled it up and opened the cage. I plucked the piegfowl out and almost tucked the letter into the tube attached to its leg. Then decided against it.

I hadn't given the princes the whole truth about Aereala yet. Maybe they'd react differently if they knew. I had to give them that chance. I sighed and placed the piegfowl back in. Maybe this was just me backing out.

"Your Majesty," Ayren said, "it's getting late. His Majesty

asked me to ensure you're in your chambers before nightfall. It's less safe at night."

"He's setting curfews now?"

"He's worried. There have been multiple threats on your life."

I sighed through my nose. "Lead the way."

The guard dipped his head, before continuing to walk alongside me. "Pardon my insolence, Your Majesty, but I wanted to ask who that letter was for. You must excuse me, for I overheard your conversation with your friend in the courtyard earlier."

"It's for... someone I can trust," I said. "You don't have to worry."

"Uh huh." The guard chuckled to himself. "Of course. You're to be our future queen, so you'll be on the Constanrian's side, yes?"

"You doubt me?" I asked, raising an eyebrow.

"Oh no, not at all. I was just... voicing my reasoning."

As we strolled through the cream-colored corridors of the eastern wing, I spotted Gaius talking to his mother. It struck me that Miriel Everborne wasn't queen anymore—her husband was dead. Queen dowager would be her proper title.

Next to Miriel was her daughter, Anatolia. The princess who'd foretold my death. A chill ran through me as her shocking blue eyes caught mine. She was holding a stuffed toy of a horse and still wore a shroud of innocence because of how young she was.

This had all started from her three simple words.

I was about to walk past them when Miriel called my name.

I turned around, dread in my stomach. Before I left, I'd spent more time with her, hoping to foster a better relationship. I thought it had worked, but now none of that friendliness remained in her eyes.

"Your Majesty," I said, my eyes flicking to Gaius then back to her.

"You're back," she said. "Nice of you to return after all the trouble you've caused."

I blinked. "Rylan told me it was Vancel who had stirred the pot."

"Using your name. Gisiroth tried to cut you from the Everbornes, but my sons protecting you sent the message loud and clear. It was easy for Vancel to sully my husband's name after that."

I bit my tongue, holding back a retort. This was a grieving woman. "I'm sorry for your loss, Your Majesty."

"If you were, you would have thrown yourself from the edge of a cliff to save us all this trouble."

"I bid you a good evening." I bowed. "If you would excuse me."

When she didn't stop me, I turned around, shoulders feeling heavy. Another reminder that Constanria perhaps was not the place for me. Other than the princes (and lovable Frederick, of course), nobody wanted me here.

The decision had been made. Vanjar would send someone to take me back to Beyestirya...

...if she wasn't feeling too betrayed by my initial leaving.

Footsteps tapped beside me. I lifted my head to see

Gaius. The soft orange glow of the lanterns hanging from the walls lit his hard-jawed face. He brushed his hand across his short hair. "I'm sorry about Mother. She'd only just stopped crying. When I saw her, she broke down in tears, and she's been bitter since."

"I understand. How long was she with Gisiroth again?"

"Four hundred years."

"Longer than I can imagine."

Gaius tried to hide it, but I could tell he was hurting too. His stiffened shoulders and the tight line of his lips gave it away.

"How are you taking it?" I asked. I wished I could stay here longer to help them with their grieving.

"Can't believe the old bastard's dead." He took my gloved hand and rubbed his thumb across its back. "To be honest, I don't know if Rylan can match up to Father. He was a strict father but a good king. He always stuck true to his beliefs, which always seemed good for the country, and it isn't fair that he died—" He peered down. "What are you doing?"

"I thought you might need a hug."

The guards around me probably noticed, but they were good at acting like they weren't there. I tried not to bother them, even if their presence did feel a little weird.

Gaius returned my embrace, his chest lifting and lowering as he breathed. I could hear the soft beating of his heart. I rested my cheek on his skin, which created that nice tingle between us. I closed my eyes and breathed in his earthy scent, thinking that if I left, I wouldn't be able to feel more of this.

"Gaius, what if…" *Should I tell him?* Or would that ruin the whole plan?

"What if?"

I decided against it. "What if Frederick was so successful with his diet that he ended up getting abs?"

"Good… for him?" He squinted. "I don't really see where you're going with this."

"And he became the hottest in all of Constanria, and Kael gets jealous, so Kael decides to name Frederick his enemy." I paused. "What if Kael decides to challenge Frederick to something ridiculous?"

Gaius was smiling. "I don't think that title's going to him. I have a claim on that one. Kael should be challenging me."

"I don't know…" I tapped my chin. "Kael's kind of hot, too."

"And do you have a preference?"

"Depends on the time of the day."

"Oh? And what time of the day do I belong to?"

"The… I need someone to lean on kind of time? It's usually at night, when I get moody."

"You don't let it out like other girls do."

"It's nice to have company after a bad day."

"Kael's good to lean on. He's tall enough—"

A guard coughed, interrupting our moment. I was reminded we weren't alone, so I pulled away from Gaius's warm touch. The air felt much cooler, especially since winter was coming.

It wasn't nearly as freezing as Beyestirya was.

If I went back, I was *not* looking forward to having to wear that thick, get-in-the-way-of-everything dress, to function as a human being and a walking ornament. Those with lots of dragon blood could strut around in their undies and still be perfectly fine, and they'd smile and wave at me, asking me how was my day. "Jealous of your non-freezing ass" was something I often thought of replying with, but I usually settled on "Fine."

Gaius's jaw ticked with annoyance as he looked at the guards. He shooed them away, then said to me, "I'll walk you back. There won't be anybody trying to hurt you with me around, so they're unnecessary."

The captain gave me a quick salute before leaving.

I peered up at Gaius. "Didn't Rylan say they had to be with me at all times?"

"He's overdoing it. But he's careful like that. Can't make mistakes when you're king."

He slipped my gloves off and pocketed them.

"Gaius, you shouldn't—"

He grabbed my hand and squeezed. "Don't need to wear them when you're with us." He shot me a smirk. "In fact, you don't have to wear anything at all when we're alone together."

"Gaius!"

"It's the truth. I'd much prefer your body bare." His blue eyes traveled the length of me, and somehow I felt like he was undressing me.

I bit the inside of my cheek, eying the two maids strolling toward us.

When I opened the door of my room, Kael was already lying on my bed. He was snoring. Gaius picked a log from the fireplace and threw it at Kael. It bounced off Kael and to the ground. Gaius then summoned fire in his hand and threw it at the pile of logs. The wood caught the fire, sparking with life, and lit up the room.

Kael lifted his head up, rubbing his eyes. He groaned. "I was waiting so long I fell asleep."

"You've messed up Sera's sheets." Gaius sniffed and walked to a pitcher on my side table. He poured a glass of water for himself. "What are you doing here?"

"I wanted to visit Sera. What's wrong with that?"

"Nothing. Except you messed up her sheets." Gaius looked at the line of paintings above Kael, which still portrayed the four princes in too-serious fashion. "I still hate how Rylan put me at the edge," he muttered.

"Doesn't matter that I've messed it up," Kael said. "It wasn't going to stay neat for long, anyway. I promised to show Sera a good time, so you're free to leave now, brother." Kael flopped to his belly, perched his chin on his hand, and waved Gaius away. His gaze fell on me.

Gaius strode to the window and slumped onto a couch. "I'll stay."

Kael lifted a brow. "He wants to watch."

"I need to rest," I said, my hands going clammy.

"You can rest after."

The nervous, new-to-sex me wanted to tuck her tail between her legs and run. I remembered how much it hurt the first time with Micah.

"Micah and Rylan?" I asked.

"We only promised to share the first time together," Gaius said, then sipped on his water as if everything was right in the world. The calmness he showed only made me more jittery. My gaze dropped to between his legs, and there, I saw a bulge that I had to quickly tear my eyes from.

Kael pushed the blanket aside and patted it.

I decided to summon my inner Kael and throw all fucks to the wind. I didn't have much time to spend with the princes anyway. Might as well make the most of it. I hopped on the bed, and as soon as I did, Kael's lips assaulted mine.

I gripped his shoulder, and a low chuckle rumbled from his throat. I tucked my other hand into his silky hair as I breathed him in.

He tasted salty and sweet at the same time.

"You don't have to be so gentle with her this time," Gaius said. "Or are you still sore, Sera?"

A little bit, I thought, but Kael caught my lips again before I could respond.

I looked toward Gaius, and he was still sipping on that cup of water, which didn't look like it'd been emptied at all.

Our eyes locked. His eyes darkened. My insides churned and I felt the need to squeeze my thighs together.

"Look at me," Kael said, his voice having lost the playful inflection it usually had. He gripped my hair, tugging a bit too roughly, and forced me to meet his eyes, which had turned a bright yellow.

I traced the ridges of his stomach. His body was *hot*. Far hotter than I'd felt it before, almost burning to the touch.

"You're quivering," he said. "Are you scared?"

I shook my head, trying to find words, but I was grinding my hips against his, wanting him inside me, and my mind had numbed too much for me to speak.

I watched the fan across the room spinning, round and

round, like my thoughts were. I was still mad with the princes for their decisions, but I loved them so much. Especially when they touched me like this. It simply felt too good to be with them.

Kael's fingers dug into my waist. His grip was so hard that I thought he might bruise me. He let go of my waist and reached down, finding my center. Smirking, he pressed through the fabric of my robe and rubbed against me. My hips met the rhythm of his hand. It wasn't enough, and suddenly the clothes that kept me warm felt constraining. I wanted them off.

"You'd be afraid if you could hear what my dragon's thinking now," Kael said.

I licked my lips. "What is it thinking?"

"That I should fuck you until you're screaming my name. Until my scent's all over you and that you're certain you belong to me and me alone." He pushed my head back and nipped my neck gently. Not enough to hurt, but enough to send tingles through my body. He continued to move his lips down my body, biting my skin teasingly.

I was on fire.

"You have to share," Gaius said. "She doesn't belong to you alone."

Kael growled. "Don't remind me."

"I don't want you to get too greedy."

Kael sat up. I didn't want him to leave. I grabbed for him, wanting to drag him down and command him to continue pleasuring me. I could never have too much of Kael.

He grabbed both sides of my robe.

Rrrripppp.

My dress lay in pieces, tossed between the sheets.

I breathed harder, chest rising and falling. Kael glanced at my breasts, before dipping his gaze to the rest of me. He lodged his fingers between my bra and skin.

"Don't," I said. "That's my favorite—"

He tore it apart anyway. I didn't have much time to mourn the loss of my favorite undergarment, because Kael was back to working his magic. He took a nipple in his mouth and worked it with his tongue. I sucked in a deep breath through my teeth. He pinched my other nub between his fingers.

I threw my head back and moaned, arching my back.

He was hard and grinding against my panties—another annoying layer of fabric. I reached for them and struggled to get them off, but Kael helped me out and ripped them straight off.

"Having fun, Sera?" Gaius asked. He had walked up to the pitcher to pour himself another glass of water. He stood next to me, his face right above mine, perfectly chiseled and showing amusement.

"Y-y-ou... you could join," I said.

"I thought I'd let Kael have a turn. Then, when you're alone with me, you'll know just how much better I am."

This didn't have to be a competition, but Kael took it as one. As soon as Gaius said the words, he bit gently on my nub and slipped his finger inside of me, stroking quickly but in all the right places.

I reached down and gripped his wrist. It was a bit too intense, and I had to purse my lips to stifle a moan.

"You don't have to silence yourself," Kael murmured, his hot breath tickling my neck.

I was stubborn, so I continued trying to keep quiet, but Kael pulled his member out, and as soon as he entered me, I cried out his name.

I'd expected a sharp pain like with Micah. I tensed. But as soon as Kael was in me, filling, stretching, blinding me, pleasure filled my core. My toes curled in response, and I was pretty sure I had scratched Kael's back by holding on to him too hard.

He didn't go slow, not like Micah had. He pulled back and slammed into me, not restraining himself. He grabbed my hair and tugged at it gently, enough for a little bit of pain to bite my scalp. It only added to the experience. More excitement coursed through me. My heart thumped against my ribcage.

"Damn," Kael said, throwing his head back. "Micah was right. She feels too good. Must have been torture to stop."

"Fuck," Gaius said. "I can't just watch anymore." He stroked my head. I looked up and saw the need in his eyes. He ran his fingers from my neck to my stomach, his hot touch driving me crazy. Combined with Kael's pounding, it drove me past the edge.

Gaius fastened my wrist against the bed. I wasn't sure what to expect when I found his cock next to my face. He didn't say anything, didn't ask, and pressed it to my lips. I opened them, inviting him in, and tasted the salty wetness on his tip.

He was almost too much. The both of them were.

The three of us found a rhythm, one that was too fast for

me to catch up. It was surreal. I had asked for this many times, but I didn't think we'd get to this stage, and now that I'd gotten what I wanted, it was better than I'd ever imagined, and perhaps more than I bargained for.

"You're being too rough," Gaius said to Kael. He was pushing deeper into my mouth, one hand on the back of my head, guiding me.

"You're one to talk," Kael replied. "She's struggling to take your size."

"It's not about how fast you go. It's about hitting the right spots."

"Like this?" Kael pulled nearly all the way out and forced himself back in. Twice. Stars lit in my eyes. I wrapped my fingers around his arms, steadying myself, but tension rose in my center. It coiled there, before exploding through me, filling my senses.

Kael growled. "Fuck, she's coming. I-it's too much." He quickened, before slamming one final thrust into me. He spilled his seed inside my folds, his member pulsing.

Gaius drew out of my lips. He stroked himself. He looked so large up close, and I questioned how I'd managed to fit him in my mouth in the first place. He let out a huge sigh as he found his release.

We'd made a huge mess. The remnants of my clothes were strewn all over the place, and my skin was sticky and gross.

I needed a shower.

But the princes didn't think the same. Kael flopped to my side while Gaius crawled to the bed.

Kael hugged me to him. "Come to me when you want to have a good time, Sera, because my brothers can't compare."

Gaius snorted. "You wish."

I was exhausted, and the aches that had been numbed by the lust began to seep back in.

"You were a bit too intense," I said, still reveling in the hardness of the princes' bodies.

"Isn't that the point?" Kael said.

"Sometimes a girl's got to take a break."

"I can do slow." He winked at me.

"This is nice," I said, making myself comfortable in our messy cuddle.

"Yep," Gaius replied. "And we're going to have forever together to do things like this."

My chest tightened at Gaius's words.

If only.

"Aereala's coming," I said, finally blurting it out. They had to know. I was afraid of hurting them, but they deserved the truth.

"What?" Kael said. "No, no. I think you and I were the ones who just did that."

I laughed at that, even though I wasn't quite in the mood to. "She's visiting the physical realm. That thing I 'joked' about in Kaldaross... I wasn't lying. I'm her vessel, guys. She's coming to stop the famine, but I won't be around after that."

They both stilled.

Time was suspended.

I was afraid Gaius might erupt in anger again, but instead, he squeezed me really tightly, like he was holding on to me for dear life. On his face, I saw tears pouring down.

My chest sank. I reached up and wiped the tears away.

Kael had been stunned into silence. His blue eyes were wide in shock.

"This is for the good of the Drae Lands," I said. "Aereala will be coming, so you don't have to war with Beyestirya. We just have to work together."

Gaius's voice was throaty when he replied, "When?"

"I don't know. She told me that she'd do it when enough of her power gathers. I can't say for sure."

"A year? Two? Or none at all?"

Kael tucked me closer to him. "We'll just have to make the best of it."

"The war?" I asked.

"Will still happen," Gaius said. "Beyestiryan troops have been spotted on the move. Rylan has no choice."

At that moment, my heart dipped to my knees.

I really did have to send that letter.

CHAPTER TWENTY-FIVE

KAEL AND GAIUS had given me the best sexual experience of my nineteen years, but they didn't mention how horrid the aftermath would be.

It had been two days since we'd lain together in bed. They hadn't told the other two brothers of what I'd mentioned. Perhaps it was their way of grieving. In silence. Alone. I didn't see much of them around. I'd expected that they'd want to spend more time with me.

I felt like I'd been ripped into two, both emotionally and physically. I hoped nobody noticed that I walked funny when I entered the Council of Intelligence.

Inside, it reminded me of the Assembly of Scholars, just that it was far more brightly lit, since it wasn't buried underground. Sunlight beamed through its glass windows. Dead crops lay all over the place, along with papers and scrolls.

When I picked up a dead leaf and it lit up with color, some Constanrians stopped to look. But they walked away, intimidated by the guards surrounding me. I sighed and turned to Micah, who'd been kind enough to accompany me here.

"They still hate me." There was no question about that. Their hate had simmered when I left, festering like a neglected wound.

Micah strolled alongside me. "They're scared."

"Doesn't mean that they should go around pointing fingers at the first person they can blame."

"The prophecy Anatolia gave sounded too convincing." Micah frowned. "My little sister shouldn't be spouting nonsense."

I laughed sheepishly and avoided his gaze. Did I really have to break it to them twice? Maybe I should have waited until all four of them were gathered. Why hadn't Gaius and Kael done the hard work for me?

For some reason, I'd imagined many of my Constanrian colleagues running to me with open arms, saying they'd missed my presence. Before my curse had been revealed, we did share three good years.

I guessed it didn't matter. Once Aereala came and solved their problems, I wouldn't be around to see how they viewed me anymore.

It kind of sucked that I had to be so melodramatic. I kept trying to keep my chin up, but a death sentence wasn't exactly an easy thing to face.

The Council of Intelligence had lost its familiarity. Strange. This place, with its stained-glass windows and marble pillars, used to feel like home. But I found myself missing the assembly in Beyestirya and all its friendly faces.

Micah and I found a corner on the second floor. The scholars at the two tables beside us stared at me hesitantly. The guards, not under my instruction, shooed them away, before going on patrol. I wanted to stop my guards, until I saw the relief on the scholars' faces. They'd prefer not to sit too close to me.

Figures.

Whatever. I didn't need people like them sitting next to me anyway.

"Thanks for accompanying me," I said to Micah, as I sorted through the reports Frederick had given me. "I know you have a lot to do with Rylan."

Micah smiled. "It's all right. I like spending time with you."

So sweet. Micah was less talkative than the other princes, but whenever he spoke, he was the kindest. "It's only when you and your brothers are around that the guards don't crowd around and make me feel like I can't breathe."

"The security is necessary."

"Gaius didn't think so."

"He's less discerning than others. I know it's annoying, but you need it. Rylan continues to get requests for your head. He's going to send out a decree saying that anyone who dares threaten you will be whipped."

"Whipped? That's a bit harsh, isn't it?"

"For threatening and slandering you? Whipping is perhaps too lenient. If I were him, I'd deal a more severe sentence." He took out a piece of candy and unwrapped it. Popping it into his mouth, he said, "Beheading, probably."

Had I just thought he was sweet? Maybe I had to reconsider my assessment.

Micah circled the candy around his mouth. I looked at the documents. Things had moved so fast during the time I was away. All this data looked completely different from what I remembered, and it was taking a while for me to process everything.

No more harvests were coming in. The Constanrian scholars had tried new techniques—more spells, similar to the heat-resistant one I created; more irrigation systems; new soils. All those attempts didn't work. The scholars had moved from prevention to mitigation, and instead of trying to stop the famine, they fiddled with logistics. Whether people made it through the famine or not had become a matter of properly delegating supplies.

With this, they were deciding who got to live and who had to die.

Their primary form of information was now census data and inventory. Numbers piled in front of me, too many to sift through. Too overwhelming.

Instead of spearheading my department, I'd gotten left behind.

"You don't have to be here," Micah said.

"Where else should I be?" I'd worked in the council for the last few years. I couldn't imagine a different life in the palace. "This is my job."

Micah's expression darkened. "You're going to be queen soon, right? You'll have other duties. Social ones. Like Miriel, you'll have to garner favor in the court."

Social duties sounded even harder than reading through all this. "I'm not going to be queen."

"No? " Micah tipped his head. "That's what everyone has been saying."

"I promised you. I won't." I just hadn't managed to sit down and have quiet time with Rylan yet. I needed to break it to him.

But he was too busy planning war.

I flipped to the next page. "I won't get the chance to, anyway."

Micah frowned. "Of course you will. You're not making any sense."

Shifting from the topic, I said, "What do think... of these new events?"

"Rylan being king?"

I nodded.

"It's not as bad as I thought it'd be."

"You thought it might be bad?"

"Growing up, I wanted everything he had. I dreaded the day he'd be king. It meant I'd failed at taking the throne. But no, it's not really the duties or power I wanted. I was never close to getting them anyway. Nobody would accept a bastard son like me. I'd have to kill Rylan to stand a chance, and even then, there was Kael and Gaius. I love them. I just longed to be accepted." His eyes pierced mine. "And I'm accepted by you and my brothers. I don't care for the power anymore. So I'm okay with it. I'll be here to stick by Rylan."

He shrugged. "Gisiroth hardly talked to me anyway. I actually like Rylan being king. It's strange to not have a father. But Rylan's going to give me a high rank in the

Council of Fortitude. He's trying to make Kael the head, but that brother of mine hates duties. The paperwork would crush him. Maybe I'll be head instead."

"Isn't the position voted on?"

"Not when there's war. It's in our constitution, written by the first king. In times of war, the king is allowed to pick leaders for both councils."

Fuck the war. I didn't know what to think about it anymore. It made me tired.

He reached over and squeezed my hand. "About you being queen, though. Don't say yes. Don't belong to just him."

"I thought you said you were okay?"

"I still get jealous." He kissed my temple, wearing a wide grin. He leaned back into his chair and pried open the book he had been reading—one about math problems. It still puzzled me how he could read math for pleasure.

I drifted from the accounting documents sitting in front of me, and my attention turned to Micah. His hair was growing out a bit longer than usual. His lips were full; his eyelashes longer than his brothers. Eyes—cool and striking, reminding me of the sky.

"You're staring," Micah said, flipping to the next page.

"Can't help it," I replied. "You look so much better than numbers do."

"Numbers can be pretty, too."

"Not as pretty as you."

He shut his book. The sides of his lips curled up. "Are you trying to tempt me, Sera?"

"Depends. What am I tempting you to do?"

As he stared at my mouth, he ran his tongue across his lower lip. "My brothers told me you were too sore to do anything for the next few days. That we should let you rest."

"I like to test my boundaries." They hadn't touched me since, probably to make it easier for themselves to hold back.

Micah reached for my face, but before his fingers brushed my skin, Ayren interrupted us.

He had his hand rested on the back of a squire. The young man twiddled his thumbs.

"He said he wanted to see you, Your Majesty," Ayren said.

"For what?" I asked.

The squire shifted his feet. "I-it's very important..."

"Pass it here," Micah said.

The squire's gaze darted to the ground, then to me. "I was told not to let anyone but Her Majesty see this, Your Highness. I'm sorry, but I can't give this to you."

"I'm your prince."

"I know, but I can't. I was told to destroy this message if Her Majesty doesn't get it."

I reached out, and the squire quickly placed the letter in my hand. I unrolled it. It was smaller than my palm.

It read:

Be at the courtyard of the northeast wing tomorrow evening. Try not to bring too many others with you.

The squire zipped off as soon as he could.

"What does it say?" Micah asked. He tried to snatch the letter from me, but I tore it up, perhaps too abruptly.

"Stupid death threats," I muttered, giving him my best peeved face.

"Death threats?" Micah's forehead creased.

"I don't want to talk about it."

Micah didn't look convinced, but he let the matter rest and went back to his book.

Ayren left us to our own devices soon after. I tried to focus on the documents Frederick had given me, but I couldn't. Not with that message.

Was it Vanjar? I'd sent her the letter right after talking to Gaius and Kael. I wanted to go back to stop Beyestirya from attacking.

Should I listen to it? What if it wasn't someone from Beyestirya but some enemy I didn't know who wanted my head? There wasn't any shortage of them in the palace. And how was I supposed to get there alone?

I attempted to focus on the documents in front of me. The Emilia region was getting fewer rations because they were the most likely to get attacked by Beyestirya.

But as I continued to read, the numbers blurred in front of me. They were replaced with a plan. One that involved Frederick.

———

At five thirty, right before the sun set, Frederick knocked on my door, like I'd asked him to. He greeted me with a large sack of things.

"We'll have to check that first," Ayren said, before he let Frederick through.

"Let him through," I said, wondering what all those things he carried were.

Ayren started, "But—"

"Frederick is my closest friend. It's too insulting to him for you to even suggest he might hurt me." I hoped my commanding queen voice sounded convincing. "Let him through. Don't make me repeat myself."

I waved Frederick in, and Ayren obliged, but not before giving a Frederick a long, hard stare.

I kicked the door shut as soon as Frederick stepped through and pulled him into the room, far away from the door so the guards couldn't hear.

"What're all these things?" I asked.

Frederick shot me a disgruntled look. "Explain to me what this is all about. I went through a lot of trouble for these." He lifted the sack and shook it.

"Do you have the soul beads?" I asked, snatching the sack from him.

"No." He looked perplexed.

"Why not?"

"With less livestock, the council's being really tight with soul beads. I'd need to write out a *convincing* ten-page report to get them. It takes a day to get approval. So I figured I'd come up with something else. Why do you need a disguise?"

"To sneak out, of course."

"For what?"

I looked into the bag and poured the items onto my bed,

but not before checking my door once more just in case a guard barged in. Feeling uneasy, I walked to the door and locked it, before striding back to my bed. On the bed lay a rope, some servant clothes, bindings, makeup, and some theater props.

"These should do," I said. Frederick really was resourceful. I had to smile at his efforts, but it didn't last long. I was too nervous.

What if the person who'd sent that letter didn't wait for long?

Did I even want to meet him or her?

"Peas explain," Frederick said.

"I need to go somewhere."

He pointed to the door.

"No, not like that. I mean like, I can't be with these guards."

"Why?"

"Because I received a letter."

"From who?" Frederick crossed his arms.

I threw a servant's dress at his face. "I don't know."

He peeled it off. "That doesn't sound safe."

"It's not. Which is why I need you there with me. I think it might be Vanjar or her men. I need to go back to Beyestirya, stop this war, then—"

Then what? Turn into some sacrificial dynfowl? But I had a plan to buy me more time with Aereala. Maybe it'd play out with the goddess, and I could go back to the princes once I stopped the war.

Aereala's teats. I was really rushing into this, wasn't I? What if Vanjar wanted me to go with her? I needed time to say goodbye to the princes, too. This was all happening far too quickly.

I picked up a male servant's outfit and the bindings before walking to my bathroom.

"What am I supposed to do with this dress?" Frederick asked.

"Wear it."

"What?"

I slammed the bathroom door behind me. I hastily dressed up, wrapping the bindings around my breasts to flatten them. They were uncomfortably tight and it was slightly hard to breathe. When I walked out, Frederick was still dressed in his robes.

I raised a brow. "Why aren't you clothed?"

"Because it's ridiculous! I don't need to be in a disguise."

I sifted through the theater props, finding a fake mustache. It didn't match my hair color, but thankfully, Frederick had also brought a short black wig and a hat. The servants around here didn't usually wear hats. I'd be a strangely dressed male servant, but at least unrecognizable. I pasted the mustache above my mouth. "How is it?"

"Hideous."

"Convincing?"

"No."

I peeled it off—perhaps too quickly and roughly, because I winced at the sharp pain. I didn't let the pain bother me, instead throwing a wig at Frederick.

"And what's this?" Frederick asked.

"Wear that too."

"We're sneaking out, not getting ready for a play."

"Look. People know you're close to me. They might give my disguise another look if they recognize you. It's better if you're in one, too, and the farther away you are from your regular persona, the better."

Frederick stared at me wide-eyed. After a long pause, he threw his hands up. "Fine."

"Thanks. You're the best friend ever. I love you."

He shut the bathroom door behind him.

I glanced at my satin gloves. They weren't going to work. They'd be a dead giveaway. I pulled them off my fingers and replaced them with leather ones, hoping people wouldn't be able to make the connection between my gloves and my curse. The outfit left some of my arms exposed, but it'd have to do. I'd just have to be careful.

My bathroom door swung open.

Frederick stepped out wearing a dress.

"Beautiful," I said, stifling a laugh.

"Really?" Frederick said, resting his hands on his hips. Not a hint of amusement showed on his expression. "You sure? I thought the yellow might be too much with my ginger hair."

"Okay, maybe a dress was a bit much."

"I am so surprised."

"I totally forgot about your stubble. It's not the most inconspicuous thing."

Frederick rolled his eyes. He picked up a servant outfit, some glasses, and another wig from my bed. Huffing, he strode back into my bathroom.

He came out minutes later as a different, poorer version

of himself. To me it still looked like Frederick, but strangers would have a hard time making the connection.

When we were done getting ready, which, luckily, didn't take long, I threw my window open.

Frederick watched me. "You're not looking to climb down, are you?"

I fastened the rope ladder to the window ledge and threw it down the building.

"That does *not* look safe," Frederick added.

I tugged at the ladder. "Safe enough."

I lived on the fourth floor. A cobblestone path and some bushes waited for us at the bottom. It wasn't too high up, so if an accident happened, neither of us would die. We'd suffer terrible injuries, however, and my stomach churned at the thought. I pulled at the ladder one more time, as hard as I could, just to make sure it was as secure as it could be.

I gestured to the exit. "You first."

"Why me?" His voice had risen a few notches.

"Because if you fall, I can make sure the rope is secure from the top. And if I fall, it's probably better for you to catch me instead of the other way around because of our weight difference."

Frederick looked over the ledge, peering down. He backed away from the window. "Okay... You're right. Why are you always right? It's annoying. Just give me a moment. I don't like heights."

We climbed down without too many problems—except for one side of the ladder snapping when it was my turn. I held on to its ropes for dear life, cursing Aereala's name. My knee slammed against the building, sending a jolt of pain up my right thigh. It still ached when I fumbled down the rest of the ladder, which was only attached on one side and hung at an awkward angle. When my feet hit the ground, relief surged through me. Scowling, I rubbed my knee.

"Secure, huh?" Frederick asked, wearing a smug grin.

I slapped him lightly on the shoulder. "You would've caught me if I fell, right?"

He shifted his gaze to the ground and shrugged.

Nobody recognized us when we strode through the palace. We got some strange looks because of our outfits and made some servants do double takes, but no alarms were raised.

We reached the meeting location in ten minutes. It was the closest wing to the princes' quarters.

The courtyard we entered was devoid of life.

It was the worst I'd seen since coming back to the palace. Everything was gray. Dead leaves, some rotting, filled the small stream trickling through, leaving an acrid taste in the air. It looked like death itself had an agenda with this place and decided to suck the life out of it. Not a hint of color graced the area. Had the epidemic already spread this wide?

There was nobody here.

A wind blew through the courtyard, shaking the leaves of a small, grayed tree. Some leaves fell on the gravel.

"Are you certain this is the right place?" Frederick asked, tugging my sleeve.

We weren't fully in the courtyard yet, and I hoped the person waiting hadn't spotted us.

"I want you to hide in the bushes," I said in a low voice.

Frederick reeled back. "These bushes look gross."

"Please? If anything happens to me, run back and tell the princes straight away. You're my backup."

"I can't run that fast. I've been working out, but it takes time to build stamina."

"Hurry and hide." I elbowed him.

Frederick groaned and shot me an annoyed look. "You're always dragging me into things."

"I love you," I said again. I winked at him as he stalked away to hide in one of the grayed bushes.

I strode into the courtyard, taking a glance at Frederick as I did.

His bottom stuck out. He looked at me for confirmation, and I gestured for him to move. He did, hiding his bottom, and then flashed me a thumbs-up from the shrub.

I pulled the letter out from my pocket and gave it another look. "Yep. It said the northeast." Why wasn't anyone here?

As if answering my thought, a woman's voice sounded from behind me. "Sera?"

I spun around. Vanjar strode toward me, wearing leather armor and pants, with a sword strapped to her side. I wasn't used to seeing her without one of her pretty dresses. She carried the rugged look well. Then again, Vanjar could probably wear two coconuts as a top and still look stunning.

Vanjar spread her arms open, inviting me in for a friendly hug. I accepted it, folding my arms around her before pulling away quickly.

"You didn't have to come here," I said.

Vanjar smiled. "I wanted to make sure you returned. Baekeil gave me permission." Her smile dropped. "We don't have much time. I'll have to take you out of the palace in human form. It'll attract too much attention if I shift. Once we're out of here, we'll head straight back to Beyestirya. I'm so glad you managed to get here—"

The bushes rustled, and Frederick strode out, some leaves stuck in his hair. He brushed some leaves out, but missed the debris.

So much for hiding. That was short-lived.

Vanjar reached for the hilt of her sword. I placed my hand on hers, halting her. "He's a friend."

"Sorry." He shrugged. "I figured since you gave her a hug she's someone we can trust."

"She is," I said.

Frederick frowned. "You're leaving, Sera? So soon?"

"Does it have to be this soon?" I asked Vanjar.

She nodded. "I'm here on borrowed time. And I don't want to risk sneaking around even more, lest I get caught. The palace has patrols everywhere. I used up a good amount of soul magic getting here, especially since my body isn't as in tune with the art. If I drag this out, I'm afraid my disguises won't last."

I dipped my gaze to the ground. The place felt colder for no good reason. "I haven't said goodbye."

Vanjar's expression softened. She grabbed my forearm and gave it a reassuring squeeze. "I'm sorry, Sera."

"So, what?" I asked her. "You're going to carry me out of here?"

It was one thing to be in the princes' arms, but Vanjar? She didn't look strong enough. Not with her slender figure and delicately sensual frame.

"Don't underestimate me. I'm a hidrae myself." She

paused. "But it'll probably be conspicuous if I'm seen flying around with another woman in my arms, disguise or not. Meet me at the front gate. Few should recognize you wearing this. It took me a long, hard look to figure it out."

This is it.

I sucked in a deep breath. "All right. I'll see you there."

Before reality had any time to settle in, palace guards, wearing Rylan's blues and clunky armor, appeared from all sides. The passageways, the roofs. They left no opening for escape. Far too many to fight off.

Vanjar looked upward, panic written all over her.

My pulse spiked, and Frederick inched closer to me. I saw a lump travel down his throat.

Micah appeared from the edge of the rooftop, gorgeous, bathed in the glow of the setting sun. Muscular, tall, and imposing. His cold eyes met mine from under his red fringe.

"Welcome to Constanria, cousin," Micah said.

But not a hint of welcome lit his features.

CHAPTER TWENTY-SIX

I SAT in my own room as a prisoner under interrogation.

Rylan paced around it. Micah, who had found me out, leaned next to the window. The rope ladder I'd used to escape was still strapped to the window ledge. It hung there, a reminder of my crime.

Kael and Gaius walked in. They shifted their gazes to me before looking away, Kael at the ceiling and Gaius at the wall next to us.

Gaius said, "We just heard from the squire. Is it true?"

"Sera here tried to sell us out." Rylan sounded bitter.

I shook my head. "No, that's not it."

Gaius's expression darkened, while Kael looked confused.

"Why?" Gaius asked, turning to me.

"I... I don't want war."

"So you told the enemy our plans?" Rylan asked. "Make us lose the war? Do you realize that means death?"

"That's not it!"

Micah's piercing gaze burned my side. He had read the letter in the library before I tore it up, but he didn't say anything. Instead, he'd planned that ambush. "Why did you betray us, Sera?"

Sera. Not the pet name they'd given me. He was distancing himself, and that made my heartbeat quicken.

"I wasn't going to let her know of your plans," I said. "I thought that maybe if I were there, you four would be less inclined to attack. The Beyestiryans will also listen to my opinions. I'd be able to stop them should they want to order a charge. If I go there and tell them it's Aereala's will, they'll listen, and if they're not attacking Constanria because of my presence, you won't have reason to order a charge either."

Rylan closed in on me. He looked so angry, and I drew back, afraid he might lash out. Instead, he got down to one knee in front of me, reaching for my hand. He rested his head on my lap. "Why are you so silly?"

"Silly? I was trying to stop a war and you guys wouldn't listen."

"We can't avoid this. It's a struggle over resources. They'll come, or we'll have to go, regardless of where you are. I'd rather you stick by our side. You are my weakness, Sera love. *Ours.* And if they have you when war breaks out, I'm not sure if I could take it." He picked my hand up and kissed my palm. "They'll use you against us."

"I *will* stop the war," I said. "Like how I managed to get you that conference with Baekeil. Which you blew, by the way. Let me go back with Vanjar." I didn't know where the princes had left her. Micah had rounded us up, sent Frederick on his way, and taken Vanjar. I hoped she didn't sit in some cold dungeon. She'd treated us with so much hospitality when we were in her country, and I was the one who'd drawn her here.

"Why are you so keen to leave us?" Gaius asked, not able to mask the hurt on his face.

"I love you," I said. "You have to know that. But I can't wait here for Aereala to fix things. Should I just sit here and let people die, while I wait for a goddess to answer my prayers?"

"Aereala to fix things?" Micah asked.

All four pairs of blue eyes fell on me. My heart beat faster. I hadn't told Rylan and Micah yet. I shared understanding glances with Gaius and Kael.

I decided to make it quick but painful. "Aereala will take over my body to restore the crops. Famine will be solved, but she hasn't given me an indication of when. I won't survive."

Tension dripped through the air, and everything seemed to still.

My words hung in the air. I saw them slowly sink in.

Rylan's eyes flashed. The world seemed to spin around us.

Rylan let go of me, as if my touch were poison. He didn't say another word. Instead, he stood and left, slamming the door behind him.

I'd expected a severe reaction, but not one this cold.

I got up, ready to chase after him, but Gaius halted me. "Stay. It's okay," he said. "He's hurt. I'll talk to him."

I nodded, and Gaius was out the door too, leaving me with Micah and Kael.

Micah sank onto the bed. "Is this true?" he asked.

Kael had known the truth. Despite that, he didn't take hearing it a second time well. I ran my fingers over the crease of his brow and drew him in.

Micah took me in an embrace. He kissed me like he needed me, as if I was air itself. I breathed him in, needing him, too.

"Yes." I nodded.

Micah's face looked calm, but he had one hand in a fist, so tight that the white of his knuckles showed. "And even with this, with less time, you were going to leave us. What were you thinking?"

"I was going to stay at first. I wanted to spend as much time as possible with you guys. But then Rylan called for war, and I thought about the dead. Men and women and children, all wasted lives. I have to stretch the peace out. Until the matter is resolved. And I can only do that in Beyestirya."

Kael sat on the bed, too. He tugged me to him and planted a kiss on my forehead. "If you think we're going to let you leave after this, then you're sorely mistaken."

"Do you think Rylan will let me go?"

"*I* won't let you go."

"You'll have to eventually."

Kael drew back and stared at me. His eyes were watering, and the sight shook me. Kael wasn't the kind of person to get sad. He was the type to not care for anything. That was how he was so happy all the time.

But he cared for *me*.

It touched me so much that it hurt on a physical level. I squeezed my arms around him.

We lay down on the bed, me sandwiched between Micah and Kael.

It was peaceful.

Kael rested his hand on my cheek, looking at me with a sea of emotion in his eyes, while Micah held my wrist and placed kisses on my neck.

But the peace wasn't going to last.

Because we were attacked by my three ingorias. They hopped over Kael and Micah, toward me, stepping over our bodies.

"Ow!" Kael said. "Do their nails ever get trimmed? They're sharp."

"Aren't you supposed to be a dragon?" Micah said. "Getting defeated by nails."

"I have delicate skin when in human form."

"What, because of your impeccable skincare routine?"

Their bickering sounded forced this time, like they were trying to distract themselves from the news. I laughed anyway, because I needed a distraction too.

Mayhem slobbered all over Micah.

"They need their teeth brushed as well," Micah said, pushing Mayhem away. "It stinks."

"He's a sweetheart," I said. I let him lick my face.

"I'm not kissing you anymore."

I chuckled. Mayhem's tongue felt like sandpaper, but I was used to it. "We can take a shower after this."

"Together?" Kael said, making faces at Aura.

"Does the experience come in a package?" I asked.

"If Micah, joins, then two." He winked.

We spent the next hour playing with the ingorias, and with Micah telling me about more silly things Kael used to do as a younger adventurer.

Kael had once tried to fight five draekeri in an arena, promising not to shift, and he almost lost. He let the event be public, and allowed bets, while betting on himself. Eventually, he'd won, and he sat on a fat pile of money after that. It happened before I was born.

"And now he's getting destroyed by ingoria nails," Micah finished. "Pups, no less."

"Can I still call them pups?" I asked. "They're huge." My bed creaked with their weight, and I worried it might break.

"You fought their mother, didn't you?" Kael said. "These *are* pups."

"Did I tell you about that time Kael ripped his pants?" Micah asked. There were tears in his eyes but a smile on his lips.

I leaned my ear toward him. "Please elaborate."

Kael scowled. His nose was red. "Hey! That was after a really bad attempt at getting at Gaius. I wanted him to stop frowning for a day."

"You made him stop, all right. He wouldn't stop laughing. *At you.*"

A devilish grin split Micah's face. "It started when—"

Kael reached over and cupped his hands over Micah's lips. "Don't you dare tell her."

"Okay," I said. "Now I must hear."

Kael narrowed his eyes. "If you tell her, I'll tell her about your first time horse riding."

"Can you guys stop dangling tidbits of information and not finish?" I said. "Now you've got me interested."

Kael removed his hands from Micah's lips.

"Deal," Micah said. "I'll keep mum." He made a zipping motion over his mouth.

"What!" I smacked Micah with my pillow, and Aura joined in my attack, assaulting Micah with her tongue. "That's not fair!"

"So," Kael said, pulling me in. He sniffed me and made a face. "Shower time?"

———

Shower time ended up becoming nap time. I wasn't sure how it happened. One minute we were playing with the ingorias and making jabs at each other, and the next, all three of us dozed off. I guess being between Micah and Kael felt too comfortable, because drifting off to sleep snuck up on me and I was none the wiser.

A nudge on my shoulder woke me up.

I opened my eyes, seeing Gaius hovering over me. His eyes were still dark. He needed Mayhem to lick all that broodiness out of him. "Rylan's in his study," he said. "It's late and he still won't go to sleep."

"How is he taking it?" I asked.

"He's toughing it out."

"And you?"

"Not very well."

Micah and Kael woke. They parted from me, and I untangled myself from their embraces. I was getting a little too hot lying next to them, underneath the sheets. The ingorias seemed to have thought so too. They'd hopped off the bed and settled on the ground.

"Could it be possible Aereala's message might have just been you falling sick?" Gaius asked. "And that it was just a dream?"

"It's a possibility."

"I'll hold on to that, then."

"I'm going to have a talk with the goddess to figure this out."

"A... talk? With the goddess? You can summon her?"

"Hasn't been working so far, but maybe I haven't tried hard enough."

I got to my feet and ran my fingers through my messy hair. I grabbed a brush from my bedside and began taming the beast on my head. "Let me wash up before talking to Rylan," I said, laughing sheepishly. "I have slobber all over me."

"My brothers really went too far, huh?" Gaius said, his expression lightening.

"It wasn't our fault," Kael said. "She can't control her pets."

"They like licking people," I replied.

Micah scrunched his nose up. "Ugh. I can't believe I fell asleep with this gunk on my face."

I waved them goodbye and stepped into my bathroom.

I took a five-minute shower and came out with a simple robe. I toweled my hair dry, feeling fresh. Part of me dreaded meeting Rylan again. His reaction had been the worst, and I didn't want him to yell at me. What if I made it worse, somehow? Said the wrong thing?

"Do you want to come?" I asked Gaius. He was keeping his brutish persona up well, but maybe I needed to talk to him, too.

"I'm harder than you think," Gaius said.

My gaze dropped to his crotch.

"That's not what I mean."

"I'm kidding."

I kissed his jaw and stalked out the door. I ran my hands across the decorations lining the corridor as I strode to Rylan's study, which wasn't too far from my room.

I walked past his door, preparing words in my mind:

Aereala's just trying to save the entire race of dragon-kind. Don't fault her.

Or:

I'll see you in the spirit realm once it's all over. There are dead birds that are freaky there, but we can freak together in the afterlife. It'll be fun.

Yeah, I doubted I'd do a good job comforting him. How did one recover from a death sentence like this? It was like making fun of a terminal illness.

I imagined Kael pointing at someone with rock-skin disease and talking of their dreadful skincare routine: "*What do you use you wash your face every day? Wasps?*"

Sounded similar to: "*At least your body will be used to host a god. A huge upgrade from your current personality, if you ask me. You won't be here to see it, but the rest of us will.*"

Nah. I doubted Kael would go that far. Maybe these terrible lines were just my pathetic way of shrugging this off.

As I entered Rylan's study, I stopped in my tracks.

Another woman was there.

Dark hair, in curls that were far less perfect than usual. Leather clothes I'd seen in the courtyard.

Vanjar.

Rylan looked from her to me.

She followed his gaze, turning around to greet me. "Hi, Sera."

Rylan gestured to the empty chair next to Vanjar. I sat down on its hard surface. It wasn't the least bit comfortable. I'd spotted dragon-stone shackles around Vanjar's wrists before I sat. It was likely to suppress her dragon side.

So much for talking to him alone.

At least I didn't have to make it worse with those terrible lines I'd prepared.

"As I mentioned," Vanjar said, returning her gray eyes to Rylan, "Beyestirya has no intention of attacking Constanria. Your time and questions are for nothing. I merely wanted to bring Sera back. Upon *her* request." She slapped a piece of paper on the table. I recognized my own handwriting on it before Rylan picked it up. He skimmed through it before putting it down, showing little regard for the letter.

"Sera wants to go back with you," Rylan said, studying me. "She thinks it'll stop the war. But she's too late."

"What war?" Vanjar said. "I want to keep the peace. It's what Aereala wants us to do. Sera told us that."

"Your husband doesn't share your sentiments," Rylan said.

Vanjar stiffened. "What do you mean?"

"I received a report minutes ago. An army has stormed

through the Mishram Plains and is at Gaean's pit. Luckily, we anticipated this with our scouts. Your husband made his moves far earlier. Three days ago, we spotted him preparing for war. We have forces at Gaean's pit, positioned at their fort. A battle is happening as we speak. Men are dying as we speak."

Wow. He spoke of the death of innocents like it was inconsequential. A fly on the wall. He didn't bat his eyelids, frown, or do anything I would. I'd probably sound angrier.

Because I was angry.

At both sides.

Why couldn't everybody just get along? Why were people so quick to rush to clashing heads and pointing fingers and swords? Slapping and piercing and killing each other as if the Drae Lands didn't have enough suffering already? Why was it so much to ask them to shake hands, embrace, and cooperate?

Why in Aereala's name did I even care?

Maybe it was because I had to die for these people. I wanted them to be a race worth dying for. I was sick of this.

"My husband said nothing of this," Vanjar said.

"He probably used your disappearance and capture as an excuse to rile the troops," Rylan said.

Vanjar shook her head. "Oh, Baekeil."

"What shall I do with you now, cousin?" Rylan asked.

Vanjar looked up with a sneer. "I am a prisoner of war now, aren't I? Do I have a choice?"

"Will you help us?"

"I'm the enemy, aren't I? My allegiance stands with my husband. Why should I help you?"

"Funny," I said. "I remember me saying the same thing to you last time."

"And you stuck with your lovers till the very end."

"No. I sent that message to you, didn't I? They wanted war and they made me have to go against them. I couldn't betray myself." I took a step closer. "What do you think we should do? What do you think is right?"

Vanjar tensed. "Baekeil wants war too."

"I'm not asking you about your husband. I'm asking about your opinion."

She pressed her lips together. Finally, she said, "I think we should find peace. I want my children to be happy. My people to be happy."

"Then work with us. Convince your husband to turn back. War has begun, but it's not too late." *I hoped.* And if I could convince Vanjar here, maybe I didn't have to go back to Beyestirya. It seemed to be working...

Then she shook her head. "If my husband turns back, your betrothed will just bite us as we retreat."

"Rylan?" I asked, hope rising in me. He knew the truth of Aereala. I didn't want him to be a warmongering king. That wasn't how I wanted to see him, and I trusted him to make what I felt was the right decision this time.

He sighed. "Beyestirya has attacked us already. It's not my decision to make. Right now, all I can do is defend Constanria." He placed his hands on the desk, leaning closer to Vanjar. "But you both can make a difference. I'll send you back to them, Sera, if only to stop them. And Vanjar, entreat your husband. Let us find peace."

Vanjar offered a hand.

Rylan glanced at it, as if contemplating whether to take it. When he did, relief surged through me, and I longed to kiss him for his decision.

"We'll head to Gaean's pit tomorrow," Rylan said. "And we'll put an end to all this."

CHAPTER TWENTY-SEVEN

THE NIGHT WAS COLD.

Rylan noticed me shivering and grabbed my hand to place it in his pocket. I inched closer to him, wanting more of his comfort.

We had just finished talking to Vanjar and decided to leave in the morn. Rylan and I strode in the dark, the pavement lit by the moonlight.

Fireflies, with their green, glowing bodies, fluttered about us.

According to Rylan, the Constanrian soldiers had been pushed back by Beyestirya's and retreated into the mountains of Gaean's pit. There was a fort there, guarded on most sides. The enemy forces were now beginning a siege, and the two armies stood at a standstill. Tomorrow, with Vanjar's help, we were going to send the Beyestiryan soldiers home packing.

"Sorry about walking out on you," Rylan said. "I just..."

"I didn't want to break it to you guys. I thought I could've handled it. I told Gaius about it once. Long ago. He thought I was joking. He was on the verge of a breakdown."

"It's not something you should suffer alone."

We continued to walk in silence. I had the sudden urge to kiss Rylan. To trace the tattoos that wrapped around his body, and to hear him whisper sweet nothings into my ear.

"I have bad news," Rylan said. "But I'm not sure if I should let you know. Not after what you've gone through."

Not what I was hoping for him to say.

"I can handle it." *I think.* Maybe everything really was too much, and I should have bathed in the bliss of ignorance. Still, curiosity got the better of me. I had to know.

"Your mother..." Rylan rubbed the back of his neck.

"What does she want this time?" I sighed.

"It's not that." He shifted his gaze to the ground. "There's no easy way to say this, Sera love."

A pit grew in my stomach. "I can take it," I said, but doubt trickled in me, and I was afraid I couldn't.

He drew a deep breath then turned to face me. "There was a raid on their home. I made sure that your family was taken care of, sending all the required food and supplies they'd need so you didn't have to worry about them. But the famine is hitting hard, and the neighbors noticed what your parents had. Things they didn't have. They robbed your home. There was a scuffle. You father and sister are fine, but your mother..."

This was Rylan's sick way of getting back at me, right? His form of a practical joke, so that I suffered for telling him about Aereala.

My mind blanked, and it took a moment for sense to fill it.

Rylan waited. He studied me and gauged my reaction.

"She didn't make it," I said.

"Two stab wounds to the chest. She was sent to a physician, but it was too late by then."

My chest tightened. Previously, when I still lived with them, I had imagined my life with my parents dead. It was a terrible thing for a daughter to think, but they hadn't treated me well after my curse manifested.

But despite my curse, they had kept me clothed, protected me from those who wanted to have me strung up. Mother especially.

I'd fallen sick a few times after my curse was revealed. She got grumpy when I did, but she cooked for me and brought me to the healer. Most of the time, the healer sent me away. They didn't want anything to do with me.

But Mother banged on the door, almost knocked it down, and made sure I got the right medicine.

Her words could be vicious, but ultimately, she was still a mother to me, albeit not a very good one.

And now she was dead.

"The last time I saw Mother," I said, tightening my hold on Rylan, "it was during one of my trips back home. From the council. She made potatoes and mushrooms again. I got sick of it as a child, but when I came here to the palace, I started missing her cooking. The chefs here are good, but they can't replicate nostalgia.

"She was actually cheery that day. Definitely moreso compared to years ago, when we were cleaning the latrines.

Her new life was treating her well, and she actually gave me a hug. She made sure none of my skin came into contact with hers, of course, so it was kind of awkward. But it'd been a long time since Mother embraced me, so it made me happy that whole day. I can't remember what the last thing she said was."

Rylan didn't interrupt my rambling. He continued walking, my hand in his pocket. I followed him to nowhere in particular, wandering around the palace as my emotions raced.

"Funny how I'm remembering all the nice things about her now that she's gone." I laughed, but there was no joy in it. "I'm usually complaining about her."

"You can cry, you know," Rylan said.

"I..." My childhood had trained me to hold it in.

"You're shaking." He wrapped one arm around me and held my head to his chest. I breathed in his smoky scent. I felt the rise and fall of his chest. "You can let it out."

I shut my eyes. I didn't think I needed Rylan's permission, but as soon as he gave it to me, the waterworks began.

It was an ugly cry. The complete package of messy weeping, with its hiccups and snorts and snot. But Rylan stood by me as I grieved my heart out and mourned the loss of my mother.

I didn't realize how much I loved Ashryn Cadriel until now. I always knew I did, in a twisted way. Her parenting had messed me up, but I'd messed her up, too, and I believed she loved me in the same strange way I did her.

I sobbed and cried and tore my heart out in front of Rylan

as he rubbed my tears away. He was sturdy and calm, my tree in these winds.

"I'd seen the crops die," I said. "Saw others suffer for it. Those... they were difficult to watch but... now... *my mother*."

Rylan stroked the back of my head. "I'll protect you. My brothers and I will make sure nothing like this happens again. That no more harm comes to you."

"All right," I said, my tears calming down, even though I didn't believe him.

"All right," he echoed. He gave me a smile that didn't reach his eyes, and in his gaze, I saw fear.

They couldn't protect me, because they weren't going to face Aereala. I was. I couldn't let this go on. Other families, not just mine, were affected too.

Rylan let me cry for as long as I wanted, though the tears ran out quickly. He brought me to my room, striding past the ingorias as he did, and tucked me into my bed before crawling in with me. The other princes had already left.

"I'm so happy I'm finally going to get some sleep," Rylan said, cuddling with me.

"So that toy Kael gave you didn't work?" I asked.

"Nothing beats the real deal." He kissed my cheek. "Your presence is the best thing to soothe me to sleep."

"It must have helped a little bit." My feeble attempt at a joke was shaky on my lips.

"Maybe just a little."

"Really?"

He snorted. "No. Go to sleep."

But he didn't sleep. At least not for long. I knew because I couldn't sleep too.

I was not the kind of person to take grieving well.

Rylan had eventually fallen asleep on my bed, although the sun was rising in a couple of hours, so he wasn't going to get much rest. We were supposed to have an early day tomorrow, to bring Vanjar to Gaean's pit to find Baekeil.

I pried Rylan's legs and arms off me, wanting to go for a stroll.

Mother was dead.

I was in denial. She was still going to send me those letters, right? Even though they sounded painful most of the time, at least they were from home and told me she was fine.

How had Father and Bianca taken this? They must have been hurting more, since they were closer to Mother.

I found myself back at the lake I'd once seen Micah throwing rocks at. No one else was here this time.

I picked up a flat rock and tried to skip it over the waters. It sank like my aching heart, straight into the depths.

Still not good at this.

The next rock I tried plopped through the surface again. It made me mad at the lake. Uncontrollable anger surged through me, and I began throwing and tossing and kicking rocks at the waters, as if it was the lake that had wronged me, and not those men who had taken my mother's life.

It was a good thing no one was here to see me, or they'd think I'd lost my mind. I began muttering curses at the gods. "*Aereala*, you stinking piece of dragon's arse. Why can't you just fix all this? You're a god, right? Aren't gods supposed to be omnipotent? But you're sitting helpless under your stupid big tree, and—" I released a loud half scream, half grunt, and kicked more rocks at the lake. The princes would probably think I was deep in my menstrual cycle if they saw me like this. "I need to have a talk with you, because you sitting there under that creepy tree isn't going to do anything. More people are dying every day because of this famine. It's... it's real... and it's hitting us badly." I knelt on the ground, feeling tired. I flipped one more rock into the lake, and it broke the surface. The attempt looked feeble compared to what I'd just been doing.

Aereala answered my prayer—if you could have called that a prayer, anyway—and the dizzy spell that took me in the Assembly of Scholars returned. I welcomed it. It made it hard to keep on my feet, so rested my body on the grass and shut my eyes. The airy sensation took me.

My head lolled as my consciousness faded, and when I opened my eyes, I met the pink skies of the spiritual realm.

There was no tree in sight, but I saw a huge waterfall whose water looked like gems. It reflected a prismatic set of colors, so sparkly and sharp that it felt like the waters might cut me if I went too close.

In the river that the waterfall was connected to, were fish—equally as colorful. There were hundreds of them, flipping their fins in the sparkling waters.

"You complained about the tree," Aereala said. "So, I thought a change of scenery might be good." *Her beauty never failed to awe me. Her hair seemed to have a life of its own, floating in the still air of the spiritual realm. I had to admit that I felt a little bit of jealousy, too. Aereala would be how I'd look like if I'd been perfect.*

She wasn't looking at me, instead talking to the air. I realized she couldn't see me, because I had to be in contact with her for her to do so, so I reached my hand out and placed it on hers.

She turned to me.

"Why did you summon me?" I asked. "Are your powers ready?"

"Oh? I didn't summon you. You were the one who called for me, and so I answered."

She hadn't answered all those other times I tried. Perhaps I hadn't been aggressive enough. I made a mental note that next time I wanted to summon Aereala, I'd have to find a lake, violently throw rocks at it, and curse her name. I'd have to record it as a pagan ritual for future religious scholars.

"When will your powers be ready?" I asked.

"My concept of time is not the same as yours. But to try and simplify it in your terms... Five years? Ten?"

"That's a huge difference. You know that, right? Also, we'd all be dead by then."

"Not all. It's unfortunate, but there will be many remaining to pick up the pieces and rebuild."

"You care for dragon-kind, don't you?"

She frowned. I wondered how she did that without forming a single crease on her brow. "Yes, which is why this is saddening for me."

"And you want to minimize the loss?"

"Yes." She nodded.

"Then I have a proposal for you."

Her eyes lit up with amusement, like a human's would when watching a fly on the wall speak. "A proposal?"

"It's a stretch, and I don't even know if it's possible, but it'll buy us some time. If it works, it can temporarily stave off the effects of the famine. More people will survive, and those silly dragons won't kill each other over nothing."

She walked toward a large boulder, her hand never leaving mine, so I had to follow. I realized I'd never seen Aereala walk before. Her footsteps were weightless. Light. It was like elegant drifting instead of walking.

She crossed her legs and assumed a dainty, graceful sitting position. "I'm interested," she said, lifting my hand in hers. "Tell me more."

I sucked in a deep breath and curled my free hand into a fist. "Okay, so..."

This was my one chance.

And I seriously hoped it was going to work.

CHAPTER TWENTY-EIGHT

MICAH

Sera was nowhere to be found.

Gone.

It drove Micah crazy. It felt like his heart might explode from not knowing. Why hadn't she left a word?

Or had that prophecy come true? Had Aereala taken her away so quickly?

But that would mean that Sera was dead and would never come back. He didn't know how he could accept that reality.

Rylan had woken up without her and alerted his brothers of her disappearance. Rylan tried searching all over the palace and was late with his meeting for the Beyestiryan king, but he couldn't find her.

Micah was still numbed by the news. His first reaction was to call for a search. The entire royal guard was now out, flying around Constanria, trying to find her. Kael and Gaius couldn't control their worry, and they took off with the guards too.

Gaius was actually the first to look for her. He had left without saying a word. He wanted to accompany Rylan to the meeting, but he never had a lid on his temper, and losing Sera seemed to have made him mad. Gaius always had to act on his anger.

And Kael? Kael just did whatever he felt was right at the moment, and so he followed Gaius.

"I want to join the search for Sera," Rylan said, as they strode together to the palace's entrance. "But I can't delay this meeting with Beyestirya, or they might decide not to wait anymore and attack." The dark circles around Rylan's eyes stood out. His hair was disheveled, his braid messily tied.

Micah considered suggesting Rylan neaten up, but it was nearing afternoon, and time ticked by. None of them were in the mood for grooming anyway.

"You shouldn't be left alone to face Beyestirya," Micah said.

"Thanks." Rylan looked at him. "I know how much you want to look for her."

It surprised Micah that he'd managed to control himself and stay. It surprised him even more to realize how much he cared for Rylan. As a child, Micah had always hated Rylan, but perhaps all that hate had been born of admiration, and now that Sera had helped him get over his jealousy, he could love his brother again.

Where was that spitfire of a girl? He needed her in his

life. Couldn't get enough of her. To have her disappear so abruptly didn't make sense to him.

They met Vanjar at the palace's entrance, where there was a large clearing for them to shift into dragons.

"Took you boys long enough. Can you remove these now?" Vanjar asked. She raised her hands, showing the dragon-stone shackles around her wrists.

The smile on her face fell, and she frowned. "What's wrong?"

"Sera's missing," Rylan replied. He took a key from his pocket and freed Vanjar's hands.

"Missing? Did she run off or something? Is that why the whole palace has been in chaos this morning?" Vanjar eyed Rylan with suspicion. "Are you hiding her?"

"No," Rylan growled. He was normally calm, but all of them were easily ticked off today. "We don't know where she is."

"She was your bargaining chip."

"No, she was not. I never was going to give her away."

And now none of them had her.

Vanjar didn't seem convinced, but she had no choice but to accept Rylan's explanation. They shifted into dragons, took off, and headed toward Gaean's pit.

As they flew past the Emilia region, everything looked *different*. More alive. The crops there, which had been abandoned to rot, had their color returned. They swayed in the wind, as if rejoicing in their new life.

Was this Sera's doing?

Or was it Aereala's?

Micah was supposed to be relieved at the new landscape,

but the more he looked at it, the more dread filled his stomach, because it was chiseled in his mind that Aereala had taken Sera, and that he was never to see his beloved again.

They met the Beyestiryan army at the edge of Gaean's pit, where it bordered the Mishram Plains. Swarms of soldiers and dragons and beasts were positioned at the border, a force to reckon with. The women and children weren't there. Micah supposed Vanjar wasn't lying when she mentioned they were only training to keep them busy.

Constanria's own forces were nothing to scoff at either. They stood strong and ready for attack, littering the cliffs of the mountain range. Their numbers were fewer, but they had geography as their advantage. In front of the valley was a barricade, built long ago for purposes of war. Should the majority of the Beyestiryan army break through it and spill through the valley, the Constanrian soldiers could easily take them out with a volley of weapons.

The aerial battle would decide who won this round, but none seemed keen to start just yet. The battle, regardless of who won, would cost many lives.

Micah hoped it didn't have to come to that. He and he brothers had thought war was imminent, but Sera gave them —showed them—an alternative.

Baekeil rose from his troops, red wings spread behind his back. He had the same kingly presence Rylan did, and it was hard to miss him.

He followed Micah, Rylan, and Vanjar to a rocky outcrop, where they shifted back to human form and donned their clothes.

Baekeil wasted no time with formalities. He rushed to his

wife and kissed her on the lips. "I was afraid they had you. I called for the war as soon as the men I sent with you returned, saying you've been captured."

Jealousy spiked through Micah. He imagined Vanjar being Sera, and Baekeil being him.

"You were brash, my love," Vanjar said. "My cousins didn't hurt me."

"I shouldn't have let you go. I ceased to rest after you left. I should have let someone else go in your place."

"I'm alive and well."

"And I'm relieved for it."

Baekeil turned toward Micah and Rylan, his expression hardening to ice as he did.

"We're here to renegotiate," Rylan said. "About war."

"My troops have backed yours into a corner."

"A corner that might spell doom for yours due to the advantages it brings us."

Baekeil parted from Vanjar, but still held her hand. "Shall we test that?"

Rylan sighed. It didn't seem like he had much energy for negotiations such as these. Micah could understand. His thoughts were somewhere else—with Sera. "It seems like... like Aereala... She has blessed us today," Rylan said.

The words sank in Micah, growing heavy in his heart. He knew exactly what that "blessing" had cost them.

Perhaps he was too selfish, and he felt guilty for thinking so, but he didn't mind a war. And the deaths of many. If it meant sacrificing Sera to stop that, he'd pick Sera.

But he knew Sera would never be able to accept it if she lived with that knowledge, and he wanted her to be happy.

"Flying here," Micah said, "I estimated the number of crops we can harvest will be enough to feed your men until next year. We have sufficient stores to tide us over for a harsh winter, although many will be hungry during this time. But it's enough to survive if we ration it well."

Vanjar turned to her husband. "You've seen the new crops, haven't you?"

Baekeil nodded. "The ash fields awakened this morning, for no apparent reason. But my men are happy. Their morale, and mine too, has lifted."

"It's Aereala's blessing," Vanjar said.

"Sera's," Micah said.

Vanjar and Baekeil turned to him, looking puzzled.

"It feels like Sera's doing," Micah continued. "That Aereala worked through her." As he said it, acceptance coursed through him, and deep anguish took hold of his heart. He hadn't cried in countless years, so long that he couldn't remember when he last did. But losing Sera was enough to tear him to shreds, and when he had a quiet moment, he knew he wouldn't be able to hold it in.

With enough food for everyone, the negotiations went smoothly. Baekeil warmed up to Rylan, who hid his anguish well. By the end of it all, Baekeil was calling Rylan a friend, inviting him to Beyestirya for a visit.

The enemy troops took off toward the sunset. They exited through the main road, surrounded by yellow fields, glowing with life. Vanjar followed her husband home. The Constanrian troops filed off too, platoon by platoon, returning to Raynea.

"Do you think we'll find her?" Micah asked his brother.

Rylan looked *so* tired. He'd just lost their father, the man he'd looked up to all his life, and received all the responsibilities that came with that. Now, he'd lost the love of their lives, too. It seemed too much for him to bear. He walked toward the edge of a cliff, sat down, and swung his legs over it. "If Aereala took her," Rylan said, "then what are we to do about it?"

The sunset silhouetted Rylan's form. In those shadows, Rylan looked so small, unlike the imposing figure he had to portray amongst his men. Micah sat down next to him. He patted his brother on his back—a weak form of comfort. Looking at Rylan, Micah saw the tears dripping from his brother's eyes, despite Rylan's stoic expression.

They stared at the horizon together in mourning. Watching his brother cry was the breaking point for Micah, and he let his tears fall, too. He didn't know what to believe in after this. He used to worship Aereala, but she had taken away his most beloved treasure.

How was one to love a god when he felt so wronged?

He closed his eyes and made one last prayer—to have Sera back. He didn't think it would be answered.

"Hey!"

Grief must have made him hallucinate, because he was hearing Sera's voice.

"Hey, assholes!"

Micah peeled his eyes open, and there, a tiny figure in the field, was what he thought was another hallucination. Sera stumbled toward them. Her features became clearer as she stalked closer.

She was a mess.

Her hair had leaves stuck in it, and she was still wearing her nightgown, which had been torn in places and was covered in dirt. Her skin bore splotches of brown all over.

But even then, despite the state she was in, she was the most beautiful thing Micah had ever seen.

Rylan hopped off the cliff, summoning his black wings as he did. He rushed toward Sera, acting like he needed her as much as he did air. Micah was quick to follow.

Rylan tugged her into an embrace.

Micah couldn't wait to get his hands on her. He needed to touch her, breathe in her scent, hear her voice. To cement in his mind that she was still alive and the real thing. He pulled her from his brother's embrace and took her for his own. He caught her lips. She was sweetness and spice mixed together. The taste of home.

"Wow," Sera said. "Were you guys crying? Your eyes are red. I'm touched."

"We thought we lost you," Micah said, his breathing sporadic. His heart thumped wildly. Reality had yet to sink in, and he was still afraid she might be gone for good.

"What happened?" Rylan asked. "Why are the fields back to life? Where did you go?"

"I had a talk with Aereala and we came to an agreement. I figured out a way to send some of her power to this world. Through spells." She looked to Micah with her green eyes. "Micah, you're hugging me a little too tightly. My ribs hurt."

Micah loosened his grip on her. "Through spells?"

"My experiments in the Assembly of Scholars gave me that idea. Aereala created the spells we use in soul magic.

Apparently, she just finds words that she feels makes sense to her and randomly prescribes a cost to them. Spells are a conduit for the spiritual realm, just like she intended me to be. But they're not as effective. And I made her make me an incredibly strong spell, just to save these crops. She thought it was silly at first, because it'll drain her powers and she would have to delay saving the world for good. The goddess doesn't think in temporary terms, apparently... I feel terribly, *terribly* sick, however. Using her well of power inside me seems to take a toll." Now that she mentioned it, Micah noticed the beads of sweat on her brow.

"But it isn't as effective? So the matter isn't resolved?" Rylan asked.

"It is for now." Sera smiled. "I am exhausted. Not to mention covered with grime. Take me home so I can have a shower and a long sleep. How were the negotiations with Beyestirya?" She circled her arms around Micah's neck. Micah tucked his arms between her knees and used his other arm to support her back.

"Easy," Rylan replied. "There's enough food for all of us now. We just had to agree on how to apportion it."

"That's a relief. I'm glad this was all worth it, then."

Sera sighed, hugging Micah tighter. He was a believer now. He thanked the goddess profusely for returning her to him, so he could see light in his world once again.

But Sera's words made him scared.

For now.

Two words, so simple, but terrifying.

He feared he might have to go through this day again and mourn the loss of Sera twice. He looked down at her. She'd fallen asleep in his arms. She seemed so comfortable despite being hundreds of feet off the ground.

He decided to ignore his fears and relish the moment. Her presence gave him bliss, and he'd cherish that bliss for as long as he could.

THANK YOU FOR READING!

I hoped you enjoyed the second book of the Sera's Curse series. I still don't have a publication date for the third book yet, but I'm aiming to release it in 2018.

For giveaways, swag, early ARC copies and announcements, you can follow me on my FB group here: https://bit.ly/2KySdV6

And, if you haven't downloaded your copy for Golden Embrace (novella from the *Soul of a Dragon* universe), you still can by joining my mailing list here:

http://eepurl.com/dk8WTH

facebook.com/ClaraHartleyBooks

ANNEX

Types of Dragon-kind

Hidrae

Full-sized dragon shifters, known to be the most powerful of their kind. They can shift into dragons as large as those of ancient times. They are highly uncommon, and so far, the only known hidrae are a handful of nobles, and those of the royal family. They also bear the traits of drerkyn when they half shift.

Draerin

They can shift into dragons as well, albeit of a variety much smaller than hidrae. They also bear the traits of drerkyn when they half shift.

Drerkyn

Dragon-kind with half-dragon forms when they shift. They can sprout wings, horns, and talons.

Darmar

The weakest dragon-kind, only able to bear superficial traits when they shift, such as yellow eyes or patches of scales. They have slightly stronger constitutions than humans. They used to be rare, but have become numerous over the last thousand years, since they have higher birth rates.

Beasts

Geckari

Large, lizard-like creatures that are used as a form of transport, especially for large loads.

Ingor

Wolflike creatures who are commonly raised in select conditions. The effort it requires to raise them makes them very expensive.

Ingoria

Cousin to the Ingor. They are larger, rarer versions, found in the wild.

Dynfowl

Chicken-like creatures.

Inca

Ugly canines who are often lazy and large. Perfect as

livestock, and a meat that is often eaten by the upper middle class.

Draeox
A creature that looks like a bull.

Balebeast
A subspecies to the draeox that is faster, smaller, and more sinewy.

Piegfowls
A species of bird with blue plumage. They function as messenger birds, with a good homing sense that allows them to travel back to wherever they have been imprinted, no matter where they are.

Wyngoat
A mountain goat with three horns.

Mammotharians
Mammoth-like creatures that travel in groups through Beyestirya.

Places

The Drae Lands
The entire continent of dragon-kind. Thousands of years ago, under the rule of the Dragon Mother, it was known as Ayesrial.

Gaia

An entire continent of humans, said to have been abandoned thousands of years ago by order of Rayse Everstone, first dragon king of Constanria. The event is known as the Great Separation.

Beyestirya

A country of dragon-kind bordering Constanria. It is a landlocked country, and its outer regions are facing the worst of the high summer, causing a food shortage in the inner regions. Most of the country faces winter ten months out of sixteen.

Kaldaross

The capital of Beyestirya. It is half the size of Raynea.

Raynea

The capital of Constanria.

Constanria

A country of dragon-kind that borders the Black Ocean. It's the largest kingdom in all of the Drae Lands. Previously ruled by King Gisiroth Everborne, currently ruled by Rylan Everborne.

Languages

High Dragon Tongue

The ancient language spoken by the old dragons.

Common Tongue

The language spoken by all Constanrians.

Historical and Religious Figures

The Dragon Mother

The old, false goddess of Constanria. She had a million-year reign over the region, suppressing it with her lust for power and intense use of soul magic.

Constance Everstone

The first queen, who started the Great Separation and built the Drae Lands to what it is today.

Rayse Everstone

The first king of the Drae Lands.

Aesryn

The previous ruler of the Drae Lands, who kept it under her dictatorship for a million years. She was defeated by Constance and Rayse Everstone.

Sect of the Holy Pair

The main religion of Constanria, although there are outliers who also worship the Dragon Mother and Constance. They believe in the two gods—Aereala and Gaean.

Aereala

The female god of the Holy Pair. She is said to control the heaven and the skies.

Gaean
The male god of the Holy Pair. He is said to control the earth.

Spells

Invongar respodalis vin garlis ron siras—A failed spell.

Plantia Involuntis—A spell used to invigorate herbs.

Arcio involus—A spell used for plant growth.

Plantia arcio—Another failed spell.

Glacilis provoto—An ice spell.

Illusio volantaris—An illusion spell.

Paraci involuntis—A successful spell, to increase the rate of plant growth.

Lucio—A basic light spell.

Es rea misreagou—The spell used to harvest bright souls.

Kisla misreagou—The spell used to harvest dull souls.

Couela misreagou—The spell used to store souls in soul beads.

Juraca borivilia—A spell to make bombs out of metal objects.

Miscellaneous

Gaeanea *Root*

A starchy herb that has poisonous properties, but a sweet aftertaste. Humans are the most susceptible and can die within an hour of ingesting the herb.

Hydrocus

A large fish with a bulbous head. Said to be rare in Constanria.

Grinche Grass

A vegetable similar to lettuce.

Atira

An elevator

Acecia Berries

Berries dragon-kind use as contraception. It ruins the womb of a woman temporarily, and it is not yet known if it has any lasting effects on childbirth. Studies are still being carried out for it.

Fireoak

A type of oak.

Magic

Soul Magic

An ancient artform that was banned by Constance Everstone. The magic works by harvesting souls, and chanting spells to use them. Many spells were lost through the ages, after the ban on the art.

Dark Magic

Corrupted soul magic, which utilizes the spells of sentient beings, namely humans and dragon-kind. Immensely powerful, but also said to drive the user mad.

Soul Beads

Beads used to store souls for easy casting.

Bright Souls

Each being contains two kinds of souls, bright souls and dull souls. Bright souls contain the select and unique properties of the creature it belongs to.

Dull Souls

Dull souls are the main essence of all creatures. Every creature has them, although to varying amounts.

Made in the USA
Middletown, DE
16 May 2022

65827640R00234